TIME FOR A LITTLE PAYBACK

"Stupid move, female." Nick closed his hand around her wrist and yanked. "I warned you."

Cynna gasped and fell into him. But before she could pull away, he turned and dragged her behind him.

"Nick..."

He headed for the tunnel on the left, wrapped his fingers around the first set of steel bars he came to, and threw the door open.

He flung her into the dark holding cell and stepped in after her.

She sucked in a breath as he drew close, but didn't struggle when he grasped her arm, yanked it upward, and snapped a metal cuff high on the wall over her wrist. Didn't once turn away while he reached for her left arm, jerked that one up as well, and snapped the second cuff over her other wrist.

That dark energy hummed and rolled inside as he stepped back. His gaze slid over her newly dark hair, the white, almost angelic sweater falling open at her chest, the tips of her breasts pressing against the soft cotton, and her slim hips and long legs encased in the formfitting jeans. Arousal stirred in his belly, mixed with the darkness, then slinked downward until he was hard as stone.

"Nick. Listen to me." Her hands curled into fists. "I—"

"What did you say to me in that cell when you brought those nymphs to me?" Power rippled in his veins as he braced his hands on the stones beside her head and moved in so close his body was a breath from hers.

"I—"

He brushed the tip of his nose against her ear and lowered his voice to a menacing whisper. "I think it was something along the lines of...this isn't a game."

TITLES BY
ELISABETH NAUGHTON

Eternal Guardians Series
(Paranormal Romance)
TWISTED
BOUND
ENSLAVED
ENRAPTURED
TEMPTED
ENTWINED
MARKED

Aegis Series
(Romantic Suspense)
EXTREME MEASURES
SINFUL SECONDS
FIRST EXPOSURE
ACAPULCO HEAT
(in the Bodyguards in Bed Anthology)

Stolen Series
(Romantic Suspense)
STOLEN CHANCES
STOLEN SEDUCTION
STOLEN HEAT
STOLEN FURY

Against All Odds Series
(Contemporary Romance)
HOLD ON TO ME
WAIT FOR ME

Firebrand Series
(Paranormal Romance)
POSSESSED BY DESIRE
SLAVE TO PASSION
BOUND TO SEDUCTION

Anthologies
SINFUL SECONDS
WICKED FIRSTS
DARK NIGHTS-
DANGEROUS MEN
BODYGUARDS IN BED

TWISTED

ETERNAL GUARDIANS

ELISABETH NAUGHTON

EN

For You,
my loyal Eternal Guardians fans.
Finally, Nick.

.

"Here, therefore, huge and mighty warrior though you be, here shall you die."
—Homer, THE ILIAD

CHAPTER ONE

She'd made a deal with the devil. A sadistic, twisted, perverted devil.

As if there was really any other kind.

Of course, the fact he was a depraved son of a bitch didn't really bother Cynna. She'd known exactly what she was getting into. She'd weighed the cost and the reward before agreeing. No, what bothered her was the fact her devil wasn't your run-of-the-mill I'll-take-your-soul-and-you-can-have-your-wildest-fantasy kind of guy. *Her* devil continued to take, even after that initial transaction. And what he still wanted from her…

Sickness pooled in her stomach. A sickness she'd learned long ago to fight back. In this place, nausea meant weakness, and weakness equaled death. And if there was one thing she wasn't willing to give up, even for the greatest revenge in all the world, it was her will to live. He could take her soul. He could take her body. He could even take her freedom. She wouldn't balk at any of those. But he'd never have her will. Not while she had an ounce of fight left within her.

"How is our boy today, my sweet?"

Cynna's body instinctively stiffened at the sound of Zagreus's deep voice coming up behind her, but she willed her muscles to relax inch by inch. Leaning her weight onto her right leg and wishing she wore pants instead of the stupid leather miniskirt and knee-high stiletto boots he insisted she parade around in, she crossed her arms over her chest and stared down into the arena below.

Three satyrs holding sharp, vile-looking weapons circled a shirtless man swinging a blade as long as his forearm. His feet were bare, his jeans riding low on his lean hips, his torso strong and cut under the lights hanging from above. Muscles flexed in his arms and beneath his skin. His shaggy blond hair fell into his face, and a thick beard covered his jaw. But it was the scars on his back that drew her attention. Thin white lines that crisscrossed all over his skin, as if he'd been whipped and tortured long before he'd found himself prisoner in this wretched lair. "Holding his own. So far."

"He's fighting." Zagreus stepped up against her spine, his heat washing over her in a hot, sticky wave. He placed his hands on her shoulders, making her wish she was dressed in something other than this skintight black corset top—something else he insisted she wear. "That's an improvement."

Cynna wasn't so sure. The man might be wielding that blade like a pro, but he was doing it on his terms, not theirs, and as soon as Zagreus realized that, his amicable mood would head straight for the shitter.

Zagreus's fingers kneaded Cynna's bare skin, and she swallowed back the bile sliding up her throat. His palms were wide, his fingers long. She knew from experience he could use his hands for pleasure and pain—she'd been on the receiving end of both—but today, any touch from him felt wrong. And it had since the man below had come into her world.

The satyr on the right charged, and Cynna's stomach curled into a knot. The man ducked beneath the sword, narrowly missed being decapitated, swiveled, and arced out with his blade. It caught the satyr across the chest, and he stumbled back. The satyr on the left lunged. The man hit the ground with a thud, rolled, then popped back up, catching the second satyr in the leg.

He was stealth and danger and precision and coiled strength, and Cynna's blood hummed as she watched his body twist and turn and beat back the monsters with a rhythm that looked more like a dance than a battle. Blood gushed from the satyr's wound. The beast dropped his weapon—a pitchfork-like trident with long angled teeth—and howled. The third, realizing it was his chance, lurched off the ground and hurled himself toward the man who held her riveted attention.

Their bodies collided in a crunch of bones and tendons and sinew. Weapons went flying. Fists connected with jaws. They rolled across the sand of the training arena. High above, Cynna tensed as she watched the man take hit after hit. At her back, Zagreus's excitement permeated the air around her, as did his whispered "Come on. Unleash the monster."

His fingers dug into her shoulders. Pain spiraled from the spot, shooting up and down her spine, but she didn't move. Her eyes were fixed on the struggle below. Sand flew up into the air. Blood and sweat coated their bodies. Grunts echoed off the walls. They rolled again, and the satyr got the upper hand, pinning the man to the arena floor. One hand pressed down hard on his shoulder while the other closed in a vise around his throat.

Cynna's adrenaline surged, and a tight, hard lump formed in her chest, causing her breath to catch.

Muscles flexed beneath the pale skin of the man's arms. He wrapped one giant hand around the satyr's covering his throat, and tried to pull the satyr's fingers free of his windpipe. His other arm flew out to the side, grappling for the blade just out of his reach. His eyes bulged. His face turned red.

Cynna's palms grew sweaty, and she swallowed hard, knowing what it felt to be held like that, willing him to break free. To live. Though why, she couldn't say.

The satyr chuckled, a dark menacing sound that drifted up to the rafters in a throaty growl. "You are no savior. Just a worthless, weak mortal about to visit the fires of Hades."

"Not. Without. You."

The man's neck muscles strained. His fingertips found the handle of the blade. Releasing his grip on the satyr's hand at his neck, he shoved against the satyr's shoulder, lifted his knee, and nailed the satyr in the balls. The satyr gasped in pain. The man closed his hand around the handle of the blade, yanked it close, then thrust it into the satyr's belly.

The beast's eyes flew wide. Blood spurted from the wound. The man pushed hard, knocking the satyr off him, then stumbled to his feet.

Blood covered the man's bare chest, his damp hair fell into his eyes, and sweat dripped off his tight muscles as he looked down at the writhing satyr. The satyr gasped one last time, then his arms landed against the sand of the arena with a thud, and he fell silent.

Chest heaving, the man turned his attention toward the remaining two beasts, both injured but not finished. Not yet.

"Yes," Zagreus whispered near Cynna's temple, his hot breath flaming her already overheated skin, his excitement palpable in the thick air. "Finish them. Let the darkness free."

As if he heard him, the man turned and looked up into the spectator area where they stood. A deep scar cut across the left side of his face, disappearing beneath his beard, but his piercing, amber gaze didn't hover on Zagreus. It landed on Cynna. And held. As if they were the only two in the room.

Her pulse picked up speed as she watched his eyes narrow. As disgust filled his features. Chest rising and falling with his deep breaths, he threw the blade on the ground, spit, and stepped back from the carnage he'd just caused. And as his blistering gaze continued to hold hers, something in his eyes cut to the very center of her. She'd been watching him defy Zagreus's will for months, but this was the first time he'd done it while staring at *her*. The first time she felt as if…he was testing *her*.

The injured satyrs both growled and slowly pushed to their feet. Blood matted in the thick hair of their chests. The white paint in a stripe over their bare skulls dripped onto their shoulders from their own sweat, forming blobs of slick white goo to run down their dark skin like war paint. The pants they wore were tattered and ripped in different places from the fight, but the clothing didn't hide their grotesque hooves or the curve of their animal legs. And the rage she saw in both their faces told her they were about to change the tides of this battle.

The satyrs advanced on the defenseless man once more, and Cynna's adrenaline spiked all over again. But his gaze didn't shift their way. He continued to stare up at Cynna with those scorching eyes, continued to look through her as if he could see her soul and knew it was black. Continued to pin her with his singular focus as if *she* were the real threat.

She licked her lips. Glanced between him and the beasts. *Turn and look, you idiot.*

Zagreus's fingers curled into her flesh at the shoulders. The pain amplified outward from the spot, but she barely cared. Her heart rate jumped as her gaze continued to flick from the man to the satyrs and back again. Was Zagreus really going to let them kill him? That wouldn't help his cause. He wouldn't allow his prized possession to die, right here, right now…would he?

Sweat formed along her skin. Her pulse turned to a roar in her ears. The satyr on the right growled. The one on the left pushed his hooves against the ground and charged. Both their faces twisted in fury.

Move. Defend yourself. Pick up your fucking blade!

She wanted to scream the words. To hurl herself into the arena. But she didn't dare move. The man continued to stand still and silent, staring up at her with those smoldering, mysterious, fiery eyes.

Run!

The satyr on the right lifted his blade for the kill move.

"Halt!" Zagreus let go of her and lurched toward the railing, his fingers curling around the metal pole until they turned white.

The satyrs skidded to a stop, their blades still lifted in fury, their chests rising and falling with their labored breaths.

"Stand down," Zagreus growled.

A breath of relief whooshed out of Cynna's lungs.

They lowered their weapons, but the venom in their eyes said they weren't happy. They'd tasted blood and wanted more. And yet, the man didn't even spare them a glance. He continued to look past them, past Zagreus, and focus only on her.

"Son of a fucking bitch," Zagreus muttered under his breath. He turned away from the ring, his face contorted in anger, and looked toward Cynna. She stiffened, covering any reaction, working for blasé when she felt anything but. "I gave you a simple job. To *break* him. And you've failed."

Panic slithered in to mix with the fear. But panic, like nausea, was a weakness she wasn't about to let show. She forced her gaze away from the man below and focused on the devil she'd sold herself to.

Her shoulders tensed, her chin lifted, her back straightening with a strength she pulled from the very center of her being. "He has the blood of Krónos in his veins. His will has proved to be stronger than most."

Zagreus chewed on the inside of his lip. He was taller than Cynna. Even a few steps below her near the railing, she had to look up at him. To most he was a sex god—tanned, dark, muscular, with a body carved to tempt and a face to seduce. But Cynna knew the cunning devil he was beneath. And being Hades's son, his appetites, and his quest for power, knew no limits.

"His will must be broken if he's to come into his god powers. And I need his god powers to best my father and those other fucking gods who think they own this world and the next. If he refuses to cooperate, we'll just have to find another way."

Cynna's eyes narrowed. They'd already tortured the man in every way imaginable. They'd whipped him until he'd bled. Stretched him on racks. Beaten him until he was black and blue and broken. And through it all, she'd watched—even ordered his torture because she had to—while inside she'd only wanted to vomit and run. But every time he'd healed, his superhuman genes repaired every ounce of damage they'd inflicted, much to her surprise—and relief.

They'd brought him to the brink of physical pain, and he'd yet to crack, so she couldn't imagine what else they could do to him. "Like what?"

A dark, perverse light flared in Zagreus's eyes. "We'll use the nymphs."

Oh shit. She'd been wrong. There was another way to torture him. One she hadn't even considered.

"If we can't break him physically," Zagreus said, "you will break him...sexually."

He shifted away from her and looked down into the arena. "Take him back to his cell." Guards stationed at the doors moved in from the shadows and jerked on the man's arms. "Have him cleaned up, then chain him to the wall. My sweet Cynna has something special planned for him."

Zagreus turned that sickening smile her way and winked, just once. "Don't you, *agapi?*"

Cynna's gaze strayed from Zagreus's victorious grin down to Nick, standing taut in the center of the ring, being held at each arm by the guards, his face drenched in sweat, his body in blood, his intense amber gaze never once straying from her face.

Zagreus stepped up next to her and leaned close to her ear. "Break him, Cynna. Use the nymphs to bring him to the brink again and again, no matter how long it takes. Because if you can't, if you fail me now, you remember what I said would happen, don't you?"

Cynna's stomach caved in, and fear—true fear—rolled through her veins. Yeah, she remembered. He'd promised to break *her.* Mind, body, soul...*her* will. Until there was nothing left.

Only she'd never be able to hold out. Not like Nick.

Slowly, she nodded. And stared into the scarred face of her victim. Hating—despising—everything she'd agreed to all in the name of revenge.

"Good girl," Zagreus whispered. "You do this right, *agapi*, and your reward will be most pleasurable. That, I promise."

CHAPTER TWO

Nick wasn't sure what was going on, but he knew whatever Zagreus had planned for him next wasn't going to be good.

Soldiers—no, not soldiers, Zagreus's hired satyr mercenaries—led him through the long, dark hallway toward his cell, illuminated every ten feet by torches attached to the rock walls. Water dripped down to form puddles where the floor was uneven. A cool chill spread through the corridor, being so far below ground, but Nick had gotten used to it over the last few months. What he would never get used to, though, were the moans, the screams, the crack of leather hitting flesh. The cries of ultimate misery and the hopeless despair that reverberated through the tunnels both night and day.

The dark energy he fought—energy he'd always thought had come from his mother, Atalanta, but now knew was straight-up evil delivered from his fucking father, Krónos, the most malicious of all the gods—rolled and churned inside, electrifying him, exciting and arousing him, even though disgust brewed in his stomach over what was being done to the other poor souls trapped in this living hell. He'd tried everything to tune the sounds out, but they were always there, taunting the darkness, calling to it, begging him to just let go.

He ground his teeth against it. Focused on the rocks below his bare feet, on the way the metal cuffs bit into his wrists, on moving forward one step at a time. He slowed when he reached the threshold to his cell, but the satyr behind shoved him hard, forcing him to stumble into the beast ahead.

"Keep moving."

The satyr at his front turned and shoved him back. Weak from the fight and loss of blood, Nick staggered but caught himself before he went down. A stench rose up around him, one he blocked out. All satyrs smelled like death. Something else he hadn't grown used to during his months of captivity.

They led him into the baths, and today he was thankful to find the cavern empty. He didn't have the energy to scrap with some of the other inmates who were often brought here to bathe at the same time. The ones who were trying to hold on to some semblance of control by acting aggressive in front of the guards, hoping it would grant them a day or two of life. They didn't realize that every person imprisoned here had a purpose, or that most lasted only a few days. And as soon as they gave in, Zagreus lost interest and they were truly dead.

Three large pools took up space in the center of the cavern. Stalactites hung from the ceiling. A bench had been carved out along the far right side, and fresh towels had been laid out in advance.

The satyr on the right tossed Nick a small plastic bag. "The prince wants you cleaned before we take you back to your cell. Do it quickly."

As the satyrs turned away to stand guard at the door, Nick looked down at the package in his hands. Soap and a disposable plastic razor.

The razor had potential. His gaze skipped over the thick rock walls, then to the backs of the two satyrs he could see. Two he could take down with a weapon as simple as a razor blade. Three was pushing it. And if he succeeded, odds were good he'd be caught before he could figure out how the hell to get out of this maze of a prison.

Plus there was the harsh reality he'd lost a fair amount of blood in that last fight and was more tired than he wanted to admit. Now was not the time to plan his big escape. He stripped off what was left of his torn pants and stepped into the pool.

Cool water surrounded him, and he winced when it hit a cut on his leg and another on his shoulder, then sighed as the liquid cradled his sore body. He dunked beneath the surface and let the water rush over his face and swirl above his head, pulling the grime from his hair and beard. No, he didn't have a clue what Zagreus had planned next, but he was thankful for the chance to rid himself of the filth and stench and blood of those satyrs. If only until the next unfair battle.

He came back up, flicked the wet hair out of his eyes, and opened the small bag. After washing his shaggy hair and the rangy beard, he scrubbed the soap all over his skin, then rinsed, feeling more human with every passing second. When he was clean, he glanced toward the razor sitting on the side of the pool and frowned because he knew that thing was gonna hurt like hell tugging through all the hair on his jaw. He considered leaving his damn face just the way it was, then thought better of it. If the satyrs had given him a razor, it meant either he was shaving himself or they were. And he didn't want those fuckers anywhere near him.

He did his best without a mirror and scissors, wincing every time he nicked himself. After rinsing, he climbed out of the pool, reached for a towel, then hesitated with his hand on the soft cotton as his gaze caught on the cuffs around his wrists and the markings on his forearm. Markings that made him think of his soul mate.

He wondered where she was and what she was doing. Whether or not her newborn child had survived the daemon attack at the half-breed colony. If his brother, Demetrius, his twin and—thanks to the fucking gods—also her soul mate, was taking care of her right this minute or out running useless missions with his Argonauts.

If she ever thought of the sacrifice Nick had made for her.

Anger pushed in. An anger he'd lived with many long years. He waited for the familiar burst of longing that always followed, for the soul mate pull, which was like a magnet, dragging him toward Isadora. Yes, it was there, calling to him, but it wasn't as intense as before. And he couldn't help but wonder why.

Maybe he was finally hardening inside, losing what little humanity he had left. Or maybe Isadora's bond with Demetrius was so strong Nick just didn't matter anymore. His brother and Isadora were bound to each other now, with all the pomp and circumstance the stupid Argolean ceremony imposed. But more than that, they'd solidified their side of the soul mate bond through the act of making love, something Nick *seriously* didn't want to think about.

His own bond with Isadora had never been sealed like that. Not that he hadn't considered it…only a bazillion times. But even as he fantasized about the possibility again, he knew it was no longer even an option. He was going to die in this miserable place. It was only a matter of time. Which meant his brother was going to wind up with her all to himself. Just as the son of a bitch wanted.

The thought was more depressing than Nick wanted to admit, so he pushed his mind back to the battle in the arena. And this time when the dark energy surged, he relished it. Yeah, his death might be imminent, but he wasn't dead yet. And before he went out, he planned to take a few satyrs and that sick fuck Zagreus with him.

"Enough," the taller of the two guards barked, looking over his shoulder. "Leave the clothes. Wrap yourself in a towel."

The towel was new. Usually—*if* Nick was granted a turn in the baths—he was required to dress in the same filthy garments he'd worn the day before. He eyed the now-dull razor once again and for a fleeting moment considered his chances against the three guards, then dismissed it. If Zagreus wanted him clean, it meant someone was coming to see him. And someone coming to see him meant he might have a better chance at a vengeance even more destructive.

"My sweet Cynna has something special planned for him."

His fingers stilled on the towel at his waist, and a rolling heat spread all through his torso, his hips, and down into his groin.

Cynna... The name fit. The female who'd directed his torture these last six months was sin in every way imaginable. Caramel skin, long blonde hair that didn't match her coloring, almond-shaped, exotic eyes, and a body...

That arousal sharpened, bringing his cock to life as he imagined her pert breasts, which were always on display in some revealing corset top, her small waist, and those long, slender legs she flaunted in the black leather stiletto boots she wore everywhere.

He couldn't quite read her relationship with Zagreus. The sadistic god was attached to her, though Nick was sure it wasn't love that kept her around. And though she didn't flinch when Zagreus touched her, she didn't warm to the god or melt into him the way Isadora did when his brother touched their soul mate. No, Cynna's link to Zagreus was something more, something darker, and every time Nick saw the dead look in her eyes when Zagreus drew near, he grew more and more convinced she wasn't the captor in this twisted version of hell like they both wanted him to believe.

The guards came in as Nick finished knotting his towel. One stood to the right holding a spear, glaring at Nick. The red gash across his cheek was Nick's doing, from yesterday, when the son of a bitch had come at him in the hall for no apparent reason. Nick had gotten in three good punches before a handful of guards had come to the fucker's rescue. Nick smirked.

"Something funny, mortal?" the injured guard growled.

Nick didn't answer. Taunting would only garner him a beating. And though he'd love to have another go at this prick, right now he was too interested in seeing what Cynna had planned to care what these two thought.

They led him out of the baths and back down the corridor toward his cell. The rocks were cool against his feet, and a chill swept through the tunnel, bringing the fine hairs along his nape to attention.

The guards swung the steel door open and pushed him into his cell. No windows, no light. The injured guard lit a torch on the wall, illuminating the damp space made up of nothing but rock walls and his pile of blankets where he slept in the corner.

They maneuvered him around until he was standing in the center of the room, facing the door. One guard uncuffed his wrists, and for a moment, he thought of taking them down. But voices were already resonating through the corridor, growing stronger, coming closer. And one stood out, causing his stomach to tighten and arousal to rush back through his body, bringing every other thought to a halt.

The click of heels sounded as the guards hooked chains to D-bolts in the ceiling Nick didn't remember being there, then reached for his arms. As they attached the first chain to his left wrist, stretching his limb up and away from his body, he winced, the injury in his shoulder sending a sharp shot of pain across his muscles. They grasped his other arm and locked him to the chain, then closed the metal cuffs around his ankles, kicked his legs shoulder-width apart, and chained those to hooks in the floor as well.

Cynna appeared in the doorway to the room.

The pain dissipated as Nick focused on her. She was wearing the same revealing outfit she'd had on when she'd watched his fight in the training ring, and it distracted him from what was going on around him. Excited him. Sent a wicked thrill through the dark part of what was left of his soul.

"Mistress," the injured guard said, standing straight. "The prisoner is ready."

Cynna's gaze flicked over Nick, over his bare torso and the small white towel covering his awakening erection, then up to his face to hover on the scar on his left cheek. Without sparing a look toward the guards, she said, "Leave us."

Her voice was like sandpaper and velvet, a voice made for sin, just like her body. In her hands she held a jar.

Two females—no, nymphs—rushed into the room as soon as the guards left. One was blonde, the other with short dark hair. They were both petite, both submissive with their eyes cast downward, and both were wearing flimsy pale pink dresses made from thin fabric that barely hid their bodies from view. They were also wearing metal collars. Collars he'd seen on other submissives in the tunnels. Collars that marked them as sex slaves.

Nick's stomach tightened. His gaze skipped past the females, toward the steel door, which was now closed, and through the small window to see who was watching.

Darkness reflected in the glass. But that didn't mean they were alone. Zagreus was always somewhere watching Nick's torture. Feeding off it. Waiting for him to break.

Turning to the dark-haired nymph on her right, Cynna handed the female the jar and said, "Use this. But do not touch him anywhere save where he bleeds."

The nymph nodded and approached, her cheeks a deep cherry red, her breaths shallow. She unscrewed the lid and set it on the rocks at her feet, then gathered a scoop of whatever was in the jar and lowered to her knees in front of him.

Nick sucked in a breath. She was inches away, his groin hidden only by the small towel. Her fingers grazed the wound on his thigh, a tickling sensation that made his muscles tense, but the healing balm was cool where it coated the gash. He relaxed as she rubbed the balm into the wound, feeling the jagged skin already knitting back together, feeling his body healing faster than it would on its own, feeling a heat he didn't expect warming his skin.

"Enough," Cynna said. "Now the other one."

The dark-haired nymph pushed to her feet, still didn't look Nick in the eye, and moved around behind him. Again he felt her fingers gliding over his skin, and he tensed, then the balm slathered the wound in his shoulder, slowly warming his skin, repairing the damage and relaxing him from the outside in.

Cynna's deep brown eyes remained blank as she watched the nymph work. No emotion crossed her face. No pleasure or excitement over what was to come, as Zagreus always showed. Nothing but emptiness. An emptiness Nick had gotten used to seeing on her flawless face.

Only…that wasn't true. When he'd been in the ring earlier, when he'd dropped his weapon in defiance of Zagreus's desire to make him fight, he'd seen something in her eyes then. Something that had looked a lot like panic.

"That's enough," Cynna said.

The nymph's fingers lifted from Nick's skin, and she stepped back. Moving around him, she knelt to pick up the lid, recapped the jar, then sank back against the far wall near the other nymph.

Cynna moved forward, her eyes never wavering from Nick's, and the scent of jasmine hit him as it always did when she drew close, filling his senses, messing with his mind. She was tall for a female, at least five ten, and in those ridiculously high-heeled boots, only a few inches shorter than him. Today her blonde hair was swept over one shoulder, a blue streak near her temple contrasting sharply with her caramel skin. Her face was heavily made up, her eyes rimmed in thick black, making her look every bit the dominatrix. And though he knew he should be anxious over whatever she and Zagreus had cooked up for him next, he wasn't. Because there was something about her that interested him. Perplexed him. Made him want to know more.

He'd never admit it, but the mystery of who she was and how she'd come to be here had saved him. Saved him from going mad or giving in to all that dark energy Zagreus was waiting to claim.

"You just…won't…break."

Her words were a whisper, a frustration, a surprise. She never spoke to him. Though he'd spent more time with her than anyone else in this hellhole, she never addressed him directly. She gave the commands to her grunts, and they did her dirty work. She never even got near him.

Something about today was different, though. A tiny voice in the back of his head screamed what was about to happen in this cell was on a whole different level from what he'd been through before.

She stepped close, so close he could feel her heat but not close enough to touch, then moved to her right, slowly making her way around him. His stomach tightened, and that blistering arousal came rushing back.

"This isn't a game." Her warm breath fanned his nape, sending a shiver across his bare skin. And in his wounds, where the nymph had spread the balm, heat gathered and grew, radiating outward, heading for his belly. "You cannot beat Zagreus. No one wins against the Prince of Darkness."

Nick's arms flexed, and the chains rattled above his head. He didn't want to beat the fucker, he only wanted to destroy him. Not just for what he'd put Nick through during the last few months, but for what he put everyone in this wretched place through— Cynna, his gut told him, included.

"I can't stop what he has planned for you." She circled around and stopped directly in front of him again. "Give in, and you save yourself the torment. Give in, and this ends now."

"Give in," Nick repeated, staring into her dark eyes. But unlike before, they weren't empty. They weren't dead. There was something there. Something that looked a lot like…desperation.

Was she warning him of something horrendous to come? Why would she do that? She was Zagreus's puppet. Or was she simply afraid of what would happen if he didn't break?

"You want me to give in?" he asked.

She didn't answer. Only stared at him.

"The way you gave in?"

The desperation in her eyes faded and was replaced with that lifeless, vacant look, the one he'd seen so many times when she'd ordered Zagreus's satyrs to torture him. Without a word, she stepped back, but she didn't break eye contact.

"You were warned," she said in a low voice. "Females?"

Nick's gaze swept from her to the nymphs, approaching from opposite sides. The blonde, the one who'd stood in the back of the room, reached him first, grasped the towel at his hips, and yanked it away. The other drew close and moaned as she stared at his dick. And though he couldn't see their eyes, he could see their faces, flushed now with lust, with an obsession he knew was his next form of torture.

Shit...

They both sank to their knees in front of him. And holy fuck...heat—a heat he *did not* want—spread from his wounds and straight into his cock. Whatever that nymph had slathered all over his wounds hadn't just healed him, it was making him instantly hard. He wrapped his hands around the chains above and tried to move away, but his legs were locked in place, his body on full display. And when he felt a hand land against his thigh and warm breath skitter across his bare hips, he couldn't stop the groan that rumbled from his chest.

"Do with him as you please." Cynna's husky voice echoed in the room.

The nymphs both stilled and turned to look her way, but Cynna didn't spare them a glance.

Torchlight reflected in her blank, dead eyes locked on his, and not a single emotion flickered anywhere in her expression. "Bring him to the edge as many times as you like, but do not let him come. If you do, your punishment will be severe. Now. Begin."

CHAPTER THREE

Cynna couldn't breathe.

She'd been forced to do some horrendous things in the year she'd been with Zagreus, but this—watching what those nymphs were doing to Nick—this was the worst.

Her stomach tossed. nymph on her knees bobbed her head between his legs. The other tweaked his nipples. Each time he neared release, they would let go and switch positions, then restart his torment all over again. Thankfully, Cynna had positioned herself far enough back so she couldn't see the specifics, but she could see Nick. His sandy blond hair was drenched, he was hanging limply by his arms, and his legs were no longer holding his body upright.

She couldn't look into his eyes. Couldn't focus on his insanely handsome face—dammit—now that his beard was gone. Five minutes into the session, she'd had to stare at a spot on the far wall behind his head and disassociate herself from what was happening. That was how she got through everything Zagreus made her do— mentally shut down from the moment, drifted in her mind, focused on the reason she'd sold herself to the sadistic god in the first place.

Only today—now—she hadn't been able to do that. Every moan, every labored breath, every time Nick rattled those chains while the nymphs took him to the brink with their mouths, with their hands, it cut through her mental barrier, dragged her back to the moment, made her stomach toss with a queasiness she only barely held down.

"Enough." She turned away as the nymphs reluctantly released him, unable to look at the beads of sweat sliding down the rugged and mysterious scar on the left side of his face, more prominent now that he'd shaved. Unwilling to draw in another image of his chiseled, naked, very aroused body and what the nymphs had done, she ushered the slave girls out into the hall and quickly followed.

Zagreus had two satyrs waiting for them. Two who grabbed the nymphs and dragged them away, moaning and shaking. Cynna didn't want to think about what the satyrs were going to do to the nymphs. Didn't want to think about the fact that what those females were feeling was a high like that from a drug, one they couldn't control. Didn't want to acknowledge that by being forced to use them to torment Nick, she'd also been guaranteeing their impending torture.

"*Agapi.*"

My love. Revulsion sent a shudder down Cynna's spine, but she swallowed hard and looked toward Zagreus, stalking toward her down the long, cold corridor. She wasn't his love. Nor did she ever want to be.

"How is our prisoner?"

Her spine stiffened, and she met his dark gaze, knew not to back away from it. "He didn't break, if that's what you're wondering."

A wide, evil smile spread across Zagreus's lips. "I wouldn't want him to break too soon. Takes all the fun out of it, don't you think?"

Cynna's eyes narrowed. Since Zagreus had bound her gift in his lair, she couldn't tell when he was lying or being truthful, and she hated that—hated how that crippled her—but something told her this time, he was being honest. He got a sick sort of pleasure putting her in shocking situations. And right now he knew she wanted to run, and he was loving every moment of her misery.

She lifted her chin, refusing to show even an ounce of weakness. "The same two tomorrow?"

His smile widened, and his hand slid around her nape and up into her hair, dragging her toward his dark, dangerous heat. She didn't stiffen, didn't react, didn't flinch, because doing so would make whatever he had planned much, much worse.

"No, *agapi.* Tomorrow I think those two will be deliciously incapacitated. We'll find another. But tonight, my dear, sweet Cynna…" He brushed her hair over her shoulder and lowered his mouth to her neck, then bit down. Pain resonated from the spot, but she didn't dare move. "Tonight I want you to recreate for me what you watched in that cell. And when I'm convinced you were thorough enough in your observation, then I'll give you what our nymphs are getting now."

As if on cue, a scream ripped through the cavern.

Cynna's eyelids dropped, and inside, though revulsion churned and pushed up her chest, she repeated the words that had gotten her through this and so much more.

Disassociate. Disappear. Cease to exist.

With him, she wasn't a person, she was a thing. But she could endure being a thing for now, because the promise of revenge was worth this one small price.

Soon, very soon, this would be a memory, and the one who'd destroyed her life would pay.

Or so that was what she whispered to herself in the quiet of the night to hold back the dark part of her soul. The part she feared would soon consume her.

"Did you see their faces?" Orpheus chuckled as he and the queen of Argolea walked through the main doors of the castle and into the elaborate foyer. "Man, I really wish I'd had a camera. I thought Lord Timaeus's jaw was going to hit the floor."

"Mine nearly did when you had those servants sweep in with champagne to celebrate your induction," Isadora mumbled, crossing the great Alpha seal in the glossy marble floor. "There is something called tradition you need to be aware of, Orpheus."

"Tradition's overrated." He grinned as they headed up the curved staircase. "Man, this is gonna be fun."

Isadora wasn't so sure. Lord Lucian had stayed on with the Council of Elders—the governing body that advised the monarchy—as long as he could, but his health was rapidly deteriorating after five hundred years, and the Council was finally forced to find a replacement for his seat. Tradition held that the most senior male member of each founding family be instilled, but the Council clearly wasn't thrilled with their two choices: Orpheus, the troublemaking eldest nephew of Lord Lucian, or his younger Argonaut brother, Gryphon. While an Argonaut had never sat on the Council, Gryphon had been considered the lesser of two evils until his captivity in the Underworld forever changed him. The

Council was now hesitant to seat Gryphon, not just because they were unsure of his mental stability these days, but because they suspected his governing decisions would be influenced by his relationship with his mate, Maelea, the daughter of Zeus and Persephone.

That left Orpheus, the black sheep of the family, half-witch, half-Argolean, and a major thorn in the Council's side. Orpheus never did anything anyone expected, Isadora included. The Council's choice was either to seat him, or overhaul the entire governing process, which they were hesitant to do because tradition—to them—was the most sacred of rituals. But Isadora was still nervous about the entire situation. Yes, Orpheus had come through for her several times, and yes, he was now serving with the Argonauts, but he was still unpredictable. He didn't care what anyone thought, he often went against protocol, and he loved to antagonize the Council, something she feared was going to come back and bite her in the ass.

"Just remember you're not simply representing your family," she said to him as they rounded the banister at the second landing. "You're representing the Argonauts as well. Whether the Council will admit it or not, seating an Argonaut is a historic event."

He tugged on her sleeve, drawing her to a stop. "Hold on. You don't think I can handle this, do you, Isa?"

Isadora looked up at his irritated gray eyes. Not *Your Highness*, not *My Queen*, simply Isa. He'd called her that for years, and while she didn't have a problem with it in private, in public it just went one step further in showing his lack of respect for their way of life. "I think your disdain for the Council comes through loud and clear."

"They deserve nothing but disdain. And you're the first who should recognize that. They tried to execute your mate, or have you forgotten?"

Nausea rolled through her belly when she remembered Demetrius strung up in the council chamber, but she pushed it aside. "No, I haven't forgotten, nor will I ever. But tradition has fueled this country for thousands of years. It can't be changed on a dime. What I'm trying to do is instill change within the parameters our people are used to. If I move too quickly, the Council will rally the people and rise up against me. We're a hairbreadth away from a coup, Orpheus, especially with the Misos here. What I need you to do is pick your battles and not antagonize the lords just for the fun of it."

"No one wants the Misos taken care of more than me."

Isadora knew that too. After Orpheus's brother, Gryphon, had returned from the Underworld, the Misos—or half-breeds, as the Council liked to call them, half-Argoleans, half-humans—took him in when no one else would, even his own people. Though Orpheus himself wasn't a half-breed, he felt a kinship with the people who'd helped his brother. And he'd been instrumental in assisting in their evacuation to Argolea after the Misos colony in the human realm had been attacked by Hades and his son, Zagreus. He hated the fact the Council was targeting the Misos as much as Isadora did.

"I may prove you wrong, you know," he said, resuming his steps. "I have been known to do that a time or two."

He had, he was right, and Isadora knew she was worrying about something that might never happen, but then that was her job as queen. To worry about everyone—him, the Council, the Argonauts, Nick...

A space inside her chest squeezed tight when she thought of Nick, and a profound sense of loss swept through her. He'd sacrificed himself to save her life when Hades had come to claim her soul, and she'd never had a chance to thank him, never had a chance to tell him she was sorry for the way they'd argued just before Hades's arrival. She loved Demetrius, had no desire to be with anyone else, but she understood Nick's pull to her. He'd been cursed by the gods more than any other, not simply because he'd been given a soul mate he couldn't have, but because he'd been given the same one as his brother. And she'd chosen Demetrius.

She needed to find him. Needed to set at least some part of this nightmare right by rescuing him from Hades and Zagreus. It didn't matter that he was Krónos's son. All that mattered was finding him.

Voices sounded from the office ahead, and, straightening her spine, Isadora followed Orpheus toward the open door. She'd told Theron, the leader of the Argonauts, she would stop by after the Council proceedings to let him know how it had gone, but more than anything, she was anxious to hear if he had any news on Nick.

Titus was sitting behind Theron's desk when she entered, his dark, wavy hair tied at his nape, his gloved hands paging through virtual screens. Theron stood behind him, his thick arms crossed over his chest, his expression grim as he studied whatever Titus was pointing out.

"It's all doom and gloom around here," Orpheus muttered as he stepped into the room. "Feels like the Council chambers."

Both Argonauts looked their direction, and Theron's dark brows lifted. "How did it go?"

"Obviously better than it's going here," Orpheus muttered, dropping onto an arm of a nearby sofa. "Where's Gryph?"

"With Cerek and Demetrius," Theron answered, "running down a lead in the human realm. They're not back yet."

Isadora caught the flash of worry in Orpheus's eyes. He was always worried when Gryphon went anywhere without him.

She focused on Theron. "A good lead?"

"None of our leads are good at this point," Titus huffed, shutting off the virtual screen.

Disappointment washed through Isadora, but she tried not to let it show.

"We'll find him," Theron said. "The guys are investigating a Nereid settlement off the coast of Florida. We know it's a long shot, but Zagreus has a thing for nymphs. We're hoping they might know something. Demetrius wanted to check this one out himself."

Demetrius wanted to check out every lead himself. Though he and his twin had never been close, he felt as responsible for Nick's imprisonment as Isadora did. Maybe more, because he believed he should have been the one to save her, not Nick.

Which was another reason Isadora needed to find Nick. So her mate could stop feeling guilty. Since Nick's disappearance, Demetrius had become more and more withdrawn, spending every hour looking for his brother or stressing over something out of his control. Their relationship was taking a serious hit. As was the time he spent with their daughter.

"So," Theron said, looking across the room toward Orpheus. "Is it official?"

"Yes," Isadora sighed. She was tired. Tired of worrying, tired of fighting the Council, but most of all, she just wanted her family together and in one piece. "You're looking at the newest Council member."

Orpheus's shit-eating grin made her roll her eyes.

"Gods help us," Titus muttered.

"The gods can't help you this time," Orpheus said, chuckling.

Footsteps echoed in the hall, and, seconds later, Skyla stepped into the room, followed by Theron's mate, Casey.

"Well?" Skyla asked, looking toward Orpheus.

Orpheus held out his hand toward her. "Call me Lord Orpheus. The great and powerful."

Skyla let her mate pull her to his side, but the look in her meadow-green eyes was hesitant as his arm wound around her waist. "Good gods. Is this what I have to put up with from now on?"

Orpheus's grin widened. "Baby, you love it." His brows lifted. "They're gonna give me this really cool robe. I'm thinking commando's the only way to go."

Across the room, Titus sighed. "Told ya this was a bad idea."

Casey rested a hand on her very round belly as she stood next to Theron and tipped her head. "It could have been worse. They could have made him Council leader. Then we'd all be in trouble."

Everyone laughed except Isadora. She rubbed her fingers over the pulse between her eyes, finding no humor in the situation, especially because she'd just listened to the lords drone on and on about the "problem" in their realm.

She dropped her hand and looked toward Theron. "The Council denied my aid request for the Misos, which means we have a situation. They're pushing for forced segregation, using the excuse that most of them have already moved outside the city. But the bottom line is they want to isolate the Misos in what's left of the Kyrenia settlement permanently."

"Of course they do," Skyla said, resting her forearm on Orpheus's shoulder and brushing her long blonde hair back from her face. "Because they're different. Anyone who's different is a threat to the Council's way of life. In that respect, they're just like the gods. And by that thinking, Maelea, Natasa, even I should be segregated with them."

"You're not going anywhere, Siren," Orpheus said firmly, his teasing tone long gone.

"Only because I have the backing of the Argonauts," Skyla answered her mate. "Those people don't."

Skyla felt as strongly about the Misos as Orpheus. They all did.

Isadora's frustration jumped another notch, and she moved toward the arching windows that looked out over the sparkling view of the city. They needed to be focusing on locating the water element—the last of the four classical elements they required to complete the Orb of Krónos, the magic disk that had the power to control Krónos's imprisonment in the Underworld. All the gods wanted the Orb that held the strength to start the war to end all wars, and the Argonauts had it—had it and were on the verge of being able to destroy it once and for all to protect not only their world, but all worlds. But their focus was now split between the Orb and Nick. And with the Council making threats against the Misos, that focus was waning even more.

"I have no problem with the Misos choosing to congregate together outside the city," Isadora said, "but not by force."

"What are you proposing?" Theron asked, eyeing her cautiously.

What *was* she proposing? Something that would draw her guardians away from their search for Nick and the remaining element. Something she hated to do but which she couldn't see another way around.

She turned to face the room. "I think the Council's going to move on the Misos once they have them segregated. They destroyed the Kyrenia settlement once before because the witches inhabited it, and they wanted to prevent them from rising to power. They forced what remained to the fringes of society. As Skyla said, they see any bit of difference as a threat."

"Fuckers," Orpheus muttered.

Theron ignored his interjection and focused on Isadora. "Have you seen something to indicate this?"

Her gift of foresight wasn't always reliable, especially when it related directly to her. And this definitely did. But what she had seen… Her stomach rolled all over again. She wasn't ready to share that with anyone, because she was hoping like hell it wouldn't come true.

"No." That was the truth. What she'd seen had nothing to do with the Misos. "But I feel it."

"I think she's right," Casey said, her soft brown hair swaying as she turned to look up at her mate. "I read about what the Council did to the Kyrenia settlement. A repeat of that would cut Isadora's power at the knees and make her look weak to the inhabitants of Argolea."

The burning of the Kyrenia settlement was a dark part of Argolea's history. It hadn't happened all that long ago, but Isadora remembered the stories about the suffering. Her father, the king, had granted the Council permission to eradicate what he deemed "a viable threat" from the witches, and though Isadora hadn't been strong enough to stand up to him or the Council then, she was determined there would never be a repeat.

"All life has value here," she said, "regardless of race, gender, or affiliation. And I'm not about to let Nick's legacy be destroyed. Protecting his people is the least we can do after everything he's done for us."

Casey smiled at her sister, but Isadora didn't have the strength to smile back. If the Council had their way, Casey would be segregated right along with the Misos. She was a true half-breed, but because she was the king's illegitimate daughter and the mate now to the leader of the Argonauts, they turned a blind eye to her.

"You're talking about pulling the monarchy's private guards and stationing them at the Misos settlement," Theron said.

"And Argonauts."

"And Argonauts," he muttered, clearly not approving of this plan. "That will leave the castle vulnerable."

It would. But Isadora couldn't see another way around it. "We tried keeping the Misos within the castle walls, but that didn't work. I don't blame them for wanting to get away from this place. Any kind of segregation is a prison, no matter how elaborate the facility may be. But if the Council gets their way and forces segregation, things are going to escalate quickly."

When the leader of the Argonauts clenched his jaw, Isadora sighed. "The job of the Argonauts was never to protect the monarchy or this castle, Theron. The Argonauts were established to protect the human realm, and the Misos are part of that. You know I'm right."

Theron didn't answer, but a vein ticked in his temple. One that told her he wasn't happy.

"Demetrius will never go along with this," Casey warned.

"This isn't Demetrius's call," Isadora said, looking at her sister. "It's mine." Demetrius was where he needed to be right now—looking for Nick—and it was time she did what she needed to do—take care of Nick's people.

She focused on Theron once more. "Tomorrow, I want you to take however many soldiers and Argonauts you need and secure the Misos. The rest of the Argonauts I want split into two groups. One looking for the remaining water element, and the other helping Demetrius search for Nick."

"My queen—" Theron started.

"That's my decision," she said firmly.

Shuffling sounded by the door before he could argue with her, and Isadora looked that direction. Max, her eleven-year-old nephew, stepped into the room carrying a smiling Elysia. Behind him, his mother and Isadora's other sister, Callia, followed.

The baby cooed, and Isadora's mood jumped at the sight of her happy daughter. Elysia was only six months old, but she was growing fast, and she looked huge in Max's arms.

The baby wrapped her chubby little fingers around a fistful of Max's shaggy blond hair, then pulled. The two had a special relationship. If Max was anywhere close, Elysia wanted to be near him.

"Ouch," Max said. "She's definitely got Argonaut genes. She's getting stronger every day."

Callia grinned behind him. "Babies tend to do that."

Orpheus let go of Skyla and pushed from the couch before Isadora could reach for her daughter. "Gimme that kid."

He swept Elysia up in his arms and moved over to the windows, bouncing the infant and talking to her in a singsongy sweet voice that sounded nothing like the smart-ass half witch who loved to antagonize the Council.

"Titus," Callia said, "Natasa's looking for you. I passed her in the library."

Titus's hazel eyes lit, and he quickly pushed away from Theron's desk. "That means my job here is done."

As he rushed out the door in search of his new mate, Skyla dropped onto the couch with a scowl. "Someone take that baby away from the lord of shits and giggles over there."

Orpheus turned from the window and shot her a wicked hot look. "Scared, Siren?"

Skyla arched a brow his way. "Of a baby? No. Of you and your not-so-bright ideas? Absolutely. You're not getting one, Daemon, so stop looking at me like that."

Orpheus grinned and refocused on Elysia in his arms. "Don't worry, my beautiful Lys. We'll talk some sense into her."

Skyla huffed. Elysia grabbed Orpheus's nose with her little hand. Laughter rang out in the room. From everyone but Isadora and Theron.

Lowering herself into a chair, Isadora ran her fingers over her forehead and tried to ignore the disapproving looks coming from the leader of the Argonauts.

Theron was worried about her. But this was bigger than the monarchy and the Argonauts. It was something she wouldn't back down from.

"Hey." Callia leaned against the arm of her chair, her auburn hair swaying with the movement. "You okay? You don't look so hot."

"I'm just tired," Isadora said. And missing Demetrius. And worried about Nick. And, based on that vision she'd had, hoping she wasn't making a giant mistake by putting herself smack dab in the middle of his people.

Callia smiled. "Everything's going to work out."

"Will it?" Isadora looked up at her sister. "How can you be sure?"

"Because the Fates aren't done with any of us. You just have to have faith."

Faith wasn't something Isadora put much stock in these days. Because she knew in the bottom of her heart that faith wasn't going to save Nick or his people. Action would. She glanced toward her happy daughter smiling up at Orpheus, and wished they could all feel that kind of joy again, Nick especially.

But something told her not even faith was going to be enough to stop this impending doom she sensed was coming in the pit of her stomach.

CHAPTER FOUR

Cynna pushed her way out from under Zagreus and stumbled from his giant platform bed. She didn't worry about waking him. After one of his "sessions," he slept like the dead, and tonight he'd been especially rough, which meant he was extremely tired.

Bastard.

She glared down at him, asleep on his stomach, completely naked, the blanket pushed to the floor. A serpent tattoo wrapped around his right shoulder and arm, and she could just see the edges of the scorpion on his left biceps. His body was all muscle, perfect in every way, but then, being a god, she expected nothing less. But never, not once in all the time she'd been here, had she ever felt anything for him besides resignation. Something she was surprised he'd never picked up on.

Her body ached—her back, her knees, her chest, her wrists— and though her stomach turned at the things she'd let him do to her, she knew she had no one to blame but herself. She never told him no. She never stood against him. Part of her rationalized it was because he was immortal, and it would do no good. But another part—a twisted part—knew it was because there was a place inside her that craved the darkness, even if she tried to rationalize she was simply using him as he was using her.

Disgusted with herself, she turned away, grabbed her clothes from the floor, crossed to his dresser and yanked the drawer open. She grasped the first shirt her hand closed around, slammed it shut, then stalked out of the room.

In the living area of his bedchamber, she jerked on his long-sleeved T-shirt, wincing at the ache in her shoulders, hating the smell and the way the cotton felt against her skin, but refusing to bind herself back up in that tight corset he made her parade around in. After tugging on her skirt, she slid on her boots, bent over to zip them closed, then caught sight of her wrists.

Bruises had already formed. Usually, he kept his "marks" where no one else could see them, but tonight he hadn't cared, as if he'd wanted to brand her as his property. And that meant tomorrow she'd have to work extra hard to cover them so none of his satyrs saw and decided it was time to have a go at her.

Fucking idiot. Her this time, not him. Because she wasn't strong enough to put a stop to something she knew was wrong.

She tugged the sleeves down to cover the marks, and as she did, her mind skipped to the dungeons, and *her* scarred prisoner. That was what Zagreus called him. Hers. As if he were a gift rather than a living being. Nothing in this godforsaken place was hers, though, and neither would she want it, but a place deep in the recesses of her mind was starting to wonder if anything *outside* it would ever be hers either.

Her jaw clenched. She pushed upright and marched out of his bedchamber, not wanting to think too much about that just yet. Stone steps led downward. Zagreus's lair was an underground tunnel compound in the cenote system of the Yucatan. The god was so perverse, he actually got extra pleasure knowing humans were frolicking at resorts and vacation destinations directly above his torture chambers, and if a few "accidentally" stumbled across his lair thanks to morbid curiosity—as he claimed to the Olympians whenever he was caught with a human—well then, that wasn't his fault, now was it?

Stalactites hung from the ceiling. She passed a porthole window alive with water and fish and coral but didn't stop to appreciate the view. There was nothing to appreciate in this miserable place, and every day she wondered why the hell she'd sold herself to Zagreus in the first place.

For revenge. To see them pay.

Yeah, but if he wasn't going to follow through on his end of the deal... Her stomach rolled, and a thought rippled through her mind, slowing her feet.

If he wasn't going to follow through, then she'd be stuck here forever, repeating what she'd had to do today, reliving what she'd endured tonight.

Her spine tingled, but she refused to accept that reality as she pushed her feet onward. By the time she reached her floor and headed across the landing, all she wanted was a few hours of peace before Zagreus forced her to do it all again.

Halfway to the arch that opened to a cluster of rooms, hers included, a voice called, "Mistress?"

Fuck.

She looked toward the redheaded Nereid, standing near the stairs with a wary expression. She wasn't a pleasure slave like the Maenads, the orgiastic nymphs trained by the god of ecstasy, Dionysus, which Zagreus had hauled back from the Amazons and whom he'd insisted on using on Nick earlier today. No, she was simply one of Zagreus's many servants who existed on the fringes of this nightmare, trying hard to blend into the shadows. Something Cynna could never do. "What?"

The Nereid—Cynna couldn't remember her name—took a hesitant step forward. "I've been looking for you. We have a…a problem."

Cynna didn't want to deal with any problems. It wasn't her responsibility. She turned back for her room. "Find a satyr and have him take care of it."

"I can't. They won't do anything. It's about your prisoner."

Cynna's feet stilled steps to freedom. And she thought of Nick in the dungeon.

Skata. Her eyelids dropped for a brief second before she opened them and glanced over her shoulder. "What about him?"

"He's… There's something wrong with him. His wounds have not healed the way they should. He's not well."

Not well. Double *skata.* It had to be the salve. She'd told Zagreus not to use it to enhance his reaction to the nymphs, but the son of a bitch never listened to her.

Indecision warred within her. She only wanted to go back to her room and wallow in her own misery for a few hours, not deal with someone else's, but she couldn't do that now. If his wounds weren't healing correctly, then she was the one who would eventually pay. Because, after all, he was *her* prisoner, and every bit of his torture—and care—was her responsibility.

Jaw clenching, she glared at the Nereid. "If you're bothering me with unnecessary trifles—"

"Rhene. My name is Rhene. And I'm not, I promise, Mistress. Come. Quickly."

Rhene grasped her thin skirt and hurried toward the stairs, leading Cynna into the bowels of the compound. They passed through the stone arches into the prison. Two satyrs stood guard at the entrance, eyeing Cynna and the nymph with more than contempt as they passed. There was interest there. Interest Cynna forced herself to ignore every single day. The only thing that kept her alive in this place was the fact Zagreus had claimed her as his. The minute he lost interest, she was dead.

Moans ricocheted through the cavern, and a chill spread down Cynna's spine as her heels clicked along the stone floor. Water dripped from the rocks around her, as if weeping, like the prisoners in the cells. Her stomach tossed as it always did when she came down here, but she focused on getting through the next few minutes.

Rhene stopped when she reached Nick's door. "Here. Look."

Peering through the window high in the door, Cynna swept her gaze over the dark space. The satyrs had taken him down from his chains. The room looked empty, and for a moment, panic sprang up. Then she caught sight of him, crumpled in the corner, his head leaning against the adjacent wall, his arms wrapped around his waist, his entire body shaking and covered in a thin layer of sweat.

That son-of-a-bitch fucking Zagreus. Infection had already set in. Nick might have superhuman genes that could repair any wound, but that salve had trapped bacteria inside before his body had a chance to heal itself. And now it was festering.

She looked down at Rhene. "Bring me a bed. I want a fresh mattress, not a dirty one, blankets, and clean towels."

Rhene's eyes grew wide. "But Zagreus—"

"Zagreus is not here. This prisoner is going to die unless we help him. You were in charge of his care while I was away. Do you want his death on your head?"

Fear flashed in Rhene's eyes, and she quickly shook her head.

"Then take care of it," Cynna snapped. "Bring everything I've asked for. Along with medicinal herbs and the healer's kit. And do it quickly."

Rhene turned and sighed as she headed back for the entrance of the prison.

Alone, Cynna chewed on the inside of her lip as she looked into the cell. She couldn't just go in. Even sick and feverish, Nick was strong. And she wasn't stupid enough to put herself in any kind of situation where he could retaliate against her—because he had every reason to want to do so.

Steeling her nerves, she marched up to the guard's station. The keeper of the prison—Lykos—eyed her with heat and lust as she approached, just as he always did. "Mistress. To what do we owe this unexpected...pleasure?"

Just the way he said "pleasure" sent a shudder down her spine. Lykos had a wicked streak in him. One Zagreus approved of and often let loose. She'd seen what the satyr had done to a couple of nymphs with his hands and a cane, and she didn't want the bastard anywhere near her. She also didn't want him to *know* she didn't want him near her.

"The prisoner in fourteen is ill. I have to treat him, but he needs to be shackled first."

Lykos's gaze skipped past her down the dark corridor, then back again. "I've had no instruction from the prince."

"Nor will you. I just left his bed." She tipped her head. "But I could wake him for you if you'd like, and he could tell you himself."

Wariness crept into Lykos's eyes. Waking Zagreus was never a good thing, and even he didn't want to be on the receiving end of the Prince of Darkness's wrath. Without a word, he grabbed shackles from a shelf behind him, then brushed past Cynna and headed down the hall.

She waited while the grind of metal sounded, and he unlocked the door, then pushed it open. Nick didn't move, just opened his eyes and squinted at the light spilling into the room.

"Hands," Lykos barked.

Nick's face was pale and slicked with sweat. His chest rose and fell with quick, uneven jerks. He still didn't move his body away from the rocks or lift his head, but he did manage to slide his chained arms in front of him, enough so Lykos could remove the restraints that kept him attached to the wall and close the shackles around his wrists.

Some kind of commotion sounded from the hallway. Cynna turned just as Rhene and two more satyrs appeared, dragging a metal bedframe and a bare mattress with them.

Cynna pointed to the far wall. "There."

The first satyr set down the frame; the other dropped the mattress on top. Rhene lit the torch on the far wall, then set a leather satchel to the left of the door.

When the satyrs straightened, Cynna nodded toward Nick. "Move him to the bed."

The guards wrapped their hands around his arms and hauled him to his feet. He grimaced but didn't make a sound. The same towel Nick had worn earlier was wrapped around his hips again, but Cynna's attention focused on the wound on his leg. Or what was left of it. No longer open and oozing as it had been earlier today, but healed over, swollen, and red.

The last thing she needed was for him to get blood poisoning and die. If that happened, her death was imminent. And as much as she hated the fact her fate was now tied to his, she also didn't want him to die, because she was afraid if he did, that darkness threatening her soul really would win. Suddenly, he was all that stood between her and an eternity of misery every part of her knew she deserved.

She thought about telling them to be gentle but held her tongue. They laid him on the bed, and he groaned. Lykos ran a chain to his cuffs and locked it to a ring along the top of the bedframe. The ring could slide the width of the bed, but it still forced his arms over his head. He rolled to his side so his bent arms were in front of him, exhaled a long breath, and shivered.

She'd done terrible things while she'd been here. Horrendous, awful things she never should have participated in. A niggling voice in the back of her head whispered this was her penance.

"Leave us," Cynna said.

When Lykos shot her a glare, she pinned him with a hard look. "Do you want to be the one to stay and oversee this?"

A *no way in hell* look flashed in his eyes, and he crossed to the door. Cynna held out her hand as he drew near. "The key."

"Mistress, that is unwise. If the prince discovers—"

"The key," she said louder.

His expression shifted to *it's your funeral*, but he dropped the key in her palm and motioned for the other satyrs to follow.

When they were gone, Cynna drew one steadying breath. Nick's eyes were closed, his body limp against the bare mattress, his marked forearms near his face, his knees tucked up to his waist.

He looked as if he were sleeping, but she knew it was delirium from the fever racking his body, not rest.

She shouldn't be in this cell. She shouldn't even be in this realm. What she'd done... There was no redemption for what she'd done. But she was here now, and for the first time in ages, she was determined to do the right thing. Even if tomorrow fate forced her back to doing wrong.

The nymph at her side shifted her feet, and any hope Cynna had of wallowing in her own misery slid to the wayside. She zeroed in on the wound on Nick's leg. "Rhene, close the door. I'm going to need your help."

Rhene's shoulders dropped, but she shuffled toward the door as instructed. Seconds later, an ominous clank echoed through the room.

"Now," Cynna said, "hand me a knife."

Nick opened his eyes and looked up at the rock ceiling above.

Torchlight flickered off the stones, illuminating the space, which was strange because usually he was left in darkness unless he was being put through one of his torture sessions.

He shifted, tried to move his arms, but realized they were cuffed together and attached to a chain above his head. Something soft pressed against his back. Rolling to his side, he pushed up on his shoulder and glanced around. Yeah, this was still his cell, but he was in a bed—a real bed. His hips and legs were covered by a thin blanket, and across the room—

Every muscle went still as he looked over the female sitting on his pallet of blankets in the corner, her head resting against the rocks, her eyes closed, her long legs stretched out in front of her.

Cynna.

His pulse picked up speed. He glanced toward the door, trying to figure out what was going on, but it was tightly shut. Looking back at her, he realized she wasn't dressed as she normally was when she came to him. Yes, she was still wearing those ridiculous boots and that short skirt that showed off her toned legs, but instead of the corset that pushed out her breasts, she was dressed in a loose, long-sleeved T-shirt that seemed to swallow her whole. A T-shirt that was smeared with blood.

He tried to shift more upright and was thankful to discover his feet weren't shackled. The chain along the top of the metal bedframe slid along the bar while he moved, and he was able to lean back against the wall. His mind tumbled with possibilities as he tried not to make any noise. If she'd done something to piss Zagreus off, he didn't doubt the sick son of a bitch would toss her in Nick's cell just to see what Nick would do. And right now, he didn't know what he wanted to do. This was the female who'd directed his torture over the last six months. He had every reason to want to retaliate against her. But she was also the one person he hadn't been able to stop thinking about in the same amount of time, proving he was as sick as everyone else in this godsforsaken place.

The chains rattled, and he froze, but she was already waking— her eyes fluttering open, her head lifting from the wall, her gaze searching and finding his across the dim room.

For a split second, guilt crept into her eyes, then she blinked and it was gone as if it had never happened. And as she pushed to her feet and smoothed down her short little skirt, Nick wondered if it had happened at all or if he was finally losing his fucking mind and hallucinating.

She crossed the room and reached for the blanket. His muscles bunched, and he drew his legs up, ready to kick out if he had to.

Her hand stilled inches from touching him. "I'm not here to hurt you. I'm here to help. You were injured."

He didn't know how to read her. He was always injured in this damn place, but no one had ever tried to help him in any way. "Why should I trust you?"

That guilt flashed in her chocolate, way-too-familiar eyes once more. Another quick spark that was there, then quickly gone. And not for the first time, he had that strange sense that he'd met her before. Or someone like her. He just couldn't figure out where.

"You have no reason to," she answered in that velvety voice, the one that always amped him up. "But if I'm right, and you don't let me help, you will die. Not even your superhuman genes can heal you from this."

Part of him wanted to die, to be finished with this hell, but another part wasn't ready. Because he hadn't figured out how to take Zagreus with him yet.

She reached for the blanket again, and this time he let her, not because he trusted her, but because he sensed she wasn't totally lying. There was something wrong with him, some kind of infection making him weaker than he should be. Something he should have healed from on his own.

She pushed the blanket aside to reveal his bare leg. Cool air washed over his skin, reminding him he was naked beneath the fabric and covered in a thin layer of sweat. A shiver racked his body.

But the cold was quickly replaced by heat. Surprised, he looked down to see her kneeling in front of him, much like the nymphs yesterday. But unlike them, she wasn't teasing. Her soft fingers carefully removed a bandage from around his thigh, one he didn't remember receiving. And every brush of her hand against his leg sent awareness spiraling all through his limbs.

She pulled the cloth away, then her warm, electric touch skimmed the outside of a jagged, already healing incision.

"Hmm." She moved away, and chill air swept over him again, but then she was back, kneeling in front of him once more, her body inches from his, her heated touch sending another shiver down his spine, this one not from the temperature.

Blood rushed into his cock, proving he wasn't as sick as he thought. He fought back his body's reaction as her warm breath tickled his skin, bringing the hairs along his leg to attention. She smoothed some kind of ointment over the incision, and he sucked in air when warm tingles spread through his skin and permeated his muscles. But they didn't shoot straight to his groin as they had yesterday. This was a healing warmth, not an arousing one. At least the balm was. She was another matter entirely.

He was quiet while she wiped her hands on a rag, then reached for fresh bandages from a bag near her feet. Her blonde hair hung past her shoulders, one thick blue streak brushing her temple as she looked down at her work. Her skin was shades darker than his, like warm, gooey caramel, and he found himself fascinated at the contrast. Fascinated again by her—who she was, how she'd come to be in a hellhole like this, and what she was doing with a sick fuck like Zagreus.

"You smell like him," he muttered.

"And you smell like sweat," she answered, not looking up. "Neither of us are getting any awards for how we smell."

For some reason, that eased the knot growing in the pit of his stomach. Then he saw the marks on her wrists. Cuts and bruises he knew all too well, because he lived with them daily thanks to the restraints. Cuts and bruises that hadn't been on her skin earlier.

"What happened to your wrists?"

Her fingers faltered on the bandage, then she resumed wrapping and secured the end. "Nothing."

Bullshit it was nothing. His gaze traveled up her arms, to the collar of the long-sleeved, too-big T-shirt she wore. The neck gaped open, showing just a hint of skin above her breasts. Skin that also looked inflamed. Reaching out with his cuffed hands, he hooked his finger in the collar and tugged so he could see better.

She'd been struck there, with a whip or flogger, he couldn't tell which.

She jerked back and slapped a hand over her chest, pressing the shirt closed. Disbelief flashed in her eyes, followed by a quick burst of horror she masked quickly.

She pushed to her feet and glared down at him. "I could have you beaten for that."

"You already have." And suddenly, a beating was the least of his concerns. His gaze skipped to her wrists. "What did he do to you?"

She grasped her supplies from the floor and shoved them back into the bag, averting her eyes, moving quickly now to get away from him. "Nothing I didn't ask him to do."

He'd hit a nerve. There was more she wasn't saying. A lot more. That feeling that she was as much a prisoner in this hell as he slammed into Nick again.

"Your infection is down," she said, still not looking his way. "You'll be fine in another day."

She grasped the bag, crossed to the door, and slid a key into the lock from the inside. Nick wanted to ask what, exactly, they were healing him for, but then his gaze rolled over her. Over her frazzled appearance, the dark circles under her eyes, and her unkempt hair. And he realized she was exhausted. She obviously hadn't slept much, and it had to be morning. She'd come to him sometime in the night and stayed.

He wanted to ask why. Why it had been her, why she hadn't sent someone else, why she even cared if he lived or died. But he couldn't. Because part of him didn't want to hear the answer. And another part—the dark part—didn't want to give her any reason never to come back.

Metal scraped metal, the hinges creaked, and then the thick steel door swung inward. She took one step into the corridor.

"Cynna."

Her feet stilled, but she didn't turn. And in the silence, Nick's pulse shot up. It was the first time he'd said her name, and he liked the sound of it. Liked the way it rolled off his tongue. Liked—more than anything—that she reacted. And suddenly wanted to hear her say his name back in that sinful voice of hers. Just once.

His throat grew thick, and desire seared all through his body. A desire he now knew was focused solely on her. "Thank you."

She didn't answer. He didn't expect her to. But his body was hot and tight regardless. And as the cell door clanged shut in her wake, a bitter truth rang out.

He wanted her. He wanted her naked and spread before him, crying out in that sexy, dominatrix voice. He wanted her on her knees, driving him wild with her sinful mouth, wanted her bound and bent over, shaking from his deep thrusts. He wanted her even knowing it was twisted in every way imaginable and that she should be the one person he hated above all others. But he couldn't stop himself from wanting. Because wanting her gave him something to focus on.

And because for the first time in he didn't know how long, he wanted someone other than his soul mate.

CHAPTER FIVE

"That is not the answer I was hoping to hear."

Standing across Zagreus's palatial office, Hades, the god-king of the Underworld and Zagreus's pain-in-the-ass father, turned from the underwater-glass view he'd been staring at and pinned his son with a scathing look.

Zagreus fought from rolling his eyes and kicked back in his chair. "These things take time. You brought him here for a reason. You can't rush perfection."

Hades turned fully to face him. "You've had six months. His strength is growing—I can feel it—but you've yet to break him. If you cannot do so soon, I'll be forced to take him back."

Zagreus huffed. Hades would never take Nick to the Underworld. The closer Nick was to Krónos, the more likely the elder god would find out and send one of his minions from Tartarus to abduct him. Then all hell—literally—would break loose. No, Hades wouldn't risk losing his prize to his father, which meant Nick was Zagreus's until the job was done.

"I don't have to take him to the Underworld," Hades said, reading his son's mind. "I could let your mother finish what you started."

Oh no. No way in hell. Zagreus sat forward and slapped his hand against the stone desk, hating more than anything that his father was reading his mind and conjuring powers so Zagreus couldn't block him. He wasn't handing Nick over to Persephone, the Queen of the Dead. She was as power hungry as Hades and would double-cross them all in a heartbeat to gain access to Krónos's powers. "She'll not touch him. He's mine."

Hades crossed the floor in a wisp of black and slammed his palms on the desk, towering over his son in a fury of darkness. "No, he is *mine*. And you'll not soon forget that fact, or I will tear away from you the one thing you care most about in this world."

Zagreus stared up at his father, a mixture of malice and hatred coursing through his veins. "You wouldn't dare."

"Push me, and you'll discover exactly what I dare."

Zagreus wanted nothing but to push his fucking father right out of this world for good, but until he broke Nick and harnessed the demigod's unused powers for himself, he would never be able to do that. Hades was too strong, and even though Zagreus was a god, he couldn't beat his father. Not in ability, at least. In cunning, though, he'd learned from the master and was determined to win this game.

He relaxed back into his seat, feigning indifference. "I care not what happens to the demigod. I simply do not want to see Mother sink her claws into him. There's no telling what she would unleash."

"Nor do I," Hades said, straightening. "Your mother is my last choice, which is why I brought him to you first. We have a deal, my son. Don't make me remind you."

A deal that was heavily weighted on Hades's side. "*Serve me or I will decimate everything you have built.*" Who in their right mind would say no to that?

Zagreus drummed his fingers along the stone table, fighting back his contempt. "I've not forgotten the deal. And I'm living up to my end of it. He will break soon."

"You have a month," Hades announced. "A month to finish what I started, or I will come and claim him. I'll know the moment his powers are unleashed, so do not try to screw me on this."

Hades knew his son well, but Zagreus wasn't planning to double-cross the god for the reasons his father expected. He didn't give a shit about the human realm, the land Hades and his two brothers, Zeus and Poseidon, were each clamoring for. No, he wanted a kingdom more perfect. A world more enticing. A race way more responsive than those simpering humans the gods loved to toy with. He wanted Argolea all to himself.

Hades moved for the door, but stopped before he reached the threshold and looked back. "For you own good, son, you should rid yourself of the female."

A fury Zagreus only barely held back whipped through him with the force of a tornado. "You'll not touch her."

"I wouldn't dream of it. Unless you fuck with me. But mark my words. You've grown soft where she is concerned. If you keep her, she will be your undoing."

"Like Mother Dearest is yours?"

A wicked, evil grin twisted the god-king of the Underworld's lips. "Your mother is strength reincarnated. The female you've attached yourself to is nothing but destruction. Find another to fuck and rid yourself of her before she ruins you for all eternity."

Hades poofed into the ether as quickly as he'd arrived. And alone, Zagreus looked across the dim room, flickering with a blue-green light from the underwater window.

His father was wrong. Cynna was not any sort of destruction. She was his way out. The one shining beacon of hope in his endless fucking life of misery. And she would never dare stand against him. He made sure of that on a continual basis.

But even as he tried to convince himself of that fact, his mind skipped back to the fight yesterday in the ring. To the way she'd been watching the prisoner below. To the look that had been in her eyes. A look he'd noticed but hadn't thought much about until right this minute.

Fear.

Worry.

Compassion.

The first two didn't concern him. But the last caused an odd tightness to condense in his chest.

The dark energy inside—the energy that kept him powerful—welled like a living, breathing creature in the pit of his soul, wrapping gnarled tentacles around his thoughts, spurring his actions. He pushed out of his chair before he could stop himself and stalked through the caverns until he found the stairs, then skipped steps to get to her floor.

He didn't knock when he reached her room, simply turned the doorknob and stepped inside. The lights were off, the only illumination the same eerie blue-green light from an underwater window much like the one in his office. He looked around, that dark energy snarling and swirling every second he didn't see her. And then he spotted her, sound asleep on her stomach in the middle of the bed, her head tipped his way on the pillow, her blonde hair spilling over her back and partially blocking her perfect face.

Crossing to the bed, he sat on the edge of the mattress and brushed a blue-streaked lock away from her temple. She'd taken off her boots but nothing else. She'd been so exhausted after she'd left his bedchamber last night, she hadn't even bothered to climb under the covers. His gaze slid over her body, over the short skirt that showed off her wicked legs and his long-sleeved T-shirt that was three sizes too big for her. A burst of relief stole through him as he took in every delectable inch of her.

Remind her who's in control. Make sure she never forgets...

Thoughts spun out of control. Dark, warped, angry thoughts that were fueled by the shadow energy churning inside, the energy that was rooted to the Underworld and which fed his powers. His fingers tangled in the ends of her hair, and he squeezed his hand into a tight fist, a blinding urge to yank on her scalp, to wake her with pain consuming him. But he struggled against it. Giving in to that energy kept him strong, but he hated the outcome. Hated what it made him do. Especially to her.

Slowly, he released his grip on her hair and smoothed his fingers down the silky blonde locks. He'd scored a major victory when she'd come to him looking for a deal, and he couldn't let her go. Not if he ever hoped to break free of his father's control. He could lose his underground kingdom, he could even lose his satyrs—he wouldn't care—but he wasn't about to lose her and the promise of freedom she'd become.

"Sleep, my sweet Cynna. We still have much work to do."

He pushed from the bed and stared down at her. The dark energy still raged inside, but this time, he fought it back. This time, he wasn't going to let it control him.

Because this time, he finally had a way out.

Cynna couldn't shake the chill.

Seated at one end of the long dining table while conversation drifted around her, she stared into the crackling fire in the big stone fireplace and watched the flames lick and skip over the charred wood. Where did Zagreus get the wood? His lair was in an underground cave system. Someone had to leave and bring it back. Why couldn't she have been given *that* job instead of being branded the mistress of pain and torture?

And why, in the name of all the gods, had Nick thanked her after everything she'd done to him?

The flame popped and sizzled as it rolled over the log, consuming it from the outside in. She felt like that piece of wood. Like there was nothing she could do to stop the fire from devouring her. Like she was trapped with no escape. Like she was destined to be nothing more than a cold, dark shell of her former self, much as that log would be ash by morning.

Thank you.

Thank you.

Another shiver rippled down her spine. She didn't deserve Nick's thanks after the things she'd done. She didn't deserve anything but vengeance from him. And in no way should he be thanking her for prolonging his never-ending torture.

Thank you...

"*Agapi?*"

It took several seconds to realize Zagreus was talking to her. Tearing her gaze from the fire, Cynna looked to her left, toward the head of the table where he sat leaning against the armrest of his chair, watching her with assessing, black-as-night eyes.

Blinking several times, she fought from swallowing and showing any ounce of that weakness he thrived upon. "Yes?"

"You've had little to say tonight. Do you not think the session went well?"

He was talking about Nick's torment by the nymphs. Zagreus had given Nick a day to recuperate after Lykos had informed the god his prized prisoner hadn't healed correctly after the use of that salve. Cynna had been surprised by the break in schedule, but she'd been so tired from everything, she'd spent all day sleeping—another tidbit that had surprised her...that Zagreus had *let* her rest. Usually he gave no thought to her wants or needs.

Her gaze flicked to Lykos, seated across from her. She'd also been dismayed to learn the satyr had *not* informed Zagreus she'd spent the night in Nick's cell taking care of him. She wasn't sure what Lykos's motives were, but neither was she about to ask.

She forced the image of Nick's torture from her mind. She couldn't think about it. She'd barely been able to stomach being in the same room. The only way she'd been able to get through it was to zone out like she always did when someone was tortured in front of her. But even now—a full day later—she could hear his strangled groans. She could feel the rattle of his chains in the rock walls around her. And at any moment, she expected her body to break out into a cold sweat—the same sweat that had coated his pale skin.

She was a coward. She knew it. For not standing up to Zagreus, for letting this go on, for doing nothing to help those in pain in the dungeons below.

Thank you…

"*Agapi?*"

Blinking rapidly, she looked to her left again. To Zagreus's curious expression.

Holy *skata*. She needed to focus on the here and now. Needed to pull her shit together and remember what was important. Needed—more than anything—to get out of this damn dining room and away from Zagreus before he saw her vulnerability and pounced.

"How the session went is of no matter," she said in a voice she worked to keep even.

"And why is that, my sweet Cynna?" Zagreus reached for the decanter and refilled his wine goblet. "I saw what those nymphs were doing." He smirked at Lykos. "No human could hold out much longer against that."

Lykos chuckled. He knew full well what the nymphs were capable of—if forced. *The bastard.*

"No human would," Cynna agreed. "But he is not fully human, now is he?"

Zagreus carefully set his goblet down and pinned her with a hard, calculating look. "What are you saying?"

What was she saying? Something she probably shouldn't. But she was tired of kowtowing to Zagreus. And his minions. "He won't break from this. He's too strong."

Zagreus's eyes narrowed and sharpened, and though the fine hairs along her nape stood straight, she lifted her chin, refusing to back down.

After several long seconds, he looked toward the satyr for confirmation. "Lykos?"

Lykos's heated stare and snarled grin told her he knew she was walking a very fine line and that he couldn't wait to see her fall off her perch. It also told her he'd be there to claim her when she did. "He'll break, my prince. It's only a matter of time. The female does not know of what she speaks."

Cynna was sick and tired of taking Lykos's shit. She slapped a hand on the table and leaned forward. "I know more than you will ever know about the people of his world, beast."

Every muscle in Lykos's body tensed, and a growl rose in his throat.

Zagreus chuckled and cut into his bloody steak. "Too bad we can't just sic Cynna on him. She could break any man with that mouth." He speared a piece of meat with his knife, his humor fading. "Time is the issue here, now isn't it?"

Anger pumped off Lykos in waves. He stared at Cynna with malice and contempt brewing in his dark eyes, but she was done letting him take potshots at her. Especially in front of Zagreus. *Come on, you bastard, come at me, right now.*

The satyr's hand curled into a fist against the scarred wooden surface of the table. He glanced toward Zagreus and back at her, judging his chances.

Zagreus chewed, then swallowed and took a sip of wine as if nothing were happening. He might get rough with her from time to time, but if one of his satyrs laid a hand on her, Zagreus would rip his throat out with his bare hands. She'd watched him do it. And she couldn't wait to see him do it again, right now.

Zagreus set his wine down. "The nymphs were good, but we're going to need to step things up. I want to see progress. Lykos, you've more knowledge of the nymphs' secret talents than I. Which one can get the job done?"

Lykos relaxed back into his chair, but fire still brewed in his eyes. A fire seared with the promise of retribution. "Nesaea," he said, answering the prince but continuing to stare at Cynna. "She's shown a high pain tolerance. I think she likes giving as much as receiving."

Zagreus chuckled and cut another bite of bloody meat. "I know a female like that myself."

That was all Cynna could take. She couldn't sit here a minute longer and put up with Lykos's venomous looks or listen to the various ways he and Zagreus were going to use the nymphs to break Nick or continue to ignore either of their derogatory comments directed at her.

She pushed back from the table. "If you'll excuse me."

Zagreus's utensils stilled over his plate. "You've barely touched your dinner."

Her gaze flicked to Lykos. "I've suddenly lost my appetite."

Zagreus sat back and considered her. "You worry me, *agapi*. I do not like to be worried."

She hesitated. The last thing she needed was any kind of extra attention from the Prince of Darkness. But what concerned her most was the look in his stormy dark eyes. A look she'd seen before but tried to ignore. One that hinted of some kind of vulnerability. Of a whisper of…humanity.

Which was an asinine thought. There was no humanity in him. He was a devil. One spawned from Hades himself. One who took great pleasure in pain and craved only torture. Finding something…anything…redeeming in Zagreus only signaled just how far he'd sucked her into this mind fuck.

Working to relax her jaw, she forced the contempt from her voice when she said, "No need to worry. I'm just tired. I had a rough night."

That look lingered in his eyes. Only this time she saw a flash of…

No, she had to be wrong. The Prince of Darkness couldn't possibly feel guilty for what he'd done to her last night.

He blinked, and the look passed. As if it had never happened. Reaching for his wine goblet, he said, "In that case, I suppose I can let you go. This once." He glanced her way and winked. "Rest up, my love. I need you in tip-top shape for what is yet to come."

Cynna's stomach rolled, but she forced herself not to answer. Turning out of the dining room, she told herself she was just tired; that was why she was seeing things that weren't there. She moved through the stone doorway, heading for the circular stairs in the middle of the compound that led to freedom.

No, not freedom. A miniscule respite from hell. Something Nick would never have.

The suite was dim when she stepped inside and closed the door at her back, the only illumination from the underwater window casting that blue-green shimmer of light across the floor. Her room was one of the larger ones in the compound. It had the same rock walls and ceiling as every other room, but it was softer, more feminine, and she knew Zagreus went to great lengths to keep her well pampered.

A plush white carpet lay across the stone floor; a king-size, distressed, white four-poster bed sat along one wall. Her sitting area was comprised of two oversize chairs and a long couch—also done in white—and along the opposite wall were her books. Books from all over the world. Stories of adventures and romance and mysteries she often read to unwind. Stories that took her away from this nightmare and gave her something else to think about. To dream about. To want.

But that was all they were. Stories. They weren't real. There was no such thing as happily ever after. She knew that better than anyone.

Pushing away from the door, she crossed the floor and turned into her closet. Like the rest of her suite, it was grand, rows and rows of clothes Zagreus rewarded her with for good behavior. Half of which she'd never worn. More corsets and slutty skirts and foot-cramping stiletto boots? No, thank you.

After unzipping her current torture shoes, she tossed them aside, tugged off her skirt, and managed to unlace the air-constricting high-necked corset enough so she could shimmy out of it. She ripped off the thick bracelets she'd worn to cover the marks on her wrists, kicked it all aside, not caring where it landed, then moved into her bathroom.

She flipped on the water and stepped under the shower spray. Closing her eyes, she drew in a deep breath, then let it out again as the hot water pounded her skin. Aside from her books, this was the only pleasure she got in this place. But even that tiny bit of relief was dimmed when she thought of Nick again in the dungeons. He had no relief there, no chance for respite, not even an ounce of hope to get him through to the next day.

Bracing her hand against the rock wall, she opened her eyes as water cascaded down her face, dragging her makeup with it. Hope was a dangerous thing. Hope had brought her to Zagreus. Hope had convinced her to accept his deal. And hope was keeping her alive, day after miserable day, because it gave her something to think about other than how wretched her life had become.

But that hope was fading. Zagreus wasn't going to live up to his end of their bargain. She'd seen it in his eyes last night when she'd asked him how things were going on his end. She'd felt it with every strike of that flogger. But mostly she sensed it in what was left of her heart. And the longer she stayed here…the longer she did what he commanded without taking a stand, the more of herself she was going to lose until she really was nothing but a cold, black ember like the wood in his fireplace.

This wasn't who she was supposed to be. This wasn't the woman her mother had raised. And if either of her parents could see her now…

She closed her eyes, dropped her head under the spray again, and pursed her lips to hold back the groan from working its way up her throat. She'd done all this for them. But they wouldn't want this. They wouldn't understand. And every minute she stood here, bending to Zagreus's will, was another minute she moved further away from what was left of their memory.

"What we did yesterday doesn't matter. It's what we do today that determines who we are."

Her mother's voice rolled through her mind, and her thoughts centered on Nick in the dungeon below.

She couldn't free him. She couldn't save him without killing them both. But she could do something to ease his suffering. Something no one else dared do.

Nerves bunched and gathered in her stomach, making her pulse beat faster, making her breaths come quicker. She opened her eyes and stared at the rocks in front of her while her heart pounded hard, wondering if she had the strength to really go through with it.

CHAPTER SIX

Seated on the floor in his cell, his back resting against the cool rocks, Nick squinted through the darkness to look up at the ceiling above his head.

He couldn't see it, but he knew the chains shackled to his wrists looped up through hooks in the ceiling, then disappeared into small pipes high along the wall. Right now the chains were loose, allowing enough slack so he could sit and move around the back half of the room, but the tension was controlled by a button near his cell door. A button he'd stared at hour upon hour, trying to figure how in all of hell he could access it from clear across the room.

His gaze strayed to his arms resting on his bent knees, then to the metal cuffs, barely visible in the dark. The only light shone from beneath the door and the one small window that looked out at the hall, but it was enough so he could see his callused palms as he turned his wrists, then the scabs on the backs of his hands.

Ancient Greek text ran down his forearms and intertwined his fingers. Text that marked him as an Argonaut. Text that had dictated his life until he'd been brought here, made him think he could be a leader for his people, made him think he was something honorable.

But he wasn't honorable. He wasn't even an Argonaut. He was Krónos's son—which, in a sick sort of way, explained a lot—and though just the thought turned his stomach, right about now he wasn't averse to a little of his so-called father's power. Because if he could figure out how the fuck to harness some of those almighty gifts Zagreus thought he had in him, he could break out of this shithole and rain holy hell down on the Prince of Darkness and any other god who got in his way.

Metal scraped metal across the room. Lifting his head, Nick tensed and squinted through the darkness to see what was happening.

The door creaked, and torchlight from the hallway flooded the opening, forcing him to blink several times at the increased light. But he didn't need to see who was stepping into his room to know who it was. He could smell her. The sweet scent of jasmine preceded her everywhere she went, and his entire body responded in an instant, tightening in anticipation.

"Stand." Cynna's velvety voice slid over him like a caress, bringing every inch of his skin to life.

Slowly, he pushed to his feet, the chains on his wrists rattling as he moved. Torture at night wasn't a surprise. He'd learned not to relax even in utter darkness, because he never knew when they were going to come for him, but her being here now was a shocker. As was the fact the door was closing behind her, locking them in together alone.

The room grew dark again. She pushed that button on the wall near the door, and the tension in the chains grew taut, dragging his arms up and away from his body, forcing him to step out from the wall. She let the motor hum for several seconds as his arms were lifted, then pushed Stop when his elbows were at a right angle. Not exactly comfortable, but not as painful as when the satyrs wrenched his arms over his head, pulling on his sockets, making him grapple to hold himself upright.

The stones were cold on the soles of his feet, and brisk air washed over his spine. Today—thankfully—he wasn't naked to start. The cotton drawstring pants might be thin, but they gave him at least a little protection from whatever was coming. Shifting his arms, he wrapped his hands around the chains for balance. Fabric rustled, and then the torch on the far wall flared to life, casting warm illumination over the cell. He looked away as his eyes adjusted to the light, then slowly slid his gaze back her way and nearly swallowed his tongue.

She wasn't decked out in her usual dominatrix getup. Tonight her blonde hair was pulled back into a neat tail, showing off the supple line of her jaw, and her face was void of makeup, making her look years younger than before. Instead of the skintight corset and skimpy skirt she always wore, she was dressed in a thin black tank and loose-fitting, soft pink cotton pajama pants that accentuated her natural curves. But what surprised him most was the fact her feet were as bare as his. As if she hadn't planned to come down to the dungeon tonight. As if she'd rushed and forgotten shoes.

He watched her carefully, wondering what she was up to, wondering what she had planned. Aside from the other night when he'd been sick and she'd tended his wound, she never came alone. Quietly, she set a small bag on the floor near the door, withdrew something he couldn't see and slipped it into her pocket, then pulled out a white plastic bottle and turned to face him.

Her dark eyes found his and held. Eyes that didn't look as flat and dead as they had in days past. She twirled the bottle in her hand several times, then stepped forward. Heat gathered in his belly and slinked downward as she drew close, and his skin tingled at the prospect of her touch. A touch he shouldn't want but couldn't seem to stop fantasizing about.

Her sultry heat encircled him as she drew near. She uncapped the bottle and held it to his lips. "Drink."

When he hesitated, she tipped her head, and something gentle passed over her eyes. Something he couldn't quite read. "It's only water. I promise."

His mouth felt suddenly dry. Fresh water was a rarity in this place. One he craved.

She pressed the tip of the bottle to his lips, and he opened slowly, feeling the smooth plastic against his skin. In a rush, cool, clear water washed over his tongue, flooding his mouth, awakening his taste buds, making him groan.

One side of her lips ticked up, just a touch, just enough to change the entire look of her face. In an instant, she went from hard and jaded to soft and...gorgeous. "I guess it's safe to say you like that."

He did. But not just the water. He liked that she was the one pouring it into his mouth. Blood rushed from his belly into his cock as he watched her watching him. And excitement he knew he shouldn't be feeling energized his body and made his pulse beat hard in his arteries.

"Careful," she said in that sexy, alluring voice as she pulled the water bottle away. "I don't want you to get sick."

Sickness was the last thing on his mind. She had suddenly become the center of everything. He licked his lips while she capped the bottle and set it down, watching her every movement.

Drawing a deep breath, she stood in front of him once more and nodded toward his leg. "I need to check your wound."

She didn't wait for his answer, simply lowered to the floor and braced her hands on her thighs. And in the silence, as he waited for that first touch, Nick couldn't help but think back to those nymphs kneeling in front of him yesterday just like this, to the way they'd ripped off his towel, to the things they'd done with their hands and mouths.

His cock stiffened and swelled, but not with remembered arousal. No, this arousal was purely from the prospect of watching Cynna kneeling so submissively in front of him, preparing to touch him in any way she wanted.

And *skata*, how fucking twisted was it that he knew some kind of torture was coming, but he couldn't wait to see what she did next?

His pulse roared as her soft fingers grasped the hem of his left pant leg. The pants were loose enough for her to push the thin cotton all the way up his knee, past his wound. Tingles raced across his skin as she lifted the fabric higher, and he swallowed hard, fighting back his traitorous body's reaction. Only when she bunched the fabric together around his upper thigh did he realize his ankles weren't shackled as they had been yesterday.

He was always shackled—arms, legs—and the guards knew never to get close enough to his mouth where he could bite. But tonight, either she'd forgotten he was capable of retaliation, or she just didn't care. If he wanted, he could wrap his legs around her and squeeze the life out of her in a matter of seconds.

But even as the thought circled, he knew he wouldn't do it. Not because she didn't deserve it after everything she'd put him through, but because that dark place inside him was anxious to see where this was headed. And because every time her silky fingers brushed his skin, the electrical vibrations shooting through his limbs were better than anything he'd felt in a long time, even if he was chained and completely at her mercy. Even knowing things could turn straight to shit.

She freed the end of the bandage and slowly unrolled it from around his thigh. As the last of the cotton pulled free, cool air washed over his skin but was immediately replaced by her heat as she shifted forward to get a good look at his wound. And just seeing her lean in like that, so close to his groin, her warm breath fanning the sensitive skin of his inner thigh, his cock pulsed and grew painfully hard.

"This looks better." She pressed her fingers all around the wound. A dull ache radiated outward from the spot, but it was quickly replaced with the heat of her fingers and more of those tiny electrical vibrations that felt so damn good.

Slowly, she lowered her hand and eased back onto her heels. "Cutting the wound open obviously worked."

His pant leg fell to the floor, covering his skin once more. Disappointment was swift. He wanted her to go on touching him. Didn't even care if it was just his wound. He wanted her hands on his body, anywhere. Everywhere.

Pushing against her knees, she rose to her feet, then moved around behind him. His muscles bunched when he could no longer see her, but he could feel her. Close. Once again her body heat washed over him, followed by her warm, seductive breath skimming the sensitive skin of his nape.

"This looks better too." Her fingers landed against the wound on his upper right shoulder, and an uncontrollable shiver raced down his spine.

Her hand stilled. "Are you cold?"

Cold? No way in Hades. He was fucking hot. Hot and hard and aching right now. And even though he knew he shouldn't be, he didn't want her to stop.

"No," he managed in a voice even he could tell was thick and heavy with desire. Did she hear it? She hadn't made any overtly sexual moves, but he was already harder than he'd been with the nymphs, even though they'd pulled out every technique they knew and she was barely touching him. And she had to know it. The thin cotton pants weren't hiding anything.

"The salve trapped infection in your wound," she said, probing the edges of the cut on his back much as she'd done the one on his thigh. "I've no doubt you'd have healed fine without it. This one wasn't as bad, but the injury on your thigh needed to be reopened."

"What was in the salve?" He wanted to keep her talking. If she was volunteering information, he was going to use it.

"Healing herbs that sealed your wounds."

And...?

"And," she went on as if she'd heard his thought, "a chemical to enhance your reaction."

That explained the heat. And the fact he'd been instantly hard even though those nymphs hadn't interested him in the least. It also explained how they'd been able to hold him on the edge of release for hours.

Orgasm denial was an effective torture technique. Zagreus obviously hadn't been able to break him physically, so he was trying to break him sexually. Nick had only been through one session, but just that one had been worse than all the physical shit he'd been subjected to in the six months he'd been there. He wasn't sure how he'd make it through months of this kind of torture without losing his mind, especially when just looking at Cynna—just smelling her wild scent and knowing she was watching—made him instantly hard, jump-starting each session and making it all that much easier for the nymphs.

Her fingers moved from the wound on his back to his spine, then gently traced a line to the top of his low-slung drawstring pants, forcing another shiver to rack his body. "You have many scars. Scars that were here long before Zagreus brought you to this place. I've seen these before. Or ones like them. Where did you get them?"

Shock registered. That she'd noticed. That she was asking. An answer hovered on the tip of his tongue, but he held it back, unsure what she was looking for. Even though she hadn't done anything to torment him—yet—he knew full well there were other ways to torture a prisoner. Mental ways that would fuck with his head. And though she was totally hot and every part of him desperately wanted her touch, he wasn't about to give her any advantage.

He didn't answer, and in the silence, she trailed her hands back up to his neck, then to his jawbone. And then very gently, she skimmed her fingers over the jagged scar that ran across his left cheek and ended near the corner of his mouth.

He stiffened. His pulse beat hard in the silence.

"Scars are tattoos with darker histories," she said quietly, tracing the uneven skin to the edge of his lips. "I wonder what this one would say if it could speak."

He waited for her to ask. Waited for more, but it never came. Sighing, she lifted her hand from his face and set it back on his shoulder, then her fingers gently brushed his back again in a languid, sensual way that made the hairs on his skin stand at attention and another shiver ripple down his spine.

"Your constant defiance frustrates Zagreus," she said. "He senses you're growing stronger. He's going to double his efforts soon."

Frustrating the shit-for-brains Zagreus was the only pleasure Nick got anymore. He scoffed. "I think he already doubled his efforts yesterday."

Her hands skimmed across his shoulders, and gods, that felt good, like she was tickling his skin. He fought from closing his eyes and relaxing into the wicked sensations running up and down his spine.

"Yesterday was only a sampling of what he has planned for you. The females he's trapped here are Maenad nymphs, trained by the god Dionysus. They thrive on sexual energy. He will use them on you again and again until you can't take it anymore."

So the nymphs weren't willing participants either, just as Nick had guessed. They were prisoners too, being forced to do something they probably didn't want to do but couldn't stop once they got going.

Like Cynna?

Her touch made his mind skip to what she was doing now. And that made him think of what he'd endured.

Death by sex. Though Nick liked sex as much as the next guy and had plenty of his own dark desires—most centering around Cynna these days—the thought of being tortured like that, by those females, turned his stomach.

Her hands slid under his arms and around his ribs until they rested against his chest. Then she moved closer, her heat seeping into his back, her succulent breasts pressing against his spine, her lean hips cradling his ass. And feeling her so close shut down his brain function, brought his full attention to where she touched him, pushed aside every other thought. His pulse picked up speed, and heat shot from beneath her hands, to his belly and straight into his groin, making him even thicker and harder.

"He wants you to break," she whispered close to his ear. The fingers of her right hand slid lower until they grazed his nipple. His cock jumped, and his stomach caved in as electricity arced from the spot and ricocheted into his balls. "He's waiting for you to break so he can have what's inside you."

Her fingers rolled his nipple into a stiff peak, and Nick bit his lip and fought from groaning at the erotic thrill. He knew Zagreus was waiting for him to somehow give in so he could harness the powers Krónos had hidden in him for safekeeping, but Nick didn't know how Zagreus planned to do that, or what it would entail.

He opened his mouth to ask, but Cynna trailed her other hand to his opposite nipple, twisting and pinching in the same way, distracting him from his question. Pain mixed with pleasure to send a burst of carnal desire all through his body. Instinctively, he rocked his hips forward, wanting resistance there, wanting her touch lower.

Her breath caught. It was so subtle he almost didn't hear it. But it was enough to keep him from giving in. From letting go the way his body wanted.

She scraped her nails across his nipple, sending sparks of pleasure-pain across his skin, and he bit his lip. Against his ear, her warm breath radiated, causing more tiny tremors to ripple through his limbs. "You can't let that happen. No matter what he wants, don't give it to him."

Give in...don't give in... She was sending mixed messages, telling him one thing one day and another the next. He tried to make sense of what she was doing but couldn't because the haze of arousal was clouding everything, especially his ability to think.

She's fucking with your head. Zagreus sent her. Don't fall for her games. Stay in control.

He ground his teeth against her wicked fingers continuing to tease and torment his oversensitized nipples. Worked like hell not to lose himself in what she was doing to his body. "When you were here with the nymphs, you told me I couldn't hold out. That it was only a matter of time. Why the change of heart?"

"I told you what he wanted you to hear. He was watching."

And Zagreus wasn't watching now? Nick wasn't sure he believed that. The fucker always seemed to know what was happening in his lair.

"Why are you telling me all this?"

Her fingers stilled against his nipples. "Because your defiance gives others hope. And hope is something many here have lived too long without."

Her words were so quiet, such a subtle whisper, he almost missed them. But they were real. Echoing in his head, radiating down through his chest, awakening something inside him he thought had died. And though he didn't want to believe it, an ominous feeling in his gut told him that hope she talked about wasn't for others, but for her.

A thousand questions raced through his mind—who she really was, how she'd ended up in this hellhole, what the fuck she was doing with Zagreus—but every single one came to a screeching halt when those tantalizing fingers started moving south, over his abs, heading for the edge of his thin cotton pants.

He sucked in a breath and held it. Heat gathered beneath her fingers, seeping into the skin of his lower belly, ratcheting his arousal up another sinful notch. Finally, she reached the drawstring at his waistband, found one end, and pulled.

Every ounce of blood in his body seemed to pool in his groin. His cock throbbed, aching to be touched. His stomach caved in. His breaths grew fast and shallow as she tugged the tie free, then slowly eased her hand inside, sliding her tantalizing fingers beneath the cotton, then lower until the very tips grazed the base of his cock.

His teeth sank into his bottom lip, and he gripped the chains tightly over his head so he wouldn't moan. But it didn't stop her. The tiny gasp behind him caused his cock to twitch against her fingers.

The hand at his chest dropped to his hips, pushing his pants lower, freeing his erection. But instead of grasping him as he wanted, she let go and pulled her hands back. Something clicked in the silence.

He tensed, unsure what she had planned next. Then her hands returned. She wrapped her long, slim fingers around his cock and squeezed. Only this time they were slick. And he realized—*holy fuck*—she'd coated her palm with lube.

His eyes fell closed, and though he knew he shouldn't, he couldn't stop his hips from flexing forward, pushing his shaft into her tight, wet grip.

"So hard," she whispered, trailing the fingers of her other hand back up to twist and tease his nipple once more. "You ache for release, don't you, warrior?"

Gods, yes, he did. Right now it was all he could think about. She loosened her grip, slid her hand up to the tip, then back down to the base, and the sensation was so erotic, so hot, Nick's balls contracted, and he rocked into her hand again, wanting her to move faster, needing her to drive him to the edge, even though somewhere in the back of his head he knew she wouldn't take him over.

She stroked him again, base to tip, then hesitated and spread the tiny bit of fluid that had leaked free from the tip up and under the flared head to the taut gathering of nerve endings below. His whole body trembled.

"So big," she whispered in that seductive, sexy, dominatrix voice right in his ear, closing her hand around him once more. "Zagreus hates you for that too." She trailed her hand low again, squeezed the base, then slid her fingers higher, pumping him gently, making his cock swell even more. The heat of her pelvis pressed against his ass, driving him completely mad. "The females here all fantasize about this. About seeing you come. There's power in sex. Power in giving it, power in releasing it. Zagreus is afraid for you to have that power."

Nick didn't give a fuck about Zagreus. All he could focus on was the slick glide of her hand, moving faster, using long, tight strokes that were making him absolutely wild. He groaned, couldn't stop from pushing into her grip, felt his release barreling so utterly close.

Just a little more…

He thrust forward again and again, couldn't let her stop. Burned hotter than he had in…forever.

More, more, more…

"Yes, that's it." The hand at his nipple pinched hard, then released. And then he felt her silky fingers close around his balls and squeeze. "Come, warrior. Come right now. For me."

The orgasm shot down his spine, detonated in his balls, and exploded through his cock, robbing him of sight, of sound, of breath. Hot jets coated her hand, but she didn't stop stroking his length, didn't stop pumping even as his body twitched and shook with the power of his release. It had been so long—months and months of frustration—and she was drawing it all out, milking him of every drop, not letting go until there was nothing left.

His body trembled. Every muscle felt weak and spent. If it weren't for the chains, he would have collapsed, he was sure of it. Finally, she slowed her strokes, but against his ear, her warm, sinful breath radiated, sending tiny tremors up and down his spine, reminding him he wasn't alone, that he wasn't in control, that she held the power.

Gently, she let go of him and stepped back. Cool air washed over his sweat-dampened spine, replacing her sultry heat, and brushed his sensitive cock, making him shiver.

She crossed the floor and reached into the bag she'd set by the door. Nick couldn't see what she was doing, but in the silence, his brain slowly started to click back into gear.

He was suddenly more vulnerable than he'd ever been. If she wanted to hurt him, to torture him, right now he wouldn't be able to mentally or physically prepare himself. He tensed, tried to straighten in his chains, tried to pull himself together, but his body wasn't listening yet. The orgasm had completely wrecked him and was still pulsing through every cell and muscle.

She moved back to him, reached for the bottle she'd set on the floor, then lifted the water back to his lips. "Drink."

He opened his mouth and swallowed the cool, refreshing liquid, keeping his eyes locked on hers, unsure what she had planned next. In her hand, she held something, something he couldn't quite see.

"Good. That's enough."

She lowered the bottle, then poured the water over the object in her hand. And then, with her dark eyes locked on his, she stepped close. Seconds later, cool, wet cotton brushed over his sensitive cock, and he jerked.

Her gaze flicked down, to where she was cleaning the last remnants of his release from his body. Even though he was spent, blood still pooled in his groin with every brush of her fingers. If she noticed, she didn't show it, just went about what she was doing in a methodical, almost clinical way. Without a word, she tucked him back into his pants, and tied them at his waist.

His brain was having trouble catching up. He kept waiting for her to lash out, to do something aggressive, to punish him in some way, but she didn't. After tying his pants, she tossed the rag in her bag, then pushed the button near the wall. The motor in the ceiling hummed, and slack reformed in his chains, dropping his arms to his sides. He groaned at the ache in his muscles, tried to hold himself up, but his legs were weak, and he listened to his body and sank to the floor against the wall. Reaching for her bag from the floor, she slung it over her shoulder, then slid a small key into the lock on the door.

"Rest while you can," she said without turning. "And drink."

His gaze flicked to the water bottle she'd left within his reach, then back to her. Torchlight fell over her, highlighting blonde hair he knew wasn't her real color, making her skin seem even darker. "I've no idea what time they'll come for you tomorrow."

She pulled the cell door open. Metal groaned. And his chest pinched when he realized she was leaving. After not punishing him like he'd expected, but pleasuring him.

"Why?"

It was the only word he could get out. His throat was thick, his brain still foggy, but none of this—none of what she'd done last night when she'd tended his wound or tonight when she'd brought him to a blistering climax—made sense.

She hesitated, one hand on the door handle, then turned her head back into the room, just enough so he could see the supple line of her jaw and the plump perfection of her lips. But she didn't meet his eyes. And as it had before, that feeling that she was as much a prisoner as he slammed into him.

Which would be worse? To be tortured? Or to be forced to torture others and live with the knowledge of what you've done day after day after miserable day?

"Because I'm not the monster Zagreus is," she whispered. "Not yet, anyway."

CHAPTER SEVEN

Cynna was shaking by the time she made it back to her room.

She dropped the bag on the floor, closed the door with a snap, and leaned back against the cool wood, gasping for air.

What she'd just done... It went against everything Zagreus had commanded her to do. She lifted a trembling hand to her forehead and stopped. Nick's scent was all over her. Her body hummed with sexual excitement and her own need for release. Watching Nick's body shake, feeling the power of his orgasm rocket through her hand... She could only imagine what that would taste like in her mouth. What it would feel like spreading through her own body.

She lowered her hand and drew in a deep breath. She had to get his scent off her. She couldn't keep smelling it, couldn't keep wanting. Because wanting in this place was as dangerous as hope.

She rushed into her bathroom, didn't bother with the light. When she reached the sink, she flipped on the water and scrubbed her hands with soap beneath the stream. It didn't help. She could still smell him on her clothes, on her skin where she'd pressed up against his back. The only way to get rid of him was to shower. To get naked. To—

"That was... How should I put this?" a male voice said at her back. "Interesting, *agapi*."

A cold gust whooshed through Cynna, bringing every thought and need and want to a bone-chilling halt.

Her hands shook again as she flipped off the water, but this time not from arousal. This time true fear quaked in her muscles as she turned to face Zagreus.

He leaned against the doorway to her bedroom, his body relaxed, his arms crossed over his chest. But his eyes... They blazed with a fury she knew he was about to unleash.

She swallowed hard as he pushed away from the wall, as he ambled toward her, all coiled muscle and simmering power she knew could grind her into dust, and stopped directly in front of her. He leaned down, close to her ear, the heat of his body making her skin twitch, and drew in a deep whiff. "You smell of my uncle."

Her eyes slid closed at the sound of his snarled words, and her heart pounded hard in her chest. She'd let herself forget that very small fact. As Krónos's bastard son, that made Nick Hades's half brother and Zagreus's uncle. And even though Nick had yet to unleash those powers his father had hidden inside him, when he did, Nick would one day be more powerful than Zagreus, a reality the god at her front never forgot.

"You wound me, *agapi*."

Skata, this was it. He was going to kill her. Right here. Right now. He was not a god who gave second chances, but surprisingly... She didn't want one.

The knowledge caused her pulse to slow, pushed the cold outward from the center of her chest. Yeah, she might die, but she didn't care anymore. Because at least she'd done one selfless thing in this hellhole. When Nick had thanked her the other night, she'd known she hadn't deserved it, but tonight... Tonight she'd given him a tiny piece of pleasure in the middle of an endless misery while she'd taken nothing for herself. And for that she could be proud. Proud because even if she spent all eternity in the fire of Hades's hell paying for all the awful things she'd done in life, at least she'd go knowing her soul wasn't completely black. Not like Zagreus's.

Slowly, she lifted her gaze to his. The god was close. Mere inches away. And the rage building inside him... She could see it in his eyes, in his taut muscles, in the lines on his perfectly sculpted face. She wasn't stupid enough to egg him on, but she wasn't backing down either. Not anymore.

"Yes," she said in a voice she knew shook even though she tried to stop it. "I did."

His face turned red. His jaw hardened until it was as rigid as stone. She braced herself for his wrath, but it didn't come. Instead, he stepped back, his hands in fists at his sides, his muscles straining as if he were fighting to hold something back. Not looking away from her eyes, he called, "Guards?"

Shuffling sounded in the other room. Cynna's gaze jumped past Zagreus to the hulking satyrs rushing by him, one of whom she recognized as Lykos.

"I've been waiting for this," Lykos growled.

Panic spread through every inch of Cynna's body. She shifted, tried to move to the side, but the two beasts caught her by the arms before she could get away.

Zagreus stepped into her bedroom. The satyrs dragged her kicking and struggling through the doorway. Zagreus nodded toward the bed. "There."

"No." *No, no, no, no, no...* She thrashed, tried to fight against them, but their grips were too strong. She'd been wrong. He wasn't going to kill her. Not yet, at least. He was going to let Lykos and the other satyr have their way with her first. She'd seen what Lykos could do to a female. She'd never survive it. She didn't want to survive it. She struggled, kicked out, tried to nail him in the balls but missed.

"On her back," Zagreus ordered.

The satyrs maneuvered her like a rag doll. Cynna tried to fight, but they were too strong. One pinned her arms above her head; the other wrenched down on her legs. The bed dipped, and she sensed Zagreus move in close, felt his big hand tug her pants down at the hip. Winced as something sharp stabbed into her flesh.

A burn ripped through her muscle and spread through her leg and belly. She screamed, tried to kick out, but her muscles were growing lax, her limbs heavy. Whatever he'd injected into her was immobilizing her within seconds.

"Shh, *agapi*. That's it. Let it work. You know you deserve this."

Tears pooled in Cynna's eyes. She tried to roll to her side but couldn't. This was how Nick felt. What it was like to know misery was coming, powerless to stop it. She did deserve this. But not because she'd defied Zagreus. She deserved it because she hadn't defied him sooner.

"That's better." Zagreus's hands landed against her bare belly, tracing a slow circle where her tank had ridden up. She could feel it. Could feel Lykos's hands gripping her wrists and the other satyr petting her legs. Her stomach rolled, and sickness threatened. She could feel everything, but she couldn't react.

"Get it," Zagreus said to Lykos. Then, "No, in her arm."

A sharp stab pierced the flesh of her inner arm, this needle bigger than the other—way bigger—and something passed into her skin. Something solid. Cynna cried out, but she still couldn't move.

"That's so I can find you again, my love." Zagreus ran his fingers over her belly, pushing her tank higher until cool air washed over her breasts, baring them to the beasts holding her down. Growls echoed in the room. Growls of lust and approval she didn't want to think about.

"I was very upset when I discovered what you'd done," Zagreus said, still touching her, "but then I realized how we could use it to our advantage. You were right, *agapi*. He's not going to break at the hands of the nymphs. But he will break thanks to you. I saw it in his eyes when you pleasured him. He wants you." The tips of his fingers traced over her nipples. "Oh, how I understand that wanting." He pinched one tip until pain shot through her breast. "And I'm going to let him have you. For a price."

"Release her," Zagreus ordered. "And leave us."

Lykos growled low in his throat. Pain forgotten, Cynna stopped her useless struggling and tried to focus on what was happening around her. Even though she couldn't turn her head to look, she recognized the sound of the satyr's fury.

Zagreus's head snapped up. "Do not tempt me, satyr. I'd like nothing more than to rip someone's throat out, and right now I don't care if it's yours."

Hands lifted from her body, but still she couldn't move. Tension crackled in the room, mixing with a cacophony of lust and rage, and though Cynna still couldn't see them, she knew a power struggle when she heard it. Also knew if she wasn't careful, she'd get caught in the middle.

The other satyr, the one Cynna hadn't gotten a good look at, growled, "Come on. We'll find the nymphs."

Tense seconds passed, then footsteps sounded, followed by a door slamming.

"Smart satyr," Zagreus muttered.

Cynna wasn't so sure. Zagreus had just taken away the one thing Lykos wanted more than power. And he'd be gunning for her the next chance he got. But even that thought faded as Cynna realized Zagreus's footsteps were moving away from the bed.

Recognizing this might be her only chance, she tried to roll to her side but couldn't. Frustration and fear and anger welled inside her, but the drug he'd given her was doing its job, and she couldn't move a single muscle.

"My sweet, sweet Cynna," he whispered, coming close once more. "This is only temporary, *agapi*. Until we can be together again." She tensed as he lifted her upper body, as he sat in the pillows behind her and cradled her head in his lap. Bringing a goblet to her lips, he tilted her head up. "Drink."

She'd said the same word to Nick earlier. Zagreus had to know. But this wasn't cool refreshing water as she'd given Nick. Before the thick, warm fluid reached her lips, she knew it was blood. His blood.

It poured into her mouth and down her throat. She gagged, coughed, tried to force it out, but her tongue wasn't working. The salty, metallic liquid gurgled between her lips and slid down her chin. He tipped the cup higher, holding her mouth to the edge. "Drink it all."

Tears spilled over her eyelids. She couldn't breathe, was sure she was going to choke to death. And then he was pulling the cup away, rubbing his bloodstained fingers through her hair, smoothing his hand down her cheek. "That's all. No more. You did well. Breathe now."

Cynna couldn't do anything else. But she wasn't well. She could feel his blood settling in the pit of her stomach, sending a rolling, nasty heat all through her body.

"That's it. Let my blood become part of you. I know this won't be easy, but to break him, we have to give him something to live for. That's you, my love. You were right, and I should have listened sooner. This is the only way."

She didn't know what he meant, but a fire was building in her veins. One she was suddenly afraid would consume her.

"You're going to earn his trust." Zagreus stroked her hair as if she were a pet rather than a person. "You're going to make him think you're saving him, make him fall for you. He won't be able to resist. He's halfway there already. All he needs is a little push. And when he finally turns his back on that useless hero honor and chooses you over his precious people, then we'll have what we want. Then I'll come and reclaim you both."

He leaned close to her ear, so close his hot breath was all she felt. That and his bloody hand closing tight around her jaw to squeeze until pain made her eyes water and darkness creep in at the edge of her vision. "But remember that you are mine. No matter how you fuck him. Whether it's with your hand or mouth or your slutty little body, never forget you belong to me. My blood flows in your veins now. Mine and no one else's. We made a deal, and you will never be free of me. Not until I have what I want. That I promise."

He let go of her jaw. And vaguely, she felt his hands traveling down her neck, across her bare breasts and over her abdomen, but she didn't care. That darkness was claiming her, pulling her under, drawing her into a murky abyss. And she relished it. Because there she wouldn't have to endure whatever else he had planned for her. And there she couldn't worry about what he was going to do to Nick.

"Sleep now, *agapi*. And know I will come for you. Soon."

Soft humming woke Isadora.

Rolling to her side, she peered through the open doorway of her bedroom that led into the nursery. A low light burned in the darkness, and her daughter's happy coo drifted from the other room, but it was the sweet male voice that pulled her from the bed.

She ran her fingers through her shoulder-length hair as she crossed the room, her pulse picking up, her stomach tightening as it always did when he was close. The sleeves of her silky blue pajamas fell past her fingers as she reached for the doorjamb, and her feet drew to a stop.

Warmth curled outward from her chest and expanded through her limbs. Demetrius stood near their daughter's crib, cradling Elysia in one of his big arms, letting her hold on to the index finger of his other hand with her little fist while he swayed and hummed a lullaby Isadora recognized from her youth.

The Argonauts all seemed surprised at the softness he exuded when he was near his daughter, but Isadora had known it was in him for a long time. Ever since those days they'd spent on that deserted island together, when she'd gotten her first true glimpse of the real man, not the closed-off and hardened guardian he wanted the world to see.

He was still dressed in the black pants and long-sleeved thick shirt he always wore when he was fighting in the human realm. A smudge of dirt smeared his cheek, and his dark hair was tousled around his face, as if he'd run his fingers through it several times in frustration. He'd obviously come right to the castle after crossing back into Argolea, but she could tell without even asking that he still hadn't found his brother. She felt it as surely as she felt that Nick was still alive.

"I wish that was my welcome-home greeting."

His humming cut off, and he turned to face her, surprise evident in his black eyes. "Did we wake you?"

"Yes." She stepped away from the door and moved into the room to stand next to him, peering down at their daughter. Her brown eyes were all Isadora, but that thick black hair and that tiny dent in her chin were her father's, and every time Isadora looked at Elysia, she saw the man she loved. "And it's a good way to wake."

She reached for Elysia's other hand, and the baby cooed and gripped Isadora's finger, locking the three of them together.

This was what Isadora wanted. Her family all in one place. But that niggling vision she'd had wouldn't leave her, and she feared their separation of late was only the beginning of the end.

She looked up when she realized Demetrius was staring at her. He was still swaying, but concern now shadowed his eyes, and his features were drawn tight as he studied her. "What?" she asked.

He let go of Elysia's hand and placed his palm over Isadora's forehead. "Are you ill? You look pale."

Sighing, Isadora released the baby and pushed his hand away. She hated when everyone worried over her like she was some glass doll. And that wasn't the way she wanted her mate to touch her, not after the days they'd been apart. "I'm fine, Demetrius. Just tired. There's been a lot going on here, but then you wouldn't know because you haven't been around."

It was a dig. But she couldn't seem to stop herself from saying it. Turning out of the nursery so they didn't argue in front of their daughter, she crossed to the windows in their bedroom and folded her arms over her chest. Frustration clouded her mind as she looked out at the sparkling view of the Olympic Ocean under the full-moon light. Followed by a wave of confusion that she found herself being short with him when what she really wanted was him home and with her.

The door to the nursery closed softly, then Demetrius's footsteps crossed the floor. But he didn't touch her. He stopped several feet away as if he couldn't read her mood and wasn't sure how to proceed.

Well, that makes two of us.

"I'm back for good," he said in a low voice. "No more weeks away at a time."

She focused on the lap of water against the beach far below, shimmering in the moonlight. "You talked to Theron, didn't you?"

"I need to be here."

No, he'd talked to Theron and found out what she'd decided about the Misos and the Council. "We're perfectly safe here in the castle. I don't need you sacrificing your duties out of guilt."

He moved close, his body heat wrapping around her, warming her, and then his big hands landed against her upper arms, gently turning her to face him. "You are never a sacrifice, *kardia*."

Tears burned in her eyes. Useless tears she didn't understand.

His hands slid up to cup her face and tip her gaze up to his. Confusion clouded his features. "What's wrong?" he whispered.

She didn't know. And that frustrated her more than anything. It was more than that vision—a vision she wasn't about to accept. It was more than what was happening with the Misos and the Council. It was even bigger than the distance that was stretching between them. It was something else. Something she couldn't grasp yet. "I'm just tired," she managed. "And I miss you. So much."

He pulled her in close, wrapped his arm around her, and slid one hand into her hair. "I've missed you too. You have no idea how much. I'm sorry I haven't been here. I'm sorry I left you to deal with everything on your own. I won't do that again."

As she fought back the stupid tears, she rested her head against his chest and closed her arms around his back, drawing in a deep whiff of his masculine scent, loving his heat, loving his strength, loving *him* more than she ever thought she could. "No, you're doing what you need to be doing. I want you to find Nick. We can't let the gods have control of him if he really does have Krónos's powers inside him. I'm just…"

"What?" His fingers paused their gentle massage against her scalp.

"I'm lonely without you."

"*Kardia…*" He eased back, then bent his head and brushed his lips over hers. "I'm here. I'll always be here for you. No matter what. You are my everything."

The kiss was sweet. A soft brush of skin against skin, but the moment his flesh touched hers, she wanted more. Needed their connection if for no other reason than to prove to herself that this overwhelming desire to find Nick wasn't personal. He wasn't the man she loved. This one was. This one was her life.

She lifted to her toes, slid her tongue along the seam of his lips, then groaned when he opened and kissed her deeply. His hands tightened around her back, and at her front, she felt his body's reaction, felt his muscles tighten and his erection swell against her belly.

"Prove it to me," she whispered. "Prove it to me right now."

He drew back, just enough so he could look down at her in the dim light. "On one condition."

"Anything." Right now she'd promise whatever he wanted just to be close to him.

He brushed a lock of hair way from her temple in a move that was so tender, her heart rolled beneath her ribs. "After, you let me make you something to eat. You're thinner than when I left."

She pushed down the irritation, the reminder that he still thought of her as weak, and rose back to her toes. "After. But right now all I want is you."

*E*scape.

The word pulsed in Cynna's head, growing louder with every passing second.

Her eyes popped open, and a searing burn slid up her throat. Rolling to her side, she coughed, trying to expel the vileness inside her.

Her body shook with her coughing fit. When it passed, she blinked and looked around. She was lying on her side on the bed in her room. Something sticky covered her fingers. Something red and—

Her eyes grew wide as she looked down at the dried blood on her hand and the puddle of red on the mattress beneath her. She jolted out of the bed and raced for the bathroom before she lost what was in her stomach.

Pain radiated outward from her belly. Backing away from the toilet, she leaned against the wall while she tried to catch her breath. Her mind was a foggy mess. She patted her arms and legs, looking for wounds but couldn't find any. What had happened? Where had all the blood come from? The last thing she remembered was being in Nick's cell, her hands traveling over his body, bringing him to release, then coming back here to her room and—

Zagreus...

Oh shit.

Bits and pieces flashed in her memory. Him, the satyrs, her fighting frantically. But she couldn't piece them together, couldn't form a coherent picture of what they'd done to her. Panic spread through her veins, and she frantically checked every part of her body, looking for marks, for wounds, looking for what Zagreus had been up to.

The only thing she found was a slightly swollen red bump on the inside of her right forearm and a tiny puncture wound in her skin. The rest of her body was untouched.

Relief stole through her. A relief that he hadn't let his satyrs have their way with her, that he hadn't raped her. It might be stupid, but giving herself to Zagreus was one thing. Having him take without her consent was something altogether different. And since she was only just barely holding it together these days, she feared something like that might send her over the edge.

Escape.

The word drowned out everything else. Whatever Zagreus had done to her was a result of her going to Nick last night. And that meant Zagreus didn't trust her and that this was only the beginning. It also meant Nick was in as much danger as her.

Escape...

She'd thought of escaping just after she'd come here, after she'd made that deal with Zagreus and realized what he wanted from her. But it had seemed like such an enormous undertaking, one she wouldn't be able to do herself with so many of Zagreus's satyrs lurking about. But with Nick's help...

Escape. Go now.

Slowly, she inched her way up the wall until she was standing, then leaned forward and braced her hands on her thighs as she breathed and worked not to get sick again. From the corner of her eye, she caught her reflection in the mirror.

Blood stained her mouth, her chin. Dried blood was gathered in her hair. Hand shaking, she touched her finger to her lips, trying—fighting—to remember how it had gotten there, but couldn't. Her stomach rolled again, and she only just made it to the toilet before she retched once more.

She had to get out of here. She couldn't stay. Not anymore. Something in her gut told her whatever Zagreus had done to her last night was nothing compared to what he intended to do next.

A plan formulated in her head. A plan that would free her for good.

Only she wasn't going alone.

CHAPTER EIGHT

Nick couldn't sit still.

He paced the back of his cell, the shackles and chains on his wrists rattling as he moved. He knew it was night. Even though his cell was dark, he kept track of time and figured it had to be about two in the morning. A good twenty-four hours since Cynna had last come to see him.

She hadn't been by at all today. No one had come for him, in fact, which was odd. In the six months he'd been here, he couldn't remember a single day where they hadn't poked or taunted or tortured him in some way. Except for yesterday and all of tonight.

The scars on his back tingled, a sign something was happening behind the scenes, something that wasn't good. Had Zagreus seen what she'd done? Was this his new form of torture? Pleasure, then silence, then...*son of a bitch*...worry?

He didn't like worrying. It was the one thing he hadn't missed since he'd been here. All his life was filled with worry—for his people, for the colony, for his soul mate—and even though he'd been tortured in horrendous ways since being dragged to this hellhole, at least during it he'd had a respite from that useless emotion.

His mind drifted to Isadora, and his pacing slowed. An echo of...something...passed through his chest. A tug toward her, as always, but also a feeling that something was off. As she was his soul mate, he could always tell when she was in danger or sick or hurt, and though this feeling wasn't warning him of one of those possibilities, it was telling him something wasn't right.

The door to his cell creaked before he could speculate further, and he turned, looking toward the light spilling into the room. Tensing, he braced his bare feet against the stone floor, expecting a satyr or even Zagreus himself to barge into the room. But the figure who stepped through the door wasn't large or hulking or beast. It was slim, curvaceous, and female, and before he even saw her face, he knew it was Cynna. Knew because that sweet jasmine scent of hers preceded her into the room, mixing with her sultry heat to wash over every inch of his skin, reminding him of what she'd done last night with her tantalizing hands.

The door closed with a soft clink. He couldn't see her anymore, but in that split second she'd stood in the light, he'd noticed her long hair was once again pulled back from her face. But *unlike* last night, she wasn't barefoot and dressed in loose, flowing, comfortable clothing. Tonight she was decked out in slim-fitting black pants, ankle boots, and a lightweight jacket.

"We don't have a lot of time," she whispered.

She didn't light the torch, but her boot steps drew close, the sound intermixing with the buzz in his head like an ominous warning. Her fingers grazed his hands, then closed over his wrist. Metal clicked against metal, signaling…she was freeing his cuffs.

It took only a split second to realize this was the chance he'd been waiting for.

The cuffs opened and clanked against the floor. Her fingers lifted from his skin, then she turned for the door. But before she could get a step away, he captured her forearm, whipped her back to face him, and closed his hand around her throat.

She gasped, and even though the room was dark, he watched the whites of her eyes grow wide in her face.

"What kind of games are you playing with me?" He backed her against the stone wall and held her immobile.

Her free hand darted up and clawed against his wrist, but she didn't try to push him away. "I'm…trying to…help you."

"Why now?"

"Because…"

When her words died out, he realized he was crushing her windpipe. He loosened his grip, just enough so she could draw in a breath and answer.

"Because," she said stronger, "I'm your only chance. If Zagreus can't break you, he's going to be forced to hand you over to Hades. He's running out of time, and he's getting anxious. And if Hades gets a hold of you, he's going to take you to the Underworld, where you'll never be free."

Nick definitely didn't want that. Sure, Orpheus had ventured in and out of the Underworld, but he'd done so with a map and a Siren and surprise on his side. If Nick was sent to the Underworld, Hades and even his fucking father, Krónos, would know, and he'd never escape.

The scars on Nick's back tingled again, telling him nothing was as it seemed. He tightened his hand around her throat. "Why should I trust you?"

Her eyes widened again, and he knew he was hurting her, but he'd been beaten, cut, broken, stretched, and teased under this female's direction. He wasn't stupid enough to think one simple moment of pleasure had changed her heart.

"You…shouldn't, but…" She dropped her hand to her side, releasing her hold on his wrist, giving him the power to do whatever he pleased, then met his gaze head-on. "Not all prisons have bars."

His eyes searched her dark ones, looking for deceit, looking for anything that would tell him she was playing the part of Zagreus's puppet. But he didn't see it. The only thing he saw was determination. The kind that comes from knowing you have nothing left to lose.

He let go of her throat and stepped back. She swallowed once, then massaged her neck. "The guards are switching shifts soon. If we're going, we have to go now."

She moved away and reached for something from the floor. A zipper rasped in the darkness, then fabric brushed his hands. "These were the best I could find. Taken from another prisoner. Dress quickly."

Jeans, a T-shirt, and boots. Nick didn't care who they'd come from, he was just thankful he wouldn't have to escape in nothing but these paper-thin cotton pants. He dressed rapidly, shoving his feet into the boots and breathing a sigh of relief that they fit. When he finished, he moved to the door, where Cynna was peeking through the small window, looking out into the hallway.

Her body heat seeped into his skin, and that sweet scent filled his head. Every other time she'd come to him, she'd exuded confidence, but tonight he felt the worry radiating from her body, felt the fear, and he knew then that the female who'd stood by unreadable and expressionless through every moment of his torture was not the real her. This was. This one was the true Cynna.

"The guard just went by." She reached for the door handle. "Now's our chance."

He caught her arm before she could move. "What happens to you if we're caught?"

"Zagreus will kill me."

"Then why are you helping me?"

Slowly, her eyes turned up to his. She was a full head shorter than him, dark where he was light, soft where he was hard, and though he knew he was wasting time, he needed to know this answer more than he needed air to breathe.

"Because neither one of us should ever have been here," she whispered. "And because if I don't do the right thing now, I'm afraid I never will."

His heart pounded hard against his ribs. He searched her eyes, looking for the lie. All he saw was truth.

He tightened his hand around her arm. "If this is some kind of trap—"

"Then you can kill me yourself. Assuming the guards don't do it first. They hate me more than you."

Her words ricocheted in his head. He wanted to ask what she meant by that, but he didn't have time. She was already reaching for the door, pulling gently from his grip.

"There's a back exit from the prison that runs up to the surface. I have a master key that opens all the doors, but we have to get to the exit first without being caught."

"Weapons would be good," he muttered as she pulled the door open slowly so it didn't creak too much.

"I know where we can find some. Stay close."

She looked both ways. Finding it clear, she crept out into the corridor. Nick's gaze shot around as he followed. But as they moved through the dark stone hallway, he realized the doors around them opened to other cells. And the sounds coming from those cells—the moans, the cries for help, the agony—they all ignited the dark energy inside, sending it skipping through his belly and chest with both excitement and disgust.

He fought the darkness and followed Cynna around a corner. She led him through a tunnel to the right, then stopped in front of a door he'd never seen. After sliding the key in the lock, she turned, then pushed the door open with her shoulder.

Weapons lined the back wall. They were in some kind of armory. She didn't illuminate a torch on the wall, but there was enough light coming from the corridor to see the racks of knives and swords and weapons with jagged teeth intended to tear through flesh. Cynna crossed to a row of knives, chose two, and strapped them to her thighs. Then she moved to a case holding a selection of daggers, hooked a harness over her shoulders that crisscrossed her back, and slid two arm-length daggers into the holders.

"Hurry," she whispered. "The guards will be making the rounds again soon."

Nick moved toward the cabinet, wishing for a damn gun. Bullets weren't generally effective against Hades's daemons, but they were with satyrs. Finding no firearms, he chose a parazonium—an ancient Greek sword similar to one he'd left at the colony. He lifted the weapon in his right hand, tested the weight, and swung it back and forth. Satisfied, he reached for knives similar to the ones Cynna had chosen, but with curved handles and jagged blades, grabbed a couple of throwing stars, which he tucked into his pockets, then reached for a mace—a club-like weapon with a long wood handle and multiple sharp teeth protruding from the metallic ball at the end.

Cynna eyed the weapons he'd picked, but didn't say anything and turned back for the door. She hesitated just before opening it. "The stairs aren't far. But we may run into satyrs. They'll sound the alarm if they see us."

Which meant they couldn't be seen. Or reported.

Cynna pulled the door open and slinked back into the corridor. Torchlight reflected off the weapons at her back. Nick stayed close, but her scent—that sweet jasmine aroma—was distracting. As was the heat radiating from her skin and her own adrenaline he felt pulsing in the air.

Something had happened. Something between the time she'd pleasured him and now. Something that had propelled her to take this risk when she hadn't before. Nick wanted to ask just what that was, but knew this wasn't the time. The minute they got free, though, he was determined she'd come clean. He wasn't letting her off the hook for any of it.

They rounded three different corners. The rock tunnels seemed to go on forever. Water dripped down the walls and pooled in puddles along the floor. Torchlight grew sparse the farther they went, but the moans around them didn't stop. And every cry of agony, every sound of tormented pain, rippled in Nick's limbs and radiated across his chest.

Cynna drew to a stop in front of another door and reached for the key from her pocket. Her hand shook as she slipped it into the lock and turned. The lock gave with a click, then she wrapped her fingers around the handle and pulled. Metal creaked through the dark corridor as the door swung outward toward them.

A set of stone stairs disappeared up into darkness. Cynna took a step past the door. "This way. Almost there."

A scream ripped through the cavern before Nick could move inside, and that energy—the dark energy he fought day in and day out—leapt with both exhilaration and repulsion.

He captured Cynna at the arm. "Wait."

She turned to look at him, her face shadowed, her dark eyes narrowed as they leveled on his. "What?"

Nick glanced back down the empty corridor to his left. The scream was now a muffled sob. A sound he recognized. One he'd made more times than he could count in this hellhole.

He looked back at Cynna. "We can't leave them."

Confusion clouded her eyes, then cleared as she realized what he was saying. Her gaze darted to her right, past the door. "We can't get them all out. There are too many."

"We can give some a chance. The same chance you're giving me."

Indecision swam in her familiar eyes as she looked back at him. She'd told him she was freeing him because it was the right thing to do. He needed to believe she'd meant that. Needed to know there was something good left inside her, even after all the bad shit he'd seen her do. Needed to know she wasn't Zagreus's puppet after all.

"The guards will hear," she whispered. "There's no way we can keep them all quiet."

"I can't leave without trying."

Her eyes held his, and a thousand different emotions swam in her deep brown irises. Too many to name. But he recognized fear, and compassion, and, mostly, self-preservation.

Several tense seconds passed. Neither of them spoke. Neither looked away. Finally, her eyes closed, and she muttered, "*Skata.*"

She pulled her arm from his grip and stepped around him. "Several will die because of this. That's not my fault."

He wouldn't hold her accountable for that. But relief rippled through him just the same. Relief that he'd pegged her right, from the start. He turned and followed. "If they stay here, they're already dead, and you know it."

She didn't answer. He didn't expect her to. But something in his chest warmed with her decision.

She stopped in front of the first cell door they came to and pulled the key from her pocket once more. "This is the stupidest idea ever. You want to free prisoners who will probably try to kill us on their way out."

"I'll make sure they don't."

She scoffed and pulled the door open. A creak sounded through the empty corridor. "Good luck with that."

She stepped into the dark room. The cell was like his, made of rocks with no illumination. A figure sat along the back wall in the shadows. Cynna pulled a cylindrical metal object from her pocket and shoved it in Nick's hand, then stepped forward. "I don't want to die today. Not now, when I'm finally doing something good."

Nick flicked on the flashlight in his hand and shined it over the back wall. Cynna was already kneeling next to the prisoner, a man wearing only thin cotton pants as Nick had been, with hair down to his shoulders and a long beard. He was thin, bony in places he should have been strong, and though it was hard to see in the dim light, he looked to be advancing toward old age.

"Wh-what do you want with me now?" the man asked.

He wasn't strong enough to overpower Cynna. Not even close. But that didn't ease Nick's anxiety any. He tightened his hand around the mace, just in case. "Relax, old man. We're freeing you."

The cuffs opened from the man's wrists and clattered against the ground. Cynna pushed to her feet. "Go out the corridor to the right. Steps run up to the surface. Follow them all the way. Don't look back."

She turned and swept past Nick without a look.

"Wh-why are you helping me?" the old man asked, slowly pushing to his feet.

Nick didn't know who the hell the man was or what he'd done to be imprisoned here, but now was not the time to ask. "Because we can."

Nick followed Cynna back down the dark hallway, holding the flashlight up each time they entered a cell while she moved toward the prisoner. They freed six males and eight females, all different ages and races. Most were frail and dirty and dazed, and few gave them any trouble. The majority didn't even recognize them. But one female did. One recognized Nick instantly, her eyes growing wide when he stepped into her cell. And the minute he flashed his light over her, Nick knew her as well.

The dark-haired nymph. The one who'd brought him to the brink of sexual frustration only days ago. Except now she looked nothing like she had then. Her hair was stringy and matted, dirt covered her skin, dried blood was smeared across her arms and calves, and her face was bruised and swollen along one whole side.

Someone had beaten the hell out of her after she'd left him. Someone he was sure was a satyr.

Anger ripped through Nick. A dark, rolling, menacing anger.

"Go out the corridor to the right," Cynna said, freeing the nymph's cuffs. "There's a—"

"Thank you." The moment the nymph was free, she bolted from the floor and threw her arms around Nick's waist, holding on tight. "Thank you," she repeated. "I'll do whatever you want. Just don't leave me here."

Nick held his arms out wide, unsure what to do. He looked toward Cynna for help. Pushing to her feet, Cynna scowled the nymph's way and perched a hand on her hip.

"Okay, you're free." Nick reached around and pried the nymph's hands from his back. She was surprisingly strong for being so small and injured. "Listen, before the guards arrive."

The nymph tipped her head back and looked up, her eyes wide and filled with gratitude. "I'll do anything. Anything you want. Just keep me with you."

"Enough with the begging already." Cynna grasped the nymph by the back of the dress and pried her away from Nick.

The nymph glanced toward Cynna, then back at Nick. Confusion clouded her eyes. She obviously recognized Cynna too. Before she could get the question out, Cynna said, "We've got more prisoners to free. Go now, before we change our minds."

The nymph cast Nick one last longing look, then rushed past him out into the hall.

When she was gone, Cynna clenched her jaw and moved toward the door, muttering, "Clingy nymphs."

Nick turned and followed. "Where's the other one?"

"I don't know."

Cynna obviously knew who he meant, but that answer wasn't good enough for Nick. They moved out into the dimly lit corridor, and another moan echoed down the hall, causing the darkness inside to surge all over again.

"Is she alive?" he asked.

Cynna slid the key in another lock. "I don't know."

"But you know what happened to both of them."

She turned the key. "Once they left me, their fates were out of my hands."

Nick braced a hand on the door above her head before she could pull it open. "But you know what happened to them," he repeated.

Cynna's shoulders dropped. "Don't make me do this now. If you do, we'll never get to them all."

They couldn't get to them all no matter what they did. And Nick needed to know the answer to his question before they moved on. "They weren't willing participants, were they? That nymph was a prisoner, just like me. She was innocent."

Cynna's stilled, but she didn't remove her hand from the door handle or turn to look at him. "No one here is innocent. Not truly. But yes, everyone is a prisoner. Some are just required to do...more...than others."

Like her.

His stomach tightened with the reality he'd been right—on both counts—and he dropped his hand and stepped back so she could open the door. He just wasn't sure what it meant toward her reasons for freeing him or how that changed what he knew of her relationship with Zagreus.

Straightening, she pulled on the handle. The metal clanged, then hinges squeaked. She moved into the cell. Hands damp, he lifted the flashlight and followed, shining the light over the back of the room. A female sat leaning against the wall, her dark hair falling to her waist, her pale blue eyes wide and unfocused.

"We're here to free you." Not wanting to think about Cynna and Zagreus right now, Nick stepped past Cynna, wrapped a hand around the female's thin arm, and hauled her to her feet.

The female's eyes grew even wider. "You can't."

Cynna slid the key in the cuffs at the female's wrists. "Follow the tunnel to the right. There's a set of stairs—"

"I know where the stairs are." The female tugged her arm back and knocked the key free.

"Dammit." Cynna knelt to pick it up.

"The guards will be here in minutes," Nick said.

"Then you'd best go before they arrive," the female answered. She pulled her arm from his hand, stepped back, then sat against the wall once more. "I can't leave."

She'd clearly been brainwashed. No one who was thinking clearly would choose this hell over freedom. "Listen, we—"

"No, you listen, son." She turned those pale blue eyes upward. Eyes filled with a wisdom that sent a familiar warning through Nick's blood. "It's safer for everyone if I remain."

Nick didn't have a clue what she meant. He opened his mouth to ask, but she cut him off by saying, "You can do one thing for me, though."

"What?"

"Find Epimetheus. Tell him… Tell him not to come after me. I know he's been looking."

Holy shit. Nick's stomach tightened. This was Pandora. The first human woman created by the gods. The keeper of all the evils of humanity. That darkness inside jerked with delight. He glanced around the cell for a jar or urn or box of some kind, but found nothing but cold, empty stone.

"It's not here," Pandora whispered as if reading his mind. "It's well hidden."

Voices and footsteps drifted from the hall. Cynna rushed to the door and peeked out, then muttered, "*Skata.*" She turned back to face the room. "The guards are coming."

"Go now," Pandora said, looking up at Nick. "There is no other choice."

Nick hesitated. If she was the scourge of the world, he couldn't leave her in Zagreus's hands. And that dark part of himself, the part linked to Krónos, wanted her with him. Wanted the powers she could unleash.

"You can't control them," Pandora said, reading his mind again. "No one can. Not even me. Zagreus has already tried everything to get me to tell him where it is, but I won't. If you free me, however, I will be attracted to it, and he will follow. And if that happens, the world as you know it will cease to exist."

"Nick," Cynna said, drawing a dagger from her back. "We have to go *now*."

Nick still hesitated. They were out of time, and they all knew it. And yet, he still struggled with the choice before him. This was power like nothing he'd ever know. This was his chance to wield it without giving in to his father. "I'll send someone back for you."

"Don't," Pandora whispered as he stepped toward the door. "Humanity is safe so long as I remain here."

Possibly. Though the vile part of Nick wouldn't believe that. And the honorable part—the part he struggled to bring to the forefront—knew no one deserved this kind of imprisonment. Not even her.

Tearing his gaze from Pandora, he moved up behind Cynna and peered over her head into the corridor. "How many?"

"Three, I think. They passed and turned down a tunnel to the right. We're clear. But we don't have time to free any others."

No, they didn't. Not if they wanted to live. And Nick wanted to live. Now more than ever.

He glanced back toward Pandora as Cynna drew the door open. "I'll find your husband. I'll tell him."

"He's not my husband, Guardian."

Considering what Nick knew of the gods' unions, he had no idea what she meant, but that one word—*guardian*—overrode his curiosity as he followed Cynna back into the dimly lit corridor. The female had obviously seen the ancient Greek text on his arms. But he wasn't a guardian. And just the fact he'd toyed with the idea of taking her regardless of her warnings proved he didn't deserve to be one either.

They moved back down the corridor in silence. Cell doors on each side were once again closed, hiding the fact their prisoners were now gone. The only open door sat at the far end of the hall. The door that led to freedom.

Cynna released a breath as they drew close. "Finally."

Yeah, finally. But Nick wasn't able to share in her relief. Because he was suddenly wondering if there could ever be any kind of freedom for someone like him. Or if he was just trading one kind of prison for another.

Cynna moved for the open door. Just as she reached the threshold, a satyr stepped in her path. One Nick recognized as in charge down here in the dungeons. One holding a blade as long as his arm.

Adrenaline flooded Nick's body. He reached around for the parazonium strapped to his back.

"Going somewhere, Mistress?" the satyr growled. Behind him, two more satyrs moved into position. "Now where's the fun in that?"

CHAPTER NINE

Cynna gasped and dropped back a step. Lykos's eyes glowed red with fury as he moved close, malice twisting his face. She'd seen the satyr pissed but knew this was something altogether different. Hand shaking, she reached back for the weapon strapped to her back.

"Oh, you're not going to need that, Mistress." Lykos arced out with his arm before Cynna could grasp her blade. The back of his hand connected with her cheek, knocking her back and down.

A sharp shot of pain rushed across her face. She grunted and fell into Nick. Strong arms closed around her, breaking her fall. But he didn't pull her up like she expected. Instead, he laid her on the ground, hissed, "Stay down," then stepped over her.

"You want to play now, human?" Lykos snarled. "Okay, we'll play."

Cynna's ears were ringing. She gave her head a swift shake and looked up. Nick was crouched down in a fighting stance, the blade held loosely in his hand, waiting for the attack. "Play is all I think you know how to do, satyr."

Nick swung out with the blade, slicing into Lykos's arm. Blood welled, and the beast jerked back.

The two satyrs behind Lykos growled and charged. But Lykos stopped them by lifting his arm and barking, "He's mine."

Fury suffused Lykos's face as he took a step to his right. "I'm going to enjoy slicing you into bits, human. And when I'm done, I'll give that bitch everything she deserves."

Cynna braced her hands on the ground and scooted back, her gaze never leaving Lykos's face. The satyr focused on Nick, but the two behind him were staring straight at her. Sizing her up. Waiting for her to join in the fight.

She glanced toward the open door and the stairs that led up to the surface. If she made a run for it, they'd follow. She wouldn't get far. Her gaze darted back to Nick, moving to his right as Lykos began to circle around him. She'd seen him hold his own against two, three, even four satyrs, but none of the ones Zagreus had tossed into the ring with Nick were Lykos. There was a reason he was Zagreus's number two. Because he was a ruthless son of a bitch and the strongest satyr in this hellhole.

She couldn't run. No matter how much she wanted to get away. She hadn't freed Nick so he could die here.

Lykos charged. Nick ducked under the satyr's arm and slammed his elbow into Lykos's back. Lykos cried out and whipped around. Blade met blade. Grunts and the sounds of fists slamming bone resonated in the corridor. Cynna pushed to her feet, her hands inching up the cold stone wall. She glanced past Nick and Lykos, toward the two satyrs beyond. They were both still staring at her. And the one on the left was salivating.

"Cynna, watch out!"

Nick's voice dragged Cynna's gaze back to the fight.

Nick slammed his fist into Lykos's jaw, shoving the satyr into the rocks. He gripped the satyr's wrist and smashed it against the wall, knocking the blade free from his gnarled fingers. "Behind you!"

Cynna grasped the blade from her back and whipped around. Two more satyrs were barreling down on them. Bracing her feet against the uneven ground, she slashed out with her blade, catching the first across the chest just as he reached her.

The satyr dropped back and howled. Growls echoed at her back. Followed by more footsteps, smacks, bone hitting bone and cracking against rock. Sweat slicked her skin as she kicked the first satyr away and stabbed at the second. Her blade sank deep into soft flesh, and he grunted, then fell back on his ass. She yanked her weapon free and ducked, just missing the blade of the first who'd lurched back to his feet and swung his blade like a major league slugger.

Metal clanged against metal in the corridor as Cynna's blade collided with the satyr's. She ducked another blow and looked for Nick in the chaos. He was covered in sweat and blood, holding his own against all three now with both the blade and the mace he'd picked up in the armory, but if any more showed up, they were going to—

The pounding of heavy footfalls sounded from the tunnels. Forget *if*. They were about to be overrun.

Cynna twisted, ducked, and struck out with her blade, catching the satyr at her front in the neck. His eyes flew wide; he gasped and then dropped to the ground. Breathing heavily, she brushed the hair out of her eyes and turned, ready to grab Nick and get the fuck out of there. But before she could make a move, something sharp stabbed into her side, just under her ribs.

She gasped. Jerked back. Her eyes flew wide. The satyr still on his ass, the one she'd caught in the chest, grinned up at her with an evil, twisted light flickering in his eyes.

Son of a bitch...

Pain, disbelief, and rage spiraled through Cynna. Pressing a hand against her side, she ground her teeth and swung out, slicing clean through the satyr's throat. Blood gushed from his carotid artery, killing his victorious grin. He fell back, his head cracking hard against the rocks.

Wincing, she turned toward Nick and leaned into the rocks, drawing a deep breath. A glance down confirmed she was bleeding. Heavily. Dropping her weapon, she tugged off her jacket and bit her lip to keep from crying out at the pain. After tying the jacket around her torso, she picked up her blade again.

The footsteps grew louder. Voices ricocheted off the rocks. Holy Hades, they were out of time. "Nick!"

Nick had taken down one satyr, but Lykos and the other were coming at him from different angles. Blade in one hand, the mace in the other, he kicked out at Lykos, twisted away from the second satyr's blade, and swung out with the mace.

Lykos ducked under Nick's mace and twirled around behind him, trapping Nick between the two beasts. Nick whipped his blade toward the satyr on his other side, missed, and glanced over his shoulder at Lykos.

Lykos growled and advanced. The other satyr followed suit. Nick swung out at the first satyr and sliced through his arm. Grunting, Cynna pushed away from the wall and stumbled forward. Sweat slicked her skin, dripped down into her eyes but

Lykos's back was angled her way. And she knew if she didn't help now, Nick might not get out of this alive.

Ignoring the pain in her side, she lunged forward, shoving her blade outward as hard as she could.

Metal pierced flesh, skewering Lykos in the back. The satyr howled. But before Cynna could grasp his shoulder and shove the blade deeper, a voice she knew almost as well as her own flooded the tunnel.

"Where is that shit-for-brains satyr?"

Zagreus. That was Zagreus's voice. Cynna whirled toward the sound, every inch of her body surging with adrenaline.

Nick kicked the second satyr to the ground and pulled his blade free of the beast's chest. He tried to see down the hall. Scowling, he muttered, "Fuck, we gotta go."

Lykos stumbled back into the wall, one hand covering the wound clear through to his belly, blood oozing from the spot to stain his torn shirt. His chest rose and fell with his uneven breaths as he glared Cynna's way. "You won't get far, bitch. He'll find you."

Cynna's vision turned red, and she gripped her blade to deliver the death blow, but Nick grabbed her by the sleeve. "There's no time. Go." He hauled her toward the open door and the steps that ran to freedom. "Fucking go."

Cynna struggled to pull free of his grip so she could finally finish this, once and for all, but Nick held her too tightly. She shot him an infuriated look back, then realized his sudden urgency.

Zagreus stalked straight toward them. A firestorm of fury and vengeance and the promise of death rolled like thunder in his black as sin eyes.

Flashes of what had happened in her room, what had propelled her to run, echoed in Cynna's mind. The blood. Being unable to move. Zagreus's voice.

"My blood flows in your veins now. You will never be free of me. Not until I have what I want..."

Horror rocketed through her entire body, replacing every other thought and emotion and instinct.

She scrambled for the stairs. Nick pulled her into the stairwell and slammed the door shut behind them. Grasping her arm, he tugged her with him as he moved up the steps, and this time, she didn't fight him. "Don't stop moving. Keep going. We're almost free."

Free…

The word was a ghost. A fantasy. A dream.

A lie.

Reality chilled every inch of her skin. She was never going to be free. Lykos had been right. She might escape these walls, but she would always be Zagreus's prisoner. She'd made a deal with the devil, and one way or another, it would haunt her, forever.

Wet palm fronds slapped Nick across the face. Swiping the rain out of his eyes, he drew a deep breath of humid air while he waited for Cynna to catch up, then paused to look around.

They'd been on the move for well over an hour. Closer to two, he guessed. As soon as they'd come up those stairs from Zagreus's lair, they'd found themselves shrouded in darkness with only a scattering of light from above to illuminate their way. Tall palms rose to the sky. Thick underbrush made it virtually impossible to move fast. He'd been captured in summer, which meant it had to be January now, but you'd never know by their surroundings. Insects hummed in the darkness. Every now and then the brush rustled. And the sounds combined with the heat, the humidity, the tropical foliage… It all told him they were in some kind of jungle. Where, though, he wasn't sure.

He didn't have a clue where the prisoners they'd released had gone. He'd heard voices as they'd wrestled their way through the jungle, but hadn't seen a single soul. He also hadn't heard any of Zagreus's satyrs on their trail. A fact that set the scars on his back tingling with suspicion.

Heavy breaths sounded at his back. He turned as Cynna stepped up to his side, lowered the blade in her hand to the ground, and leaned against a tree. "I'm slowing you down." She braced her hand at her side and sucked in another breath. "You should go on without me."

Nick looked down at her hand, pressing into her left side under her ribs. A sprinkling of moonlight shone down, just enough to illuminate the thick redness coating her fingers. "You're injured?"

"It's nothing."

He moved closer, pushed her hand away, and tugged the jacket from around her waist so he could see the torn fabric beneath.

"I said it's nothing."

He lifted the hem of her shirt. A two-inch, bloody gash cut across her side. "That's not nothing."

Wincing, she pulled back. Warm, red blood pooled from the wound. "I'll…be fine."

No, she wouldn't be. Not if she didn't get that tended. Conflicting emotions rippled through Nick. Yes, she'd overseen some of his worst torture in Zagreus's caves, but she'd also freed him, something she didn't have to do. And, clearly, she'd paid the price.

He lowered her shirt. "Where are we?"

Cynna cinched the coat tight around her waist once more, grimacing with the movement, then leaned back against the trunk of the tree. "The Yucatan. Belize."

Central America. *Motherfucker.* That didn't give them a lot of options.

Wisps of that odd blonde hair stuck to her temple and cheek. Her face was pale. From this angle, he could now see blood had soaked clear through her jacket. In another hour, she'd be too weak to walk, which meant putting more space between them and Zagreus was only going to get tougher.

"They're not following," he said.

Her breathing slowed, and her muscles tensed, but she didn't open her eyes. "Yeah. I…I noticed."

"What's your take on that?"

"I'm not sure."

Not sure. He didn't believe that for a second. His internal alarms screamed she knew a hell of a lot more than she was saying.

He scanned the dark jungle. He had a choice. He could ditch her ass here, like she'd suggested, or keep her with him. The first made total sense, considering their history. He didn't owe her a thing. But the second…

His scars tingled again, and something in his gut told him letting her go wasn't the right choice. At least not yet.

He didn't have time to argue with himself. He turned back to face her. "I need to get to a phone."

"There's a coastal highway that angles inland." She drew another deep breath. "You're bound to hit a village or two if you keep heading west."

He grasped her weapon from the ground and slid it into the sheath at his back, took the extra knives she'd grabbed from the armory and left in her pockets and added them to his collection, then reached for her arm, pulling her away from the tree. "Come on."

"What...?" Her dark eyes popped open, and surprise rippled over her features. "You'll make better time without me."

"I know." Hooking her forearm over his shoulder, he wrapped his arm around her waist so she could lean on him, then started walking, forcing her along with him.

"If Zagreus did send his satyrs after us—"

"Then you won't be able to tell them which way I went, now will you?" He slapped a palm frond out of his way, spraying water over both their faces.

She sputtered and shook the dew from her eyes. "You think I'd do that? I killed his guards. Trust me, at this point he probably wants me dead more than you."

"I'm not so sure about that. And Zagreus never wanted me dead. That's the point. Until I figure out your angle and how you're involved in all this, you're my prisoner."

Her muscles tightened at his side.

"Don't like that, do you?" he asked. "The tables being turned?"

"I've been a prisoner longer than you can imagine," she said quietly, stumbling next to him. "And you can't hold me. Not if you truly want to be free."

He glanced down at her, but she didn't meet his gaze. Her eyes were focused ahead, and her breaths lifted her chest rapidly, her body fighting, he knew, what had to be intense pain as they moved. But his scars vibrated once more as he looked at her profile in the moonlight—the high cheekbones, the elegant jawline, and the slope of her nose that was more familiar than he'd realized until just this moment—telling him she wasn't at all what he'd pegged. The problem was, at this point, he didn't know who she was. Or what she was really after.

He shook the cobwebs from his head, reminding himself not to lose his common sense where she was concerned. She might have rocked his world when she'd pleasured him in that cell, then surprised the shit out of him when she'd set him free, but she was a long way from being his ally. And the sooner he remembered that fact, the better off he'd be.

"At this point, female, you're in no shape to fight me."

She gave no response, and the fact she didn't try to pull away told him she knew he was right and that she didn't have the strength to argue.

They walked another twenty minutes before Nick noticed lights twinkling between palm fronds ahead. Cynna's breaths grew slower, and with every step she leaned into him more rather than supporting her own weight.

He narrowed his eyes to see through the foliage. Twenty, maybe thirty houses. Most dark. Based on the position of the moon, they were in the wee hours of morning, and the majority of the inhabitants in the village ahead were sound asleep. He tuned in to his senses. Counted seventy-five humans in the area, max.

Whoa.

He blinked against the lights. His tracking abilities had always been good, but being able to sense every human in the area... That was something new. Something that set off a wave of unease all through his abdomen and made those scars vibrate even more.

"What's...wrong?" Cynna asked.

"Nothing." He eased her toward a palm tree and unhooked her arm from his shoulder. She didn't put up any resistance, just slid to the ground, leaned her head back against the base of the tree, and closed her eyes. Kneeling next to her, Nick studied the bloodstain growing larger on her side.

Shit. That needed tending now. Not later. Especially if he planned to keep her alive to figure out what was really going on.

He tugged her blade from the sheath at his back, laid it on her lap, and closed her fingers over the handle. "Hang on to this."

Her eyes crept open. "Abandoning your prisoner? Not a smart move. I'll be gone before you can blink."

"I'll take my chances, female. Stay quiet."

He didn't wait for her answer. He pushed through the brush, then hesitated on the edge of the jungle as he looked toward the village. The houses were small, made of stucco, no bigger than three to four rooms. But power lines ran to each one, telling him they had to have phones.

He bypassed the first two—someone was awake inside each one. How he knew he wasn't sure, but he felt it. Zeroing in on the third, he tuned in to his senses again. Heavy human breaths sounded from inside. Two adults. Three children. All sound asleep.

He stepped up to the door and wrapped his fingers around the handle. Locked.

A frown pulled at his lips. He was just about to let go and check the back of the house when a burst of energy radiated against his palm.

He glanced down. That odd electrical charge pulsed between the cool metal and his warmer flesh. Then a click sounded in the quiet night air, and the doorknob turned in his hand.

Nick let go and pulled his hand back. Looked down at his palm, then at the door handle. Carefully, he reached for the knob again and found…sure enough…the thing was no longer locked.

Holy fuck. His senses told him the humans inside were still sound asleep, which meant…he'd just *thought* that damn door open.

His hands grew sweaty, and he pulled back again. He'd never had the power of telekinesis before. Yeah, sure, as a demigod, he'd been blessed with certain gifts. His were the ability to hear amplified sounds and to see objects from great distances. Gifts that had made him an incredible hunter and tracker and had helped him protect his people from Atalanta's daemons. But this—being able to manipulate matter with just his mind, if that was what he'd just done—this was something entirely new. And, a voice in the back of his head warned, something that could be incredibly dangerous.

"He senses you're growing stronger."

Cynna had said those words to him. In his cell, before she'd pleasured him. At the time, she'd been warning Nick about Zagreus's plans to double his efforts with the nymphs, but until this moment, Nick hadn't cued in to her meaning.

Now he did. Now he knew that if Zagreus suspected Nick's link to Krónos was giving him abilities he hadn't had before, then it meant it was entirely possible the Prince of Darkness had let Nick go on purpose. To what end, Nick still didn't know, but the fact the devil had released Cynna with him meant she was somehow deeply linked to Nick's freedom. Or his potential servitude to the gods.

Those scars on his back vibrated stronger, but he didn't have time to speculate about that reality further. Before any of the humans awoke, he needed to find that phone.

Cautiously, he pushed the door open and stepped into the small, dark house. A living area with a rug, two chairs, and beat-up end tables took up the space to his left. A U-shaped kitchen sat to his right. Ahead, an open doorway led to a bathroom and two small bedrooms.

He moved into the bathroom, didn't bother with the light, and opened the cabinet under the sink. Finding antiseptic and bandages, he shoved them into his pockets, then headed back into the living area. A grunt echoed from the bedroom to the left, and he hesitated. Seconds later, heavy breathing returned, signaling the human had gone back to sleep.

Nick scanned the dark room in search of a phone. The house might be worn. The furniture might be old. But the Chevy out front was a newer model, and in today's world, everyone had a cell phone.

He spotted it in the kitchen, plugged into a charger. Reaching for the device, he ran his finger over the screen and typed in the first four passcode numbers that came to his mind. The screen unlocked, illuminating the room in an eerie white light.

Wicked. He could get used to that.

His thumb hesitated over the Phone button. And out of nowhere, his mind drifted to his soul mate, Isadora.

Would she help him if he reached out to her? He'd gotten the message loud and clear the last time they'd been alone together: she didn't want him. She didn't feel the soul mate draw as he did. She'd chosen Demetrius over him, and that decision was never going to change. But for the first time in…Nick couldn't remember how long…he didn't care.

He looked down at the phone, pushing thoughts of Isadora from his mind. There was only one person he trusted to help him get out of this mess. Only one person he dared turn to right now.

The only question was whether or not the fucker would agree to help.

CHAPTER TEN

Cynna startled awake.

A shiver racked her body as she glanced around the dark jungle, searching for the source of the sound that had awoken her. Shadows danced in front of her eyes, a mixture of palm fronds and darkness she couldn't see clearly.

She swiped the sweat from her brow and tried to sit more upright against the base of the tree where she'd drifted to sleep, grimacing at the pain shooting across her side with the simple movement. *Skata*, she was in bad shape. Holding her breath, she glanced down but couldn't get a good view of the wound.

She shivered again. Her spine was damp, her muscles weak, and, based on the thin sheen of sweat coating her skin, she was pretty sure she already had a fever. She gritted her teeth and leaned forward. Some kind of bird or bat or creature she didn't want to think about howled high above, and the brush rustled to her right.

Animals. Nothing more. She wasn't quite sure how she knew, but she was confident Zagreus hadn't sent anyone after them. Lykos—

A whisper of…something swept through her mind. A memory she couldn't quite bring into view. One of her and Zagreus and Lykos in her room. Her pulse picked up, and sweat slid down her spine. Something had happened there. Something she couldn't quite remember but which she knew was important.

Fingers shaking, she untied the jacket from her waist and dropped it on the ground. Then she reached for the edge of her shirt, drew a deep breath, and pulled the fabric away from the wound.

Blinding pain spiraled outward from the spot, but she bit down hard on her lip to keep from crying out. Through watery vision, she looked down at the wound, jagged and red and still bleeding.

Her head grew light. Letting go of her shirt, she closed her eyes and leaned back against the base of the tree, working to suck back air.

She was going to die out here, and no one would know. No one would even care. And why should they? All the bad shit she'd done was finally catching up with her. What she'd done to Lykos, the months she'd bent to Zagreus's will, and Nick—especially all the horrible things she'd overseen with Nick. She'd be the first to admit she deserved every bit of misery piling on her now.

A wave of regret rushed over her, one so strong it made her want to let go, give up, quit fighting this unwinnable battle. The rustling to her right grew louder, and she knew if some kind of animal had smelled the blood, she needed to get a grip on her weapon so she could defend herself. But she no longer cared. Her blade lay on the ground at her side, but she didn't reach for it, didn't even want it anymore. All she wanted was peace. And to forget everything she now couldn't change.

"I see you made it far."

Cynna's heart rate jerked. Nick wasn't supposed to be here now, not when she'd finally decided enough was enough. Dragging in slow breaths, she pried her eyelids open and looked up.

She couldn't see him very well. He was nothing more than a watery silhouette in the darkness, but she could smell him. That unique sandalwood and earthy pine scent she remembered from his cell. And she could feel his body heat growing closer, warming her chilled skin in a way that reminded her...she wasn't dead. At least not yet.

He knelt at her side, set something she couldn't see on the ground beside her, then reached for her shoulders. "You need to lie down."

Her brain wasn't working, and she didn't have the strength to fight him, but she tried. When his hands landed on her overheated skin, she struggled, but he pulled her away from the tree easily, shifted her around, and laid her out on the damp ground. Pain spiraled across her skin once more with the movement, and she bit her lip against a groan.

"Sorry."

Sorry? *He* was apologizing to *her*? Gods, this was so fucked up. "You were supposed to leave." Dammit. She hated how weak she was. Hated that he'd come back and was seeing her like this. Hated even more that his hands felt so good and that part of her was rejoicing over the fact he'd returned. "Wh-what are you doing…back here?"

"Helping you."

"I don't need…your help."

He lifted her shirt from the wound. She tried to push him away, but he laid her arm on the ground, then scooted closer so her forearm was pressed against his knee, preventing her from moving it. "Oh yeah, because it looks like you're doing so well on your own."

She was too tired to try to stop him. He tugged the waistband of her pants down, exposing more of her flesh. Cool air washed over her belly, but she didn't dare look down again. Was afraid she'd get sick if she tried. Blinking several times, she stared up at the swaying dark fronds above and tried like hell to pull them into focus.

"Hold still," he said. "This might sting."

Something wet and cool spilled over her abdomen and side, making her suck in a breath. A sharp stab shot all across the wound, and she bit down on her lip against the pain dancing over her flesh.

"Hydrogen peroxide," he mumbled, pouring more liquid over her skin. "It'll clean it out until we can get it stitched."

Cynna closed her eyes and breathed deep. He rubbed a rag all around the wound, wiping the blood from her skin, then applied some kind of dressing to the gash. When he was done, he pulled her shirt back down and pressed his palm against her forehead.

She focused on slow breaths until the pain receded to a dull throb. Fabric rustled, then she felt his hands on her shoulders, lifting her up. Agony ripped through her side all over again but it was quickly replaced with another sensation. This one of heat and electricity as he slid behind her, stretched his legs out on either side of her, laid her head back on his shoulder, and then lifted something toward her lips.

"Drink."

He pressed a plastic bottle to her lips, and Cynna immediately opened. Cool, fresh liquid spilled over her tongue, moistening her bone-dry mouth.

Water. He was giving her water. Just as she'd given him water in his cell. She swallowed. This time she couldn't help but groan.

"Easy," he whispered, drawing the bottle back.

She'd said the very same to him. The irony wasn't lost on her. Nor was the warmth growing in her belly over the fact he was taking care of her.

No one took care of her. Not since her parents had died. She'd been on her own so long, she'd forgotten what it was like. And she both loved and hated it now, because she found herself wanting to lean on him. Wanting to let someone else carry the load for a while. Even if it was the one person who should hate her more than any other.

When she'd drunk her fill, she leaned her head back and closed her eyes. He capped the water bottle and set it on the ground at his side, then ran one big hand over her scalp, drawing her damp hair back from her face.

Holy gods, this was…so wrong, his being nice to her in any way. But it felt so incredibly right, she didn't have the strength to fight it any longer.

They sat in silence for several long minutes. Then quietly, he said, "You're Argolean."

Surprise rippled through her. She'd never told him her heritage. Then she realized he must have seen the Alpha birthmark on her hip. The marking all Argoleans were born with, signaling their race.

There was no reason to lie. Not now. "Yes."

He was silent for several seconds, then said, "Your Council prohibits Argoleans from crossing into the human realm. How the hell did you wind up with Zagreus?"

A burst of anger whipped through her at the mention of the Council of Elders, the governing body that advised the monarchy of Argolea, but tonight it melded with the hatred and stupidity swirling inside her at the sound of Zagreus's name.

Memories bombarded her. Ones she didn't want to see tonight. She forced them back and told herself the specifics weren't important. But she knew she couldn't tell him everything. Even though Nick wasn't technically an Argonaut, he had the markings on his forearms, and she knew from Zagreus that he'd aligned himself with the Eternal Guardians.

Her first instinct was to lie, but he was being nice to her. And with his increased strengths of late, she didn't know if he could tell when she was lying. She figured a partial truth was her best bet. "My family was murdered. When I was old enough, I crossed into the human realm via the witch's portals. And I went looking for Zagreus."

"Why?"

Why? Because it had seemed like a good idea at the time. Because she'd heard stories of the Prince of Darkness's ruthlessness. Because she knew Zagreus was the only person who could train her to fight and set her plan for revenge in motion.

But she couldn't tell Nick any of that, so she simply said, "Because I knew he was a god who was always looking for a deal. And because he promised to help me find the person who killed my family and make them pay."

Nick's hand went back to stroking her hair, and gods, that felt good. Too good. Her eyes drifted closed once more.

"Revenge always comes with a price."

His voice was low, just above a whisper, but it made her lashes flutter and her eyelids open once more. She stared out into the darkness, seeing nothing but shadows and mist as she thought about that price.

Not just her freedom. But the very heart of who she was. Or who she'd once been.

She hadn't known when she'd made that deal with Zagreus that it would bring her to this moment. To questioning everything she'd done and believed in. But now...now she wondered if revenge was really the solution. She still wanted retribution against the one who'd destroyed her family, but she didn't want to lose her soul in the process. And she wasn't willing to go through with her plan if it meant taking someone else's soul with her.

"So what changed your mind?" he asked in that same deep, sexy voice, the one that made her think about everything *but* revenge. "What made you finally decide to walk away from something you so desperately wanted?"

You did.

The words hovered on her lips but she couldn't bring herself to say them.

"Did you find a phone?" she asked, changing the subject.

"Yeah." His chest vibrated with his words, the sensation passing from him into her, warming her insides. "I also found us a car. In a few minutes, we'll head that direction and rendezvous with someone who can help us get the hell out of this damn jungle."

Us. We. He still intended to keep her with him. Warmth bloomed in her belly all over again, followed by a tiny burst of panic. "You...you called the Argonauts?"

"Hell, no."

Relief and confusion clouded her thoughts. "But you're one of them. Why wouldn't you call them?"

"I've never been one of them. And they're the last people I'd call in a pinch, trust me."

Curiosity got the best of her. The Argonauts weren't on her top-ten friend list by any means, but the animosity she heard in Nick's voice was strong, and it made her wonder what they'd done to cause such a vehement reaction.

"You were gifted with the markings."

"Cursed is more like it. Don't get any ideas, female. I'm no hero."

But...he was. The fact he'd insisted on freeing those prisoners and tended her wounds and was comforting her now when he should want her dead only confirmed that fact.

Her pulse picked up speed, but she told herself not to get worked up. He'd already told her she was now his prisoner. Common sense said if he was taking care of her, it was only to make sure she didn't die, in case he needed her for leverage down the line against Zagreus.

"Wh-why wouldn't you turn to the guardians for help?"

He was silent for several seconds, and she was sure he wasn't going to answer. But then he surprised her by saying, "Because calling them means alerting my soul mate to the fact I'm still alive. And I'm not in the mood to deal with that shit right now."

Soul mate...

Something in her chest pinched. Something she recognized as jealousy but felt so out of place, she knew it was a ridiculous emotion.

She focused on a dark palm frond ahead. "You have a soul mate? One would think you'd be anxious to see her. Or maybe it's a him."

He snorted. "Do I give off that vibe? Man, I am out of practice."

Oh, hell no, he didn't give off that vibe. But she wasn't about to tell him that right now.

"It's a her," he went on. "And she's the last person I want to see or think about. Trust me, having a soul mate is not a blessing. It's a curse."

"How so?"

"You don't know about the Argonauts' soul mate curse? You're Argolean."

"I was raised outside Tiyrns. My parents were refugees hiding from the Council's strict laws. The Argonauts and anything that happened within the capital were not things we focused on."

"Lucky you," he mumbled.

He shifted against the tree at his back, forcing her to sink farther into the warmth of his chest, and he wrapped his arm around her good side, laying his hand on her thigh as he continued to stroke her hair with the other. Warmth infused her skin all over again, making her relax back into him. Making her feel…safe. Which was something so totally foreign, she didn't know how to react.

"The way the story goes," he said, "Hera had a special hatred for Heracles, and when Zeus established the realm of Argolea, she retaliated by cursing Heracles and all the Eternal Guardians with a soul mate. The one person in the world they would be forever drawn to but who was the worst possible match for them. The person who would torment their existence. Since I was born with the guardian markings, even though I'm not technically one of them, I lucked out. My soul mate is bonded to my brother."

Oh, ouch. Yeah, she could see how that would be a curse. "And she—this female—is able to just ignore the soul mate curse? She's not tortured by it? How is that possible?"

"Because she isn't cursed. Only those of us with the markings feel the draw. She's perfectly happy in her protected realm, playing house with my brother. They even have a child now."

That had to bite. Not only had Cynna overseen Nick's physical torture the last few months, but now she knew the poor guy was emotionally tortured on a daily basis.

"How often did you see her...you know, before?" Before Zagreus had imprisoned him and she'd put him through another kind of hell.

"As little as possible."

There was definite animosity there, and her hatred for the guardians and everything Argolean jumped another notch.

Which was fucking ludicrous, because he was nothing to her. Nothing but someone she'd felt obligated to free.

Yeah, right. Keep telling yourself that, girlie...

A plethora of emotions churned inside her, ones she wasn't ready to face. When his hand lifted from her hair, she was both disappointed and relieved.

"We need to get moving," he said. "I parked the truck about a mile from here. Do you think you can walk, or do I need to carry you?"

"Walk." Definitely walk. She lifted her head from his shoulder, gritted her teeth, and sat upright, moving away from him. "But you should just go without me."

"We've already been through that. Not happening."

Even though pain ripped through her side, she turned to look at him, frustrated and...confused as hell. "*Why* are you doing this?"

His amber eyes narrowed and held hers. And though she couldn't read his thoughts, she felt his determination in the intensity of his stare. "Because you told me in that cell that you were freeing me because neither one of us should have been there. And because if you didn't do the right thing then, you were afraid you never would. For now, I'm keeping you with me for the very same reason."

She searched her feelings and locked on to her gift, the one that was now working since she was free of Zagreus's hold, and realized...he was being honest. He wasn't saving her just because he might eventually use her as leverage. He was saving her because he could.

Her heart raced against her ribs, and her cheeks grew hot. She watched carefully as his knees bent and he pushed to his feet, then stepped around her and held out his hand. "You can either go with me willingly, or you can fight me. But either way, I'm getting you out of this jungle. What's it going to be, Cynna?"

She looked from his face to his hand and swallowed hard. He didn't see himself as a hero, but that was exactly what he was, saving his enemy when he had every reason not to. And in that moment, as she stared at his wide palm and long fingers and thought back over the terrible events in her life that had brought her to this moment, she felt something inside shift. Something that had been hard and dark for so long, she was sure it would never bend. Something that was softening…because of him.

Anger and hatred were easy. But forgiveness—especially forgiving herself for the awful things she'd done and could never change—that was the true challenge.

And the unknown aftermath of what she chose right now scared her more than Zagreus ever had.

"I'm not happy with these results."

Isadora looked away from the window and the view of the harbor she'd been staring at from Callia's office and eyed her sister. "And I don't like you worrying about something that's clearly not a big deal."

Leaning against the edge of her desk in the medical clinic she ran, Callia frowned, tucked a lock of auburn hair behind her ear, and shot Isadora an irritating-as-hell I'm-always-right look. "You've lost almost ten pounds in a month, your skin is sallow, and you yourself told me you're exhausted."

Isadora dropped her crossed arms. "Is this sisterly love? Pointing out all my flaws? Because if it is, I can definitely do without."

"No, this is the queen's official healer telling her something isn't right."

"I have a six-month-old and a kingdom to run. Cut me some slack. I'm just a tad bit run down."

"This is more than exhaustion, and you know it."

Isadora drew in a deep breath to hold her temper in check. She didn't know what *this* was, but she didn't like her sister worrying. Demetrius did that enough for everyone. And lately he'd been way worse than usual.

"Look." She turned fully from the window. "You did a scan, and you didn't find anything, did you?"

As a healer, Callia had the ability to sense disease and injury within the body, and, in most cases, her gift gave her the power to heal it. "No. Nothing that would explain your symptoms."

"And you're not feeling any strange effects yourself, are you?"

Callia frowned. "No. I'm not."

Since the three sisters—Isadora, Callia, and Casey—were all linked by their bloodline through the king to the Horae, the ancient goddesses of the order of nature, whatever ailment one sister suffered, the others did as well. "Then it's nothing."

The door to the office pushed open before Callia could respond, and Casey stuck her dark head into the room. "I'm not too late, am I?"

Isadora glanced back toward Callia. "You called her?"

"Yes, I did." Callia pushed away from her desk. "This is heavy, and I think the three of us need to discuss it."

"Oh, for gods' sake." Isadora rolled her eyes and moved back toward the window.

"Okay, fill me in." Casey stepped into the room and closed the door at her back. Placing a hand on her belly, she rubbed her palm over the baby that would be here in only a few short months while Callia explained Isadora's test results.

"I haven't felt anything," Casey said when her sister finished.

"That's what I needed to know," Callia answered. "I haven't either. But something is definitely going on with Isadora."

Exasperation toyed with what little patience Isadora had left. "I'm a new mom, I've got a mate who can't stop blaming himself for his brother's disappearance, an Argonaut who loves to antagonize the Council, the Misos to get set up in their new settlement, and the fate of the world hanging in the balance as we search for Nick, who may or may not be the key to releasing Krónos from Tartarus and starting the apocalypse. If anything's going on, it's that I'm just a *tiny* bit stretched in all directions. So you can both stop speculating about what's wrong with me and just let me get back to my job."

She stepped toward the door, but Casey moved into her path.

"Whoa." Wide-eyed, Casey looked toward Callia. "I think I know why you and I aren't feeling anything."

"Why?" Callia asked.

Casey glanced down at her belly, then back at Callia.

"Because you're pregnant?" Callia asked.

Good gods. Isadora clenched her jaw. They weren't even listening to her now. She didn't have time for this. She needed to get back to the Kyrenia settlement, where the Argonauts were working to get basic services set up for the Misos before the Council came in and declared martial law.

"Remember when Isadora hemorrhaged after delivering Elysia, and you immediately felt the effects?"

Callia nodded. "Yes."

"I didn't feel them," Casey said. "I was here in Argolea, but I didn't feel anything. I was already pregnant then. I just didn't know yet."

Callia's brow dropped. "You're speculating that because you were pregnant, it caused you not to feel any adverse effects from our connection?"

"No," Casey answered. "Not just because I was pregnant. Because I was pregnant with an Argonaut's child. Genetically, the Argonauts are stronger than humans and Misos, right?" She splayed her fingers over the roundness of her belly. "Isn't it highly possible this baby is strong enough to keep me from feeling any ill effects Isadora is experiencing?"

"Yes," Callia said, a crease forming between her brows. "That's entirely possible. It's just…"

"Just what?" Casey asked.

"Well." Callia shifted her weight. "If that's the case, then I should be feeling the same things as Isadora. I'm not pregnant."

"Are you sure about that?" Casey tipped her head. "You told me a few weeks ago that you and Zander were hoping to give Max a sibling soon."

A faraway look filled Callia's violet eyes, and she glanced around the room as if not seeing it. Slowly, her eyes widened, and she turned quickly for a door that led into an exam room. "I-I'll be right back."

She was gone without another word.

Isadora frowned at her sister when they were alone. "This is a stretch. Even for you."

"Why?" Casey asked. "Because you don't think it's possible?"

"No, because there's nothing wrong with me. And I need you and Callia to back me up on this so I can get Demetrius to stop worrying. He has more important things to deal with right now."

Carefully, because her center of gravity had shifted thanks to the pregnancy, Casey lowered herself to the arm of the sofa. "Still no word on Nick?"

Isadora wrapped an arm around her waist and pinched the bridge of her nose. "No, nothing. It's like he's completely vanished off the face of the planet."

"If Hades has him, that's entirely possible."

Casey had been to the Underworld, when Hades had taken her there in an attempt to convince her to give up her life for the sake of a prophecy and his attempt to hold the goddess Atalanta in check. At the time, she'd been raining havoc over a portion of the Underworld and he'd wanted to keep her under his control. His plan had backfired, however, when Isadora made a deal with the god-king of the Underworld to save her sister's life. A deal that had led to that moment when Isadora had been dying and Nick had made the same deal to save hers. Only Hades hadn't wanted Nick's soul like he'd wanted Isadora's. No, what he still wanted was Krónos's powers, which were locked inside Nick.

"No," Isadora said. "He's in the human realm somewhere. Hades wouldn't risk taking him to the Underworld where Krónos could influence him. He's left him with his son until he can access those powers."

"Did you foresee that?" Casey asked.

"No." Isadora rubbed her fingers across her brow, wishing the tension headache taking up space behind her eyes would just go away. She felt Nick was still in the human realm. The same way she felt he was alive. Which was weird because she'd never been able to sense something like that before.

She dropped her hand. "Even if Zagreus doesn't succeed and Nick is—"

The door to the exam room pushed open, and Callia's ashen face filled the space.

"Callia?" Casey asked, pushing to her feet. "What's wrong?"

"You were right. I just ran the test. I'm…pregnant."

A slow smile spread across Casey's lips, and she stepped forward and gripped her sister's hand. "That's wonderful. Zander will be so excited. When are you—"

"No." Callia's eyes locked on Casey's. "It's not good news at all. It means you were right. Whatever's affecting Isadora is not affecting us because of the Argonaut genes we're carrying. And as rapidly as Isadora is weakening, it means whatever's happening with her is serious."

A chill spread down Isadora's spine. And that vision she'd had before, of her future with her mate, flashed in front of her eyes. Only this future wasn't the future she'd planned on. And the man in the center of it wasn't Demetrius.

Isadora's stomach tightened. Cautiously, to Callia, she said, "You told me you didn't sense any disease or illness in me."

"I didn't," Callia answered. "But we're all linked to the Horae. It's possible whatever this is, it's hidden."

Skata. That did not make Isadora feel any better. She held up a suddenly shaking hand. "Okay, not that I buy in to any of this, but I want to go on record as stating that I'm sick and tired of being the sister who's sick and tired. One of you be sick for a change and let me have a break. How about that?"

Callia didn't react to her joke. In fact, Isadora wasn't even sure her sister heard her. The healer moved around her desk and reached for a book from the shelf along the wall. "I need to do some research." To Isadora, she said, "I don't want you going out to the Kyrenia settlement. It's too strenuous for you. Until I figure out what's going on, you need to stay close to the castle."

Irritation pulsed inside Isadora. "I have work to do."

"No one's stopping you. Delegate it from here." When Isadora huffed, Callia dropped the book on her desk. "This is important. It isn't just about you. It's about all of us. You're weakening rapidly. Whatever's going on with you is more than just stress and lack of sleep. It's something that will eventually affect Casey and me as well."

Isadora's stomach tightened at the fear she heard in her sister's voice. "Okay," she said cautiously. "I'll stay close."

"Good." Callia looked toward Casey. "In the meantime, I could use your help."

"Name it."

"I need to check the ancient texts. For anything related to the Horae. If I can't figure out what's going on medically, then that means it has to be something genetic."

"Yeah, I can do that."

Callia nodded, sat in her chair, and flipped the book open.

"Callia," Casey said. "What about Zander?"

Callia's hand stilled on the page, and she exhaled a long breath. "I'll tell him."

"He's going to be thrilled."

"I know." Callia shook her head and turned a page. "But this isn't exactly something to celebrate. If we can't stop Isadora from growing weaker, and she continues to decline and eventually dies—"

"*What?*" Isadora's head snapped up. Dies? No way. Now her sisters were getting way ahead of themselves. "I'm fine. A little tired but fine. This is complete paranoia at its—"

"Oh, holy gods," Casey breathed.

The color drained from her cheeks, and she placed a protective hand over her belly. And in a flash, a whole new understanding dawned, bringing a wave of dizziness to Isadora's head.

Callia looked up. "Yeah. It means we will too. And Zander, because I'm his weakness. I already abandoned one child to the world alone. I won't do it a second time. Whatever it takes, we're going to figure this out. After everything we've been through, I refuse to accept that this is the end."

CHAPTER ELEVEN

"Dammit." Nick ground his teeth together as the Chevy he'd snagged from the small village slowed and sputtered out. He cut the wheel to the right, jostling the vehicle over holes in the side of the narrow dirt road.

The rig came to a stop. At his side, Cynna startled awake and lifted her head from the passenger window where she'd been leaning. "Wh-what happened?"

"Ran out of gas."

She grimaced, pressed a hand against her side as she sat up straighter, and looked out the windshield with cloudy eyes. "Where are we?"

Nick didn't have a clue. It was still dark outside, probably around five a.m., he guessed from the position of the moon. They hadn't passed a settlement for at least an hour, and the jungle rose on both sides of the one-lane road, encroaching in several spots like monstrous tentacles. If there was an actual airstrip out here, he'd eat his own damn shoes. It'd be just like Ari to fuck with him on this.

He checked the coordinates on the cell phone he'd taken from that house and frowned. "It's not far from here. We're gonna have to walk the rest of the way."

The greenish glow from the dashboard illuminated her pale face and the way she winced. She leaned back against the seat, still pressing her hand to her side. "Maybe I should just stay here."

Dammit... He'd told himself he was getting her out of this jungle, and he meant it, whether she cooperated or not. He wasn't sure what he'd do with her after, but something in his gut wouldn't leave her behind for Zagreus to find and torture. Not after she'd risked her life to free him. Not when she might still be important.

He climbed out of the truck, stalked around the hood, then pulled the passenger door open. Sliding his arm under her knees, he lifted her out of the truck. She bit back a groan, and he knew the movement had to cause her excruciating pain, but she didn't protest. "It's only about a mile away."

Survival skills. This female had them. After everything she'd been through, that made perfect sense. But one thought wouldn't leave his head as he carried her into the jungle. One thing she'd told him when he'd been tending her wound, which he didn't like. The bitter reality that she'd *chosen* to make a deal with Zagreus all for the sake of revenge.

"Not all prisons have walls…"

No, they didn't. He knew that better than most. It was highly possible she hadn't known what she was getting into and that her deal had become its own form of torture. But still…what kind of hatred must a person harbor to make a deal with the Prince of Darkness? What kind of anger had to drive them?

The same kind of hatred you had for your mother. The same anger you feel right now for your father for cursing your life.

An odd tingle took up space in his chest. He zeroed in on his senses, hoping something new would make him able to read Cynna's mind so he could figure out what she wasn't telling him, but that clearly wasn't a gift he'd acquired. Because, no, he wasn't that fucking lucky, now was he?

The trees ended abruptly, and Nick stepped out into a wide, green field with one tiny shack a hundred yards away.

"Wh-what is this?" Cynna asked.

He thought she'd fallen asleep. She'd been silent during the entire trek, her muscles lax in his arms. "I'm not sure. I think it's the airstrip."

The grass in the middle of the field was shorter than along the edges but still knee-high. There was no sign of life anywhere close. If this was the airstrip Ari had told him about, it was a primitive one and seldom used. Which meant the chief inhabitants of the area were probably drug runners and cartels.

Fucking fantastic. The last thing he wanted to deal with right now was humans.

He set Cynna down twenty yards from the shack. "Stay here. I'll be right back."

She didn't argue. Just lay down in the grass, shivered, and closed her eyes. And as he pushed to his feet and looked down at her, a whisper of worry rippled through him—worry he knew he shouldn't be feeling but couldn't shake.

She's not a person. She's insurance.

He turned away, repeating the words in his head. But the way she looked—vulnerable, broken, weak—flashed over and over in his mind, keeping him from thinking about anything but her.

The shack was easy to break into. Inside he found a mower, machetes for cutting jungle foliage, shovels, work gloves, and a few odds-and-ends-type survival materials.

He didn't know how long they'd be out here waiting, so he grabbed what he thought they'd need, then headed back to Cynna. The area was still dark, and he checked the phone in his pocket to see if he'd gotten any messages, but the screen was blank.

Damn, Ari.

Irritation mounting, he covered Cynna with a blanket he'd grabbed from the shack. "Here, lift up."

She blinked several times and slowly lifted her head from the ground. But her face blanched from the simple movement. Telling himself it wasn't his problem, he shoved another blanket under the side of her face, then went to work finding wood to build a fire.

She lay back down and closed her eyes once more. "Thanks."

The word was softly spoken. Almost a whisper. And so damn strange coming from her, he didn't know what to think. This whole situation was bizarre. As was the odd desire to sit with her again like he'd done in the jungle, to run his hand down her blonde hair and comfort the person who'd tortured him for the last six months.

Shit. You're clearly losing it, man.

He exhaled a long breath and gathered an armful of wood. Prisoner. She was his prisoner now. And the sooner he remembered that fact, the better off he'd be.

He came back, stacked the wood, then used the lighter he'd found in the shack to ignite the wood. The flames started slowly, then quickly licked their way up the twigs and branches.

Nick sat back and rested his forearms on his knees as he stared into the fire. It wasn't cold enough out here to need heat. He'd built it to keep animals away and to illuminate the area so Ari could find the airstrip. He hadn't built it because Cynna was cold, dammit.

Denial, dude. First sign you're fucked.

"Who is this friend we're waiting for?"

Cynna's mumbled words dragged Nick from his messed-up thoughts, and he glanced to his left where she was lying at his side. With her eyes closed and the moonlight making her hair appear even more blonde, she looked almost like an angel. His chest constricted with unfamiliar emotions. "Just a guy I've known for several years."

"A human?"

"No."

"What is he?"

Nick looked back at the fire, thinking of a way to describe Ari. "He used to be Argolean."

Her eyes slowly slid open. "Used to be? How do you 'used to be' something?"

Nick tried not to look, but couldn't stop himself from glancing sideways at her. At her pale features, the sweat dampening her brow, and the firelight dancing in her glassy eyes.

Dammit. He didn't *feel* things for other people. Not individuals, anyway. For his race…yes. And that had only started because helping the Misos thrive was a way to get back at the Argolean Council who'd shunned him as a child. But even with that singular goal, at his core he was a loner. And, knowing now his parents were, for good reason. So no way in hell should he be *feeling* anything for any female, especially the one beside him now.

He clenched his jaw and stared into the fire. "His people think he's dead. That's how."

"Why would they think that?"

"Because he wants it that way."

She was curious. But he wasn't in the mood to give her more. Especially not when she was fucking with his head.

The hum of a motor echoed in the darkness, and Nick's senses kicked in. Glancing up, he spotted the plane, still three miles off in the inky sky. Relief washed through his veins like a vat of sweet wine. "There he is."

"Where?" Cynna looked up. "I don't see anything."

Nick pushed to his feet. "You will."

Red lights blinked in the darkness. The hum of the engine grew louder. The single-engine Cessna made a large circle over the runway, then dropped in the sky, heading right for them.

Cynna grimaced and pushed up to sitting. "He's coming in sideways."

She was right. The wings of the small plane were wagging up and down. If that fucker was showing off and crashed the plane now...

The left wheel touched down. Then the right. A roar sounded through the field as the brakes were applied. Finally, the plane slowed and turned, rumbling their direction.

The engine cut off, and the propeller died. Inside the cockpit, the pilot pulled off a headset, popped the door open, and dropped to the ground with a raucous, rolling laugh. "Hot damn, that was fun."

Nick frowned as he crossed to greet Ari. "You sure do like to make an entrance."

Ari's mismatched eyes—one a brilliant blue, the other a deep green—twinkled in the lights from the plane. He captured Nick's forearm in a tight grip and grinned, his white teeth all but glowing in the darkness. "Thought you were dead, man. Everyone did. Gotta say, though, dead isn't exactly a bad place to be. Like the hair, by the way."

Nick let go of Ari's marked forearm and ran a hand over the thick blond hair on his skull. Normally, he kept it shaved—way easier to deal with—but in the months he'd been held captive, he hadn't had the luxury. "Feels fucking weird."

Ari's always assessing, ever-wild eyes narrowed and shot a look past Nick. He lifted his chin Cynna's direction. "Who's the female?"

Reluctantly, Nick turned her way. He didn't need Ari knowing just who she was or how she was involved, especially not when he was still trying to work it all out in his head. He might have called the guy for help, but that didn't mean he trusted him. Not completely. Especially knowing Ari's quirks. "Just someone who helped me escape."

Ari drew in a deep sniff. "Not a Siren. But she smells of nymph. And that makes her of high interest."

He pushed past Nick and headed right for her.

Shit.

Nick turned and caught up. Ari was as skilled a hunter and tracker as Nick, maybe more so since living in the wild these last few years. But his methods were more than questionable.

Dressed in worn jeans, a short-sleeved gray shirt, and boots, Ari stopped in front of the fire, tucked his massive hands into his pockets, and tipped his dark head as he stared down at Cynna. The firelight seemed to dance over the puckered scars that covered the left side of his jaw, ran down his neck, and disappeared under the collar of his T-shirt. "She's Argolean."

"Yeah." Nick held his breath, wondering how the hell this was going to go down. Ari's obsession with Sirens was well known, but his interest in nymphs was personal.

"And you said she was one of Zagreus's prisoners?"

Crap. Ari was making connections. Suddenly Nick was wishing he'd left Cynna in the jungle after all. "Yeah."

Cynna pulled the blanket over her lap, but her dark eyes were still glassy as they darted from him to Ari and back again. Nick knew she was having trouble following the conversation. So was he, for that matter.

"Does she have a name, or do you just call her bitch?"

"Hey now," Cynna finally said, her spine stiffening. "Who the hell do you think you—"

"Cynna," Nick cut in, wanting only to keep the peace right now. They needed Ari's help. Not to piss the guy off. "Her name is Cynna."

"Cynna…" His mismatched eyes narrowed and held on her face. "I've heard of a female with the same name in Zagreus's keep. Looks like you've caught yourself a live one."

Before Nick could ask what he'd heard, Ari pulled a jagged knife from the small of his back and lurched around the fire.

He was big and muscular—almost as big as Nick—and Cynna recoiled as he drew close. His massive hands grasped Cynna by the shoulders and pinned her to the ground. Cynna yelped. Ari climbed over her.

"Son of a bitch." Nick sprinted around the fire. "Ari, godsdammit, let go of her."

Cynna screeched a bloodcurdling cry, and Nick's adrenaline went sky-high. He grasped Ari by the shoulder but couldn't pull the bastard off. Shifting around, he caught sight of what Ari was doing.

His knees held her pinned to the ground while the knife in his hand sliced through the flesh of her forearm.

Blood gushed from the wound. Ari dropped the knife and drove his fingers into her muscle. Cynna screamed and kicked out but couldn't get away.

"Motherfucker, Ari." Nick grabbed the male's shoulders and yanked him back. "I said to let go. She's not a fucking threat."

Ari released Cynna and stumbled back, barely missing falling into the fire. In his bloody hands, he held up something small and metallic. "Not a threat? What the fuck do you call this?"

Nick's chest heaved. He focused on the small circular device in Ari's bloodstained fingers. "Is that—"

"A tracking device. Yeah." Ari nodded toward Cynna. "You said she helped you escape. You sure she's not setting a trap for you instead? They call her the Mistress, man. I've heard all about her in my travels. She's Zagreus's whore."

Cynna moaned and rolled to her side on the ground, clutching her bloody forearm in her hand.

Chest rising and falling with his deep breaths, Nick looked down at her, fighting his first reaction to assume the worst. He tuned in to his senses. Searched his mind for what he knew as fact. And came up...completely fucking empty.

Shit. What good were powers if he couldn't access them? *Think, dammit.* She could have known. He'd sensed she wasn't telling him the whole truth earlier when he'd asked why no one was following them. She could still be working with Zagreus, luring him into some kind of trap as Ari suggested. But the way she'd repeatedly told him to leave her behind, that panicked look in her eyes when she'd come down to his cell and freed him... Those weren't things someone still working for Zagreus would do. Not if she knew she was being tracked and that staying with him would lead to his recapture.

Nick snatched the tracker from Ari, dropped it on the ground, then crushed it under his boot. Anger coiled through him. Anger because he couldn't get a solid read on Cynna. And because, thanks to him, she was now in even more pain. "I know who the hell she is. Why do you think I brought her with me?"

He knelt beside her, reached for her shoulder, and rolled her over. "Stay still."

"I didn't know," she whispered, still clutching her arm. "He came to my room after I left you. I…I couldn't remember clearly, so I didn't say anything. He was livid. He saw us." She closed her eyes and pressed her lips together, breathing through the pain. "When I awoke, I was covered in blood. I don't know what happened. I just knew I had to get out of there. That if I stayed, he was going to kill me…us. He…he could have put that…thing…in my arm then. I didn't know. I didn't know."

"Shh." Her words were hurried, rushing together, and filled with a sense of immediacy that set off a strange protective urge inside Nick. One he'd never felt before. "It's okay." He shot an irritated look over his shoulder toward Ari. "Get the hell over here and fix this."

Ari scowled but stalked their direction. "She's lying. All females lie."

Cynna's muscles contracted as he drew close, but Nick pressed his hands against her shoulders to hold her still. "Don't move. He's not going to cut you again. I'll make sure of it."

Ari knelt on her other side and rested his bloody hands on his thighs. "You should just let her die, man. More humane."

"I'm not human."

Ari chuckled, the sound dark and slightly crazed. "That'd be too fucking easy, now wouldn't it?"

Nick watched as Ari held his hands over the wound on her arm. Cynna's eyes grew wide, and she struggled beneath Nick's grip, but Nick only held her tighter.

"If you want to change your mind," Ari said, "now's the time to say so."

"Just do it," Nick growled.

Ari shook his head. "It's your damn funeral, man."

He laid his palm over Cynna's bleeding forearm. Her gaze followed, her eyes growing so wide the whites could be seen all around her dark irises. The skin beneath Ari's palm began to glow, dimly at first, then growing in intensity until it was a beaming white light, making his skin look translucent and the edges of his hand shine red.

Cynna's eyes slammed shut. Her back bowed off the ground, and an ear-piercing scream ripped from her mouth. Nick held her tighter. Long seconds passed while Ari knit the wound back together, then the glow finally dimmed. When he lifted his hand, the wound was closed, but the skin all around it was red, inflamed, and sizzling.

"Where's the other one?" Ari asked.

"On her side." Nick nodded toward the bloodstained shirt.

Ari peeled the fabric away, then laid his hand over the wound beneath her ribs and repeated the process. Seconds later, it was over. Cynna lay limp on the ground, gasping and moaning.

Ari leaned back on his heels. "You'll need to cover those. The burns will heal quickly, but they can still get infected."

Nick nodded, a wave of relief sliding through him. Relief that was as foreign as the protective urge he'd felt before. "Thanks."

Abruptly, Ari pushed to his feet and drew in a deep breath, as if sniffing the humid air. A low growl built in his throat.

Nick's head came up. He shot a look at Ari, then glanced around the dark airstrip. "What do you sense?"

Ari's head darted from side to side, and that crazed, wild look filled his mismatched eyes all over again. "Sirens."

He shot into the trees and was gone.

Blinking rapidly, Cynna looked toward Nick, still pale and glassy-eyed, but at least now no longer bleeding. "Wh-what was that?"

Nick pulled the extra bandages from his pocket, which he'd snagged from that house. "Serious psychosis, that's what that is."

He wrapped the first bandage around the blisters forming on her inner arm, then moved to her side, careful not to press on the wound. Even though it was closed, the burns had to hurt like a bitch.

"Who is he?" Her voice was weak, tired, and run-down. But at least now rest would fix that. Relief slid through him. Which, again, was a wacked reaction for him to have.

"An ex-Argonaut."

"Ex? I don't recognize the name."

"Remember I told you he faked his death? He did it after his son came of age and joined the order. His given name is Aristokles."

Cynna's brow lowered. "That sounds oddly familiar. Which Argonaut is his son?"

Being Argolean, even if she hadn't lived in Tiyrns, it made sense she'd know who the guardians were. Everyone in the damn land did. "Cerek."

"Why did he leave the order?"

Nick shrugged. "Couldn't take it anymore, I guess. You saw him. He's a little different."

She was silent for a moment while he pulled her shirt down and covered her with the blanket again. "What's with the Siren thing? Are they really out there? Why would he go looking for Zeus's warriors alone?"

Nick settled back and rested his hands on his knees, feeling a hell of a lot better than he had only minutes before. "Because he hunts them."

"Hunts Sirens?"

He nodded.

"Why?"

He shrugged again and looked toward the trees. There was no telling how long Ari would be gone. The guy was like a cat, here one minute, gone the next. And while before her questions might have irritated him, at least now they kept him from thinking about what he was going to do with her once he got her back to the colony.

"Remember I told you a soul mate is a curse, not a blessing?" She nodded. "Ari's the perfect example of that. Several years back, while he was out on a mission for the Argonauts, he came across an injured nymph. The way he tells it, she'd been hurt escaping from Zeus's clutches. He took her to Argolea, where Zeus and the other Olympians can't cross, and basically fell for her. Claimed she was his soul mate and that they were meant to be together. Some would say she was his prisoner, others, his lover. I'm not sure. I wasn't there and don't know. But according to Ari, they were madly in love. Only Zeus wanted her back. He was pissed that an Argonaut had stolen his prize. So he sent his Sirens to kidnap the nymph and bring her back. When Ari realized she was gone, he went a little ballistic and abandoned his duties to find her. Caused all kinds of trouble for the guardians. Eventually he caught up with the Sirens, and a fight resulted. The nymph was killed."

"Oh geez."

"After that, he lost it. Went on this killing spree. Any Siren he could find. It was bloody. The guardians tried to rein him in but couldn't. When an Argonaut loses his soul mate it can get nasty. Anyway, to keep peace with Olympus, they banished him to the human realm. His son, Cerek, however, didn't want to accept that ruling. He found him. Thought he could rehabilitate him and bring him back. Ari didn't want to go back, though. All he wanted to do was go on killing Sirens, chipping away at Zeus wherever he could. But he also knew Cerek would never give up on him. So he faked his death to get his kid to back off."

"In a fire," Cynna mumbled.

Nick glanced her way. "How do you know that?"

"The scars on his face and neck."

"Yeah." Nick looked back at the flames in front of him. "In a fire. One I set."

"You?"

Nick shrugged. "He asked for my help. I gave it. I held no love for the Argonauts back then."

"And now?"

His mind drifted to his soul mate and his brother, Demetrius. And though that pull toward Isadora was still there, it wasn't nearly as strong as it had once been. Something he found both odd and relieving. He shrugged again. "Now I still hold no love for them."

Cynna was silent for several moments. Softly, she said, "I didn't know about the tracker. If Zagreus put it in my arm, it means he doesn't trust me."

Nick knew she was right, but he was fighting conflicting feelings where she was concerned. And those feelings, combined with his strange increased powers and the changes in the soul mate draw made him mistrust his gut reaction. More than ever, he wasn't about to get caught being stupid. Not by Cynna. Not by anyone. "I haven't decided if I trust you yet either."

"You have every right not to trust me," she said in a tired voice. "But I promise you, I'm not working with Zagreus."

Promises were easy to make. It was keeping those promises that was the hard part. As much as Nick wanted to believe her, knowing she'd voluntarily been with Zagreus meant there was a whole other side of her he'd yet to uncover. A side he wasn't quite sure he was ready for.

He looked out at the dark jungle. "You should sleep. Ari could be gone a while. I'll wake you when it's time to leave."

She stared up at him, and he sensed she wanted to say something more, but didn't. After several long seconds, she sighed, tipped her head on the blanket beneath her cheek, and closed her eyes. "Thank you for saving my life."

A lump formed in his throat, one he didn't like. He looked back at her, eyes closed, that odd blonde hair falling across her cheek. "Don't thank me. I'm only keeping you alive as leverage."

"Doesn't matter," she said softly. "You still saved me. No one else even tried. I won't forget that."

Neither would Nick. And he had a strange feeling that fact was going to change things for him in ways he wasn't sure he was ready for.

A popping sound erupted in the trees behind him. Far off but growing closer. Nick jerked around and looked that direction.

Cynna's eyes flew open, and she pushed up on her hand. "What was that?"

"Gunfire." Nick rose to his feet and squinted to see toward the trees, his senses growing sharp, tuning in to the surroundings. Seven, no…ten men. In two vehicles. Heading their direction.

An engine revved. More gunshots exploded. Cynna pushed to stand at his side, wobbled, then gripped his arm to hold herself upright. "Gunfire?"

"Shit." Nick's pulse shot up. And not from the warmth of her palm resting against his bare skin. No, this was from the fact something bad was about to go down.

The brush rustled to his left. He reached for the blade he'd swiped from Zagreus's lair and left by the fire. Swords and axes and other handheld weapons were effective against the Prince of Darkness's minions, but gunfire meant humans. And humans shooting shit meant trouble of a whole different variety.

The rustling grew louder. Nick pushed Cynna behind him. "Run for the plane."

"But—"

Ari lurched through the brush before Cynna could finish her protest, his arms waving wildly, his eyes as wide as saucers. "Go! Run! Get the fucking engine started!"

Nick's muscles bunched, and he ushered Cynna toward the plane. She stumbled and almost fell. Swooping her into his arms, Nick picked up his speed and sprinted. Ari raced up at his side.

Nick reached the plane, set Cynna down, and jerked the door open. "What the hell did you do?"

Ari skidded to a stop, kicking up dirt and rocks. "I was wrong. Not Sirens. Not even close. Couple of whores servicing a group of drug runners."

"*Skata.*" Nick helped Cynna into the back of the plane. "Tell me you didn't."

"I only sampled one."

"Son of a fucking bitch." Nick knew exactly what Ari's "sampling" entailed. The fucker liked to play with his prey. "You didn't stop when you realized she wasn't a Siren?"

"She was hot, even if she was a whore. I have needs, asshole."

Nick climbed into the plane after Cynna and yanked the door closed. Ari slid into the pilot's seat and reached for his headset.

"I must have stumbled across their grow. No way they cared about those chicks." Rapidly, Ari pushed buttons on the instrument panel. Lights flicked on, then the engine roared, and the propeller coughed to life, spinning slowly at first and picking up speed.

Nick took the copilot's seat and reached for his seat belt while Ari maneuvered the plane toward the end of the grass runway. The tires bounced along the uneven ground, jostling them in their seats. "They're going to be through those trees any minute."

"I know, I know," Ari repeated, hands gripping the wheel.

"You've got a fucking problem, psycho."

"I'm saving your ass, aren't I?"

"Barely," Nick tossed back. Son of a bitch, he should have called the damn Argonauts instead of this nut job.

"Ah, Nick?" Cynna said from the backseat, fear filling her voice.

Nick whipped around and glanced over his shoulder, out the window. The sun was just starting to come up, casting an eerie white light through the jungle. But he easily saw what she was looking at. Two trucks emerged from the trees and barreled toward them, the beds filled with men carrying automatic weapons.

Nick's jaw ticked. "You better fly, Ari."

"Flying high's what I do best." Ari turned the plane toward the runway and punched the engine. "Hold on, fuckers. This is going to be one hell of a takeoff."

CHAPTER TWELVE

Cynna's whole body was stiff and sore. Rolling to her back, she lifted her arms over her head, stretched, and blinked several times. Slowly, her vision cleared, and she focused on a gigantic iron chandelier hanging from old-world beams and a high-pitched ceiling.

Confused, she sat up and looked around. She lay on a mattress. Fuzzy blankets covered her legs, and a fire crackled in the biggest stone fireplace she'd ever seen. But a shiver rushed down her spine, and, looking to her right, she realized it was because the glass in the tall arching windows was shattered and broken, letting in a cool breeze that sent a chill through the gigantic room.

Tossing the covers back, she pushed to her knees, then climbed to her bare feet. She'd been thankful they'd escaped those drug lords with barely a scratch, and had slept most of the flight. By the time Ari had finally landed the plane, she'd been groggy and out of it. She remembered being in a car. Then walking through something dark, but that was about it. Moving toward the broken windows, she crossed her arms over her chest to ease the chill and looked out at the view, then drew in a surprised breath.

Cliffs opened to a wide lake, which spread out before her like a crystal-blue blanket. Purple-green mountains rose all around the lake, melding with a steadily darkening sky. The first twinkle of starlight flashed high above, telling her it was early evening and that she'd slept longer than she'd thought.

Her gaze drifted down to her arm, covered in a white bandage. She tugged the edge free and studied the cut underneath. A thin red line marred her skin. Reaching for the edge of her bloodstained shirt, she pulled the cotton up and found the same on her side where she'd been pierced by that satyr's blade.

Ari had succeeded in healing her. Fuzzy memories of that whole ordeal whipped through her head. Turning away from the view, she wondered where the strange Argonaut had gone. There was no sign of him in this room. She looked around, searching for Nick, only there was no sign of him either.

Unease filtered through her chest, but it calmed when she caught sight of Nick's weapons in the corner of the room. He wouldn't have left without them. And the fact he wasn't carrying them now meant wherever they were—and she was confident they were no longer in the Yucatan—there was no immediate threat.

She breathed easier as she moved past the mattress, intent on finding him. Little furniture sat in the giant room besides the makeshift bed. A pile of wood lay scattered in the corner. A couple of couches were overturned, the cushions sliced, stuffing littering the ground. And one whole wall was blackened, as if a fire had roared through this part of the building.

This wasn't a house or even a compound. It was some kind of ruins. An archway opened to a wide hall with scuffed walls and crumbling stucco. Ahead, a giant curved staircase—or what was left of one—disappeared to upper levels. Boards were missing. What had once been intricately carved wood was now blackened and covered in soot. Another set of dilapidated stairs dropped to floors below, but she couldn't see where they led.

She stilled. Listened. Couldn't hear anything but the cry of a bird somewhere through the broken windows. Whatever this place had once been, it was clearly now abandoned.

Her stomach churned with both apprehension and dread. Gritting her teeth, she told herself standing around wasn't going to answer any of her questions. She moved for the staircase. It was battered but stable, and she grasped the railing on the right as she climbed to the next level. Another hallway opened before her, this one not quite as wide. A frayed carpet ran along the floor, and broken doors sporting holes and splintered wood hung open on hinges that looked as if they could give with a tiny gust of wind.

She glanced in rooms as she passed. The remnants of a library—books charred and torn and scattered across the floor like kindling. A dining hall—tables shattered and overturned; windows broken with tattered curtains blowing in the breeze. An office—

computer screens cracked and smashed, lying on the floor; desks splintered and busted as if someone with a sledgehammer had gone ballistic.

That unease came rushing back. She turned the corner and stopped, peering into what she knew on first look had once been a nursery. Toys were broken and ripped and scattered across the floor. Cribs lay in shambles. A rocking chair sat in pieces near a shattered window.

These weren't just ruins. This was a demolition.

Her head grew light. Her stomach a tight knot. She turned out of the ruined nursery and swiped a hand over her suddenly damp brow as she passed room after ransacked room, looking for one that wasn't in pieces. At the far end of the hall, she found a closed door that was still hanging on two hinges, wrapped her hand around the knob, and pushed.

Paper lay scattered across the floor, and a few mirrors on the walls were cracked and broken, but this room hadn't sustained the kind of damage the others had. She walked through a sitting area, then stepped into what she knew instinctively was a salon.

Swivel chairs were lined up on each side of the room. Mirrors—whole, undamaged, normal mirrors—sat in front of each one. Scissors, hairbrushes, razors, and clippers were all tucked into canisters on the workstations.

She caught her reflection in one of the closest mirrors. Her skin was still pale, her eyes a little wild after everything she'd seen, and her clothes were a mess, stained with blood and dirt. She fingered the ends of her bleach-blonde hair and stared at the image Zagreus had created.

Not her. Not who she was inside. Not who she ever wanted to be again. Suddenly, she felt the need to purge herself of everything related to the last year.

She rummaged through cupboards until she found what she needed. Tugging on clear plastic gloves, she mixed the solution she figured was closest to her natural color in a plastic bowl, then rubbed the cream into her artificial blonde locks. After wrapping her hair in a plastic bag, she secured the end, then went in search of something clean to wear.

The next level up had clearly once been sleeping quarters. These were left in shambles too, but she didn't focus on the destruction. In one room she found clean jeans that looked as if they'd fit. In another, a loose-fitting white sweater with a ballet collar. In still another, she dug through a ramshackle closet until she pulled out a pair of boots her size.

She went back down to the salon. In the back of the room, she found a full bathroom decked out with a wall-length mirror, granite counters, and a glass-enclosed shower with a rock floor. She flipped on the shower. The water sputtered as if air had been in the line, then finally flowed freely, growing warmer with every passing second. Tugging off her disgusting clothes, she stepped beneath the spray, rinsed her hair, and sighed.

Just being clean made her feel a thousand times better. She stayed in the shower as long as she could, then climbed out and dried off. After dressing in the fresh clothes, she moved back into the salon, wrapped a towel around her shoulders, found a pair of scissors, and started cutting.

She'd always hated that white-blonde Zagreus was so fond of. The blue streak had been her one attempt at defiance, but he'd liked that too, the bastard. She snipped and cut, using her fingers as a guide. When she was happy with the length, she tugged the towel off, ran her hands through the brown shoulder-length locks, then stared at her reflection.

It was like looking at the old her. Before anger and hate had driven her to become someone else. Her gaze strayed to the white sweater that showed off the length of her neck and the line of her collarbone, still bruised from Zagreus's hands. Disgust swirled in her belly, but she forced it down along with the memories, focusing instead on the fitted jeans that were so new, she guessed they'd been worn only once or twice.

Who had they belonged to? What had happened to her? And why did Cynna suddenly feel like she was stealing from a ghost?

The relief she'd felt at being clean dissipated. And the need to find Nick grew even stronger.

She turned out of the salon and continued up several flights until she reached what she guessed was the top level. Double doors hung haphazardly off their hinges, and a strong breeze blew the hair back from her face. Shivering, she walked through the broken doors, stopped at the stone railing, and looked down.

She was on some kind of balcony. Her gaze skipped over the lake beyond, then dropped to a stone courtyard far below. Large black patches marred the stones. Gray ash swirled along the ground. And in the middle of what was clearly the remains of some kind of fire, facing away from her, stood Nick.

His hands were perched on his lean hips. His head was bowed so she couldn't see his face. But the muscles in his back were tight and bunched beneath the thin black T-shirt he'd changed into, as if he carried the weight of the world there. And unease pressed down on her chest as she watched him look around the courtyard, lift one large hand and rake it through his shaggy blond hair. He dropped his arm to his side, hunched his shoulders, and knelt to the ground, lowering his head as if in defeat.

Cynna glanced across the empty balcony, then over the lake again, taking in every bit of destruction as if seeing it in a new light.

The half-breed colony. Her stomach pitched with the realization of where they were. She'd heard rumors of its existence when she'd been a child in Argolea. Her parents had even considered relocating to the colony instead of the Aegis Mountains with the witches. And she knew from her time with Zagreus that Hades, especially, had been searching for the colony for years because he suspected Maelea—the female he termed "the stain"— might be hiding out there.

This was Nick's colony. His home. His people. And she knew without even asking that it hadn't looked like this the last time he'd been here.

Emotions and her own gnarled memories of a scene much like this rolled through her chest, making her heart beat faster, making panic spread through her limbs. She turned quickly from the railing, found the stairs, and hurried to get down to the courtyard before he left. She was panting by the time she found a broken set of heavy wooden doors lying askew against a stone archway. Spotting Nick still kneeling in the middle of the blackened courtyard, she drew a breath of relief and stilled her feet to gather herself.

When she felt steady, she slowly made her way toward him. But her nerves kicked up again with every step. This hadn't been just a fire. She could sense the remnants of souls still scattered in the wind. This was all that remained of a mass cremation.

She stopped feet from him. He had to have heard her but didn't turn. Glancing around the blackened stones, she tried to think of something to say.

"Nick…" Condolences lingered on the tip of her tongue, but she couldn't get them out. Not because she wasn't sorry for what he'd lost, but because she knew no words could ease his suffering. Because they'd never eased hers.

"Three of my men took down a daemon there." He nodded toward the corner of the courtyard where a charred section of rock stood out against the gray stones. "Five satyrs cornered them before they could get away." He glanced to the right, where another blackened patch stained the ground, his shoulders tight, his eyes shadowed, a raspy tone to his voice. "Two daemons ripped apart a female trying to escape there. She had a child with her. I don't know what happened to the boy."

Oh gods… A fresh wave of trepidation washed over Cynna. "You…see them?"

"No, I *feel* them."

She glanced around the empty courtyard again, and an eerie shiver rippled down her spine as visions swam in front of her eyes. People running in every direction. Satyrs and daemons bearing down with blades and maces and vile-looking weapons intended only to kill. Bone-chilling screams floating on the breeze. The clank of sword cracking against sword ricocheting off the stones as Nick's men fought to battle them back. The crimson splatter of blood along the ground. And everywhere, fire and smoke. The night alive with angry red flames licking the sky under the dark shadows of Hades and Zagreus, watching from the hillside across the lake.

The vision cleared, and Cynna gasped and stumbled back. Sweat beaded her brow as she looked toward Nick with wide eyes. Over the months, she'd known he was growing stronger—Zagreus had sensed Nick's powers were growing too, which was why he'd been so anxious to break him sooner rather than later—but until this moment, she hadn't realized just how strong those powers had become. Whether or not he'd intended to show her that, he had. Every gruesome, horrific moment.

"They were my people. And I left them when I should have stayed and fought. I chose one life over…hundreds." His voice dropped. "I left them to die."

The anguish she heard, the misery… It cut to the heart of her. Because she knew what it was like to make that choice. To choose to live instead of fighting for those you loved. Knew because the same guilt still churned in the pit of her soul, every damn day.

Hand shaking, she took a step closer and gently touched his shoulder. "You didn't know."

He pushed to his feet and whirled on her. Surprised, she jerked her hand back. And saw then that his eyes weren't just pained. They were enraged. And blazing with a vicious darkness she'd never seen before, not even when Zagreus had taunted and beaten and tortured him in his dungeon of horrors.

"I did know. I knew I was leaving them to this nightmare. And I did it anyway."

She swallowed hard. Knew he was in a bad place. Knew the smartest thing for her right now was to walk away. He didn't trust her. He still had no reason to trust her. But something deep inside wouldn't let her leave. She'd had no one after her village had been destroyed. No one to lean on. No one to turn to for comfort. No one to help her pick up the broken pieces of a life in ruins. And that solitude had bred a hatred that had eventually pushed her toward Zagreus. She didn't want Nick to take that same dark path. Didn't want to look back on her life and regret one more thing she might have had the power to change. Didn't want to know that a warrior like him had finally reached his breaking point.

She lifted her hand to his cheek.

He closed his big hand around her wrist in a tight grip before she could touch him, his inflamed amber eyes growing wide with disbelief. "What the hell do you think you're doing?"

He was closer to the edge than she'd thought, but she wasn't backing down. "Helping you. The way I did before. Only…more."

His gaze raked her features, so intense, so calculating, she felt as if he were seeing past every barrier, deep into her soul. But she didn't recoil as she once had with Zagreus. Didn't try to hide what he was seeing. Because she needed him to know he wasn't alone.

"You never helped me," he sneered. "You're as responsible for all this as your *master*. Had it not been for you, I might have been able to break free of that hell and come back to stop this." He lifted his chin, indicating the destruction. "I might have been able to save them."

He was blaming her because she was an easy target. She recognized that, but his words still stung because a place inside knew he was right.

Her heart beat fast against her ribs. "If I'd known—"

"Don't even say it." He flung her arm away in disgust, and his eyes grew dark. As dark as her heart. "Get as far from me as possible, because right now I want you as dead as the Prince of Fucking Darkness you chose to serve."

He turned for the crumbling archway that led back into the castle. "Run hard, female. Run fast. This is the only chance I'm going to give you."

Energy tingled in the tips of Nick's fingers, fed by a darkness he only just held back. Skipping steps, he quickly dropped to the lowest level of the colony and headed for the tunnels that fanned out beneath the massive structure.

The twisting maze was a point of entry, designed to disorient and confuse any enemies who managed to get close, but Nick knew every turn, every corner, and today he needed the solace the tunnels had always given him. Needed the break from responsibility. Needed the freedom.

Only there was no freedom to be found here. Not when visions of what his people had endured played behind his eyelids like a movie set on repeat, every agonizing scream for help booming like cannon fire in his ears.

He bypassed bent, broken lockers with doors hanging askew in the anteroom, didn't even stop to see if any weaponry had been left behind, and stepped over the mangled steel door that had once formed a barrier between the castle and the cavern beneath. Moving on memory, he walked deeper into the tunnels and didn't stop until he reached the wide room where a myriad of corridors opened in all different directions.

The cries grew louder. The visions spun faster. He pressed his hands against his ears, hoping to drown out the sounds, slammed his eyes shut, and ground his teeth against the darkness.

He was breaking. He could feel Krónos's energy inside feeding off his anger and hatred and pain. Churning in his chest. Rushing through his limbs with an all-encompassing power. A power just waiting to command and destroy and annihilate.

He fought the pull. Pressed harder against his ears. Opened his mouth. And roared.

His body trembled. The sound of his scream echoed in the caverns.

"Nick." Cynna's soft, warm fingers brushed his shoulder.

He dropped his hands and whipped around. This deep in the tunnels, there was no light, but his senses were so heightened right now from Krónos's energy churning inside that he didn't need any illumination to see her standing a foot from him, her silky hair falling to her shoulders, her wide chocolate eyes alight with sadness and…pity.

The pity pushed him right to the edge. Who was she to pity him? Who the fuck was she to care?

"Don't let them win." She moved closer. "Fight it. The way you fought it these last few months."

Those months spun in his memory. Reverberated in his ears. Rushed through his veins. The crack of a whip snapping in the darkness. The sting of the leather slicing into his flesh. The cold metal of the shackles tightening against his wrists. The chains jerking his arms high over his head. The hot, wicked sensation of those nymphs' fingers gliding along his overheated skin. And a release he hadn't known he'd craved hovering out of his grasp, impossible to reach. All thanks to her.

Blood pounded in his veins. Anger and rage and desperation coalesced. That energy snapped and sizzled in his hands until he couldn't hold it back anymore. "Stupid move, female." He closed his hand around her wrist and yanked. "I warned you."

She gasped and fell into him. But before she could pull away, he turned and dragged her behind him.

"Nick…"

He headed for the tunnel on the left, wrapped his fingers around the first set of steel bars he came to, and threw the door open.

He flung her into the dark holding cell and stepped in after her.

She hit the stone wall, turned quickly, and looked back, her wide eyes searching the darkness, trying to find him. "Wh—what is this place?"

"Our version of a drunk tank. Never used until now. Fucking poetic, if you ask me."

She sucked in a breath as he drew close, but didn't struggle when he grasped her arm, yanked it upward, and snapped a metal cuff high on the wall over her wrist. Didn't once turn away while he reached for her left arm, jerked that one up as well, and snapped the second cuff over her other wrist.

That shadow energy hummed and rolled inside as he stepped back. Thanks to his enhanced senses, he could see her. See her well, even in utter darkness. His gaze slid over her newly dark hair, the white, almost angelic sweater falling open at her chest, the tips of her breasts pressing against the soft cotton, and her slim hips and long legs encased in the formfitting jeans. Arousal stirred in his belly, mixed with the darkness, then slinked downward until he was hard as stone.

"Nick. Listen to me." Her hands curled into fists. "I—"

"What did you say to me in that cell when you brought those nymphs to me?" Power rippled in his veins as he braced his hands on the stones beside her head and moved in so close his body was a breath from hers.

"I—"

He brushed the tip of his nose against her ear and lowered his voice to a menacing whisper. "I think it was something along the lines of…this isn't a game."

She swallowed hard.

He drew in a deep whiff of jasmine that supercharged his blood. And when she shivered at the slight brush of his nose against her neck, that arousal grew inside until it was a roar in his ears, blocking out everything else but her.

"But it is," he whispered, letting the edge of his lips skim her lobe. "The gods fuck with our lives because to them we're nothing more than a game. And I'm finally ready to play along. I wonder, how long will you be able to hold out? When will you break? How long do I get to torment you before you give in and beg me to finish you for good?"

She swallowed again, then shifted her weight, standing more upright against the rocks at her back. "You can do whatever you want to me. We both know I deserve it."

She did. She was right. But the fact she'd admitted it drew him back, just enough so he could see her eyes. So he could see the lies brewing in the depths of her soul.

They weren't there, though. What lingered in her unfocused gaze as it darted around the darkness was excitement. And determination. And just a hint of fear.

The excitement and fear aroused him even more. She wanted this. She liked being manhandled. But her defiance confused him. And his inability to read her set off an odd tingle in the center of his chest.

He pushed away from the wall. Gave his head a swift shake and reminded himself she'd *chosen* to be with Zagreus. She'd directed torture. She'd kept him from his people. She was at the root of every bit of pain and misery swirling inside him.

He reached for the hem of her sweater, jerked it up her arms, and yanked it over her head, letting it bunch between her shoulder blades. She held her breath but didn't move. And as his gaze ran over her once more, his body pulsed with a wicked thrill while he took in every delectable inch of her caramel skin contrasting against her stark white bra and the waistband of her fitted jeans.

"You do deserve this." Shifting his legs to the outside of both of hers, he placed his fingers on the soft skin of her belly. Her muscles jerked, and her stomach caved in. He wrapped his hands around her rib cage, lowered his nose back to her neck, and drew in a deep breath. "I just wonder how much you can take."

He bent his head, blew hot against her sensitive flesh as he trailed his nose along the length of her neck, over her collarbone, then down into the valley between her breasts. A tiny tremor ran through her. Opening his mouth, he bit into her bra and ripped the fabric with his teeth.

She gasped, but he was too caught up in the succulent globes of her breasts falling free of their confines to care. Brushing his nose over the inside of her left breast, he worked his way toward the straining tip. When she swallowed hard, he drew his nose over her areola, extended his tongue, and dragged it across the hard nub of her nipple.

A moan rumbled from her throat. Glancing up, he did it again and watched as her eyelids drifted closed, her hands fisted in the cuffs, and her head fell back.

"You like that." He laved his tongue all around the tip, cupped her other breast, and skimmed his thumb over the other nipple.

She groaned again, and her hips pushed forward, seeking his, but he angled his body away so she couldn't reach him. "Tell me you like it, Cynna."

"I...I like it."

"I bet you do." He breathed hot over her, then captured the other nipple between his thumb and forefinger and pinched. Hard.

She jerked in the restraints and cried out.

"How about now? Still like it?"

She shifted her feet back until they hit the wall, as if trying to get away. The movement only gave him resistance, and he scooted in closer, until the length of his body brushed hers and his cock pressed into her belly.

He released the pressure. Pinched again. "Tell me. Still like it?"

"Yes. I still like it. Don't...don't stop."

Either she was lying or she was as twisted as he was. The second revolved in his mind as he scraped his teeth over her nipple then shifted to her other breast, drawing the tip into his mouth to taunt and torment while he rolled and played with the first.

She groaned. Rested her head back against the rocks. Lifted her hips, trying to rub against him.

"Eager, aren't you?" He rolled her left nipple in his fingers, damp from his mouth. "Tell me how badly you want to come."

She bit her lip, rocked into him. Her body trembled and jolted with every touch of his skin against hers, every pinch of his fingers, every scrape of his teeth. Not from pain anymore, he was sure, but from pleasure. Wicked, white-hot, forbidden pleasure.

She was every man's sex fantasy. Gods knew, she'd been his for months. But it was way past time she suffered the way he had.

Releasing her breasts, he skimmed his hands down her slim rib cage, over the indent of her belly button, then flicked the clasp on her jeans. "I bet you're wet."

Her breaths grew heavy as he placed his palm against her belly and slid his fingers beneath her waistband. Moving slowly, he inched his way into the silky soft hair at the apex of her legs.

"Wet and aching. Are you wet, Cynna?"

She pressed her ass back against the rocks, giving him more room in her jeans. Bit down on her lip to keep from groaning. He watched her carefully as he slid his fingers lower, between the soft lips of her pussy, and into a river of arousal.

"Holy fuck." He braced his free hand against the rocks near her head and lowered his mouth to her neck, breathing heavily as he stroked her sex, then found the hard, tight knot of her clit. "You aren't just wet, you're fucking *drenched*."

She groaned, unable to resist lifting to meet each stroke. Zeroing in on her face, he watched while he flicked her clit again and again, while he trailed his fingers lower and teased the entrance to her pussy. While her eyes rolled back in her head and the first stirrings of her orgasm began to take hold.

"You're gonna come, aren't you?" He pushed one thick finger into her slick channel, drew out, and pressed back in with two, pumping slowly, dragging her closer to that ledge. "Tell me how bad you want to come."

Her eyes squeezed shut. She bit her lip. Shook her head. Moaned when he hit an extra sensitive spot.

"Tell me, Cynna." He twisted his fingers inside her and rubbed his thumb over her clit. "Beg me to let you come."

He stroked faster. Pressed deeper. "Do it. Beg for me."

"Oh gods." Her head fell back. Sweat slicked her skin. Her breasts pushed forward, and she rocked her hips against every thrust. "Yes, I want to come. It's right there. *Skata*, don't stop."

She opened her mouth to cry out. But before the wave crashed into her, he pulled his hand free and stepped back.

Cynna fell forward in the restraints. Groaned at having been denied what she so desperately wanted. Whimpered.

He moved in close again and braced both hands against the rocks on both sides of her head. "Had enough yet?"

Her chest rose and fell with her uneven breaths. But slowly, she lifted her head and rasped, "Never."

She was tough. But then he already knew that. She had to be to partner with Zagreus, the sick fuck.

He lowered his mouth to hers. Blew hot over her lips. Against his chest, her pulse picked up speed. She moaned and lifted to meet his kiss. But instead of taking her lips, he angled toward her ear, drew the soft flesh between his teeth, and bit down.

Her whole body contracted, and she cried out. He licked and sucked his way down her neck, knowing he was leaving marks. Scraping his teeth over her left nipple, he pinched the right one with his fingers, then dropped to his knees in front of her.

She choked in a ragged breath, opened her eyes to search for him. He grasped the waistband of her jeans and ripped through the denim like paper. A whimper met his ears while he jerked her boots free and stripped the ruined garment from her legs. Grasping the edge of her panties, he tore them from her skin and tossed them on the ground. Then he spread her legs and devoured her sex.

A scream tore from her throat. He wasn't sure if it was rooted in pleasure or shock, but he didn't care. She tasted like honey, smelled like sin. He laved his tongue over her, drew her clit into his mouth, suckled hard, then scraped his teeth across her sensitive flesh. He hated her. He craved her. Wanted to make her pay. Needed to hear her cry of release. Thrusting his fingers back inside her, he tormented her with his mouth and stroked deeper with his hand.

She was tight around him. So tight the blood pounded in his cock with his own need for release. Fighting the urge, he licked her again and again until she was panting. Until her body was drenched in sweat. Until his name was a plea on her lips.

"Nick..."

Synapses misfired. He wanted to fuck her. To thrust violently inside her. To leave her as wrecked as she'd left him. Not just physically, but sexually, mentally. Emotionally.

"Oh gods, Nick..."

He felt her orgasm about to break and drew back quickly, letting go so he was no longer touching her. So he wouldn't be tempted to take her.

She groaned again, this time in utter frustration. He pushed to his feet, and as cool air washed over his skin, he realized he was sweating too.

"Beg me to stop," he growled, leaning into her again.

"No." She swallowed hard. Shook her head. Her skin was damp everywhere. Her eyes wild. "I won't ever ask you to stop. No matter what you do."

His frustration grew to epic levels. "I'll keep you chained here." He shifted his mouth to her neck, bit down hard on the slick flesh. She cried out, and he released her. "I'll bring you to the edge again and again." He pressed his hips into hers. "Use you as my own personal sex slave."

She sagged in the shackles. "No, you won't."

"I won't?" He lifted his mouth to her jaw and nipped there too. "You don't sound so confident."

She whimpered but didn't try to move away from his teeth. "I am." Her words were pained, her body straining. "Because I know you're not the monster Zagreus is either. And no matter what you think, you never will be."

Everything stilled inside him. And something hard and dead, buried in all that darkness, struggled to the surface.

He eased back. Stared down at her. Knew she couldn't see him in the darkness. But the way her eyes were locked on his made him wonder if she could see past his face. Past his barriers. Into the depths of his very soul.

Beneath his ribs, his heart picked up speed, and along his spine, the scars carved into his flesh tingled with…doubt.

She closed her eyes and lifted her chin. Then very gently, she pressed her lips against his.

He froze. Couldn't move. And suddenly didn't know what to do next.

She tipped her head, skimmed her lips over his again. Did it until the room was spinning around him and he had no clue which way was up.

"I want you," she whispered against his mouth. "I've wanted you for months. From the first moment I saw you. I won't fight you. Never." She kissed him again. Softly. Gently. Sweetly. "Take whatever you want. As much as you want. Take every part of me."

Heat gathered in his chest, shoving aside all the darkness, replacing it with light and need, propelling him forward before he even realized what he was doing.

He lifted his hand to her jaw, opened his mouth to hers, dipped his tongue inside, and kissed her deeply. The way he'd dreamt of kissing her all those months locked in his cell. The way she was suddenly kissing him back, as if she was as desperate to taste him as he was to taste her.

She groaned, stroked her tongue against his, and leaned her body into his, her belly cradling his cock, her heat and the tips of her breasts brushing his chest and making him even harder than before.

Ah gods… His kiss turned greedy. She tasted like salvation. Like hope. Like light. And he'd had so little of each in his life, he was crazy for more. Delirious for it. Desperate. He brought his other hand up, cradling her face as he tipped her head to the side so he could taste her deeper, so he could kiss her harder, so he could get inside her.

Inside her…

He jerked his mouth back from hers. She gasped at the sudden withdrawal. Swiftly, he flicked the cuff free from her right hand, then the left, and ripped the sweater from the backs of her arms. She stumbled as soon as she was free, and her hands landed on his shoulders, but he caught her before she fell.

His eyes found hers. He waited for her to push him away. To struggle now that she was free. But she didn't. Her fingers sank into his muscles, her eyes darkened, and arousal flushed her cheeks. Then she lifted her mouth back to his and kissed him all over again. This time with a renewed sense of urgency that made his cock absolutely *throb*.

More, more, more… They were the only words he heard. The only ones that made any sense. His hands streaked down her sides, then back over her ass. He grabbed hold of each cheek and lifted, pushing his way between her legs as he pressed her back up against the wall and devoured her mouth.

He rocked against her slick heat as she kissed him. Groaned because she tasted so damn good. Burned with the heat of a thousand suns everywhere she touched. Flicking her tongue against his, she drew her hands between them, then struggled with the snap on his jeans.

She tore her mouth from his. "Too much fabric. Take these off and fuck me."

Her words were like a drug, fogging his head, driving him faster toward an insanity he couldn't stop. Harder than he was sure he'd ever been, he pressed her into the wall to hold her up, kissed her deeper, and freed himself from his jeans. Her hand closed over him as soon as he was free, dragging his cock toward all her liquid heat.

He let her take the lead and slammed his hand against the wall. She dragged the head of his cock over her clit, circled the tight knot, and shivered.

"Yes, yes," she groaned, doing it again.

Fuck. He couldn't take it anymore. He trailed his lips down her throat, closed his teeth over the soft column, and bit down. She gasped. Her body trembled. The second his cock slid across the opening of her pussy, he thrust.

She cried out as he sank deep. Groaned when he drew back, dragging his cock along her walls, then shoved in deep once more. Her fingers bit into his shoulders, slid up to his face. Tipping his head up, she closed her mouth over his in a kiss that rocked the ground right out from beneath him.

More. Faster. Deeper.

He plunged hard, fucking into her over and over, needing more. Needing everything. She wrapped her bare legs around his lower spine. Her sex squeezed tight, creating the most perfect friction. He hitched her higher in his arms so he could get as deep as possible. So he could hit that spot so far inside he knew would make her *explode.*

"Nick…" Her fingers grazed his cheekbones, and she angled his face the other way. Kissed him so sweetly. So intimately, that place inside that had burst to life seemed to grow and warm and bloom. "Come. Come, right now. For me."

She'd said that to him before. In his cell, when she'd pleasured him with her hand. And just like then, he was powerless to do anything but what she commanded.

His orgasm raced down his spine, burst in his balls, and ricocheted through every cell in his body.

Her muscles spasmed, and she clamped down around him. And then she pulled her mouth from his and completely shattered. He thrust harder, even though he was spent, wanting to draw out her orgasm. Wanting to feel it ripple through his body. Wanting to know every ounce of her pleasure.

When it faded, she fell into him. Her head landed against his neck. Her fingers slid through his damp hair. Her heat surrounded him, infused him, melded with his until he wasn't sure where he ended and she began.

Long minutes passed with only the sound of his pulse pounding in his ears and their mingled, heavy breaths echoing in the darkness. Every muscle in his body felt weak, wrung out, drained. And as the last edges of his release finally faded, he found he was glad the wall was holding them up. Because if it wasn't, he was pretty sure he'd be in a heap on the ground right now, flat on his ass.

Her fingers skimmed through his hair again, and a tingle raced over his scalp and trickled down his spine. "Mm. Thank you."

Those two words brought back another memory. Of her leaving his cell after she'd pleasured him, and his saying the very same to her.

Reality slammed into him. She was naked, pinned between him and the stone cold wall, in a cell where he hadn't planned to pleasure her but torture her.

The day spun behind his eyes. Coming to the colony, finding it in ruins, leaving Cynna sleeping while he went to search for survivors, finding nothing but death. The anger and pain and misery. Taking it out on her. Coming here then torturing and using her.

He wasn't the monster Zagreus was? He dropped his head to her shoulder, unable to hold back the groan. He'd just proved he was more like his father's fucking side of the family than anyone ever could be.

"Don't," she whispered.

He lowered her feet to the ground, then let go of her and moved back, needing space. Needing to let her go before he did something worse.

"Fuck." He tugged his pants up and scrubbed a hand over his face.

She reached for him in the darkness, found his face, and captured his jaw. "Don't. I liked it."

He stilled and stared down at her, shocked and even more the hell confused. "I left marks. Like he did."

"Yes, but the difference is I enjoyed it."

He cringed and looked away.

"I never did with him." She turned his face back to hers. "Not once. And you gave me a choice. I felt it when you freed me. He never did that. You're not like him, Nick. Not at all."

He studied her eyes in the silence. Again searched for lies. And found…only truth. Or at least a truth she foolishly wanted to believe.

His eyelids fell closed. He didn't know what he was. All he knew was that he was tired of trying to figure it out. Tired of everything. Tired of hatred and misery and most of all, tired of the never-ending struggle.

Her fingers grazed his cheek. "Let me help you."

He didn't think anyone could. And that scared him more than anything. Because for the first time in forever, he felt like she might have been the one to do just that.

If the fucking Fates had just for once been on his side.

CHAPTER THIRTEEN

"It has to be here." Seated at a table in the great library in the heart of the castle, Callia flipped a book closed and reached for another from the mountain of ancient texts she'd pulled from the stacks. "There has to be some documentation somewhere."

Demetrius felt the female's frustration as strongly as if he were seated next to her. And he was living it too. He was going nuts each day watching Isadora grow weaker and more tired for no apparent reason. Every time he tried to talk to her about it, she brushed him off with excuses about the Misos and the Council and Elysia. She might not want to face reality, but he knew in his heart something was wrong. Something Callia couldn't find medically but which was draining her of her very life force.

He tried not to dwell on the fact she was shutting him out. Tried not to think about what he'd do if he lost her. He wasn't losing her. She was the reason his heart beat. And he was determined to find a solution. Even if it meant hour after hour sitting in this dusty library, reading every damn word that had ever been written.

From the corner of his eye, he watched Zander close the book he was searching, move to stand behind Callia, and gently massage his mate's shoulders.

"We'll find it," he said to her. "Don't worry."

"I can't help but worry." Callia flicked pages faster. "You saw her this morning. I think she lost another five pounds overnight."

"*Thea*," Zander said softly. "Careful."

Callia's auburn head came up, and she slanted a look Demetrius's way, then cringed. "I'm sorry. I didn't mean that the way it sounded. She's—"

"You're right." Demetrius closed the book he'd finished and pushed to his feet. His hands were shaking, his stomach a tight knot, and he felt that pull to close himself off from everything and everyone, but he wasn't giving in to it. Isadora needed him, and he wasn't regressing back into old habits. "She's not sleeping and barely has an appetite anymore. Whatever's affecting her is drawing a physical reaction, even if you can't find it."

Callia sighed and looked back at the book in front of her. "Okay, let's run through what we know."

Demetrius moved closer and leaned against a table while Callia whipped out a notepad and started jotting notes in furious scribbles.

"She was fine a month ago."

Demetrius thought back. "I don't know. Physically, I started noticing her lack of appetite about a month ago, but the restlessness, the sleepless nights… Those have been going on for a couple of months at least."

"She chalked it up to the strains of being a new mother, which it could have been," Callia noted, "but looking back now—"

"It was probably linked to whatever this is," Demetrius finished for her.

"Yeah," Callia said. "That's what I'm thinking too."

"So what changed over the last few months?" Zander asked.

"Well, she had a baby," Callia said.

"People have babies all the time," Zander pointed out. "And they continue to every day."

Callia squeezed his hand at her shoulder, and Demetrius saw the look of worry that passed over her features. Worry for her own unborn child. She nodded. "Yes. True."

"The Misos came to Argolea," Demetrius said. "They were living in the castle until just recently."

"Yes." Callia jotted another note. "It's possible one might have passed a virus to her or that she might have come in contact with some kind of bacteria. But if that were the case, I would have seen it in my scans."

Silence stretched in the library. After several long seconds, Zander said, "Hades's contract on her soul was broken."

"I've been thinking about that." Callia shifted in her seat to look up at her mate. "Hades was pissed that he lost her. Is it possible he could have done something to her soul? Put some kind of, I don't know, spell on it?"

"No." When Callia turned to look at Demetrius, he crossed his arms over his chest, confident this had nothing to do with any kind of spell. "The gods can't dictate life or death. Only the Fates do that. And in the case of a prophecy, like the one that brought Casey to Argolea, it's preordained at birth. We'd know if that were the case now."

Callia bit her lip and looked down at her notepad again. Quietly, she said, "Nick disappeared."

Zander glanced down at his mate. "How would that have any kind of impact on Isadora, *thea*?"

Callia turned to look up at him again. "It's a long shot, but bear with me. We already know that Isadora is both Demetrius's and Nick's soul mate, right? Thanks to the whole twin thing and Hera's curse. What if the soul mate curse is somehow affecting her?"

"It doesn't work that way," Demetrius said. "The female in the equation is immune to the curse. It's only the Argonaut who feels the pull, and even then, it's more of an—"

"Emotional pull," Zander supplied, looking over Callia's head toward Demetrius. When Demetrius nodded, he glanced back down at his mate. "It's a physical pain for the Argonaut, yeah, but the draw is toward another person's soul. Not the body. And I've never heard of it weakening or threatening a guardian's life."

Callia placed her hand on the back of her chair. "I realize that, but Nick isn't a normal Argonaut, now is he? We already know he's Krónos's son. And if Atalanta was his mother, she was a goddess herself. Even if, somehow, Krónos made her mortal when he impregnated her, then that makes Nick a true demigod. And we've never had a true demigod Argonaut in the ranks, have we?"

Demetrius looked over her toward Zander and lifted his brows in question. Zander shook his head.

"No, I guess not," Zander said. "Not recently, at least. The original seven were true demigods, but that was generations ago. I still don't see how that would change anything, though."

"I'm not sure yet, myself," she answered, looking back at her book. "I'm just—"

"I think I found something." Maelea's voice sounded from somewhere in the stacks.

Callia and Zander turned her direction. Demetrius looked past them where Gryphon's mate was walking from between shelves, her jet-black hair falling past her shoulders, a faded leather book open in her hands.

She laid the open book on the table in front of Callia and pointed to a passage. "There. I knew I remembered something similar."

Callia scanned the page, and since he couldn't see the words, Demetrius watched her features. Her eyes furiously read the words, then her face paled. And that knot in his stomach clenched even tighter.

He pushed away from the table, worry and dread skittering along his already frayed nerve endings. "What does it say?"

Callia laid her hand on the worn book and looked up at Maelea. "You remember this happening?"

As Zeus and Persephone's daughter, Maelea was over three thousand years old and had seen or been privy to almost every important moment in ancient Greek history. "I remember hearing about each one, yes."

"Callia," Demetrius demanded, stepping closer. "What does it say?"

Callia sighed and looked back at him. "Aiakos, Minos, and Rhadamanthys were three mortals who were given the choice between death or becoming Judges of the Dead in the Underworld."

"Okay." Demetrius stared at her. "What do three dead mortals have to do with Isadora?"

"All three were of Zeus's line," Maelea said. "And all three were bound in life to a mate. When they became gods of the Underworld, the mate they each left behind slowly withered away until eventually death claimed them."

Demetrius looked from face to face. "I'm still not following. I'm not dead."

"No," Callia said, shaking her head. "You're not following. Death isn't the connection. Power is. As their powers grew, their mates' strengths dwindled until there was nothing left."

Demetrius stared at the female. And her words didn't immediately click. He was perfectly healthy. Nothing about him had changed. And since Isadora was his soul mate, that meant nothing should be impacting her. Because…

Oh *skata*… The blood rushed from his cheeks, and the entire room felt like it tilted right out from under his feet.

Callia turned in her seat to look up at Zander once more. "We *have* to find Nick. Hades said he needed Zagreus to harness the powers Krónos gave Nick. If that's about to happen and Nick's powers are growing, that could explain why Isadora is sick."

Zander was already stepping toward the door. "What will you do if we find him?"

Callia pushed out of her chair. "I don't know. But maybe having him here will give me a chance to figure something out."

Demetrius felt like his brain was thick pea soup. His mate's health was failing because of his brother?

His heart pounded hard in his chest, and his skin grew damp and tingly. From the first moment, her life had been cursed. By him. By Nick. The Fates couldn't be this cruel to them. They couldn't keep threatening to take away the one thing that mattered most in his life.

In a haze, Demetrius pushed away from the table, intent on following Zander, but Titus's big body filling the doorway to the library drew him to a stop.

"There you guys are." Titus's voice was breathy, as if he'd been running. Wisps of his long wavy hair fell over his temple. "We've been looking all over for you. There's movement at the colony."

"What kind of movement?" Maelea asked, stepping out from behind the table.

"Not sure," Titus said. "But someone's fired up the generators, and there are at least two people moving around inside."

Zander glanced toward Demetrius. "Where would Nick go if he somehow escaped from Zagreus's lair?"

"To the colony."

"That's exactly what Theron thought," Titus said. "We're leaving in five."

Zander kissed Callia's cheek. And with a new sense of purpose rushing through him, Demetrius headed out into the corridor. But at his back, heard Zander say, "See? I told you everything would work out."

"It hasn't yet," Callia whispered.

"Have faith, *thea*. It will."

Faith... Demetrius had never been able to summon up much of that, but for his mate, he'd find a way. No matter what he had to do, he'd find a way to save Isadora's life.

He was so silent, Cynna was sure Nick could hear her heart pounding against her ribs in the cell. And since she couldn't see him in the darkness, she had no way to judge what he was thinking.

He doesn't believe you. Now that his temper's eased and his desire's been slaked, he doesn't want to be near you. Why would you possibly think he'd want your help anyway?

Doubts rushed in. Every doubt she'd ever had where he was concerned. But she pushed them away, just like she did every doubt that had ever threatened to drag her down. Reaching for his hand and finding it in the dark, she wrapped her fingers around his and pulled him toward the open cell door. "Come on."

He didn't tug back on her hand. Didn't fight her. Didn't say anything, for that matter. She led him out into the tunnel, walking carefully on the uneven rocks with her bare feet as she headed toward the dim orange light, the corridor growing brighter with every step.

They rounded a corner, and she spotted the open doorway and the splintered door lying on the ground. Just before she reached it, Nick pulled back on her hand, stopping her. "Wait."

His face was cast in shadows as he let go of her hand, grasped the hem of his T-shirt, and tugged it off, then dropped it over her head so the soft cotton fell against her bare skin.

Until that moment, she hadn't even realized she was still naked. She'd been too focused on him. "Oh. Thanks."

"Don't thank me, Cynna. Not after that. Your back is all scratched from the rocks. You have bruises over—"

"I'm fine." She knew she had bruises. But they were the good kind of bruises, not that bad. And she, more than anyone, knew the difference.

He scowled and looked away, and she realized then that this was about more than what had just happened between them. He was good and truly wrecked. She could see it in his flat eyes and the way they wouldn't meet hers, could hear it in his gravelly voice. The hours, the days, the months were catching up with him, and suddenly she knew exactly what he needed.

"Come on." She gripped his hand again and picked her way around the broken door at her feet, then moved into the anteroom that opened to the colony.

He didn't pull back from her again, didn't fight her, didn't do anything but sigh and let her lead him. And as she pulled him up the stairs and the devastation around them grew visible, she felt his pulse pick up against hers. Felt his muscles tense in her hand. And knew he was blaming himself all over again.

She couldn't let him focus on that. Not if he was going to hold it together. They made it to the main level, and he groaned at her back. Tightening her fingers around his, she pulled him toward the charred staircase. "Don't look around. Just stay with me."

They moved up another level. By the time they reached the empty hallway she'd found earlier, his head was down, his free hand was covering his eyes, and he was massaging his temples. Stress and regret and misery radiated off him. So much she knew she had to do something fast to take his mind off it all.

She pushed the door to the salon open, pulled him inside, closed it at his back, and led him to one of the many swivel chairs lining both sides of the room. Letting go of his hand, she turned, pressed her palms against his bare chest, and pushed him down. "Sit."

"Cynna." His voice was tight, his head still tipped down so she couldn't see his face. "You need to leave. Get the hell away from here. Hades and Zagreus know where this place is."

A shiver of panic snaked through her ribs, but she shook it away. Even if Zagreus knew where the colony was located, he didn't know she and Nick were here. And by the time he figured it out, they'd be long gone.

Grabbing a comb and scissors from the table, she moved around behind him and tugged the comb through his hair. "We'll leave later."

His head lifted, and he shot her a *what the fuck are you doing?* look in the mirror.

She ignored it and continued combing. "Trust me. This will make you feel better." She pointed toward her own head, then leaned forward and used the scissors to gently cut the hair at his nape. "Just getting rid of that blonde mess did wonders for me."

His gaze bored into her through the mirror. She knew she'd just confused the hell out of him, but she didn't care. She combed, snipped, ran her fingers through the back of his hair, cutting it short. For a moment, she considered using the clippers and shaving his head like he'd had it styled the first time she'd seen him, but then thought better of it. He had great hair. Thick. Soft. She didn't want to cut it all off. Warmth slid through her belly and slinked between her legs when she remembered wrapping her fingers in all this silky goodness while he'd had her pinned to that wall and was thrusting inside her.

Oh man. That had been so very wrong. But it had felt incredibly right. And at the moment, all she could possibly think about was doing it all over again.

Sexual energy hummed through her body, amping her awareness of him as she worked her way around to his front, shaping the sides of his hair, running her fingers through the top and dropping cut strands on the floor. He didn't move. Didn't speak. But his eyes watched her every movement. And though she couldn't quite be sure because she'd yet to look directly at him, from the corner of her vision he didn't seem as bewildered anymore. Yes, there was still confusion there, but she also saw heat in his amber gaze. And…whoa. *Seriously?*…awe.

She faltered. No one was awed by her. Horrified. Disgusted. Afraid, sure. But awed? Never.

She cleared her throat. Tried to think of something— anything—to say. "What happened to Ari?"

"He left."

She waited for more, but he didn't go on. And one glance at the mirror told her he was still staring at her with those intense eyes, following her every movement.

She swallowed back the sudden nerves, set the comb and scissors on the work counter behind her, then ran her fingers all through his hair, testing the length. Satisfied with the result, she stepped to the side so he could see his reflection. "What do you think?"

He stared at the image in the mirror, and she looked at what he was seeing. A bare-chested, sexy-as-all-get-out man who'd been through hell and survived, sitting on the small swivel seat, making it look tiny in comparison. But after several heartbeats, she discovered he wasn't looking at himself. He was staring at her. And as her eyes met his in the mirror, and she caught the look of awe again in his, her pulse jumped, and heat spread all through her limbs, knocking that sexual energy up a blistering notch.

"I like it." His voice was still gravelly, but this time it was laced with just enough arousal to make her inner thighs ache.

She dragged her gaze from his and cleared her throat. Running her fingers through his hair once more, she worked for nonchalant when she said, "It should feel lighter. No more wisps falling in your eyes. It's—"

"Not mine. Yours. I like the brown. It's real. It brightens your face. It's stunning."

Her fingers froze in his hair. No one had ever called her stunning. Not Zagreus. Not even her parents.

She stood still next to him, his warmth radiating around her until her skin prickled, his gaze watching her carefully in the mirror until her pulse was a roar in her ears. And in a rush, she realized what she was doing for him here wasn't about making up for any wrong she'd committed. It wasn't even about pulling him back from his father's hold like she'd told herself in the tunnels. It was done purely to give him a piece of normalcy in a sea of unending misery. To show him that all wasn't lost. To comfort him in a way no one had before.

She could count only two people in her life she'd ever wanted to comfort like that. Her mother and father. The only two people she'd ever truly cared for.

Her hands trembled, and she quickly released his hair and stepped back. A lump formed in her throat, one that made it hard to swallow. Swiping her hands along the edge of the oversize T-shirt he'd given her, she turned quickly for the back of the salon and forced her tongue to work. "There's a shower through here. You've got hair all over you. Go get cleaned up while I find you a towel."

Leather creaked as he pushed his big body out of the swivel chair. She found a closet and pulled the door open, busily searching for that towel, telling herself the entire time that she was walking a dangerous line.

Falling for Nick? Krónos's son? No. That wasn't possible. That wasn't even *sane*. She'd helped him because it was the right thing to do. Cut his hair because he hadn't had it cut once in the months he'd been trapped in Zagreus's lair. And she'd fucked him because…well, he was hot. She was still a female with needs. And sex was a natural, physical reaction to the adrenaline rush they'd both been through. She hadn't *done that* because she felt anything for him. Because, dammit, she *wasn't* falling for him. No way in hell.

"Cynna."

She drew up sharply at the sound of his voice directly at her back and smacked her head against the shelf above. Pain spiraled across her scalp, and she reached up, rubbing the suddenly sore spot. "*Skata.*"

His large hand closed over hers, and before she realized what he was doing, he turned her around and pulled her into all his warm, muscular perfection.

Heat infused her skin, and the natural scent of him—earthy scents of sandalwood and pine—filled her senses. As did the musky remnants of the sex they'd shared only minutes ago.

His hand opened, splayed against her lower spine, then fisted the soft cotton of his shirt against her back. "Thank you," he mumbled into her hair as he held her immobile against him. "I didn't realize how much I needed that." Then softer, "Thank you."

That lump in her throat grew even larger, and though she tried to fight it, her eyes slid closed, and she drew his scent deep into her soul, every inch of him, as much as she could get, until she felt giddy and lightheaded from just his simple touch.

Oh gods. She was falling for him, dammit. For someone she had no right to even look twice at. For someone who shouldn't want to be anywhere near her. Their being anything other than enemies made absolutely no sense. And she had zero hope for any kind of future with him beyond tonight. None. The smartest play for her was to leave—no, to *run*, as he'd told her to do before—right this very second.

He lifted his palm from her scalp, slid his fingers down her bare arm, leaving tingles in his wake, then grasped her hand. "Come shower with me."

Yes. Oh gods. Her entire body tightened with the need to feel him deep inside again. *Yes…*

No!

Her pulse raced in her ears. Conflicting thoughts swirled in what was left of her gray matter. If she went with him, and he showed her even a fraction of the kindness he was showering on her now, she'd be totally lost. Give in. Step right off that cliff and not care where she landed. And if that happened, that wall she'd erected to hold herself together since her parents' death would ignite like kindling consumed by flame.

It had taken her a long time to come out of that depression-induced spiral. If she let herself fall all the way for Nick, she knew she'd end up right back in that murky abyss. And considering the last time she'd been there she'd made a deal with the Prince of Darkness, there was no telling what awful thing she'd do when this fucked-up relationship imploded.

She swallowed hard and pressed her hand against his chest. "Go start the water. I'll grab towels."

"Okay." He released his grip on her shirt. Stepped back. And shot her a wicked-hot look laced with...oh *skata*...more of that fucking awe that was chipping away at her very last bit of resolve. "Don't be long."

He walked away, his bootsteps pounding against the tile floor in time with the pulse throbbing in her arteries. And as she watched the muscles in his back ripple beneath his scarred skin as he left, she knew he was every bit the warrior she'd pegged him to be from the start. Every time she thought about the constant struggle he was waging inside, every time she remembered the misery on his face in that courtyard, she wanted to go to him, to comfort him, to be for him what no one else had ever been. But she couldn't. Not if she had any hope of surviving herself. And right now, self-preservation needed to be foremost in her mind. Because if it wasn't...

If it wasn't, she knew exactly where she'd end up.

As soon as he turned the corner, she dropped the towel in her hand and sprinted for the door.

CHAPTER FOURTEEN

Nick tipped his head back and rinsed the shampoo and soap from his body as the hot water cascaded down his skin and soothed his sore and tired muscles. Steam rose around him, warming every inch of his skin, but he didn't need it to ease that ever-present chill inside. Cynna had done that when she'd so gently cut his hair. When she'd sunk into him moments before and let him hold her. When she'd kissed him in that cell in the tunnels, then rocked his world right out from under his feet.

Blood rushed to his groin at the memory, and he grew hard and achy under the spray. He'd been fascinated by her for months. Had wanted her long before they'd taken this journey together. And now that he'd had a taste of her, he knew once wasn't going to be enough.

His body urged him to find out why the hell she wasn't naked in this shower with him already, but before he could turn and call for her, understanding slammed everything to a screeching halt.

He'd been as close to the edge as he'd ever been in those tunnels. Krónos's power had been rippling through his veins, just begging to be released with a wicked unrivaled fierceness. And yet, he hadn't let it go. Not because he'd possessed some superhuman self-control, but because Cynna had pulled him back from that edge. She'd given him something else to focus on, something better to want. And it had been enough to keep him from giving in to all that wretched darkness that would undoubtedly be the end of him and possibly the world if he let it free.

His heart picked up speed, pounding a staccato rhythm against his ribs, and he lowered his head and opened his eyes as water ran in rivulets down his face.

He needed her. Not because she was some kind of insurance against an attack from Zagreus, but because she kept him grounded, kept him sane when he felt like he was losing his slight grasp on reality. And though the rational side of his brain warned he still didn't know her well enough to make any kind of steadfast decision about her motives, his heart told him loud and clear that she wasn't here to betray him. If betrayal had been her goal, she wouldn't have comforted him like she'd just done. She wouldn't have bothered to cut his hair and make him feel human again. And she certainly wouldn't have kissed him crazy when he'd given her the chance to run.

He turned toward the shower door, desperate to feel her against him again, to taste her sinful perfection, to thank her in the only way he could. But before he could reach for the handle, the scars on his back tingled, and a new sort of awareness rushed over him.

Six people were in the castle. Not humans. Not Misos. Not satyrs or daemons. He tuned in to his senses and let the tentacle-like receptors of his mind fan out.

Argoleans. The six newcomers were definitely Argolean.

Warning bells kicked off in his head. His first thought was of Isadora—which only pissed him off. He was finally at a place where he had something—someone—else to crave, and the soul mate curse was still there, taunting him. Slamming the water off, he stepped out of the shower and reached for a towel, only to realize there wasn't one. His gaze shot through the open bathroom door toward the salon. A towel lay in a heap on the ground.

He grasped his clothes from the floor, crossed to the towel dripping wet, and scooped it up. After drying, he pulled on his jeans, shoved his feet into his boots, and realized Cynna was still wearing his shirt.

Cynna... Shit. Those warning bells turned to full-on flares.

His gaze scanned the salon, but he already knew she was gone. Tuning back in to those senses once more, he searched for her. She was still in the castle. One level down, in the main hall. Hell if he knew how he was able to track her, but he could, and right now he was glad for it.

He moved for the door. Voices—male voices—drifted from the stairwell, followed by Cynna's curt one.

"No," she snapped. "I don't have to tell you anything. And I said, let *go!*"

That darkness surged inside. Nick rounded the corner and looked down the curved and charred staircase. Cynna stood in the archway that led into the main living area, still wearing nothing but his black T-shirt, struggling against Theron's grip on her upper arm. Several other Argonauts—Titus, Zander, and Gryphon—stood around her, blocking her in.

"Take your hands off her."

They all turned as one and looked up the staircase toward him. But Theron was the one Nick focused on. And his hold on Cynna's arm. That darkness leapt and bubbled inside with the prospect of a bloodletting.

"Nick." Theron released her. "Holy *skata.*"

Cynna jerked her arm away and shot daggers into the back of the leader of the Argonaut's head. But Nick no longer cared what Theron was doing. His focus shifted to her. To the nervous look in her dark eyes, to the way she wouldn't meet his gaze, and the fact she was actively searching for somewhere to run.

Away from him.

The reality was like a sharp stab to the solar plexus. Yeah, she didn't want to be anywhere near the Argonauts—he could feel her animosity growing for them with every passing second—but this need to escape had nothing to do with them and everything to do with him.

That moment, when he'd held her in the salon, ricocheted through his memory. The way she'd tensed, then relaxed, then—reluctantly, now it seemed—agreed to join him in the shower.

She was spooked. That was why she'd taken off. That was why she was pissed now. She'd felt the same thing he had upstairs. The same deep connection that wasn't rooted in a forced and silly soul mate bond but was deeper, more immediate, more...real.

He moved down the stairs, his gaze directly on her, not willing to let her out of his sight now for even a minute. "Are you okay?"

She darted a venomous look toward Titus, standing on her right, then one at Theron again. Still not meeting Nick's eyes, she crossed her arms over her chest. "I'm fine."

Theron's dark hair swayed as he moved toward the stairs. "When did you get out? Holy *skata*, we've been frantically searching for you everywhere."

Nick ignored the leader of the Argonauts, pushed past him, and reached for Cynna's elbow. "Don't take off like that again."

Her gaze finally swung his way, but her eyes weren't soft and compassionate as they'd been upstairs. No, now they held a sharp edge. One he'd seen before. In Zagreus's lair. "I'll go wherever the hell I want. I'm not your prisoner."

So they were back to this now...

"Nick," Theron said at his back. "There are things happening in Argolea that concern you."

"Argolea?" Cynna's eyes widened, and she shot a look at Theron over Nick's shoulder. "Oh, you should definitely go."

"The Council's got a serious set of sticks up their asses," Titus said somewhere to Nick's left. "Orpheus is doing the best he can to try to keep the peace, but shit, man. It's O. We all know how well that's going over."

Zander muttered something Nick didn't catch. Something about the Council and the witches and some kind of settlement. All crap Nick couldn't care less about. And Argolea was the last place he ever wanted to visit again.

His hand tightened around Cynna's elbow, and a desperate urge to get her alone, to finish what they'd started upstairs consumed him. He tugged on her arm, drawing her a step back toward the stairs. "You're coming with me. We have unfinished business."

Cynna dug her bare heels in and struggled against his grip. "I don't think so."

"It's definitely stronger," a female voice said near Gryphon. One Nick recognized. "I could feel it as soon as we came into the castle. It's clearly coming from him."

Nick's irritated gaze darted to Maelea, whom he hadn't picked out on first glance because she'd been standing behind her mate, then to Gryphon. "You brought her here? Stupid Argonaut. The therillium ore isn't camouflaging this place anymore. Hades can find it again if he looks."

Gryphon reached for his mate's hand and drew her to his side. "We're not staying long. You need to come back with us."

"Who the hell is that?" Cynna mumbled, still pulling back from Nick's hold.

"Maelea."

Cynna's eyes widened. "Maelea…as in Zeus and Persephone's daughter?" She tugged harder against his grip. "Oh yeah. I'm *so* not getting caught with *that*. Let go of me right now."

Nick's irritation reached its breaking point. He clenched his jaw and pulled her another inch toward the stairs.

"Nick—"

"Look," Nick answered before Theron could get more than his name out, "I'm not interested in whatever crisis you've got going back in Argolea. You all know the way out, so find the fucking door on your own."

"Niko, stop."

Nick stilled at the use of his given name. His gaze shifted to the right, toward Demetrius, whom he hadn't even noticed when he'd come down the stairs because he'd been so focused on Cynna.

His brother's dark hair was messy, his skin sallow, and there was a haunted look to his black eyes. One that stopped Nick cold.

"She's sick," Demetrius said. "We're not sure what's wrong with her, but Callia thinks you might be able to help."

She.

Isadora.

His soul mate.

The swirling irritation came to a shuddering halt. Nick's gaze drifted over the faces around him, seeing nothing and no one as he searched for that connection he felt to Isadora. The soul mate draw was still there. Lurking beneath the surface. But it wasn't as strong as it had been even a month ago. Something he was grateful for but suddenly way the fuck confused by. Especially since he hadn't realized she was sick. Now, yes, he could feel that something was off, but he'd had to think about her, to focus on her to realize it. Which was a thousand times different from years past.

His brow dropped low as he looked back at his brother. "What can I do? Your bond with her is stronger."

"Not anymore," Demetrius answered in a strained voice.

Nick had no idea what Demetrius meant, but when Cynna pulled back on his grip again, his attention darted her way.

"You should go with them," she said. "They clearly need you."

And she didn't. His gaze sharpened on her dark eyes. And he saw again what he'd seen upstairs in the salon, just after he'd held her.

Fear.

Though right now, he couldn't tell if it was because of him or the Argonauts surrounding her.

Indecision skipped through his mind and then fled. She might not need him, but he definitely needed her. And there was no way he was going to Argolea without sanity on his side.

He looked back at his brother. "Fine. I'll go with you." He nodded toward the female he had yet to release. "But she's coming too."

"*What?*" Cynna tugged hard on Nick's grip. "No way in hell."

Nick only held her tighter, pulling her up against his side. Demetrius's eyes shifted her way, and though Nick's gaze didn't follow, judging from the increased beat of her pulse beneath his fingertips and the heat now rolling off her in waves where she pressed against him, he knew she was seething.

Too bad. He needed her to keep him from losing it for good. Especially now when he was heading back to the one place he swore he'd never visit again.

"Who is she?" Demetrius asked.

"I—"

"Just someone who helped me escape from Zagreus," Nick answered, cutting her off.

"She's Argolean," Theron said cautiously at Nick's back. "What was an Argolean doing with the Prince of Darkness?"

Nick huffed. "It's a long story."

"I'm right here," Cynna growled from between clenched teeth. "I can answer my own da—"

Nick squeezed her elbow until she winced.

Theron stared at her a long beat, then finally glanced toward the other Argonauts. "Fine. She can cross with us. Z?"

"On it." Zander brought his hands together so his pinkies touched. The portal between worlds popped and sizzled and opened with a sharp beam of light that illuminated the room.

A heavy weight pushed hard against Nick's chest. At his side, every muscle in Cynna's body contracted.

He leaned close to her ear while Gryphon and Maelea went through the portal, and whispered, "Don't worry. We won't stay long. And I meant what I said before. We still have unfinished business."

"Fuck you," she growled.

"Pretty sure you already did that."

"Don't remind me." She yanked back on his grip once more, her eyes like daggers, but he only held her tighter, not letting her move away. "The second you release me, I'm gone."

That pressure in his chest eased, if only for a moment. Because this, her feisty defiance, gave him something solid and real to focus on instead of the shit that was about to go down. And staying centered on her kept that poisonous darkness from bubbling to the surface. "Then I suggest you get used to my touch, female, because there's no way I'm letting you go. And that means you're gonna get a whole lot more of me real soon."

Cynna was on the verge of hyperventilating. Not only were Nick's fingers digging into her elbow, leaving bruises in their wake, but he'd dragged her through the portal and was now hauling her with him into the castle.

The Argolean castle.

Gods almighty. Gods al—*fucking*—mighty.

Perspiration dotted her forehead, collected along her back, and slid down her spine. His "soul mate" clearly knew the queen. Which meant there was a chance Cynna might run into the bitch in this horrid place. Anger and panic and disbelief tangled in her chest until she couldn't breathe.

She focused on drawing air deep into her lungs, then pushing it out so she didn't actually lose it. A gust of wind swept through the ginormous entryway, sending a shiver down her spine, and that was when she realized that not only was she in the middle of her own worst nightmare come true, she was wearing nothing but Nick's thin T-shirt. No shoes, no pants, not even underwear beneath the soft black cotton that hit her midthigh. And thanks to the fact she'd bolted before she'd even had a chance to think about clothing, that meant she was probably still sporting that just-fucked look too.

"Son of a bitch," she muttered.

"Stay close to me," Nick whispered at her side.

Fury whipped through her with the force of a tornado. "Fuck y—"

"Cynna." His gaze darted down to her while they walked behind the Argonauts. "This isn't a game."

She knew this wasn't a game, dammit. For her, it was the furthest thing from a game. It was the last possible place she wanted to be. Her own private version of hell. A—

"I know you're pissed," he said, easing his hold on her elbow a touch. "But I'm asking you to please not make the situation worse. Fifteen minutes, then we're gone. Trust me, I don't want to be here any more than you do."

His words were filled with a note of anxiety that drew her focus from her roiling anger. She chanced a look his way. His jaw was tight, the muscles a flexing beneath his scruffy skin, and his eyes were hard and guarded as he stared straight ahead.

He'd told her his soul mate was bonded to his brother. She'd witnessed the tension between the two males back at the colony even if she hadn't wanted to acknowledge it. Her mind drifted over their conversation in the jungle, when he'd been telling her about the soul mate curse, and she remembered vividly the animosity in his words when he'd mentioned the female at the center of their messy little love triangle. Using her gift, Cynna searched for any sense that he was lying, only she found nothing. He was telling the truth. Being near his soul mate gave him no kind of happiness.

"Only those of us with the markings feel the draw." He'd told her that as well, that the female in the soul mate equation wasn't affected by the curse. Which meant, being here, being close to her, had to be like a new form of torture for him. And Cynna was making it worse by freaking out.

Her jaw unclenched. The muscles in her arms relaxed. As they moved up the stairs, she sighed and figured she could either continue being a bitch…or she could get through this and then get the hell away from him for good.

"You don't have to hold me so tightly," she muttered. "I clearly can't go anywhere. And I won't. For at least fifteen minutes."

Nick's grip released her elbow, and blood rushed to the spot. She reached over and rubbed her sore elbow but was distracted when his hand closed over hers hanging at her side, his fingers intertwining with hers to keep them close. She glanced up, caught the gratitude in his amber gaze, and suddenly couldn't breathe again.

"Thank you."

Thank you...

He needed to stop saying that to her. All it did was make her feel worse. Because he had absolutely no reason to thank her, dammit. Not after the things she'd done.

She focused on slow breaths, in and out, as she walked up the stairs beside him, knowing she needed to pull away from his hand. But a dangerous place inside didn't want to let go. And just recognizing that fact sent her adrenaline spiking all over again.

"Yo, Nick." The Argonaut with the long wavy hair tied at his nape with a leather strap caught up with them just as they reached the landing on the next level and pushed a shirt into Nick's hands. "Might want to put this on before you go in there."

"Thanks, Titus." Nick took the shirt, let go of Cynna's hand, and tugged it on, the light blue button-down covering his bare chest. And though she was still irritated she remained half-naked and that no one had brought her more to wear, a tiny place inside Cynna was glad this soul mate of his who seemed to enjoy tormenting his existence wasn't going to get to see all the sculpted goodness and strong muscles Cynna had sampled only an hour or so ago.

Her body warmed at the memory of his hands running over her naked flesh, his mouth nipping at her sensitive skin, the wicked things he could do with his tongue, and instantly she wondered if this female had ever experienced any of that. As quickly as the thought hit though, she dismissed it. There was no room for jealousy in her heart. After everything she'd done, it was pretty clear she no longer had a heart, anyway.

He grabbed her hand again as they headed down a long, wide corridor with an intricately carved dome ceiling and ornate pillars lining the hall, and she let him hold her, not because she wanted to touch him, she told herself. But because she was doing exactly what he'd asked—not making a scene.

Archways opened to a library, a sitting area, what looked like offices. With every step, her anxiety shot up, and she searched each room for any sign of the queen, hoping and praying she wouldn't run into the female before she could escape. Fifteen minutes. She could give Nick fifteen minutes after everything she'd put him through.

They drew to a stop outside another open doorway, but this time Cynna couldn't see past the Argonauts to get a look in the room. Voices resonated from the open doorway, though. A female's and a male's, both clearly in deep conversation.

"No," the female said, "Lord Tiberius definitely sent spies. We've intercepted two couriers taking back detailed reports to the Council, outlining the layout of the settlement, the entrances and exits, even the Argonauts' arrival and departure times. They're looking for patterns. Waiting for the perfect time to hit."

"You really think they'll do that?" the male asked. "That would be brazen, even for them. Their political campaign hasn't even kicked into high gear yet. They risk alienating a large section of the population with a preemptive strike against an unarmed group."

"It's a calculated risk," another female said. "Eliminate them before they pose a risk. And don't forget, the witches are aiding them, which, in the eyes of the Council, gives them justification for any kind of attack."

"I guess," the male said. "But I haven't picked up on any of that yet, and I've been spending as much time with the Council as I can."

"They're not going to plan when you could overhear," the first female said. "Why would they? They know where your allegiance lies, even if they did vote you in."

"We're going to need to up security around the settlement," a third female said, this one's voice softer than the others. "Even if it means pulling the Argonauts from the human realm, I want—"

Theron knocked on the doorjamb, and the voices inside died down. But that fire in Cynna was growing all over again as the first few Argonauts stepped into the room. Just the mention of the witches and the Council made the temperature of her blood feel as if it shot up ten degrees.

"My queen." Theron bowed slightly as he stepped into the room. "There's someone I think you'd like to see."

Queen? *Queen?*

Cynna's eyes flew wide, and her heart lurched into her throat, beating so hard she felt as if she were about to choke. She instinctively pulled back, but Nick gripped her hand tightly in his and tugged her with him into the room.

The floor was made of marble. The ceiling was decked out in dark wood beams, and tall, arching windows looked out at a view of the bay, but that was all Cynna could catch. Because suddenly she couldn't think. Couldn't breathe. Couldn't stop the panic stabbing into every inch of her skin like hot, sharp knives.

"Relax," he said softly at her side. "Fifteen minutes. That's it."

No. She couldn't stay fifteen minutes. She couldn't even stay five. And forget about relaxing. She had to get the hell out of here, *right fucking now.*

Hand shaking, Cynna tried to pull away again, only to freeze when she heard the female voice from across the room exclaim, "Nick."

Her gaze lifted. A slight, petite female with white-blonde hair rose from behind a desk that looked like it could swallow her whole, and stared wide-eyed at Nick. A female Cynna knew on first look.

Cynna's heart rate shot up. Footsteps died down at her back as more people filed into the room. Standing on the far side of the desk was another male, as big as the Argonauts, and two females, one with long, golden blonde hair, and the other with shoulder-length auburn locks, looking from Nick to her and back again with veiled curiosity.

No one spoke. Silence settled over the tall room as everyone waited for... Hell, Cynna didn't know what they were waiting for.

Long seconds passed. And then Isadora's face brightened, and she moved quickly around the desk before coming to a stop directly in front of Nick.

She was smaller than Cynna realized, a full head shorter than her, pale where Cynna was dark and weak where Cynna was strong. But standing so close to the queen, every inferiority Cynna had ever felt came rushing back. And the moment the female threw her arms around Nick and hugged him tight, breaking his hold on Cynna's hand, Cynna snapped right out of her trance. Her blood didn't just hover at bubbling, it went into full-on boil.

"Nick," the queen exclaimed. "Oh my gods. I can't... I'm so..." She drew back but didn't let go of him, and a wide smile broke across her face. "I can't believe you're here."

Still no one spoke. The tension remained as high as ever in the room. And though Cynna's hands were just itching to grab the queen and tear her away from Nick, she held back. Her gaze shifted to Nick. And focused on the totally perplexed expression on his scarred face.

Isadora's smile wobbled. And her gaze darted past Nick to the tall, dark Argonaut behind him. The one Cynna had quickly realized back at the colony was Nick's brother.

"Demetrius." She let go of Nick with one hand, reached around behind him, grabbed the dark-haired Argonaut's forearm, and dragged him to her side. But, Cynna noticed, she still didn't let go of Nick with her other hand. "I can't believe it. How did you...? When—"

The auburn-haired female, the one who was standing near the queen's desk, moved close and placed two fingers on Isadora's wrist—the one connected to the hand still resting on Nick's chest. She turned and looked past Cynna toward the door. "It's stronger. Her pulse is definitely stronger."

Nick's gaze shifted that direction.

"I was afraid of that," Maelea said. "The darkness in him is much greater than the last time I was at the colony."

"What the hell is going on?" Nick asked, looking back at the auburn-haired woman, then glancing toward the queen, and finally the tall Argonaut. "You brought me all the way back here. Tell me what this is all about."

"It's about the soul mate curse," the leader of the Argonauts said somewhere behind Cynna. "And how it's affecting Isadora."

Cynna nearly choked on her tongue. "Soul mate?" She looked from Nick to the queen and back again, her eyes growing wider. "*She's* your soul mate?"

Holy hell. The queen of Argolea was his fucking soul mate?

Pressure pushed at every inch of her skin, making her lungs feel like they were about to explode. The Fates could not be that unfair. *Life* could not be that unfair. Of all the people in all the world for her to get involved with, it had to be the soul mate of the one person she hated with every fiber of her being?

She only just held back a pathetic laugh. If the situation weren't so dire, she'd be rolling on the floor with laughter. But she couldn't. Because this was her fucking fate.

Somewhere at the back of the room, someone chuckled. Followed by a whispered, "What's so funny?" and an "I'll tell you later."

But Cynna couldn't turn to see who'd spoken, because Nick's attention finally shifted her way. And in his irritated amber gaze, she saw exactly what she'd expected. He'd forgotten she was even there. "We'll talk about this later."

Cynna's heart—or what was left of it—felt like it shattered. Right there on the floor. She moved a step away and muttered, "Like hell we will."

The queen finally lowered her hand from Nick's chest and looked at her. "Who is this?"

Nick's jaw clenched, and, oh yeah, he was pissed. Well, so was Cynna. So much so she wanted to slam her fist through a wall. Or someone's face. Only she couldn't seem to stop her damn hand from shaking.

"Cynna," Nick said. "She was with me in Zagreus's lair."

"Cynna," the guy near the desk whispered to the blonde at his side. "Isn't that…?"

"Shh," the blonde muttered, cutting him off.

The queen's assessing gaze slid over Cynna, making the fine hairs along Cynna's back stand to attention. But not even a flicker of recognition passed through Isadora's eyes.

Even though she was seething, even though she wanted to do nothing but run, Cynna breathed a little easier. The queen didn't know who she was. She could get out of this if she kept her cool.

"She's Argolean," the queen said. "What was an Argolean female doing with Zagreus?"

Unfortunately, Cynna's cool went right out the window with that question, and her temper raged back to the forefront. Oh no. They were *not* going through this again. She wasn't about to sit back and let a single person—especially the queen of Argolea—make assumptions about her like she wasn't even in the room.

She straightened her spine and opened her mouth to tell the queen just what she could do with her damn questions when the blonde who'd been standing near the desk stepped forward.

"I can see these guys were acting like cavemen again and didn't even bother to give you time to get dressed before they dragged you here." Cynna's gaze snapped toward the blonde, who had a pleasant expression fixed across her pretty face. "How about you and I go find something for you to wear while they all gossip like schoolgirls?"

The fact Cynna was wearing nothing but Nick's T-shirt hit her again, but she didn't care. She didn't need clothes to put these people in their places. She'd lived with Zagreus, for fuck's sake. She could hold her own with the queen of Argolea and her stupid merry men. But before she could spout off as much, her brain kicked into gear, and she realized…this could be her way out of this nightmare.

She reined in her temper—even though it took every ounce of willpower she had—swallowed hard, and nodded once.

"Good," the female said. "I'm Skyla. Come with me."

Cynna took a step toward the door to follow the blonde, but Nick grasped her arm at the wrist before she could get too far away and drew her back. His amber gaze locked on hers, hard, steady, resolute. "Don't go far. I'll come find you in a few minutes. "

Just the fact he was finally looking at her sent that temper right back to bubbling. Two minutes ago, he'd forgotten she even existed.

She wrenched her arm from his grip. "Your fifteen minutes are up."

CHAPTER FIFTEEN

Cynna tried to settle her raging temper as she turned to follow Skyla, only to realize there were more people in the room than she'd thought. Another woman had stepped in after her, one with fire-red hair who'd sidled up next to the guy in the back wearing gloves—the one she was pretty sure had been laughing. And two other males had joined the fray, both clearly Argonauts and both as crazy handsome as the rest. Where the hell did they find these guys? Studs "R" Us?

Voices faded behind her as she followed Skyla back down the long corridor. When they reached the massive curved staircase, Skyla said, "We're going up one level."

Cynna took in every detail as they walked. The guards below in the foyer, the servants they passed, the posh surroundings and expensive furnishings. And every second she spent in this castle, surrounded by luxuries and more wealth than she could imagine, she remembered the small house she'd lived in with her parents before they'd died. The wood floor, the tiny bedrooms—one for them, and one for her—and the closet-size kitchen where she and her mother had prepared the meals. They hadn't had much, but they'd been happy. Or so she'd thought. But how could anyone ever be content with that after being surrounded by all this?

"Here we are." Skyla stopped in front of a large, arched door, turned the handle, and pushed with her hip.

Cynna followed her into the room, and once again, her jaw nearly dropped to the floor. Racks and racks of clothing lined the walls. All different sizes, for all different genders and ages. Huge bins were lined up in rows in the middle, holding socks and shoes and undergarments.

Skyla moved toward a rack on the left and pawed through until she found a pair of jeans and a long-sleeved red T-shirt, then turned and handed them to Cynna. "These should fit. You're about my size. Go ahead and grab some undergarments from the bins, and I'll find you some boots. Don't worry. Everything's new." She pointed toward a tall screen set up in front of the windows. "There's a dressing area over there."

Cynna grabbed what she needed from the bins and moved behind the screen. She tugged on the underwear, thankful that they fit, then reached for the jeans. "Must be nice to have a shopping mall in your own freakin' house."

"Yeah, it would be," Skyla said from beyond the screen. "But these aren't for the castle. They're for a refugee camp outside the city."

The queen actually cared about refugees? Cynna nearly scoffed as she buttoned the jeans and reached for the shirt.

"You know," Skyla said, "I've heard of a female named Cynna who lives with Zagreus. She's also known as the Mistress of Torture."

Cynna's arms froze, shirt over her head, and her pulse picked up speed. Swallowing hard, she pulled the garment on and tugged it down her hips. "What's your point?"

"My point is simple. The others may assume you were just a prisoner, but I think we both know differently. I want to know what Zagreus's right-hand female is doing with Nick."

Cynna smoothed her hair back from her face, reminded herself to play it cool, and stepped out from behind the screen. "What are you, the queen's personal spy?"

Skyla tipped her head. "Until recently, I spent a lot of time in the human realm dealing with Zagreus's satyrs and the messes they created. The rest of the time I spent on Olympus, with Athena."

Cynna's gaze skipped over the blonde, and she realized what she'd missed earlier. The warrior stance, the calculating look in the female's green eyes, and the coiled strength hidden beneath that attractive facade.

Skata. This changed things...quite a bit. While Cynna had no reservations about dueling with an Argonaut, she did not want to piss off Zeus. "You're a Siren."

"Was," Skyla answered. "I recently left the order." She crossed her arms over her chest. "Now answer my question. What the hell are you doing with Nick?"

She could lie, but at this point all Cynna wanted was out. And the fastest way to get out was to finish this conversation so she could split. "I helped him escape."

"Why?"

"Because Zagreus was going to turn him over to Hades."

"And you, what? Developed a conscience about that?"

Cynna's temper inched up. "I didn't want to see him in the hands of a god who could use his powers for evil against the whole world. So, yeah, I guess you could say I developed a conscience. I don't think anyone wants that."

"And Zagreus? He was just okay with you leaving?"

"No," Cynna said, glancing over the racks of clothing, "I'm sure he was pretty pissed." She looked back at the Siren. "I didn't wait around to find out."

Skyla studied her a long moment, and Cynna couldn't tell if the female believed her or not, but she didn't care anymore. For once she'd done the right thing and still she was being labeled a traitor.

"Look," she said, working hard not to lose her cool with the Siren. "Not everything is as it seems. There are all kinds of prisons, and whether you want to believe it or not, I'm not the villain here." *Not anymore, at least.*

Skyla's jaw clenched. "What's your relationship with Nick?"

This time Cynna couldn't stop her stomach from pitching. Relationship? Did they even have a relationship? Captor-captive came to mind when she remembered their time together in Zagreus's lair. Followed by lovers when her memories skipped to their hot, sweaty sex in the tunnels beneath the colony. But she dismissed both because neither were accurate pictures of what they were. The only thing that even remotely made sense was...

"Really fucked up," Cynna finally answered.

Skyla stared at her, and as the seconds ticked by, Cynna's anxiety inched up all over again.

Would the Siren try to imprison her? Was she going to take her to the queen and tell her everything Cynna had just admitted? If that happened, she might never get out of this nightmare. Her gaze darted toward the windows that looked out over a courtyard, and that fight-or-flight response kicked in, only this time flight won out, big-time.

Skyla dropped her arms and pointed toward a pair of boots and a light jacket sitting on the ground near the screen. "Those are for you. Weather's calling for snow, and I'm sure you don't want to be caught in the cold. Let's head back and see if they're done gossiping."

Relief pulsed through Cynna's body. She reached for the boots and the jacket. "Um, is there a restroom somewhere I could use?"

That assessing look crossed Skyla's features again, making Cynna think the Siren was on to her. But instead of calling her on it, the blonde pointed toward a door on the far side of the room. "Through there. Don't be long."

Cynna nodded. "I won't."

She closed the bathroom door and glanced around. It was mostly marble, as big as her whole house had been as a kid, and disgustingly fancy. But—thank the Fates—there was a window that looked out to the courtyard several stories below.

She quickly pulled on the boots and jacket, then flipped on the fan to drown out any noise. A silent prayer of thanks whipped through her when she found the window unlocked.

Pushing it up, she peered outside. There was no balcony. Nothing but a small ledge that ran the length of this wing. But that was all she needed. She climbed out, gripped the stone ledge above, and made her way down the side of the building.

And told herself she wasn't ever looking back.

"This is freakin' nuts." Nick ran both hands through his hair and dropped them to his side, leveling a hard look at his brother.

Demetrius, leaning back against the desk in Isadora's palatial office with a scowl on his hard face and his arms crossed over his massive chest, didn't respond. In fact, since they'd arrived in Argolea, the guardian hadn't said shit. Just stared at Nick like he wasn't sure whether he wanted to hug him or slam his fist into his face. Which only pissed Nick off even more. His brother wasn't one for words, but the fact he wasn't arguing against this asinine theory where *his* soul mate was concerned only kicked Nick's anxiety up about the whole situation.

He looked back at Isadora, who also had her slim arms crossed over her chest but now refused to meet his gaze, then glanced toward Theron, standing at her side, looking frustrated and guilty all at the same time. "That's not how the soul mate curse works, and you all know it. Only the one with the markings is cursed. They're the only ones who feel it."

Nick was glad Theron had ushered most of the guardians and their mates out of the room so they didn't have to listen to this crap. If he had the choice, he'd be out of here too. That darkness was bubbling inside him with every passing minute, and being near his soul mate—the one he couldn't have—wasn't helping matters. He chanced a look toward the doorway, searching for Cynna, but she still had yet to return with Skyla.

"Everything about this situation is different," Theron said, "because you're different."

Nick scoffed, rested his hands on his hips, and turned toward the window. "I'm fine."

"Maelea can sense the energy in you is growing," Theron said. "And if that's the case, then it corresponds to what happened to those three mortals who—"

"Those were three dead mortals." Okay, yeah, Maelea, a product of the Underworld herself, might be able to sense Krónos's dark energy growing inside him, but that didn't mean she knew what the hell she was talking about. Nick pressed his fingers against his chest. "Last time I checked, I was alive. And this isn't the fucking Underworld."

Theron sighed. "Yeah. But we all know you're a hell of a lot stronger than you were. Who's to say your getting stronger isn't somehow messing with the soul mate curse and making Isadora weaker."

"It's possible," Orpheus said from his spot near the windows. "I didn't really feel the soul mate pull with Skyla until my daemon started to fade. That pull definitely strengthened the weaker my daemon became."

Nick rolled his eyes and rested his hands against his hips. They were all certifiable. That was the only explanation. He scowled at Isadora, then turned his glare on his brother. "Don't tell me you're buying in to this too. This is your fucking soul mate we're talking about. The one you told me to stay the hell away from."

Demetrius's jaw ticked, but the bastard still didn't answer. Just stared at Nick with those hard, cold eyes.

"Look." Callia stepped forward, clearly sensing the tension in the room. "We don't know anything yet. It's all just speculation. But I can tell you her vitals are much improved since you got here. Isa"—she turned toward her sister—"how do you feel?"

Isadora let out a breath. She bit her lip as she looked toward Nick, then glanced at her mate near the desk. She turned back toward her sister. "Better. A little stronger. But maybe that's just a coincidence."

"See?" Nick said, holding his arms out wide. "Finally, someone with a little sense."

Callia tucked a lock of auburn hair behind her ear and frowned. "I'm sorry, but Isadora's pulse regulating when she touched you was not a coincidence." She turned toward her sister. "We'll figure this out, don't worry. Now that Nick's here, it should buy us some time."

Oh no. He wasn't staying. He looked back over the faces in the room. They didn't actually expect him to remain in this realm, did they?

Footsteps reverberated from the corridor before he could ask, and his attention shifted that direction, his pulse skipping with the hope of seeing Cynna, back to keep him centered.

Except the female who stepped into the room wasn't the one he desperately needed. It was Casey, her brown hair shimmering under the chandelier above, her violet eyes sparkling as her gaze caught on Nick. "Someone told me we had a visitor."

Nick fought back the darkness pushing him to run. Casey crossed the floor, rose up on her toes, and wrapped her arms around Nick's shoulders. But this time—unlike when Isadora had hugged him—he didn't flinch. Because Casey was not, and never had been, any kind of threat to his sanity.

"I knew you'd come back," she said softly, lowering to her feet and smiling up at him. "You're like a bad penny. You always turn up."

Nick nodded toward her rounded belly. "You've obviously been busy while I've been gone. How long?"

Casey cast a warm look toward Theron, who was talking quietly with the queen and Callia. The guardian caught her eye, sent her a worried half grin, then went back to his conversation.

Casey turned back to Nick. "Two more months."

"And how's the hero with it all?"

"A bear. Worried. Constantly." Casey grinned. "Not a whole lot different than usual."

Nick huffed.

Casey hooked her arm in his and drew him toward a couch in the sitting area of Isadora's palatial office. "The bigger question is, how are you?"

She was the first person who'd asked. The first one who even seemed to care. But then, being a half-breed—one of *his* people—maybe she was the only one who could.

Cynna cared. His mind flashed to the way Cynna had grabbed him and kissed him when he'd given her the chance to run in the tunnels. Then how she'd known he was spiraling out of control and gently taken him upstairs, cut his hair, and dragged him back from the edge of something he was sure he wouldn't have been able to pull himself free from without her.

"Nick?"

He looked to his right, where Casey was sitting next to him on the couch, one hand resting on the swell of her belly while she eyed him with curiosity. Dammit, he didn't even remember sitting. "What?"

"I asked how you were doing. After everything you've been through—"

"I'm fine," he said quickly, not wanting to delve into what he'd been through. Not with her. "I'm always fine."

She frowned like she didn't believe him. "You're not happy about being here, are you?"

He leaned forward, rested his forearms on his knees, and worked not to scowl again. The fine hairs along his back bristled. "Let's just say this isn't my favorite place in the world."

"I know. But I'm glad you're here, even if you aren't. Isadora needs you right now."

He turned to face Casey, his eyes hardening as a whisper of animosity—no, a hell of a lot more than a whisper—whipped through him. "She never needed me before. Don't tell me you're buying into all this bullshit too."

"It's not bullshit. You haven't been here, so you haven't seen her deterioration, but something is definitely affecting her. Look at her. She's thinner now than when I met her."

Nick's head shifted Isadora's way before he could stop himself, and he took a good long look at the queen, standing across the room as she spoke quietly with Callia and Theron. Yes, she was thin, but the last time he'd seen her, she'd been eight months pregnant. It was hard for him to gauge what was normal for her and what wasn't since he'd stayed as far from her as possible in the past. But as he studied her closer, even he couldn't miss the sallowness to her skin, the way her eyes were sunken in, her cheekbones more prominent than before, and the tired droop to her shoulders.

Guilt whirled around him. And the soul mate draw, the one that he'd never been able to stop, pulled at something deep in his chest.

Her chocolate gaze lifted and locked on his from across the room, almost as if she'd felt it too. And the shock of it was so sudden, so intense, it sent a shiver of surprise through Nick that made him blink and look quickly away.

"She's fighting it," Casey said at his side. "She won't admit to anyone that she's weak—especially Demetrius, because she doesn't want to hurt him—but she is. At least now you're here, and we can hopefully figure out what's going on."

"I'm not staying."

The words were raspy, forced, and didn't sound like his own. He cleared his throat.

"Of course you're staying. You just got here."

Nick looked back toward the door. Desperate now for Cynna so he could get his mind off Isadora and back on something that kept him centered. Where the hell was she?

A quick glance over his shoulder told him Demetrius was still watching him way too carefully. "I don't think that's a good idea."

He started to get up, but Casey's hand on his forearm stopped him. "Wait, Nick." When he turned her way, he caught the worry in her friendly eyes. "I know things between you and Isadora and Demetrius are...strained."

"That's putting it mildly."

A half smile curled her lip but faded quickly. "I also know being here is the last place you want to be. But if you can't stay for her, or them, then stay for me."

"You've got superhero over there. You don't need me."

"That's where you're wrong. Our people need you. And I'll always be one of them."

"Our people?" Confusion drew his brows together.

"Yeah." She stared at him. "Don't you know? After you left the colony with Hades and Zagreus—"

Casey's words cut off as Skyla stepped into the room. Alone.

Nick pushed to his feet, his eyes growing wide, searching the empty hallway beyond for Cynna. "Where is she?"

"She went out the bathroom window. Good climber, that one."

Holy fuck. "You let her *leave?*"

"Relax," Skyla said. "She can't get far. I already alerted the castle guards."

Not far? She'd clearly underestimated the female. Just like Nick.

"She's Argolean. If she gets outside, she can flash." And he'd never find her again. He headed for the door.

"She can't flash through the castle walls, even if she is in the courtyard." Skyla sighed. "Besides, something tells me she'll be back."

Nick didn't wait for more. Didn't listen to the protests behind him. He turned out the door and hustled for the stairs.

"What did you find out?" Orpheus's voice drifted into the hall behind him.

"Something quite interesting," Skyla answered.

Nick could only speculate what Cynna had told the Siren, but right now he didn't give a rip. He had to get to her before she was gone for good.

He skipped steps to make it to the first level as quickly as possible. Across the marble floor and towering entry of the castle, Cynna was just pushing her way past the door guards, heading for the outer courtyard and the castle wall beyond.

Nick didn't yell for her, didn't want to give her any reason to run. He pushed his legs forward, moving with stealth across the great Alpha seal stamped into the floor. Both guards regarded him with speculation as he drew close, but he'd visited the castle often enough in the past that they didn't pay him any extra attention. He raced down the front steps and caught up with Cynna yards from the closed front gate, grasped her by the arm, and tugged her around to face him.

"Hold up," he said. "Just where do you think you're going?"

Her eyes widened in surprise but quickly hardened. "I'm leaving."

"No, you're not."

Fury flashed in her chocolate gaze. "You don't get to decide that. You don't get to choose. I was willing to help you in any way I could, because I know you deserved it after all the shitty things I did to you. But not this. I can't." She tugged back against his grip. "I won't."

He'd seen her pissed when those satyrs had come at her. But this was different. This wasn't just anger, it was panic and fear and hurt all clashing together.

"Look," he said calmly, hoping to settle them both down. "I know you don't want to be in Argolea."

"You think this is about Argolea?" She wrenched her arm from his hold. "This isn't about Argolea. It's about her."

"Her who?"

"Her." She held up a hand toward the castle. "Your *soul mate*."

A hard knot formed in Nick's chest, and his memory skipped back over the last few minutes. She'd obviously seen his reaction to Isadora. He hadn't been able to mask it, even though he'd tried. No wonder she was pissed. Especially after the things he'd done to her in the tunnels of the colony. Especially considering the things he wanted to do to her all over again.

Nick took a step toward her. "It's not what you think. Isadora and I—"

"Oh, for gods' sake." Cynna stepped back so he couldn't touch her. "I don't care that you have a soul mate. I don't care if you have ten. What I care about is the fact it's *her*. Of all the people in all the world, your soul mate turns out to be the one person I hate more than any other. I should have expected it. I should have known, dammit."

She took another step back and waved her hands, and as he watched her frantic movements, as he saw her panic and anger growing, an odd tingle spread across the scars along his back.

"I don't care how guilty I feel over the things Zagreus made me do," she snapped. "I won't have anything to do with her. And you can't make me stay anywhere near this disgusting castle."

She turned to leave again, but Nick caught her by the arm, twisting her back to face him once more. "Hold on. What did Isadora do to you?"

Her jaw clenched, and that dead look, the one he hadn't seen in her eyes since before she'd tended his wounds in the Prince of Darkness's lair, crept back into her gaze. A look that was so sudden, so emotionless, it halted every one of those tingles and sent a chill straight down his spine.

"Everything," she said in a hard, cold voice. "She's the reason I was with Zagreus. The person I traded my freedom for to see ruined. She's the one who murdered my entire family."

CHAPTER SIXTEEN

The disbelief on Nick's scarred face told Cynna everything she needed to know.

He didn't believe her. But then, why would he? His soul mate was the queen of fucking Argolea. And he was so completely gone over her, he wouldn't believe the truth about her even if it punched him square in the face.

Metal ground against metal at her back. Cynna didn't have to look to know that the castle gates were opening. Someone was coming in. Which meant—because she couldn't flash through solid walls, even out here in the open—she now had a way out.

She pulled her arm from his grip once more and moved back a half step. "This is finished."

"Cynna—"

She closed her eyes and pictured home. Or what was left of it. And in a flash, she was floating, spinning, traveling across the distance to the only place in this miserable land where she'd ever felt she belonged.

Her feet connected with the hard ground, and she opened her eyes only to draw in a surprised gasp.

Snow littered both sides of the dirt road. Spindly barren deciduous trees void of leaves stood like decrepit statues while conifers swayed in the cool breeze. Beyond, the Aegis Mountains rose to the gray sky in shades of blue and purple. But what startled her wasn't the familiar scenery. No, it was the two-story high stone wall that had been rebuilt, the enormous wooden gate—solid, not burned or broken or filled with holes—and the soldiers. Castle soldiers from Tiyrns—she recognized their emblems—manning the entrance.

Her pulse raced, and she looked all around as she moved forward, trying to figure out what was going on.

The guard to her right leveled her with a look and held out his spear. "Halt, female. Papers are required for admittance to the Kyrenia settlement."

"Papers? What papers?"

The massive doors opened, just a crack, and a young male, close to Cynna's age, came through, nodded at the guards, and walked past. Cynna peered through the opening as the gates slowly closed. Dozens of people filled the streets. Buildings—those were actual buildings, not ruins—stood on both sides of the road.

Her skin grew hot, and she took a step forward, a new sort of panic spreading through her veins. "Who's in there? What...?"

The guard shoved a hand against her shoulder, stopping her. "Papers, female. No papers, no admittance."

"But that's my home," she said, pushing against him. "I have every right to be here. I demand to know who's using my—"

"Cynna? Is that you?"

The female voice from beyond the closing doors slowed Cynna's struggling. She knew that voice. Knew it well.

Her heart beat hard, this time not from panic but from a warmth that curled through her entire body. "Delia?"

"Open these gates, at once," Delia demanded on the other side of the door. "She's one of us."

Some kind of argument was happening. Cynna couldn't hear clearly through the closed doors. But seconds later, the heavy grind of the great wood doors parting sounded once more, and Delia's face appeared—snow-white hair hanging past her shoulders, sharp blue eyes, high cheekbones on a youthful face, and thin lips curved into a welcoming smile. To most she looked to be only in her early thirties, the same age as Cynna, but she was much, much older. And wiser. "My dear Cynna."

The witch wrapped her arms around Cynna and pulled her into a tight hug, and as the familiar scent of lemon surrounded Cynna, she closed her eyes and held on, for the first time in...years...feeling something other than alone.

"She has no papers," the guard mumbled.

Delia glanced his direction with an irritated expression. "You and your useless papers. I'll vouch for her." She looked back at Cynna, her annoyance fading. "Come. You look a fright, child. Come in out of the cold."

Delia pulled Cynna into the settlement. A shiver raced down Cynna's spine as she stepped into the courtyard, and for the first time, she registered the temperature. But even that faded as the gigantic doors closed behind her, and she looked around the bustling city of Kyrenia.

"Looks quite different, doesn't it?" Delia said at her side, one arm still wrapped around Cynna's shoulders.

"Slightly." Cynna swallowed the lump in her throat.

The last time she'd stood in this spot, just before she'd left for the human realm, Cynna had stared at nothing but ruins. Broken stone, charred wood beams, ash and dust and the remnants of a life she sometimes thought of as a dream. But these weren't ruins. Shops had been rebuilt. Homes had been restored. The fountain in the middle of the courtyard where she'd waded as a child was bubbling. Children dressed in coats and boots were playing tag and throwing snowballs while males and females shopped, chatted, and went about their business.

Cynna looked from face to face, searching for someone familiar, finding nothing but strangers. "Who are all these people?"

"Refugees," Delia answered, moving forward and pulling Cynna along with her. "The coven is helping to get them settled."

"Refugees from where?"

"The human realm. They're Misos. From the half-breed colony." When Cynna's brow dropped, Delia added, "Half-Argolean, half-human."

"I know what half-breeds are," Cynna said, trying to keep the irritation from her voice. "How did they get here?"

"The queen brought them."

"*What?*" Cynna stopped and faced her mother's oldest friend.

Delia's expression turned sad. "Hades and his son attacked the Misos colony, and the queen and the Argonauts brought them here for safekeeping."

"Here?" Cynna looked around, disbelief swirling in her chest. "To *our* home?"

"It wasn't much of a home of late. You've been gone so long, you couldn't know. The settlement has been empty and cold for years. Originally, the queen was housing the refugees in the castle in Tiyrns. But there were too many, and the Council... Well..." Delia sighed. "The Council made it clear they did not want the Misos wandering around the capital. She contacted me for advice. I suggested the Kyrenia settlement. So they were relocated here."

Just the fact that Delia, of all people, would allow the queen to use their home as a prison flared the fires of Cynna's anger right back to life.

"Banished, you mean," Cynna ground out. Yeah, that made sense. Of course the queen would lock away anyone who was different so they didn't infect her perfect Argolean society. But Cynna had no idea why she'd even bother to bring the Misos here from the human realm in the first place.

"Not banished," Delia said, her sharp voice drawing Cynna's gaze. "Saved. Did you not see the guards at the gates? Those were castle guards, pulled from the monarchy's personal detail."

"Yeah, I saw them. Chosen, obviously, to keep the Misos locked in."

"No, Cynna. To keep the Council and their spies *out*." Delia's eyes narrowed. "Has your heart been hardened so much that you cannot see what's right in front of you? Look around, child. Look at these people. Do they look like prisoners to you?"

Cynna glanced back over the faces. Smiling, laughing faces. And even though she didn't want to believe it, even she could see these people seemed content. Not miserable as she and everyone else who'd lived in Zagreus's realm had been. Not bitter and broken. Yes, some walked with crutches, others had ugly scars from what she knew were battles past, but no one seemed on edge. No one looked afraid. No one around her appeared anything but calm and relaxed and, yes, even happy.

Her skin grew cold and clammy. An odd tingle built in her chest. She glanced around again, only to realize...

She turned back to Delia. "You said they're Misos? From which colony?"

"The one in Montana. Why?"

Nick's colony. Cynna's gaze skipped back over the faces even as her mind tumbled with visions of Nick standing in that burned and broken courtyard, seeing nothing but death around him. These were Nick's people. Healthy. Whole. Alive.

That tingle turned to a warmth that flared all around her heart, making it beat faster. She needed to tell him. He thought everyone was dead. But as soon as the thought hit, reality slammed back into her.

He didn't need her to tell him anything. The queen would undoubtedly fill him in on all he needed to know. Now that he was with his soul mate, there wasn't a single thing he needed from Cynna.

That warmth died out, leaving behind cold, barren cinders, much like the ones she'd stared at in Zagreus's massive fireplace. Only then, she'd been smart enough to protect her heart. At some point since then, she'd dropped her guard, and now she wasn't just struggling with emotions she didn't want to feel. Now she knew what it meant to truly be alone.

She swallowed hard, only that ache in her chest wouldn't go away. And dammit, she didn't need this now. Not when she didn't have a clue what in the hell she was going to do next.

"Cynna?"

Delia's voice wafted through the cool air, and Cynna glanced in her direction, only to realize she was still standing in the middle of the courtyard making a fool of herself. Giving her head a mental shake, she told herself to snap out of it. "I—I need somewhere to stay."

Delia's expression softened. "You're always welcome with us, child. The coven has a house here in Kyrenia we use whenever one of us is visiting. Consider it yours. Call me selfish, but I'm hoping you'll decide to stay permanently."

Cynna wasn't ready to commit to anything just yet, but a place where no one could find her sounded just about perfect at the moment. "Thank you. I appreciate it. I—"

"Cynna."

The sound of Nick's voice drew Cynna around, and her eyes flew wide as she watched him stalk in her direction across the courtyard. How in Hades had he found her? How had he gotten through the gates? She hadn't even heard the damn things open. And why the hell was he here tormenting her?

She whipped back to Delia and wrapped her hand around the witch's wrist. "Take me there. Now."

"But—"

"Now." When Delia's gaze snapped to Nick, Cynna tightened her grip. "I don't want to talk to him."

Indecision crossed Delia's face. Behind Cynna, someone said, "Nick? Oh my gods, is that…?"

"Look, everyone, it's Nick!"

Voices drifted. Footsteps sounded. From the corner of her eye, Cynna saw a group suddenly swarming around Nick, slowing his pace. But his gaze was still locked on her, and though Cynna didn't know what the heck he wanted from her, she didn't care. She didn't want to hear any more about his soul mate or talk about what had happened to her family or rehash what was obviously finished between them. She just wanted a moment of peace.

"Please," she pleaded to Delia.

Delia's eyes darkened. Then she nodded once. "Yes."

Energy buzzed around Cynna as they flashed, and she felt herself flying. When she opened her eyes, she was standing on the porch of a two-story home that looked as if it had just been built.

"Come inside." Delia released Cynna's arm and pushed the front door open. "It's cold out here."

An entryway opened to a combo living-dining area. Stairs ran up to the second floor on the right, and a hallway led toward the back of the house. The room to her left was sparsely furnished with a couch, two side chairs, a fireplace, and an old wood dining table that looked like it sat at least six. There were no pictures hanging on the walls, no artwork, nothing to signify anyone lived here permanently.

Which was just fine with Cynna. She didn't need anyone's memories right now, including her own.

"Is it empty?" She moved into the living area and pressed her hand along the back of the soft brown couch. Exhaustion pulled at her, and she realized how tired she was after everything that had happened.

"Yes." Delia headed down the hallway that opened to a kitchen, breakfast nook, and another gathering room. "I was here wrapping up a few things and was planning to go back to the coven tonight. But if you're here, I might just stay. Are you hungry, child?"

Cynna's stomach growled at just the mention of food, and she tried to remember the last time she'd had a meal. She hadn't eaten that night she'd had dinner with Zagreus and Lykos. Hadn't eaten anything when she'd been running in the jungle with Nick because she'd been injured. Hadn't even looked for food at the colony. And then they'd come to Argolea and met Nick's soul mate and…

That pressure returned to her chest all over again, and she forced herself to breathe through the pain. She wasn't going to think about Nick and the queen. Wasn't going to think about anything.

Her stomach rumbled again, and she tugged off her jacket and laid it over a chair, then pushed her legs forward to follow Delia. "Yeah. I am. I—"

"Cynna."

Shock rippled through her once more, and she whipped around at the sound of the familiar voice. Nick stood in the middle of the living room, staring at her with those hard, determined amber eyes.

Hunger was washed away on a wave of heartbreak that had no place inside her and was followed by a quick burst of anger. "Godsdammit!"

"We're not done, female."

"Oh, we're way past done." He'd obviously used his newfound powers not only to track her and flash through solid walls, but to seriously piss her off. She pointed toward the door at his back. "Just go back to your soul mate and leave me the hell alone."

"Cynna?" Delia called. "For gods' sake, who are you yelling at? I can hear you a—"

Delia drew to a stop in the hallway, her gaze resting on Nick. Cynna had no idea if the witch could tell who—or what—he really was, but her guess was yes. As one of the eldest in the coven, Delia had the ability to see more than others.

A little of Cynna's anger ebbed. No way Delia would allow Krónos's son anywhere in her home. She had powers. Strong ones. Stronger than Nick's right now. She could banish him from the settlement and cast a spell to keep him out.

Cynna crossed her arms over her chest, feeling smug and, dammit, oddly depressed. Which was an asinine thing to feel for a man she'd tortured, abused, and who had no reason to want to be anywhere near her. Why the hell did she even care? His soul mate was—

"I suddenly remembered a meeting I'm due to attend," Delia announced. She turned toward Cynna and pulled her in for a quick hug. In Cynna's ear, she whispered, "You need to deal with this, child."

Cynna's mouth fell open. No. She had to have heard Delia wrong. She wasn't just going to leave her with this. "But—"

"I'll find you later." The witch released her, and in a flash she was gone, her powers strong enough for her to flash through walls, just like Nick.

"Cynna." Nick shot her a hard look. "We need to talk."

All that anger, humiliation, and betrayal Cynna had felt in the castle when she'd faced Isadora came raging back. She had to get out. Had to get away before she said or did something she'd regret. She moved around Nick and marched for the door. "The hell we do."

The lock flipped shut just as her hand closed around the door handle. Startled, she looked down, tried to unlock it, but the mechanism wouldn't budge. Temper flaring, she turned for the window. The shutters snapped closed with a deafening clack, darkening the room.

She whirled on Nick, that anger flaring to full-on fury. "Stop using your damn god powers and let me out."

"Not until you tell me what Isadora did to your family."

His calm, even tone was so infuriating, it was all she could take. "You want to know what she did?" she snapped. "Nothing. She did nothing."

"Then why—"

"She knew her father approved the Council's attack on this settlement. She sat back while hundreds—no, thousands—of people were slaughtered because they were different. There weren't just witches living here. There were all races, all types of people from all over the land who'd congregated here to avoid the Council's persecution. And she watched while the Council's soldiers not only murdered and raped, but razed this city to the ground. It might look different now. It might be rebuilt, but I remember. I remember my parents lying dead in the street. I remember the fires and the screams. I remember Delia grabbing me and making me run. I remember everything that your *soul mate* didn't do to stop the massacre."

His features softened, and he stepped toward her. "Cynna..."

She swatted his hand away before he could touch her and moved back. "No, don't."

Her skin was vibrating, her emotions raw and unguarded. And now that she'd spoken, she couldn't get the images out of her head. Images that were a thousand times worse than those she'd seen at his colony, because they'd been of her people. *Her* family. But though she hurt, she relished the pain because it fed the rage inside her. The rage that kept her focused and reminded her...revenge was the only thing that mattered.

"Cynna." His voice was calm—too calm—as he moved another step closer. "You don't know what it was like for her. The hold her father had on her. She couldn't have stopped it if she wanted to."

"Oh, that's bullshit." Cynna moved back another step. "She could have stopped it. She could have stepped in. She chose to sit back and do nothing while people suffered."

The way you sat back and watched Nick suffer?

A wave of heat washed over her, making her skin prickle. That was different, she told herself. What she'd done, she'd done for a reason. For restitution. For payback. For—

For your own personal gain. Just like her.

Her stomach tossed, and the air seemed to clog in her lungs. She wasn't like Isadora. She couldn't be. She—

"It was wrong," Nick whispered, his warm breath fanning her cheek, making her blink several times. Somehow she'd backed herself against the wall, and he now stood only inches away, one hand braced near her head, the fingers of his other hand running softly down her cheek to make her tremble. "What the king and the Council did to your people was wrong. But it wasn't her. She wasn't in power then. She was timid, shy, not at all like she is now. No one would ever have listened to her. If she'd known what was happening here, she wouldn't have been able to stop it."

A hot ball formed in Cynna's throat, one that made it hard to swallow. She glared up at him. "She's your soul mate. Of course you'd take her side."

Why was he standing so close? Why was he touching her? Why the hell was he even here when his soul mate was back at the castle, just waiting for him?

She shoved aside the jealousy and swiped his hand away. "Go back to her and leave me alone. I'm not the one you want, and we both know it."

She twisted to get away from him, but he caught her around the waist and pushed her back against the wall. "That's where you're wrong. I don't want her. I need you."

Cynna stilled and knew he had to be lying because...no one needed her. No one ever had.

"You're a fucking liar."

"It's not a lie." His arm tightened around her waist, and his body pressed fully into hers—his chest grazing her breasts, his thigh pushing between both of hers, his erection—oh gods, his heavenly, hard erection—nestling against her hip. "You keep me centered. You have from the start. How do you think I got through every sick thing Zagreus subjected me to? Because you were there. Because no matter what was happening to me, I could look at you and think about you, and not focus on the pain. If not for you, I'd have lost it long ago. Zagreus would control me, Krónos would be free, the gods would be at war, and the human world would be consumed by the apocalypse. You stopped it all from happening. You give me the strength to fight back."

Cynna's heart pounded hard, and her skin tingled with a heat she couldn't hold back. She braced her hands on his shoulders and tried to push him away, but he was an immovable force, and he wasn't letting her go. "You lie."

"Why would I lie? What do I get out of lying about this? I need you, Cynna, not her. I have for a long fucking time."

Her fingers curled into the fabric of his shirt, and her breaths came fast and shallow. But she was no longer sure if she was trying to push him away or pull him in closer. And her gift, the ability she'd always had to tell lie from truth, was screaming she was wrong. He believed what he was saying. Believed it as he believed nothing else.

She tried to be disgusted. Knew that was the logical reaction. But she wasn't. She was intrigued. And, dammit, incredibly excited. "That's...sick."

"Not to me. To me it's the only thing that feels right. *You're* the only thing that feels right."

His mouth was so close, his breath hot and minty, and everywhere he touched her, even through the fabric forming a barrier between them, her skin tingled. She needed to get away from him. Couldn't think when he was close like this. But the thought of letting him go back to *her*...

Her fingers tightened even more in his shirt, and she dragged him an inch closer. Electricity arced between them, like a firecracker about to explode. "I don't need you. I don't even want you."

"Now we both know who's lying," he whispered.

His head lowered to hers. She sucked in one breath and lifted to meet him. His lips parted at the first touch, and she licked into his mouth, their tongues tangling in a fiery kiss that rocketed through every cell. He pushed her harder into the wall while he devoured her mouth, while she devoured his right back. His erection stabbed into her belly. Desire roared in her veins. Wrapping her leg around his hip, desperate to feel the friction of his cock rubbing against her mound, she clawed at his shirt, needing skin. Needing heat. Needing him.

"Cynna…"

"Don't talk." She nipped at his bottom lip hard enough to make him wince. He drew his head back. She braced her hands against his chest and pushed hard. "Don't say a word."

He stumbled back a step and stared at her, his face flushed with arousal, his eyes as dark as she'd ever seen them. And somewhere in the back of her brain, a little voice screamed she needed to walk away, needed to run if she had any hope of saving herself. He might believe the things he'd said, might want her right now because of what had happened between them, but eventually, that soul mate bond would win out, and Cynna would end up heartbroken and alone.

But she didn't listen. She couldn't. Because every ounce of anger and longing and frustration and hurt was swirling inside her, making her see red, making her body tremble, making her want to prove to him—and maybe to her—that she was more real than his soul mate could ever be.

She threw her arms around his neck and kissed him hard. The weight of her body knocked him into the back of the couch, but he didn't miss a beat. His arms wrapped around her waist, dragging her in tight, and his mouth opened over hers. And then he was kissing her like he couldn't get enough, tasting her harder, deeper, making her wetter with every touch, making her forget everything but him.

His hands streaked down to the hem of her shirt, and he broke the kiss long enough to drag it up and over her head. She found his mouth again as he dropped it on the floor, then sucked in a breath when his tongue stroked over hers and his fingers flipped the clasp of her bra free. He tugged the garment from her arms, then closed his large, warm hand over her left breast and squeezed.

She groaned as electricity shot to her nipple, then raced to her core. It was wrong—wanting him like this after everything she'd done—but she couldn't stop the desire. Couldn't stop the hunger. Needed only this, here and now.

Her own hands slid down his torso and found the hem of his shirt. She pulled away so she could wrench the garment from his body. Dropping the soft cotton on the ground, she let her gaze slide over him. Over the broad, strong muscles flexing beneath his rough skin. Over the dusting of fine blond hair covering his pecs. Over the scars in all shapes and sizes that proved he was more than Zagreus or Hades thought. He wasn't just a vessel of untapped power. He was a warrior. One she'd wanted from the first moments she'd laid eyes on him.

Memories bombarded her. The day Zagreus had pulled him into the torture chamber and presented Nick to her as if he were a gift. Watching from the upper level of the arena while he fought Zagreus's satyrs, being mesmerized by every ripple of muscle each time he moved. Standing still and unmoving as that nymph had dropped to her knees in front of him in his cell, ripped off his towel, and taken him deep into her mouth.

Her blood pumped hot. Her mouth grew dry. Her sex burned. She'd hated that moment with the nymph, not just because the female had been tormenting him, but because Cynna had wanted to be the one to taste him, to stroke him, to make him moan.

"Cynna." Nick's hand slid into her hair, and his fingers flexed against her scalp, drawing her face back toward his. She opened to his kiss, dragged her tongue along his, and trailed her hands down his torso until she found the snap on his jeans.

He groaned into her mouth, used his other hand to tip her chin up higher so he could taste her deeper. She flicked the snap on his pants free, slid the zipper down while he kissed her, then pushed the waistband over his hips.

His cock sprang free, and she wrapped her hand around the thick shaft. He was hard as steel beneath her fingers, hot in her palm, and while he continued to devour her mouth, she stroked him, base to tip, squeezed the head until he moaned, then drew the moisture from the tip down his length so she could do it again.

He let go of her chin, trailed his hand down her chest and pinched her nipple. And as electricity arced straight into her sex with the mixture of pleasure and pain, she moved closer, stroked him faster, lifted her chest so he could do it again. His teeth nipped at her bottom lip, then her jaw as his fingers rolled her nipple, and then his lips were pressing hot, wicked kisses along the soft skin behind her ear, his warm breath making every inch of her body shiver.

"Gods," he whispered. "Your hand feels so good. So much better than before."

Before…

She knew what he was remembering. When he'd been chained in his cell and she'd pleasured him with her hand. Except then— like now—what she'd really wanted to do that night was taste him. Drop to her knees like that nymph. Feel his length pulse against her tongue. Draw him so deep he'd never want anyone but her.

She might not have had the courage to do it then, but now there was nothing holding her back. Letting go, she braced her hands on his belly, then slid down to her knees. He sucked in a breath. His cock stood out strong and proud in front of her. Wrapping her fingers around his steely length once more, she drew him toward her lips and glanced up at his face.

Desire darkened his eyes, flushed his cheeks, made a vein in his temple stand out against his pale skin. Keeping her eyes locked on his, she leaned closer, opened her mouth, and traced the tip of her tongue all around the head of his cock.

A groan rumbled from his chest. His hands slid into her hair, his fingertips flexing against her scalp. She did it again, running her tongue along the vein on the underside, then finally closed her lips around his length and sucked.

"Holy fuck…"

He was so thick, she had to open wide to take him deep. Flicking her tongue against him, she drew him to the back of her mouth. He groaned and flexed, his hands tightening in her hair. Wrapping her hand around him for balance, she squeezed his ass, drew back with her mouth, then took him even deeper.

His cock hit the back of her throat, pulsed and swelled. She sucked hard, released, and did it again. He dropped his head back.

Every time she drew him in, he flexed and thrust forward until her eyes watered.

"So good," he groaned, driving into her mouth. His fingers tightened in her hair. "Swallow me."

Wanting to give him a pleasure his soul mate never could, she opened her throat and took all of him, fighting her gag reflex and breathing through her nose so he could slide in one more reaching inch.

"Oh fuck, yeah. Don't stop."

He was on the edge. She could feel the sexual energy radiating off him, could sense he was about to come. She dug her fingernails into his ass and swallowed again and again, milking him with her throat muscles, needing to take him over. His cock swelled in her mouth, growing even larger. He thrust harder. She held on tight as his climax slammed into him, and he burst in her mouth, groaning long and deep with every soul-shattering pulse.

She swallowed his release, drawing out his pleasure. Slowly, she eased back and swirled her tongue around the head of his cock. He twitched with the simple touch and slumped against the back of the couch. And as she felt his muscles relax, a smile played on her lips.

She'd done that to him. She'd brought him blinding pleasure. His soul mate might have a never-ending hold over him, but the female would never be able to make him weak the way Cynna could. Because she hadn't been trained in the erotic dark arts by the master of sex and depravity the way Cynna had.

Thoughts of Zagreus rolled through Cynna's mind, bringing a tightness to her stomach and dimming her desire. And as it did, she remembered the things the Prince of Darkness had made her do. The hours she'd spent still and silent, overseeing Nick's torture in his tunnels. The way she'd let those satyrs hurt him and the time she'd stood by and watched while those nymphs had tortured him sexually.

Her skin grew hot all over again, but this time not from arousal. This time from disgust. She didn't have any place here. Nick shouldn't want to be anywhere near her. She'd railed at him about how awful his soul mate was when the truth was…she was the monster, not Isadora. The things she'd done were a thousand times worse than what Isadora had or hadn't done, because, unlike the queen, Cynna was strong enough to put a stop to them and chose not to.

She pushed quickly to her feet, swiped a shaking hand over her face, and moved back three steps. The room swayed around her. The walls grew blurry. Glancing around, she searched for her shirt.

"Cynna."

She swallowed hard. Couldn't look at Nick again. She needed air. Needed to get out. Spotting her shirt on the floor, she lunged for it. "I...I have to go."

Her fingertips grazed the soft cotton, but before she could close her hand around the garment, it vanished.

Wide-eyed, she glanced up. Nick had pulled his pants up, but they were still unbuttoned, his chiseled abs and strong shoulders flexing in the dim light as he advanced on her. And the intense look in his amber eyes screamed he wasn't about to let her go.

Her heart jackknifed. Not because of his strength or what was still unharnessed inside him, but because she knew right then that she *had* fallen for him. And if she didn't run now, he'd hurt her worse than Zagreus ever could.

She backed up until she hit the wall and dug her fingers into the plaster. "L-let me go. Just...let me go."

He closed in at her front. Danger. Sex. Heat. Lust. Everything she wanted but knew she couldn't have.

"Not happening." He wrapped his arm around her waist, tugging her tight into the warmth of his body until she gasped, then lowered his mouth a breath from hers. "Because I haven't had enough of you yet. And because, deep down, you know you haven't had nearly enough either."

CHAPTER SEVENTEEN

Cynna's hands landed against Nick's bare chest, spreading electricity all across his skin. But her dark eyes were shadowed, doubtful, and the fear that had flickered in them when he'd looked down at her moments before was still there, raging as strong as ever.

He'd seen into her mind right then, wasn't sure how, but knew she'd had a flash of Zagreus. Of the things she'd let the god do to her. Of the things she'd done for him. Of the countless times she'd stood back while his minions had tortured Nick, physically and sexually. And they were all swirling in her head now, tormenting her, making her want to run, making her think he couldn't possibly want her.

But he did. His cock swelled, proving he wanted her now more than ever. Yeah, it might be sick. And yeah, the things he was seeing should turn him off. But they didn't. Because even though part of him wanted to slam his fist into the god's face for the things he'd put her through, another part loved the fact she was excited by the same dark and twisted things Nick had always craved.

The shadow energy inside hummed with approval. He lowered his mouth to hers, took her lips in a bruising kiss. She gasped but opened at the first touch and slid her tongue along his. Pushing his erection into her belly, he closed his hand around her breast and squeezed until she moaned.

He released her mouth, lowered his head, and drew her breast to his lips. Her body trembled. Her fingers sifted into his hair. She didn't speak, but she didn't try to push him away either, and he grew even harder as she pressed her chest out as if in offering, as he laved his tongue over her nipple, as she sucked in a breath and held it while he scraped his teeth over the tip in a way he knew had to hurt but made her groan deep in her throat.

He needed to make her forget about Zagreus and focus on him. Lifting his head, he closed his lips over hers and kissed her hard again. She answered by licking into his mouth and gripping the nape of his neck until pain shot down his spine. Wrapping his arms around her, he lifted her off the floor, crossed to the table, kicked the chair out of the way, and laid her out on the solid wood.

He pictured her naked, as she'd been in his tunnels, while he leaned over and tormented her nipples with his tongue once more. And seconds later, the rest of her clothes disappeared, as if he'd willed them all away.

Cynna's eyes flew open. She pushed against his shoulders and looked down her naked body with surprise, then glanced up at him. "How did you do that?"

A slow, wicked smile pulled at his lips. "I don't know. But I like it."

Her shock slowly gave way to a rolling, heated lust that darkened her eyes. He captured her mouth once more. Her fingers slid along his nape, pulling his head more firmly down to hers, and as her lips opened to his, so did her legs, making room for him between her thighs, making him lightheaded from the raging need pumping off her in hot, rolling waves.

Yes, she wanted to run, but even she couldn't deny this connection between them anymore. And he wasn't about to let go of the only thing in his life that felt right.

His cock throbbed inside his jeans, and the need to take her, to fuck her hard and fast grew so strong, it messed with his resolve. But he wanted her to know the things she'd done in her past didn't bother him. Needed her to believe that she excited him. Every part.

He pulled back from her mouth, eased away from her body, and gripped her hips, flipping her easily to her stomach. She grunted as her belly and hands hit the table, then groaned when he kicked her legs apart and pressed against her ass.

He rolled his hips against her, letting her feel how hard he was. How hard *she* made him. She moaned and dropped her forehead against the table. Bracing a hand on the solid wood, he wrapped his arm around her waist, drawing her back and up against his chest, then breathed hot against her neck and nipped at her earlobe until she trembled.

"We're alike, you and I," he whispered against her ear. "We have the same dark desires. The same depraved needs. I know why you were with Zagreus. Not just because you wanted revenge, but because danger turns you on. The way it turns me on. Every time I saw you in that prison, I was hard. Even when I knew there would be pain." He rubbed against her ass again. "I was hard just like this."

Her eyelids dropped. "Don't tell me that."

"Why not?" He let go of the table, reached around, and pinched her nipple. She jerked, then groaned and dropped her head back against his neck, pushing her chest out once more, enticing him to do it again. "Because it scares you? Or because it excites you? Tell me, Cynna. That night you came to my cell and stroked me with your hand. When you knew someone could be watching and that I might retaliate. Tell me...were you wet?"

She swallowed hard and tensed in his arms.

"I bet you were," he whispered, trailing his hand from her breast over the arm holding her tight against him, then down her lower belly. "I bet you were as wet then as you are now."

His fingers slid into the thatch of curls at the apex of her thighs, then lower, between her swollen flesh. And the second he felt her slick honey coating his fingers, he groaned and pressed his cock against her ass all over again. "*Fuck*, female. You're dripping."

He trailed his fingers lower, across the opening of her pussy, then up to circle her clit. She moaned, gripped his forearm, and trembled against him.

He flicked her clit again. "You like it rough and dirty, don't you, Cynna?" His fingers slid lower, and he pressed one thick digit deep inside her. "The same way I do. Say it."

"Nick..." She flexed her hips, forcing him deeper.

He pumped into her body and rubbed his thumb over her clit again and again. "Say it, and I'll give you exactly what you need. No more teasing."

She groaned, turned her face into his neck. Her hot breath washed over his skin as she pushed her hips forward and back, seeking more friction, making his cock ache and his balls vibrate with his own need for release.

He drew his finger out and pressed back into her tight depths with two, rubbing that special spot he knew she wouldn't be able to resist. "Say it, Cynna."

"Oh gods." Her back bowed. She reached one arm up, wrapped it around his neck, and lifted her mouth to his.

Their lips met, their tongues tangled. She was slick and wet and tight around his fingers, hot and wild and wicked in his mouth. Everything he needed. The only thing he wanted.

"Say it, Cynna," he whispered, easing back from her mouth and thrusting deeper with his fingers. "Say you like all the wanton, sinful things I do."

"I do," she whispered, bucking against him. "I like them all."

Victory flared in his veins. He released her, pushed her forward over the table, and kicked her legs wide again. Her hands slapped against the solid surface, and she gasped in surprise, then moaned and pushed back, searching for him, telling him, oh yeah, she'd love every naughty little thing he wanted to do to her.

He pushed his pants down and pulled her hips back to the edge of the table. Fisting his aching cock, he bent his knees, then rubbed the head all along her steamy center.

She groaned and pressed her forehead against the table.

Reaching for her right hand, he pulled it to the small of her back and pinned it between their bodies. Then he leaned forward, breathed hot against her neck, and nipped at her earlobe. "I'm gonna fuck you. Just like this. So you can't move. So all you can feel is me, taking you deep, again and again. Do you want that?"

"Yes." She arched her back, rubbing the heat of her sex against his already straining cock. "*Skata*, I want it. Take me, Nick."

He gripped her wrist tight against her lower back, leaned away, and watched as he pushed in slow, feeling her tight sheath stretch around his cock. His body trembled. Sweat gathered along his spine as he fought from shoving in hard and fast. Her guttural moan rang in his ears as he wrapped his free hand around her hip, as he drew out slightly, then pressed in farther, sliding as deep as he could reach.

"Oh fuck," she gasped as he bottomed out. He held still, letting her adjust to this new depth, to his cock stretching her so wide, all the while loving the way she trembled and wiggled back against him, as if she couldn't wait for him to move. "Nick."

"You want more?"

"Yes, dammit." She turned her head so her cheek pressed into the table, then slapped her free hand against the hard wood. "Fuck me. Hard."

That dark energy inside leapt with excitement, and he couldn't hold it back anymore, didn't want to. He drew almost all the way out, then drove back in, as hard as she'd asked. She cried out, the sound a mix of pleasure and pain, and arched her back, encouraging him to do it again. Dragging his cock along her slick walls, he watched her face as he plunged deep again and again, as lust glazed her eyes, as her pussy grew hotter and wetter around him. Her moans turned to fevered cries of carnal need that echoed in his ears and pushed his hunger for her even higher.

Letting go of her arm, he grabbed her hips and jerked her body back into his, fucking into her harder and faster, the way he'd wanted since the first moment he'd met her. "Tell me you love this," he growled. "Tell me you love fucking me as much as I love fucking you."

"I do." Her fingers curled against the table. "Don't stop. Don't you dare stop."

He didn't think he could. He shoved deep, needing to get farther inside her, needing her to feel him everywhere. She pushed up on her hands and arched her back, taking him in even more. Pleasure raced down his spine. His orgasm was dangerously close. Wrapping his arm around her thigh, he slid his fingers along her steaming wet heat and found her clit, needing to feel her explode before he went over. She groaned as he flicked the taut bundle of nerves again and again. Closed her eyes. Arched even more.

She excited him, amazed him, aroused him in ways he never expected. Every sound she made, every time she trembled, every ripple of pleasure that rocked her body... It all made him hotter, higher, made him feel so fucking alive. "Come all over my cock, Cynna. Fuck back into me. Mm, yes. I need to feel you come all around me. I need it right now. Give it to me, baby."

She rocked back again and again, taking him deeper, squeezing him tighter. And just about the time he thought he wasn't going to be able to hold out any longer, she threw her head back and cried out. Her body shook, and her sex pulsed and rippled around him with the force of her orgasm. And knowing she was coming, knowing he was giving her exactly what she needed made his own orgasm shoot down his spine, detonate in his balls, and rocket through every cell in his body.

Pleasure arced through every limb, raced along his nerve endings, and exploded behind his eyes in a flash of heat and light. Her pussy continued to clench around his cock as his orgasm went on, milking him of every last drop of erotic bliss. When it finally ebbed, he realized he was breathing hard, his body was covered in a layer of sweat, and he was lying across Cynna's back, pressing her into the hard table.

He pushed up on one hand and looked down at her. Her cheek rested against the surface of the table, damp hair stuck to her temple, and her eyes were closed. But the Cheshire cat grin tugging at the corners of her mouth told him loud and clear that she'd enjoyed that. Every single moment.

Gently, he drew back, pulled free of her body, and tugged up his pants. She cringed as his sticky skin separated from hers.

"Oh my gods," she muttered. "I can't move. I think you broke me."

He chuckled. Couldn't remember the last time he'd felt like laughing. Rolling her to her back, he tugged on her limp arms until she sat up. Her eyes popped open. Her brow furrowed as she focused on him. Before she could think up another excuse why she needed to leave, he pushed his way between her legs, wrapped his arms around her slim waist, then lifted her from the table and carried her toward the couch.

Her warm palms landed on his shoulders. "Nick—"

"Don't fight me right now." He sat on the couch and leaned back into the cushions so she was draped over him. Then he reached up, pressed her face into the hollow between his shoulder and throat, and tightened his other arm around her back. "Just let me hold you for a few minutes."

"*Skata*," she whispered against his throat. "Don't do that."

"Don't do what?"

"Don't be all…sweet."

He guessed no one had ever been sweet to her. Maybe her parents, but they'd been gone so long, she probably barely remembered what it was like to have someone care.

He ran his hand down her dark hair, loving the soft texture, loving the way she sank into him and felt so right. Closing his eyes, he breathed in her intoxicating jasmine scent mixed with the heady aroma of their sex, and relaxed even more.

He needed this. Her, keeping him centered, giving him something real to focus on. When he was with her, he could push everything else to the back of his mind—what his father wanted from him, what was wrong with his soul mate, what had happened to his people. When he was with her, he felt grounded. In a way he never had before.

He trailed his fingers down the soft, delicate length of her spine, then back up again. And as he did, he remembered the marks on her caramel skin, which brought back a wave of those memories he'd caught in her mind only moments before.

"I don't care what you did with Zagreus."

Her breaths stilled against his neck.

"I mean," he went on, "I hate the things he made you do that you didn't enjoy, but I don't hate that you did them. I can't. Because I don't want some virginal little princess."

Slowly, she drew back and looked at him, confusion drawing her brows together to form a sexy little crease right between her eyes. "You don't?"

"I never did. I can't stop the soul mate draw, but that doesn't mean I like it. Or that I'm excited by it. I'm not. What excites me is that." He nodded toward the table where they'd just fucked each other blind. "What gets me hot is this." He slid his hand down her back and squeezed her firm ass. "And now that I've seen those visions in your head, all I can think about is tying you up and doing them to you myself…my way."

"Oh gods." Her eyes dropped closed, and she pressed her forehead against his shoulder. "You saw that? *Skata*. I don't like these new gifts you're getting."

He wasn't inclined to agree. Some of them, like the ability to make her clothes disappear just by imagining her naked, were pretty damn cool.

"I wasn't trying to pry. But you were projecting pretty forcefully. I couldn't stop myself from looking."

She groaned and pressed her forehead harder against his shoulder.

He ran his hand down her hair. "Don't worry. I've already pushed your former boss out of these naughty little visions. But I can't stop thinking about you wrapped all in rope, tied down with your legs spread, your skin flushed and covered in a thin layer of sweat as you wait to see what will happen next."

She groaned again, and he smiled because even though he heard the mortification in her voice, her body was growing warmer against him, telling him she really did love all the same dirty little games he did.

His hand slid beneath her hair to massage the nape of her neck. "I guarantee with me, Cynna, you'll enjoy every single thing I do. I love making you come harder than you ever have before. But most of all I love that my appetites arouse you, because they were part of me long before Hades and Zagreus got their hands on me."

"This is so fucked up. You and me. It makes no sense."

He closed his eyes and breathed her in, feeling calmer with every passing second. "Yeah, maybe. But it also feels right. And at the moment, I need as much right in my life as I can get."

She turned her face into his neck and exhaled a long breath. And as he held her and the seconds ticked by on a clock somewhere in the house, he knew he couldn't let her go. Not just because she soothed him, but because he didn't want anything to happen to her. She'd risked her life to save him from Zagreus. He needed to make sure no one else—the Prince of Darkness included—ever hurt her again. The key was getting her to trust him enough so she wouldn't run. And he could think of only one way to get her to do that.

"The scars on my back," he said softly. "You asked me where I got them. I got them here."

Her hand stilled its gentle rubbing over his collarbone. "Here?"

This wasn't anything he'd ever told anyone before, and he didn't like revisiting the past, but if it would convince her he was trustworthy, then he figured it was worth laying himself bare.

"My mother was a demigod. A warrior as tough as the Argonauts."

"Atalanta?"

"Yeah." She'd obviously heard stories about his legendary mother. "She was pissed when she wasn't chosen to serve with the Argonauts. Made a pact with Hades for immortality and revenge. But she was foolish and didn't consider the fact the god would double-cross her. She became immortal, like she wanted, but found herself confined to the Underworld serving Hades himself."

"I know this story. Delia and the others used to tell it to the young of our settlement to warn against the follies of making deals with gods." She huffed and shifted on his lap. "I clearly didn't listen."

A little of his anxiety eased. If she hadn't made that deal with Zagreus, he wouldn't be here with her now. In a sick sort of way, he was thankful she'd done that. Not that he wanted to think about thanking that son of a bitch too much right now, though.

"Yeah," he went on, pushing thoughts of Zagreus to the back of his mind. "She built her army of daemons in the Underworld, unleashed them on the human realm, targeting Misos and any Argoleans, and plotted her revenge against the Argonauts. But it didn't take her long to tire of her prison. There was only one way for her to escape. A loophole Hades put into the contract. A prophecy that stated that when two marked individuals—one human, one Argolean—were joined, it would create the perfect being, and she would be freed. Her daemons searched for the two for years in her attempt to bring them together but continued to fail. So, in a desperate bid to complete the prophecy herself, she sought out Krónos in Tartarus and made him yet another deal. She promised him that when she was eventually freed, she would then turn around and free him from his chains. All he had to do was help her create her own two 'perfect halves.'"

"I know this as well. That's how you and your brother were born. Krónos made her mortal long enough to impregnate her, then tricked an Argonaut into venturing into the highest depths of the Underworld where she, back in her immortal form, was waiting to seduce him. She was again impregnated, thus creating twins with different fathers. Superfecundation."

He glanced down at her face resting against his shoulder. "That's some story the witches shared with the young of your village."

Her eyes tipped up, and her cheeks turned a soft shade of pink as she smoothed her hand over his chest. "That part Zagreus explained to me."

Of course. Zagreus. He looked down at the coffee table and forced himself to go on. "Imagine Atalanta's outrage when Demetrius and I were born and still weren't enough to complete the prophecy."

"I imagine she was pretty pissed."

"Livid is an understatement. But she quickly adapted." He held up his forearm so she could see the ancient Greek text that ran down his arms to intertwine his fingers. "Since we both bore the Argonaut markings, she decided to use us to infiltrate the guardians, knowing her dark link to us would be enough to influence our souls. Only she didn't plan for the Argolean Council to get in the way."

Cynna pushed back and looked up at him. "What does the Council have to do with you?"

"Argonauts have fathered children with females other than their soul mates for thousands of years. Rarely does one appear with the markings, but every Argonaut is duty bound to raise any offspring marked by the gods. Atalanta knew this, so after we were born, she sent us to Argolea. Demetrius's markings were unique to his father's line. Mine were less conclusive. As we were twins, his father was required to take us both in, but he knew from the start that I was different. And he despised me for it. He was a mean son of a bitch. Had a wicked temper. If you ever wondered why Demetrius is so sullen a lot of the time, I can tell you it's not because Atalanta was his mother. It's because of that bastard."

"What happened?" Cynna asked, her brow drawn low, her gaze holding Nick's as she straddled his lap.

"Nothing, really. He basically steered clear of me. Took his frustrations out on Demetrius whenever he felt like it. That caused a lot of tension between me and my brother at a very early age. Demetrius thought I was the favored son. The older we got, the darker his mood became. It was wrong of me to sit back and do nothing to help him, but I was just a kid, and at the time, I was thankful his father wasn't pounding on me the way he was pounding on him."

"No one could blame you for that," she said softly.

Nick huffed, thinking about the brother he'd never seen eye to eye with. "Demetrius did. In a lot of ways, that animosity is at the root of our differences. Anyway, what he failed to see were the times his father would get this look in his eye and start to come after me, then change his mind and quickly turn away. I didn't understand what that was about for a long time. Truthfully, I don't think I really understood until I discovered Krónos was my real father. But he knew. Demetrius's father was part witch. He sensed the power inside me, just as Delia did, and it scared him shitless.

That's why, when I was about ten, he finally turned me over to the Council to be cleansed."

"S*kata*," Cynna whispered, her gaze flicking over his bare shoulders. "The cleansing ritual."

"Yep." Being Argolean, she clearly knew what that entailed. A ritualistic whipping to banish sin from the body. The Argolean Council's greatest gift to its people. "Usually reserved for unfaithful females but in this case inflicted on a ten-year-old boy who had no clue what he'd done wrong." He pointed at the jagged scar on the side of his face. "I moved when I wasn't supposed to."

"Oh, Nick." Pity filled her eyes. A pity he didn't need or want.

His jaw hardened. "I'm not telling you this so you'll feel sorry for me. I'm telling you so you'll understand why I hate this place as much as you. When the cleansing ritual didn't work, the Council grew scared. Someone with dormant gifts like mine, living in this land? That would forever be a challenge to their power. They wanted to kill me but didn't know my true lineage and were afraid doing so might cause some kind of retaliation from the gods. So they banished me instead. Sent a ten-year-old boy off to fend for himself in the wilds of the human world. If I died on my own, well then, that wasn't their problem, was it? But I didn't die. I learned how to survive, how to hunt, how to protect myself. And when I came across other refugees, other Argoleans who'd been banished or who'd chosen to leave this so-called utopia on their own, I taught them and their children how to survive too."

"Gods." She relaxed back into him, laying her head on his shoulder, resting her hand on his chest, right over his heart. "That's terrible. They're monsters. Every last one of them."

He brushed his hand down her naked spine, feeling pretty much the same way about the Council himself, hating that she knew and understood. "My given name is Nikomedes. I know you've heard others call me Niko. I don't usually answer to it because all it does is remind me of the Council and my days here."

"Nikomedes," she whispered. "Victory of the people." She pushed up and looked him in the eyes again. "You have a great name, Nick. One with depth of meaning. The Council knew that even when you were a boy. Look at you now. You're here. Look at your people. They live."

He still wasn't sure how that had happened, but he knew they weren't alive because of him. He'd been shocked when he'd seen so many familiar faces in the settlement when he'd gone after Cynna, then utterly thankful they'd been there. But his need to get to Cynna had been so strong, he'd barely spared them a glance. And that need now to keep her with him was even stronger, pushing aside every other thought, even those for the people she foolishly thought he'd saved.

He leaned forward and framed her face with his hands. "I need you, Cynna."

Her hands rested on his marked forearms, and her eyes softened, so much so he felt her gaze boring deep into his soul. "I'm right here."

Urgency pushed at him. Only this urgency suddenly wasn't linked to some crazy debt to protect her. It was centered solely on the fact she was the first person in forever who'd come to matter to him. "No. Not just this. I need you to stay in Argolea. And to come back to the castle with me, tonight."

The softness rushed from her eyes. Her body stiffened, and she tried to pull away, but he held her firmly, not letting her go.

"I heard everything you said about Isadora," he went on. "And I know you don't want to be near her. But I have to go back. And you…you keep me centered. In a way nothing else ever has. I need you with me so I don't lose it like I almost did at the colony. I don't want to go back. Just the thought of doing so turns my stomach. I don't want to be near any of them. I just want to be with you. But I promised my brother I'd give him and the others a few days to try to figure out what's going on with the whole stupid soul mate curse, and, well…"

The words died on his lips, and doubt pressed in as he glanced down at the couch beside them, making his hands sweat and his pulse race. Shit, how could he explain this? Why would she even agree after everything she'd lived through?

"And because you can't leave," she finished for him.

Surprise rippled through him. He looked back into her deep brown eyes, searching for something to say. For some kind of answer that made sense. But came up empty.

Gently, she tugged his hands from her face and lowered them against her thighs. "Answer one question for me. Are you in love with her?"

"No."

"Not at all?"

He hesitated. Tried to decide how to answer. "I feel a pull that keeps me connected to her, but I don't think it's love. It's...duty." Something he'd always fucking hated. Now more than ever.

She didn't respond, but her eyes searched his, and he knew she was looking for the truth. He just hoped she couldn't see what he'd omitted. That though he didn't love Isadora *now*, the soul mate curse kept the possibility open. All it would take was one simple little act.

"Okay," she finally said in a soft voice. "I'll go back with you."

Air filled his lungs, and he reached for her, sliding his arms around her slim back, dragging her close to the heat of his body. "You will?"

She braced her hands on his shoulders. "It makes me certifiable, but yeah. I will." When he leaned forward to kiss her, she stopped him by pushing her index finger against his lips. "On one condition."

"Anything."

"You keep her away from me. I'll go back for you. As long as I can handle it. But not for her. Never for her. And if at any time it's too much for me, I'm out of there. No questions asked."

"Done."

"Done?"

She obviously hadn't expected him to capitulate so quickly. But he didn't care. Because as long as she was with him, he felt like he could handle anything.

He pressed his mouth to hers, then shifted and laid her out on the couch beneath him. "Almost done." He kissed his way across her jaw to her ear, reached for her hands, and pinned them to the cushions above her head, loving the way she shivered in anticipation. "First, I need to make you come again."

A slow, sexy smile spread across her gorgeous face, and her legs fell open, giving him full access to any and every part of her. "How will you do that?"

He held her wrists still with one hand and slid the other between her legs to find her already wet and swollen. Then he groaned and, with a wicked grin, lowered his mouth to hers. "Any and every way I want, female."

CHAPTER EIGHTEEN

Cynna kicked the covers off her bare leg and breathed deep as she stared up at the dark-paneled ceiling.

She was hot, agitated, and she couldn't sleep. Not here. Not in this place. Gods almighty, she never should have agreed to this insanity.

Nick lay on his side beside her, softly snoring, the intoxicating scent of his skin and his alluring body heat drifting across the monstrous mattress to slide along her overheated flesh. She glanced at him in the spacious suite. Moonlight shone in through the arching windows, highlighting his square jawline covered in a thin layer of scruff and the jagged scar on his cheek he'd gotten during that horrific cleansing ritual.

His eyes were closed, his dark-blond hair mussed on the pillow, his muscular chest bare in the dim light and his jeans riding low on his lean hips. He was the picture of sex and sin and salvation, and though she wanted nothing more than to roll him to his back, climb over him, and do to him what he'd done to her on that couch at Delia's house, she couldn't. Not just because she knew he deserved a moment of rest, but because with every second she stayed in this castle, her anxiety inched up and the desire to claw her skin off grew that much stronger.

Sighing, she looked back up at the ceiling. After getting her situated in this room—this massive, fancy, way too expensive suite—he'd rustled up some dinner for them to share, then disappeared to do she didn't know what. She'd assumed he'd gone to talk to the queen, or maybe the Argonauts, but she hadn't wanted to ask. Not just because it wasn't her business, but because that bandage he'd returned with, the one covering the bend in his right arm, indicated he'd gotten some kind of injection or given a blood draw. And knowing the people here were messing with him physically was too much of a reminder of what Zagreus had done to him. It was also an in-your-face red flag that this whole soul mate thing was way more involved than Cynna had first assumed.

Skata. She pressed her fingers against her closed eyelids and breathed deep. She was in over her fucking head. Way past the point of reason. She'd let good—no, really hot, mind-numbing— sex color her thinking and derail her common sense. Forget about the fact she couldn't stomach being anywhere near Isadora. Every second she stayed with Nick pushed her that much closer to falling head over heels in love with the male. And though he'd said he needed only her, she knew in the center of her chest the kind of need he was talking about wasn't love. It never would be. Not when a part of him would always belong to his soul mate.

Fuck it. She tossed the covers back and carefully slid from the bed. Finding her jeans, she pulled them on, then spotted her boots and the lightweight jacket she'd tossed over a chair earlier. When he'd come back from doing gods knows what, Cynna had already been under the covers, pretending to sleep. If he'd used his god powers and figured out she was faking it, he hadn't said. He'd simply gone to take a shower, come back, and climbed in next to her. Then fallen asleep while she lay there, continuing to suffer.

Well, she was done suffering. She couldn't help him anymore. She'd been stupid to think she ever could. Crossing the floor as quietly as she could, she told herself not to look back. But her chest grew tight as she pulled the door closed softly behind her, and a lump she couldn't quite swallow took up space in her throat as she headed down the long corridor searching for the ornate staircase she'd walked up earlier.

Columns flanked the hallway. A thick, expensive carpet ran the length of the wide corridor, and closed double doors led to other rooms...probably other bedroom suites. Though she knew they were in the same wing as before, they were several floors up, and she couldn't help but wonder who was sleeping on the other side of these doors, past these walls. Was the queen's room somewhere close? Or did she have an entire floor all to herself?

Skata. Stop worrying about her and just get the hell out of here.

She passed three arches that opened to some kind of common living area. Just as she went by the last column, a sound drew her feet to a stop. A voice of some kind.

She peered into the dimly lit room. Several couches were arranged in front of a dark fireplace, and one lamp near the black windows was illuminated, but she couldn't see anyone. The room looked empty and quiet. Just when she was sure she'd imagined the sound and was about to leave, a gurgle drifted to her ears. Almost…a coo.

Brow lowered, she stepped farther into the room and came to a stop when she spotted the baby wearing pink footie pajamas, lying face-up on a blanket spread out in the middle of the carpet.

The baby spotted Cynna and cooed again, then kicked her legs in the air several times as if she were excited, reached for her feet, and grabbed both with her chubby little hands.

Apprehension slid through Cynna. She looked right and left, searching for the owner or parent or whatever you called the person who took care of a baby like this, but the room was completely empty.

The baby continued to stare at Cynna, cooed louder and swatted her arms and legs in the air faster. Then she opened her mouth and blew a raspberry that echoed all through the hall.

Cynna stepped closer until she was standing over the blanket. She didn't like kids. Didn't like babies, especially. They were loud and messy and so demanding.

"What are you doing out here all alone?" she said aloud. The baby didn't answer—of course she couldn't answer—but for some strange reason, that didn't stop Cynna from asking.

The baby kicked her legs and blew another raspberry. Then stretched her arms up as if reaching for Cynna.

Slowly, Cynna lowered to her knees. "Who leaves a baby all alone, anyway?" Reaching out, she touched the back of the baby's hand. Her skin was velvety soft. The softest thing Cynna was sure she'd ever felt. A jolt of awareness rushed through her. "Did someone forget about you?"

The baby wrapped her little hand around Cynna's finger and squeezed tight. For a tiny thing, she had an incredibly strong grip. And the way she held on made Cynna think she didn't want to be left alone again.

"Aw, you poor thing. I bet you're scared." She pulled her finger from the baby's fist, leaned forward, then slid one hand under the baby's neck and the other under her back. Lifting her from the floor, she sat back on her heels and looked down at the little bundle in her arms.

She couldn't be more than six or seven months old. Her hair was jet black, thick, and already curling past her ears, and her skin was like alabaster—shades lighter than Cynna's flesh. But what slowed Cynna's pulse were the baby's eyes. Irises like warm chocolate with flecks of black and gold. Eyes that were eerily similar to the ones Cynna saw in the mirror every day.

Footsteps sounded somewhere close, but Cynna was so entranced, she didn't have a chance to set the baby back down before a voice said, "Oh. I didn't know anyone else was awake."

Slowly she looked to her right. To where Isadora stood with one hand against an open door that looked like it led to a small kitchen, holding a bottle in the other.

Cynna's heart rate kicked up, and her face grew hot. Quickly, she looked away, laid the baby back down on the blanket, but didn't push to her feet and run. Which was weird, because…she didn't want to be anywhere near this female.

The baby kicked out her little legs and blew another raspberry. Then reached for Cynna's hand again. And she didn't know why, but Cynna gave the baby her index finger and let the infant close her fist around the digit.

"Let me guess," Isadora said, her bare feet crossing the floor to stop next to Cynna near the blanket. "You couldn't stop yourself from picking her up."

"Um." Cynna ran her free hand down the thigh of her jeans, not sure how to respond because…yeah, that was exactly how she felt. And why the hell wasn't she splitting *right this very moment?*

"Don't worry, you're not the first." Isadora sighed. "People gravitate toward Elysia, even those who don't like babies. I've suspected for a while that she has the gift of psychokinesis, but I haven't had the heart to tell her father that she's not just cute, she's a master manipulator. He thinks she can do no wrong." She knelt on the floor beside Cynna and held out the bottle. "Here. Something tells me she wants you to do this, not me."

The baby squeezed Cynna's hand tight, and before Cynna could say no, her own fingers were reaching for the bottle. Elysia gurgled a happy, excited sound.

Isadora leaned forward, scooped Elysia into her arms, then handed her to Cynna. "Tip her up just a little."

Cynna felt more awkward than she had in her whole life, but she sat back cross-legged, cradled Elysia in the crook of her arm, then held the bottle to her lips. Not missing a beat, Elysia grabbed the bottle with both hands and started noisily sucking down the milk as if a total stranger feeding her was no big deal.

"She likes you." Isadora rested her hands on her thighs. "She only lets a few people feed her. I'm hoping that's a good sign."

Somewhere in the back of Cynna's mind, she knew they made a bizarre scene and that she needed to get up and leave, but she couldn't seem to make her body obey her mind's commands. Watching as the baby drained a quarter of the bottle, she found herself amazed at the way Elysia's little lips moved and her tiny fingers gripped the bottle so fiercely.

"Nick said you helped him escape from Zagreus's lair."

The sound of Isadora's voice seemed to snap Cynna from whatever trance the baby was putting her in, and she glanced toward the queen. Isadora's white-blonde hair was rumpled, dark circles bruised the skin beneath her bottom lashes, and her light-blue pajama set looked a full size too big. But it was her eyes Cynna focused on. The same eyes Elysia shared. The same ones Cynna knew so well.

The awe and calmness she'd felt earlier, when she'd picked up the baby, trickled away, bringing back that agitation that had pushed her out of Nick's bed. "Yeah, I did. Do you have a problem with that?"

"No. No problem. In fact, I want to thank you. For bringing him back to us."

Cynna looked back down at the baby, hating the little wedge of jealousy pushing its way between her ribs. "It's my understanding *here* isn't somewhere he especially likes to be."

"No." Isadora's gaze drifted to Elysia as well. "No, it's not. I meant here to his family."

"I thought his people were his family."

"They are. But so are we. More his family than anyone else. And we protect those we care about. Fiercely."

There was a warning laced in with that declaration. One that set the hairs on the nape of Cynna's neck to attention. "I'm pretty sure Nick's capable of taking care of himself."

"I'm sure he is. But after everything he's been through, I think it's safe to say his...judgment...might be a little skewed. I just wouldn't want to see him put his trust in the wrong person, especially now when he's dealing with so many changes."

Anger and disbelief pushed their way into Cynna's chest, mingling with that jealousy that was now a raging hurricane inside. This female didn't know the first thing about her. Didn't know why she was here or what she'd done in her past. All she knew was that Cynna had helped Nick escape from Zagreus. And yet she was sitting here, making judgments about *Cynna* being bad for Nick, when *she*, with her little sickness and soul mate issue, was continually tormenting him.

"Maybe you're the one whose judgment is skewed," she said before she could stop herself. "After all, I hear you're not feeling so hot."

"No, I'm not. But that doesn't change the fact that I care about Nick and don't want to see him hurt."

Cynna glanced sharply up. "Care about him or want to use him?"

Surprise spread over Isadora's already pale face, making her skin look even whiter. "Of course I care about him. He's my daughter's uncle."

Cynna narrowed her eyes and used her gift to search for the truth in Isadora's words. Yeah, the queen was being honest. She did care for Nick because he was her husband's brother and her child's uncle, but there was another reason too. One that Cynna's gift screamed was rooted in the soul mate curse. One this female would manipulate and use to her advantage to get what she wanted, even if it ultimately destroyed Nick.

Cynna's heart beat fast, and she looked back down at the baby in her arms, no longer seeing the adorable infant but Nick's future if she left him. He'd said she kept him centered. That when she was close, he could focus on her, forget about everyone else, forget about what they wanted from him, and fight the darkness from Krónos so he could stay in control. If she left now, he wouldn't be able to do that. He'd be pulled in a thousand different directions by a hundred different people, and this female would be at the forefront, preying on his weakness for her because of the soul mate curse, slowly tormenting him in a way even Zagreus had never been able to do.

Arms shaking, Cynna quickly handed the baby to the queen and pushed to her feet.

"Where are you going?" Isadora asked, looking up.

"Back to bed. I'm suddenly tired." And anxious to see Nick. To keep him balanced. *To keep him from you.*

Frown lines formed between Isadora's eyes as she jostled Elysia and righted the bottle. "I don't mean to pry, but you don't exactly seem comfortable here at the castle. Nick mentioned you have relatives at the settlement. Maybe—"

Oh no. This chick was not kicking her out of the castle. Not now. Not when Cynna had finally decided to stay. "I'll be fine."

Not that you ever worried about me. Not that you ever worry about anyone besides yourself.

Cynna fought back the anger and resentment, then turned before she said more and headed for the hall. Working for calm when she felt anything but, she muttered, "Good night."

"Good night, Cynna," Isadora said softly at her back. "I'm sure we'll see more of each other."

Suddenly, Cynna was sure they would too. And she hated that fact.

Heart pounding, she moved quickly back to Nick's suite, closed the door behind her, and scanned the darkness. He was still asleep on the gigantic bed, only he'd shifted to his back and was now lying with one hand over his chiseled bare chest, the other resting palm-up on the pillow near his head.

Her skin warmed. Her pulse turned to a roar in her ears. She wasn't leaving him to that…female. Wasn't about to let the queen prey on his emotions, his vulnerability, his goodness. She knew in the pit of her stomach that he wouldn't ever say no to his soul mate, but she could help him stay centered. She could be his distraction. And this time, her desire to help him had nothing to do with guilt for what she'd done while she'd been in Zagreus's lair. It had only to do with these feelings for him that were already rooted so deeply inside her.

She toed off her shoes and slowly climbed over him on the bed. Her knees brushed the outsides of his hips, and she braced her hands on the mattress on each side of his head. His soft brown eyelashes feathered the skin beneath his eyes, his thin masculine lips were slightly parted and, she knew, whisper soft. She let her gaze dance over him, over every freckle, every scar, every play of bone and angle of his features. And as she did, her heart took a hard, slow tumble in her chest.

He was right. Their being together might be wrong in every logical way, but it felt so incredibly right. And for now, that would be enough.

Carefully, she leaned down and brushed her lips against his. He didn't move. Didn't respond, so she did it again. Tipping her head to the other side, she kissed him once more. Softly. Gently. Just a feather of flesh against flesh, loving the sweetness of his lips, the heat of his body, that intoxicating lightheadedness she always felt when he was close. But he still didn't wake, and disappointment slowly slinked in.

Sighing, she lifted her head and was just about to ease away when he groaned, slid his hand up into her hair, then opened to her kiss and pulled her mouth back down to his.

Ecstasy. Danger. Perfection. The words tumbled in her mind as his tongue stroked hers and his other hand drifted to her hip, then slid across her lower spine. She sank into him as he kissed her, letting him explore every inch of her mouth, kissing him back with everything she had in her. His muscles flexed as his kiss grew needy, demanding, as he tasted her deeper, and she groaned when he rolled her over and pushed all his delicious heat against her, driving her back into the mattress.

Her legs fell open. Her hands wound around his shoulders and up into his hair. She fisted the silky soft strands between her fingers and kissed him again and again, not able to get enough, needing to wash Isadora and their conversation from her mind with his intoxicating mouth.

When she was breathless, when she was ready to tear his clothes off so she could have more, he drew back and looked down at her with those sexy amber eyes. The ones that had always entranced her. Even when he'd been nothing but her prisoner. "Hi."

Heat rushed to her cheeks. It was such a normal thing to say. But they'd never had any kind of normal. And she wasn't sure how to respond. "H-hi."

"You're wearing a lot more than you were a few hours ago."

Damn. She'd forgotten to take off her pants and jacket. "I am."

His eyes narrowed. Just a touch. Just enough to tell her he was on to her. "Should I ask?"

Ask about Isadora and what they'd discussed? Um. Hell, no. "I'm surprised you didn't just look into my mind to find out."

One corner of his lips tipped up. "It doesn't work that way. I can't read your mind. I can only see your memories...if you project them." His eyes narrowed even more. "Which you're not doing at the moment."

Thank the Fates. She rested her hands against his sexy, muscular shoulders. "You'll have to teach me how to keep from doing that on a regular basis."

"Something tells me you'll be a quick learner."

Her lips curled as she focused on a tiny scar near his collarbone.

But instead of kissing her again like she wanted, he stared at her. And in the silence, her cheeks grew even warmer.

"What?" she finally asked.

"Nothing." His eyes softened. "Just... Thank you. Again."

"For what?"

"For coming back."

Her chest squeezed so tight it pulled the air right out of her lungs. And in that moment, as she stared up at him, she knew she was in love with him. Crazy, head-over-heels in love with a man who would never truly be hers.

Don't think about that now. Don't—shit... Just focus on the moment.

She swallowed hard. Dammit. She was going to get her heart broken here. There was no way around it anymore. "Don't make me regret it."

He reached for the hem of her shirt and pushed it up to her breasts, his rough fingers grazing the skin near her belly button, sending shivers of excitement straight into her sex. "Trust me, female. You won't. I promise."

She closed her eyes and fought back the sting of tears as he pressed his wicked, talented lips against her belly. And though she prayed with every ounce of her soul that he was right, her gift screamed he was telling the biggest lie of all.

CHAPTER NINETEEN

Nick felt better than he had in days. No, weeks. No…months.

He was rested. Focused. Invigorated. And he knew it was all because of Cynna and the fact she'd come back to him last night when she could have so easily run and left him for good.

He'd wanted to ask what had changed her mind, but didn't. Yeah, it was crazy. Yeah, it made no sense. But he trusted her. And he was so freakin' thankful that she'd returned to him, he didn't want to do anything to scare her off.

The halls were quiet as he made his way to the ground floor and headed for the main kitchen at the back of the castle. He'd left Cynna sleeping. After he'd thanked her with his hands and mouth and body, she'd curled into him and fallen asleep. He'd held her like that most of the night, loving the way she twined her leg between his, loving the weight of her hand against his chest, loving her heat seeping in to warm the cold places left inside him. It wasn't like him to want to snuggle, but with her he found he couldn't get enough. Because she didn't want anything from him. She wasn't waiting for him to break like Zagreus. She wasn't pulling at him like Isadora and the soul mate connection. She wasn't waiting for him to fix things and make the world better like his people.

Thoughts of his people—the Misos—slid into his mind as he walked, dampening his good mood. Before he could get lost in the guilt of a duty he didn't want to resume, voices drifted from beyond the door, slowing his feet.

"No," a male voice said. "Not even. Don't do it."

Nick recognized Phineus, the dark-haired Argonaut who had spent a good deal of time at the colony before it had been demolished. He listened closer, needing to know who else was in there before he entered. There were several people in this castle he wasn't in the mood to deal with at the moment, Isadora being at the top of his list.

"Man up, would you?" Cerek, another Argonaut, answered. "A blueberry is not going to kill you, pretty boy."

"Great. You did it. I can't eat that shit now. Not unless you want me to throw up all over this kitchen."

"You're so dramatic. Make your own damn food if you can't handle something healthy."

"I'm allergic, moron. It has nothing to do with healthy."

"That's because your forefather, Bellerophon, was a pussy and passed down inferior genes."

"You little shit. I should toast you for that."

Cerek chuckled.

Nick pushed the door open and peered inside the room. Cerek stood behind a counter, pouring batter onto a griddle, while Phineus glared at him from the other side, his arms crossed over his chest, a scowl on his model-handsome face. Other than the two bickering Argonauts, the room was empty.

"Hey," Cerek said, glancing Nick's way. "Morning. I'm making blueberry pancakes. You want? Mr. Sensitive-stomach over here isn't going to eat them."

"You're damn right I'm not." Phineus stalked toward the giant steel refrigerator across the room and yanked it open. "Stupid freakin' blueberries. Fucker knows I don't like to cook."

Cerek chuckled again.

Nick's stomach rumbled as the scent of the sizzling batter rose up in the air. "Yeah, I could eat." He stepped farther into the room, letting the door swing closed at his back. "But why are you on kitchen detail? Where's the cook?"

Cerek flipped the pancakes with a spatula. "At the settlement. The queen sent most of the castle staff over there. You might not have noticed yesterday, but this place is operating at a bare minimum. Even security's been severely downgraded."

Nick thought back to the few guards manning the entrances, and a tingle of apprehension slid through him at the thought of Isadora not being protected in the way she should be. "Why?"

"Because she's worried the Council's going to move on your people," a voice answered at Nick's back.

Nick turned to find Orpheus standing behind him.

"I've been looking for you." Orpheus ran a hand through his light-brown hair, the Argonaut markings on his forearms glinting in the fluorescent lights from above as he moved, a scowl on his usually sarcastic face. "How much did Isadora tell you about the Misos yesterday?"

An invisible weight seemed to press down on Nick's shoulders, one tinged with a responsibility he hadn't missed. "Not a lot."

Orpheus moved toward a long wooden table to his left and pulled out a chair. "Isa brought them all here after Hades and Zagreus attacked the colony. She tried to keep them in Tiyrns, but the Council threw a complete fit."

The dark energy came rushing back, a slow simmer beneath Nick's skin as he pulled out a chair across from Orpheus and sat. He didn't like the thought of his people anywhere near the Council, but he was thankful that Isadora had been able to get them to safety. Something he should have done.

More guilt rushed in. "Not a surprise."

"Yeah, well." Orpheus sighed. "They didn't make things easy for the Misos. They've got influence within the capital and used that influence to threaten and manipulate. Shopkeepers refused to sell to them. Jobs were unavailable. The Council even put forth a mandate that Misos young couldn't be taught in the same schools as Argolean young. In response, Isa tried to set up a mini city here within the castle walls so the Misos could have access to everything they needed, but this place isn't as big as your old digs. They were busting at the seams. The Kyrenia settlement in the Aegis Mountains seemed like the perfect answer."

Nick's mind skipped back over the walls surrounding the settlement, the rebuilt homes and buildings.

"It's got a dark history," Orpheus went on. "Not sure if you're familiar with it, but the witches used to inhabit Kyrenia. They created their own little city out from under the influence of the Council. Over time, it turned into a refugee settlement for any and all who were banished or chose to live on the fringes of Argolean society, not just witches. I used to trade with them back in the day. They were self-sustaining, and their numbers were continually growing. Until the Council decided they were gaining too much power and wiped them out."

"Strength in numbers," Phineus muttered from the end of the table where he was eating a bowl of cereal.

"Fuckers," Cerek muttered from the other side of the kitchen as he flipped pancakes to a plate and poured more batter on the griddle.

"No argument here." Orpheus looked back at Nick. "About twenty years ago, the Council sent in their private army and burned the place to the ground."

Nick leaned back and crossed his arms over his chest. "And the Argonauts didn't do anything to stop it?"

"We didn't know about it," Phineus said. "Most of us were on rotation in the human realm when it happened. Zander was the only one here, and by the time he caught wind of what was going on and called us all back, it was pretty much done."

Nick looked back to Orpheus, thinking about Cynna and what she'd told him about her family. "The king had to know."

"Motherfucker," Cerek mumbled from the counter, not looking up from what he was doing.

"He did know," Orpheus said, drawing Nick's gaze once more. "He okayed it. According to the Council, the witches were spreading anti-Argolean propaganda and therefore needed to be dealt with swiftly."

"The king claimed he didn't know there were others at the settlement besides witches," Phineus said, "but that's a lie. He knew. Everyone knew."

"She knew her father approved the Council's attack on this settlement. She sat back while hundreds—no, thousands—of people were slaughtered because they were different."

Cynna's words floated in Nick's head, sending a chill down his spine. If Isadora had known what had happened at Kyrenia, he believed in his gut she wouldn't have been able to change the outcome, especially not if Theron and the Argonauts had been sent away on purpose to keep them from stopping it. But it didn't change the fact Cynna was right. And a place in his heart went out to her, understanding her hatred, seeing her need for revenge in a whole new light.

Nick's eyes narrowed as he looked at Orpheus again. "So Isadora is upping security at the settlement because she's afraid the Council's going to strike again?"

"Yeah," Orpheus said. "There's been no overt threat, but she's being cautious. After Kyrenia was destroyed, the remaining witches moved deeper into the mountains, residing in tent cities that could be easily moved if the Council discovered their locations. Delia, the leader of the coven, is the keeper of the moving portals, which Isa used a few times to cross back and forth between here and the human realm without the Council or the Argonauts knowing. When Isa decided to rebuild the settlement, she asked Delia for help. The witches were more than eager to get involved. Rebuilding Kyrenia is an in-your-face fuck-you to the Council. But as yet, they're not living there in mass numbers. Only the Misos."

"Who the Council clearly doesn't want in Argolea," Nick guessed.

"Right. Things are tense here," Orpheus said. "Isa pulled Argonauts off the search for you and the search for the water element to provide more protection for Kyrenia."

Fuck. Reality carved a hole in the center of Nick's chest. His people couldn't stay in this land, not if the Council was looking for a reason to wipe them out. He needed to find them a new colony in the human realm. Someplace Hades and Zagreus didn't know about. Someplace where they could be safe.

Just the thought of starting over, of being the leader he'd grown so tired of being, pressed even more weight against his shoulders and chest. He felt boxed in, desperate for air, and that dark energy was humming even louder. Whispering…if he just let go, if he let it consume him, he'd no longer care about a race that had never done anything for him besides pull him in so many different directions he wanted to scream.

"You should go out there." Orpheus leaned back in his chair. "Look around. It would be a real morale booster for your people to see your face. It's been hard on them since you left."

More of that heavy, soul-crushing guilt rushed in, pushing out the last of Nick's good mood. This was the life he'd agreed to. Doing for others and never having anything for himself. And while once he'd thought that was enough, that leading the Misos was his way of getting back at the Council for everything they'd done to him, he knew now it wasn't. He wanted more out of life than this. Needed someone to keep him motivated, strong…happy.

Cynna.

His skin warmed at just the thought of her. At the one person in his life who didn't take, but gave.

He pushed back from the table and nodded toward the griddle, where Cerek was pulling off the last of the pancakes. "I'll take a plate of those with me."

Orpheus's chair skidded across the tile floor as he stood. "Does that mean you'll go out to the settlement?"

"Yeah," Nick said, hating that he was agreeing, knowing he had no other choice. "But first I'm gonna take Cynna some breakfast."

Cerek set a plate of pancakes, syrup, butter, and silverware on a tray and handed it to Nick. "You want coffee?"

"Do the gods like wine? Yeah. Put that shit on here too."

Cerek chuckled and grabbed two cups from the cupboard.

"About the female," Orpheus started.

"Don't." Nick didn't bother to look Orpheus's way. "She's not your concern."

Orpheus drew in a breath. "I was just gonna say…I didn't realize you were into the whole whips-and-chains thing. Considering who she used to work for, though, I'm guessing you are now."

Shit. Orpheus knew about Cynna's relationship with Zagreus. But then, Nick shouldn't be surprised. Before joining the Argonauts, Orpheus had spent plenty of time in the human realm dabbling in the dark and depraved himself.

Nick fought back that switch of dark energy. "She's no threat to you or anyone else."

"I sure the hell hope not," Orpheus muttered while Cerek crossed and set two steaming cups of coffee on Nick's tray. "Because if she is, that's gonna fuck things up royally. Not just for you, but for everyone in this damn place. Do yourself a favor, Niko. Ask her about her parents. You might learn something of interest."

Orpheus left before Nick could ask what the hell he meant. But Nick's mind was already swirling with the reality that he didn't know all that much about Cynna other than what she'd told him about her parents being killed. In fact, he knew very little about her. And suddenly her relationship with Delia, the witch, seemed of great importance.

He carried the tray back up to their room and closed the door at his back. Cynna was just stepping out of the bathroom when he entered, wearing a long black skirt that fell all the way to her bare feet, a white shirt that accentuated her breasts and made her skin look even darker, and a fitted denim jacket he itched to pull from her toned, sexy shoulders.

That darkness slowly receded as he took in every inch of her—the curves at her hips, the swell of her breasts, her dark hair pulled back from her face and tied in a neat tail, and the little silver drops that hung from her earlobes, catching the light as she moved. And just the sight of her created enough room in his chest so he could breathe again.

She looked down at herself. "That Siren chick brought me more clothes while you were out. She must think I have that girly-girl look about me, because all she left was this skirt."

Nick remembered Cynna parading around Zagreus's tunnels in that skimpy little leather miniskirt and those sexy stiletto boots. And while he'd liked that look a lot, he had to admit, he liked this girl-next-door one too. "It works for me."

She frowned. "I'd be happier in the jeans I wore yesterday, but some maid came in and took them to the laundry before I realized I was going to be left with this." She eyed the tray in his hand. "What is that?"

"Breakfast." Already feeling better, he set the tray on the table near the window and motioned her over. "Pancakes."

Her dark eyes brimmed with cautiousness as she crossed the floor and slowly lowered herself to the chair opposite him. "You cooked?"

He huffed out a half laugh, half snort as he set an empty plate in front of her and transferred pancakes, then did the same for him. "No. Cooking is not my specialty. I snagged it from the kitchen."

"Well." Her features relaxed as she lifted her fork and waited while he poured syrup all over her pancakes. "Then I'm afraid this is as far as this goes, because I don't cook either. You clearly need to be with someone who can make sure you don't starve."

No. He eyed her across the table as she bit into her breakfast. He needed to be with someone who cared about what happened to him. Someone who knew how to comfort him when he was stressed. Whose touch made him forget everything but her. Who craved him as much as he craved her. He needed to be with someone…exactly like her.

"So," he said, shaking out his napkin, working for casual because he knew he could never admit all that to her without freaking her out. "I didn't get a chance to ask you yesterday how you know the witch."

She stilled, then swallowed the bite in her mouth and quickly reached for her coffee. "You mean Delia?"

"Was she the one in that house?" He cut into his pancake.

"Yes. She was a friend of my mother's. She helped me escape when Kyrenia was attacked. I told you that before."

"So she's not a relative?"

"No. I'm not a witch, if that's what you're asking."

He wasn't. But it was nice to know she wasn't hiding any trippy spells for later use. He lifted his coffee. "How did your parents end up in Kyrenia?"

She moved the bite around in her mouth, but apprehension slid across her features for just a split second before she swallowed. "My father used to be involved in Argolean politics. After a while, he didn't agree with what the Council was doing to the refugees in Kyrenia, and as a show of defiance, he chose to relocate with them."

Nick sipped his coffee. "He was a politician? What kind?"

Cynna hesitated but didn't meet his eyes. And several long seconds passed before she said, "He was a Council member."

Whoa. Yeah, that would piss the Council off. And made Nick wonder if a big part of the reason the Council had attacked Kyrenia was in retaliation against the guy. He didn't put it past them to wipe out an entire city just to spite one person who'd turned his back on them.

"They'd been trying to force him out for years," Cynna said, finally looking up. "He was only selected to the Council to appease the dark-skinned portion of the population, which has dwindled over the years. Most were slowly forced to the fringes of society as jobs slowly became unavailable, and many wound up in Kyrenia. The witches don't discriminate." She looked back down at her plate and cut into her pancake again, only now there was a hint of anger in her eyes and words. "Unlike the Council, they don't see in shades of color, only the quality of the soul."

He understood her anger. The Council didn't like anyone who was different.

"Anyway," she went on. "He stayed on with the Council, hoping to instill change. When it became clear that wasn't going to happen, he decided to relocate to Kyrenia and help establish a new government. My mother was a refugee there."

"And she wasn't a witch?"

"No." She swallowed another bite, careful, he noticed, to keep her eyes on her plate. "Just someone who'd once lived in Tiyrns."

There was more she wasn't saying, about who her mother had been and her father's involvement with the Council and how that had impacted the attack on Kyrenia. But something in Nick's gut said now wasn't the time to push her on it.

He slid his plate back and folded his arms on the table in front of him, hating what he needed to ask next but knowing there wasn't any way around it.

"I need to go out there today. To Kyrenia. To see my people. They know I'm here. Yesterday, when I followed you, several saw me. I didn't stick around to talk to them, but I know they have to be curious. If I don't go, they'll come here to find me."

She lifted her coffee from the table. "How did you find me anyway?"

He shrugged. "I don't know. I just focused on you and knew where you were."

"Have you always been able to track people that way?"

"No."

"Hm. Another new gift."

Yeah, it was. And he wasn't sure how he felt about it. A lot of these new powers were pretty cool, but he didn't know if that meant he was getting closer to breaking like Hades and Zagreus wanted, or if he was growing stronger and somehow might be able to resist that ultimate break.

The shadow energy came raging back, but he didn't focus on it. Instead, he focused on her. "I need to ask you a favor."

She set her mug down again. "I seem to be doing you a lot of favors lately."

She was, but he sensed she didn't mind. And that relaxed him. At least enough so he could beat back the darkness. "I need you to…" No, that wasn't how he wanted to phrase it. "Would you…please…go to Kyrenia with me today?"

She lifted her dark lashes and stared at him from across the table. And as their eyes held, he picked up a memory flash, one she was projecting, though he was sure she didn't realize she was doing it. Of seeing him standing in the middle of that burned-out courtyard at the colony, staring at the blackened ground around him, his shoulders hunched, his head dropped, and the shudder that had passed through him.

Pain and guilt and anger rolled through his chest. All the emotions he'd felt that day staring at the remnants of a battle he should have stopped from happening but now could never change. But before they could consume him, he had another memory flash. This one his own. Of her taking care of him, cutting his hair, comforting him after he'd nearly lost it, making him feel human again when she had no reason to even try.

A newfound strength surged inside. One that made him feel as if he could do anything, so long as she was by his side. "Please, Cynna."

She pursed her lips and looked down at her plate. "Did you ask anyone else to go with you?"

"Only you. You're the only one I want."

Several seconds passed, and his pulse beat hard waiting for her answer. Finally, her eyes met his. "Okay. I'll go."

He reached across the table and closed his hand over hers, feeling like he could breathe again and knowing it was all because of her. "I owe you."

"No, you don't." She pulled her hand from his grip and went back to eating. But as she did, something dark passed over her features. "You don't owe me anything."

But he did. More than she would ever realize. And he planned to make it up to her as soon as he got through this.

Nick was already agitated. Cynna could see it in his tight shoulders, in the way his jaw flexed, in the sweat gathering against the palm of her hand where he held her as they walked toward the gates outside the Kyrenia settlement.

They'd flashed here from the castle in Tiyrns, but as she still wasn't able to flash through walls, even with him, they had to pass through the front gate.

He gave their names to the guards, and they waited. A few snowflakes drifted down from gray clouds above, and Cynna shivered in the lightweight denim jacket. She should have grabbed something warmer to wear, but she hadn't wanted to take the time to find a coat. Nick had been anxious to get here so he could do whatever it was he had to do and leave, and she was anxious to help him however she could.

She shivered again, and he looked down at her. "Are you cold?"

"No. I'm fine," she lied. Honestly, being cold was kind of nice. She'd been stuck in Zagreus's tunnels so long, any kind of fresh air was welcome, brisk or not.

He opened his mouth to say something, but the giant doors groaned before he could get the words out, and then his attention shifted toward the doors rolling back and the courtyard appearing before them. He drew a steadying breath and muttered, "Don't go too far. I may need you."

Cynna squeezed his hand in reassurance. "I won't."

He didn't seem to hear her. He'd already let go of her and was walking into the courtyard. Several people milling around spotted him. Excited voices rang out. A couple of children squealed. Before Cynna could get her bearings, a cluster of people formed around Nick, talking at once, people hugging him right and left, the crowd pushing her back until she was on the fringes, standing on her tiptoes to try to see over them.

Nick's voice rang out through the crowd, but Cynna only caught pieces of what he was saying. "Yes, I'm fine," and "No, nothing like that," and "Yeah, I got here as soon as I could." But with every answer, his voice grew tighter and more gravelly, and though his people probably didn't notice, she could tell every question was grating on his patience and control.

She pushed her way through the crowd to try to get closer to him, ignoring the odd looks and whispers as she went by. A few muttered, "That's her. The one from yesterday," but Cynna ignored those too. She spotted Nick at the center of the crowd, and was only about four feet away from him when a slim, athletically built blonde called, "Nick!" from across the courtyard.

His head came up. His eyes narrowed on the female. Before Cynna could reach him, he excused himself from the people around him and pushed his way out of the circle, heading right for the blonde.

Cynna tried to follow but was trapped in the crowd. The blonde's hair was pulled back into a neat tail. She wore jeans, boots, a long-sleeved T-shirt, and a light jacket. And her blue eyes absolutely lit up when they locked on Nick's.

Nick caught up with her, and the blonde threw one arm around him, hugging him tight. And though Cynna knew she had no right, a burst of jealousy whipped through her, making her wonder who this new female was and what she meant to Nick.

"Oh my gods. Nick," the blonde exclaimed, lowering to her feet. "I'm so glad to see you. You have no idea."

"It's good to see you too, Helene. Where's Kellan?"

Helene's eyes darkened as her gaze skipped over Nick's face, and her lips turned down in a sad expression. "He…didn't make it."

Cynna pushed her way to the edge of the crowd and watched the exchange. The blonde held her left arm at an odd angle against her body, the sleeve of her jacket missing, and looked up at Nick with both remorse and regret.

"When?" he asked in a low voice.

"During the raid. We lost fifty-eight before we were evacuated. It would have been more if not for the queen."

Nick dropped his head, rubbed his temples with the thumb and forefinger of one hand, and looked down at his boots. And the hunch of his shoulders, the clench of his jaw told Cynna he was fighting that darkness again. Just as he'd been at the colony.

Cynna crossed quickly to stand at his side. The blonde—Helene—glanced at her with surprise and a hint of suspicion. "Hi. I'm Helene."

"Cynna."

"You're…"

"A friend," Cynna answered.

Nick didn't look Cynna's direction. "Helene helped me run the colony."

So she'd worked with him. That explained the female's excitement upon seeing Nick again. But Cynna could tell Helene was happy to see him for other, more personal reasons, as well.

"What about Mark?" Nick asked.

Helene's blue eyes darkened once more, and she shook her head again.

Nick drew a deep breath, dropped his hand, then noticed the way Helene was holding herself. "What's wrong with your arm?"

"It's nothing."

"Tell me what happened, Helene."

She sighed. "It was chaos. There were young on the playground when the attack happened. I went out to bring them in. A daemon…"

Her voice trailed off, and Nick's shoulders went rigid, his eyes as hard as Cynna had ever seen them.

"We all got away," Helene said quickly. "None of the young were killed, but a few of us were injured."

Nick's fiery eyes shot to her arm, held close to her body. "Your arm isn't—"

"No, no," Helene cut in. "It's not like my leg. Don't worry, it's still there. It just didn't mend quite right, and Callia, the queen's personal healer, had to operate to repair the damage." She pulled her jacket back with her good arm so he could see the sling beneath and the sleeve she'd tucked inside so it didn't flop around as she moved. "See? In a few weeks, I'll be back to normal. This is just temporary."

That little bit of good news didn't seem to alleviate any of Nick's anxiety. "Who's running things here?"

"I am. Well, as much as I can. Delia is helping too, but we could really use you. The Argonauts are here now and then, and the queen herself as well. But this land, Nick… It's not at all what I expected. Their Council of Elders—"

"Nick!"

A child's voice rang out, and Nick turned to his left. A little girl, no more than seven, with dark, bouncing curls, wearing a thick coat and boots and carrying a doll in one hand, rushed toward him.

Nick dropped to his knees just as she reached him, opened his arms, and caught her in a hug. She threw both arms around his neck, her doll dangling from her fingers as she squeezed him tight. "Nick, Nick, oh, Nick. I knew you'd come back." She looked up at Helene. "Didn't Minnie and I tell you he'd come back?"

Helene laughed down at the small child. "You did, Marissa. I promise never to doubt you and your doll again."

Marissa eased back and looked into Nick's eyes, but she didn't let go of his neck. And as she did, Cynna noticed that one whole side of her face was puckered and scarred as if from some kind of fire, making the hair on the right side of her head sparse, making her eye on that side droop just a touch. "I saw you. I told them all you were okay, but no one would listen." Her gaze darted past Nick and settled on Cynna, and she grinned. "I saw you too. Hi, pretty lady."

Whoever this girl was, she'd already been through hell and back, but she didn't seem at all fazed by her scars, and since Nick wasn't looking at them as if they were new, Cynna breathed a sigh of relief and smiled. "Hi, yourself."

Marissa refocused on Nick. "I saw them. Minnie showed them to me. They're going to come for you." She leaned close to Nick's ear as if whispering a secret. "Don't let them."

Nick stiffened and pushed Marissa back, focusing on her little face. "What else did Minnie see, Marissa?"

Cynna had no idea what was going on, and she glanced toward Helene for help.

"Marissa is a soothsayer," Helene whispered. "A seer. The doll is her medium." A frown pulled at her lips. "She shouldn't be talking about this stuff right now, though."

A chill spread down Cynna's spine.

"Marissa," Helene said louder. "Nick just got here. Why don't you give him a chance to get acclimated before you start telling him what he's going to have for dinner."

Marissa grinned and let go of him. "Okay. But I want to show him my new room." Excitement filled her dark eyes again as she looked at Nick. "Do you want to see it?"

"Yeah. Sure." He laid his hand on her little shoulder and pushed to his feet, and as he did, Cynna caught the subtle movement. The way his finger hooked in the collar of the girl's coat and pulled the fabric back just an inch, revealing long, red, clawlike scars that ran down her neck and disappeared under her clothes.

His shoulders tensed. He let go of the girl and forced a smile for her before he dropped his arm to his side and said, "I'll find you in a bit."

The child ran off to rejoin a group of children kicking a ball down the street. But Nick turned his fiery gaze on Helene. "What happened to her?"

"She's fine."

"That's not what I asked. I want to know what happened."

Helene sighed. "She was inside when the attack happened. She had a vision of daemons and satyrs at the school. She came to tell me. I went running out there. I...I didn't think she'd follow."

Nick's eyes grew shadowed. And the way his muscles bunched, the way his hands clenched into fists at his sides... It shot worry straight down Cynna's spine.

She reached for his hand, hoping to soothe him, to keep him centered, but he pulled away from her touch.

"Where's her mother?" He glanced around the courtyard. People were still mingling, waiting to talk to him. "I don't see her. She never lets Marissa out of her sight. Not since the fire."

"Nick," Helene said softly.

"Where is she?"

Helene's face dropped, just as it had earlier when she'd told him about his men. "She was one of the fifty-eight."

Nick took a step back. His chest rose and fell with his rapid breaths. Every muscle in his body grew taut. His jawbone turned to a slice of steel beneath his skin. And his eyes... They were now cold, unfriendly, dead. A look Cynna instantly recognized. Because it was the same look she'd seen on her own face in the mirror when she'd finally decided to turn to Zagreus for revenge.

"Nick." Cynna reached for him.

He turned before she could touch him, stalked away, and disappeared between two buildings.

Fear and worry melded inside Cynna. She took a step to follow, but Helene's hand over her arm stopped her cold. "Wait. What's wrong with him?"

Cynna turned toward the blonde. "Who was the female?"

"A friend. One of the colonists."

"Nothing more?"

Helene let go of her arm. "Nick rescued them—the mother and Marissa—from a daemon attack years ago. They were living in the wild with her human husband. He didn't make it. Nick brought them in to the colony and promised to protect them."

And he hadn't. Cynna's heart sank. "I have to find him."

"But—"

"If he comes back by here before I get to him, don't let him leave."

A perplexed expression crossed Helene's face as Cynna stepped away. "I'll do what I can. But—"

"No buts, Helene." Panic spread through every inch of Cynna's body. "If I don't find him before it's too late, all hell could break loose. And I don't mean that figuratively."

CHAPTER TWENTY

A gust of wind lifted Cynna's ponytail, and a chill rushed down her spine. Crossing her arms over her chest, she hurried down the street, looking in every shop window she passed, searching for Nick.

He didn't know the layout of Kyrenia. Wouldn't know where to go to get away from the crowds. At this time of day—midafternoon—there was still a fair amount of people on the street doing business, but the weather was growing colder, the skies darker, and something in her gut said a storm was moving in. One that likely couldn't compare to the storm surging inside Nick right now.

She made a right and stepped over a pile of snow pushed up against a newly renovated building. Where would he go? If she could track him the way he tracked her, this would be a hell of a lot easier. Biting her lip, she glanced around, then remembered Delia's house.

It was a long shot, but it was the only place he knew. She made a left and hurried down the sidewalk, not wanting to flash in the hopes she might run into him along the way, all the while hoping—no, praying—she'd find him there.

Three blocks from Delia's house, movement between two large, empty buildings with broken windows caught her eye. She hesitated, turned back. A shadowy figure stood halfway down the darkened alley, hands pressed against the brick wall, shoulders hunched, head hanging low.

Panic spread beneath her ribs. Panic and fear and hope. Cautiously, she moved into the alley. "Nick?"

No answer. She couldn't tell if it was him. The person was big enough, but she'd breathe easier if he'd just lift his head so she could be sure. She took another step forward. "Nick, is that you?"

"Leave...Cynna."

Relief spread through every vein and cell. Her pulse slowed as she moved toward him, so thankful she'd found him in time. "There you are."

"Go," he rasped.

"No, I—"

Her steps slowed, and the words died on her lips when she got a good look at him. The light jacket he'd thrown on over his gray Henley was ripped at the seams, as if he'd flexed and the garment had shredded like tissue paper. The muscles in his arms were strained. Veins in the backs of his hands bulged. Her gaze slid higher, to his neck, red and covered in a thin layer of sweat, then to his profile, which she could just barely see with his head tipped down—his jaw, hard and rigid, his eyes squeezed shut tight, his temple pulsing with his racing heartbeat.

Another chill spread down her spine, but this one had nothing to do with the temperature. Hand shaking, she reached out to him. "Nick, just let me—"

"No." He twisted away from her touch. "Just go. I'm not in a good place. And I don't want to...hurt you...when it happens."

Her heart pounded hard in her chest. No, she wasn't giving him up to Zagreus without a fight. And Nick wasn't getting rid of her that easily. Not after everything they'd been through.

She gripped his arm before he could get two steps away. "I'm not letting you give up like that."

He whirled on her so fast, she barely saw him. His hands closed around her biceps until pain shot up her arms. But it was quickly overshadowed when he slammed her back against the side of the building, her spine and skull cracking the worn bricks.

"You think this is giving up?" He loomed over her, malice and rage and darkness swirling inside him to twist his features until he didn't look like her Nick anymore but someone who was...possessed. "I don't have a fucking choice in this. I never did." He squeezed her arms so hard, her eyes watered and her mouth fell open in a silent scream. Then he released her and turned away. "Get the hell away from me while you still have a chance."

Cynna gasped as the pain slowly receded, and rubbed her arms to ease the sting. Looking up, she watched Nick move toward the back of the alley, his shoulders shaking, his body barely holding it together as he put space between them. It was happening. He was about to break. And as soon as that happened, Zagreus would undoubtedly appear to claim his prize. He was right; she needed to run before it was too late.

But she couldn't. Because whether he knew it or not, he'd brought her back from the brink of self-destruction. And she wasn't about to let him travel down that same path.

She caught up with him and stepped right in his path. He drew to a stop and glared at her, his once mesmerizing amber eyes now nothing but hard cold pools of black. Just like Zagreus's. Swallowing back the fear curling into a hot knot in her throat, she lifted her chin. "Focus on me."

He growled and turned the other direction, but she rushed around him and stepped in his way again.

"Look at me. Stay with me."

His eyes slammed shut. He shook his head as if trying to rattle something loose. Pressed the heels of his hands against his closed eyelids.

"Listen to the sound of my voice, Nick."

He stumbled back. His body shook. His hands slid over his forehead until his fingers wrapped around the ends of his hair, pulling tight. Sweat slid down his temple. "Get. The. Fuck. Out. Of. Here."

"No," she said softly, stepping closer, knowing she needed to stay calm if she had any hope of pulling him out of this. "I'm not going anywhere. I said I'd stay with you, and I am. Focus on me. Just me. No one else."

His back hit the building. His legs sagged. His body shook harder.

She needed to reach him on a physical level. Knew he needed that connection, as he had before.

She stepped between his legs and framed his face with her hands. His skin was cold and clammy, but this time, he didn't push her away. And she focused on that rather than the way he trembled beneath her touch. "I won't let you fall. I'm right here. They can't have you. Do you hear me? I'm not letting go."

His head fell forward until his forehead rested against hers. Against the wall, his shoulders shook, and his chest rose and fell with his shallow breaths as he fought that wicked darkness inside, struggling with every labored breath.

"Leave me," he rasped.

She tightened her fingers against his jaw. "Not a chance. You're mine."

A growl rumbled from his chest, and in a sudden move, he lifted his head and closed his mouth over hers.

She sucked in a surprised breath, then moaned as he pushed away from the wall, yanked her body against his, and devoured her mouth.

Warmth spread through her veins, ignited a burn deep in her core. She slid her hands down his shoulders and around his arms, needing him, wanting every part of him.

His fingers cut into her hipbones, sending a jolt of pain across her sides, but she ignored it. Instead focused on the bruising demand of his mouth, the way his tongue raced along hers, the sinful heat of his body. But before she'd tasted her fill, he pulled away from her mouth, whipped her around, then shoved her up against the wall, face-first.

Her hands slapped the cold bricks. The air rushed out of her lungs. He kicked her legs wide with his feet, pressed his hard body up against her back, and closed his teeth over her earlobe until she flinched. "I gave you the chance to leave. Now you're going to wish you'd listened."

Her heart pounded against her ribs. Her body trembled with both anticipation and a hint of apprehension. But she knew he wouldn't hurt her. Not really. And if this was what he needed to stay focused so the darkness didn't claim him, she'd let him do whatever he wanted to her. Give him anything he asked for.

She spread her fingers against the bricks and pushed back into him. "I won't. I'm not afraid of you."

His hand rushed around her belly, then up under her tank. His hot fingers streaked across her abs, grasped the cup of her bra, and jerked it down. The strap cut into her shoulder, and she pressed her lips together against the pain, then his fingers found her nipple and squeezed hard, making her cry out from the sudden jolt.

"You should be. You should be very afraid. What's inside me is a thousand times more evil than what's in him."

He was talking about Zagreus. But he was wrong. He was strength and honor and compassion. He'd shown that to her more times than she could count. Zagreus wasn't any of those things. And until Krónos's dark energy claimed Nick for good, she'd do whatever she could to prove that fact to him.

She bit into her lip hard to keep from whimpering as he rolled her nipple between his thumb and forefinger, as he jerked the other side of her bra down and tormented the other breast. Yes, it hurt. But the shock of that initial pressure was more painful than the actual act. The longer he rolled and tweaked and twisted, the faster her pulse raced. And the stronger the tingles grew that were suddenly shooting from her breasts straight between her legs.

Her sex grew hot and achy, her body tight and eager. She pushed back into him, feeling his strong thighs against the backs of her legs and his hard erection pressing into her spine. Dropping her forehead against the wall, she struggled to find her voice. "I'm...I'm not going to fight you, Nick."

"Oh, you will." He released her nipple, closed his whole hand around her breast, and squeezed until pain lit up the entire mass. His other hand pulled free of her bra. He grasped her skirt at her thigh, hiking it up until cold air washed over her legs. Then he shoved his hand between her thighs, gripped her panties, and ripped.

She jerked in surprise, but then his fingers were sliding along her folds, sending tingles through every cell in her body, and she couldn't hold back the moan that rumbled from her throat.

"You like that?" he growled near her ear.

She closed her eyes and rocked back against him, wanting more. "Yes."

He stroked up, then down, his fingers creating a delicious friction that made her entire body shiver. "Like this?"

Oh gods... "Y-yes."

He thrust up inside her with two fingers, and she gasped. "You like being used?" His voice was hard. Cold. Cruel. Nothing she recognized. His fingers slid out, then drove back in, and his thumb circled her clit. "Is this what you did for Zagreus? Let him fuck you in a back alley like a whore?"

His ugly words dimmed her pleasure, and her eyes popped open, her gut reaction to lash out, to tell him to go to hell. But she didn't. Because she knew he'd had plenty of opportunities to say just that before and mean it, only he hadn't. Which meant this wasn't him. It was that vile piece of Krónos inside pushing him to hurt her, to make her fight back, to force her to run so it could finally claim him.

She swallowed hard and rocked back against his hand. Still not willing—never willing—to let the gods have him. "Not him, only you. I only want you. Don't stop."

He thrust deeper with his fingers, harder. And his voice grew even more menacing when he growled, "You want to get fucked? Is that what you want?"

She knew she'd probably be sore tomorrow, likely bruised, but she didn't care. Because this was too important. "Yes," she groaned, leaning back against him. "Yes. By you."

He released her breast, grasped her skirt at the back, and jerked it up. Cool air swept over the backs of her legs, then denim brushed across her bare ass as he ground the rigid length of his cock against her. "You're a wicked little slut, aren't you?"

For you. Only for you.

Her fingers curled against the wall as he continued to fuck into her with his hand. Pleasure zinged along her nerve endings. He was stroking that perfect place deep inside, driving her harder toward the crest. His thumb flicked her clit again and again. His hips pressed against her ass, his cock rubbing right between her cheeks. It was wrong…so wrong…to be enjoying this, but she couldn't help it. Because with him, she enjoyed everything—hard, rough, soft, sweet—it didn't matter how. It didn't matter when. It just mattered that it was with him.

She dropped her head back against his shoulder, couldn't hold it up, couldn't do anything but let him take her wherever he wanted to go. "Nick… Oh gods. Nick…"

He bit down hard on her earlobe, and the mixture of pleasure and pain shoved her over the edge. Her entire body was swept up in a whirlwind of light and ecstasy so intense, it stole her breath, shook her body, and dragged her straight into a tunnel of utter blackness.

When she came to, her face was pressed against the building, her chest rising and falling with her shallow breaths. Her mind was foggy, her body limp. But she recognized Nick still pressed up against her back, his forehead resting against her temple, his hot breath rushing down her neck. Yet more than anything, she knew his voice. *His* voice—not that angry, ugly thing that had been growling in her ear only moments before. This was his soft, familiar voice whispering her name over and over as she clawed herself back from a climax so strong she'd blacked out.

She was wrecked, dazed, wanted only to rest. But she didn't know how long his lucidity would last, and more than anything, she needed to drag him back to her for good.

Pushing away from the wall, she turned so she was facing him, then lifted her fingers to his scruffy jaw. Her skirt fell to her feet. Her jacket was torn at the shoulder, but she didn't care. She focused only on him. On his hands braced on either side of her, on his forehead resting on her shoulder. His body trembled as if he were dazed too, but strength simmered beneath his rigid muscles, just waiting to be unleashed. And she feared this was only the eye of the storm. That if she didn't do something fast, she'd lose him for good.

"Nick." She lifted his face away from her shoulder, pressed her mouth against the scar on his cheek, trailed her lips to his temple, then his nose, then the corner of his mouth. "Stay with me. I've got you. I'm not letting go. No matter what happens. Focus only on me."

She kissed his other cheek, his jaw, worked her way back to his mouth.

He stiffened against her. "Shit. Cynna."

"Yes." Gently, she kissed his lips. "Say my name. As many times as it takes. I'm not letting them have you." She tipped her head the other direction, kissed him again. "I won't let you fall. I won't ever let you fall."

A growl built low in his throat, and every muscle in his body tensed. And as he opened his mouth over hers, pushing his tongue forcefully between her lips and shoving her back into the wall again, she steeled herself for another wave of anger, of malevolence, of dark, viscous energy.

"Don't go too far. I may need you…"

He did need her. Not because she was special, not because she was his soul mate. But because they were alike. They understood each other. They'd both danced with the devil, and she was determined to make sure they both survived.

She opened to his bruising kiss, dragged her tongue against his even though she knew he was trying to hurt her again, and kissed him back. Trailing her fingers up into his hair, she tugged hard on the soft strands between her fingertips and met his kiss with the same ferocity, the same energy, the same strength he was showering on her. And the moment she did, something inside him shifted.

She felt it pop, like a balloon exploding. Felt it ripple all through his limbs. His muscles instantly relaxed. His kiss gentled. Against her belly he was still hard and aroused, but the anger that had been driving him—the savagery—it dissipated like water evaporating into air. And was replaced by a wave of heat and hunger and need she felt all the way to her toes.

"Cynna..." His hand slipped around her nape; his fingertips softly rubbed her skin as he kissed her, again and again. His voice grew weak, strained, but was filled with a panicked urgency, as if he were afraid he was going to lose her. "Cynna..."

Her heart swelled. She wound her hands around his waist and walked her fingers up his spine, gentling her own kiss, showing him with her mouth and body that she felt the same way, that she still wasn't leaving. "I'm right here. I'm not going anywhere. Don't stop kissing me, Nick."

One hand closed around her breast to squeeze, and his tongue tangled with hers in an erotic dance. But it wasn't the hard bruising grasp of before. This was softer, more electrifying, and tingles ignited all through her torso and shot straight back down into her sex, reigniting every ounce of her arousal. Grasping her skirt at the thigh, he dragged it up again, then carefully lifted her leg and hooked it around his hip.

"Cynna..." He rocked against her aching sex and dropped his forehead to hers, struggling to find his breath while his hard length rubbed over her clit. "Ah gods, Cynna... I need to be inside you."

He was asking, not telling. His thumb brushed over her nipple, sending shards of desire straight into her core. Giving, not taking. Her heart swelled even more because he was back. She hadn't lost him. He was still hers.

"Yes." She lifted her mouth to his and kissed him slowly, deeply, then reached for the button at his waistband and popped it free. "Yes, I need that too. But mostly, I just need you."

She slid her hand inside his pants. He groaned and sank into her kiss. As her fingertips brushed over his pulsing length, so hard and engorged, she pushed against the fabric at his hips, desperate to free him so she could feel him moving inside her.

He lifted his mouth from hers abruptly. Fear rushed back in, that she'd misread things, that he was still on the edge. But he didn't grab her or push her or even reach for her. Instead, he turned his face toward the entrance to the alley and went completely still.

"What—"

"Shh."

Her fingers froze inside his pants, the other hand against his hip, and she turned to see what he was looking at. Only she couldn't see anything but the fading afternoon light. And she didn't hear anything other than her roaring pulse and his shallow breaths.

"Nick?"

He stepped quickly away, dislodging her hands from his body, then lowered her leg and dropped her skirt. Buttoning his jeans, he said, "Someone's coming."

Cynna didn't care if someone was approaching or not. "I don't hear anything." She reached for him. "Come here."

"Shh." Gently, he pushed her hands away. "Fix your shirt. They're almost here."

Frustrated, Cynna pushed away from the wall and tugged down her shirt, hating the chill that spread over her skin after all his delicious heat. He wasn't looking at her. She needed him to look at her. "Nick—"

"I'm pretty sure he went this way," a voice called somewhere close.

Skata. Her gaze shot to the right. He was right. People were coming. Stomach tightening, Cynna stepped away from the wall and tried to smooth out her skirt. But Nick's hand around her arm stopped her.

She drew in a breath and looked up. His eyes were warm pools of liquid amber as he moved in close, cradled her face in his hands, then lowered his mouth to hers in the sweetest, softest kiss. And every bit of fear, of frustration, of worry slid right out of her with that simple brush of his lips over hers.

"Thank you," he whispered. "I know what you did." He rested his forehead against hers and drew in a shuddering breath. "I'm sorry I can't control it. Sorry I did that to you. I—"

"Shh." She lifted her fingers to his jaw and brushed them over his scruffy cheek. "No apologies. I'm not hurt. Not even close. And I meant what I said. I'm not leaving. I'll do whatever it takes—as many times as it takes—to bring you back."

He groaned, took her lips in a swift, delicious kiss, then released her. "I'll make this up to you. I promise."

He took a step away before she was ready to let him go, and as the cool afternoon air replaced all his sultry heat, her heart took a hard, irretrievable tumble. Because she knew right then that what she felt for him was stronger than love. It was the kind of emotion a person was willing to sacrifice everything for.

"Nick?" a male voice rang out from the end of the alley. "Shit, man. We've been looking all over for you."

Cynna swallowed hard and turned. Two males stalked toward them from the end of the alley. The first was tall and blond, the second more muscular, his eyes more intense. A whisper of worry rushed down her spine because she recognized both of them from the day she and Nick had been brought to the castle. The second especially, because he was the leader of the Argonauts.

"Zander," Nick said, glancing toward the blond, then shifting his gaze to the other male. "Theron. What's wrong?"

"You need to come back to the castle ASAP," Theron said.

Concern flooded Nick's features, and though Cynna knew he couldn't help it because of the whole soul mate thing, a sick feeling stirred in the pit of her stomach. "Why? Is everyone okay?"

"Everyone's fine," Theron said. "Or they will be soon. Callia's figured out what you need to do to help Isadora."

Of course this was about Isadora. Everything was always about Isadora. Cynna tried to fight back the resentment and jealousy, but couldn't squash either completely.

Nick glanced between the two again. "So the blood draw worked?"

Theron and Zander exchanged apprehensive looks. "Something like that," Theron muttered.

Cynna's pulse kicked up, and a little voice in the back of her head whispered she wasn't going to like where this was headed.

"Something like that," Nick muttered, eyeing each of them warily. "What aren't you both telling me?"

The Argonauts looked at each other once more. Zander lifted his brows as if asking a question. Theron shook his head.

Zander turned to Nick. "It's probably better if Callia and Natasa tell you."

"Natasa's involved now?" Nick asked. "Prometheus's daughter? Why do I suddenly have a bad feeling about this?"

"Because you're smart," Zander muttered under his breath.

Cynna's stomach pitched. And though she tried not to listen, that little voice grew louder and louder until it was a shrill in her ears.

Theron cut Zander a hard look, then nodded toward Nick. "Come on. The sooner you get this over with, the better. For all our sakes."

CHAPTER TWENTY-ONE

"I'm just going to wait in your room." Cynna continued up the steps of the grand staircase in the castle when Theron and Zander turned off at the third landing.

Nick captured her hand before she could get more than a step away and drew her to his side, a whisper of panic rushing down his spine at the thought of her getting too far away. "No, I need you to stay with me."

His pulse was already ticking up, and that dark energy he'd conquered thanks to her was suddenly rushing back. If she left him now, he wasn't sure what would happen. Especially since the scars on his back were tingling with an uneasiness that told him whatever the Argonauts and the queen wanted from him couldn't be good.

She exhaled a long breath but didn't try to pull away again. And as he tugged her with him and they followed the Argonauts down the long corridor that led to Isadora's private office, relief and calm filled his soul.

"This doesn't concern me," she whispered. "You didn't need me before when they were poking you with needles."

"That was different. They hadn't come up with any theories yet."

She didn't answer, just stared straight ahead as they walked. But he knew she was stressing. She didn't want to see Isadora any more than he did, especially after what had just happened between them. All he wanted was to finish what they'd started and thank her for dragging him back from the edge—again—the right way. But he couldn't do that until he got the Argonauts off his back and dealt with whatever emergency had popped up this time.

"I know it's asking a lot." He glanced sideways at her. Her jaw was clenched, her shoulders tight. Squeezing her hand, he added softly, "I'll make this up to you as well. A double thanks. I promise it'll be worth your while."

"Stop making promises to me." They reached the threshold to the office, and Theron and Zander moved into the room. As voices conversed inside, Cynna pulled her hand from Nick's and frowned, but she didn't meet his eyes. "Especially ones you might not be able to keep."

She moved into the office, and as he watched her go, a strange sense of foreboding washed over him. One that ignited a rash of ripples all along the scars on his back.

She was pissed, and she had every right to be. Especially because Isadora seemed to keep coming between them. But he wasn't lying. He would keep that promise. Not just because he owed Cynna for saving him, but because he needed to thank her in the only way he knew how. To show her what she meant to him. To tell her…

His heart lurched.

To tell her that he loved her.

His skin grew hot. The capillaries in his fingertips tingled, and the air caught in his lungs. He'd never been in love before, hadn't known what to expect, but immediately he knew this was different from the soul mate draw. It was stronger. Deeper. More immediate. And it was a choice. Not some predestined future ordained by the gods. It was…freedom…at the most basic of levels.

An uncontrollable urge to drag her out of that room, to kiss her, to tell her how he felt consumed him.

His pulse raced, his stomach tossed as he took one step forward, then another, intent on doing just that. Heads turned his way as he entered, and he registered more than just Isadora and Callia in the room, but he didn't care. He spotted Casey sitting on a couch, Theron standing behind her, Natasa across the room next to Titus, Callia and Zander speaking quietly with the queen near her desk, his brother Demetrius pacing along the far wall. But he couldn't see Cynna.

Worry rippled beneath his ribs as he looked for her. And when he finally spotted her, in the corner near the far window, one arm crossed over her chest as she gnawed on her thumbnail and peered out toward the steadily darkening sky, that tightness eased in his chest. He drew a deep, relieved breath, one that spread through every cell in his body. One that felt like it was the first of the rest of his life.

"Nick," Callia said. "I'm glad you got here so fast."

Nick wasn't. He looked past the healer and zeroed in on Cynna. He shouldn't have dropped everything with her to rush right over here. He should have told the Argonauts he'd deal with Isadora's latest crisis later. He couldn't change any of that now, anyway. But he could do something to make things right for Cynna.

He moved for the windows. "Whatever this is, it can wait. I need to—"

"No, this can't wait." Callia stepped in his path, blocking him from getting to the female he needed to reach. "As your god powers increase and your immortality strengthens, you're draining your soul mate of her life force."

"Says your theory."

"Says history," Callia tossed back.

Nick frowned and tried to step around her, but Theron moved in his way. "Listen to her, Nick."

Nick stopped and stared at the leader of the Argonauts. He didn't have time for this, didn't want to *make* time, but common sense told him if he grabbed Cynna and bolted, they'd never be left alone.

"Fine." Nick crossed his arms over his chest, wanting to get this over with as fast as possible. "You're talking about the three mortals you mentioned yesterday. The three who died and became judges of the Underworld. I've already heard this story."

"Pretty sure you haven't heard this part," Natasa mumbled from across the room. When he glanced toward the redhead, she moved away from Titus and said, "Callia asked me to do some research. Titus and I went to my father for confirmation."

Her father, Prometheus, was a Titan, and since the Argonauts had rescued him from his perpetual torture at the hands of good old Zeus, the elder god had been hiding out in the Aegis Mountains in Argolea, doing gods only knew what elder gods did these days.

Nick tamped down the irritation. "Enlighten me then. But do it quickly. Because I'm not seeing how three Underworld gods I've never heard of have anything to do with me."

"Zeus gave each of the three mortals—Aiakos, Minos, and Rhadamanthys—a choice," Natasa went on. "To either travel to the Isles of the Blessed upon their death, or become immortal in the Underworld. Immortality's a seductive lure. Each one eventually chose immortality, leaving behind a mate—a soul mate—in the human realm. A soul mate who eventually died."

She was right. The whole soul mate part of this was new, and he had a feeling he knew where this was heading. But he still wasn't seeing the solution Zander and Theron had hinted at. "Mortals don't have soul mates."

"No, but Argonauts do," Casey said from the couch. "All three were from Zeus's line. All three served with the Argonauts at different times."

Nick looked toward Casey. Her hand rested on her belly, her violet eyes as shadowed as he'd ever seen them. And there was a sadness about her, one he couldn't put his finger on. One the vibrations growing stronger across his scars told him, had to do with him. "So let me get this straight. Zeus got to handpick three mortals to be the Judges of the Dead in the Underworld. And he chose Argonauts. And Hades didn't have a problem with that?"

"It wasn't his problem to have." Theron rested a hand on Casey's shoulder. "Zeus is the King of the gods, even over Hades. And why wouldn't he choose Argonauts, just to fuck with his brother?"

"That's a total Zeus thing to do," Zander muttered.

"I verified everything with my father," Natasa said. "It's all true. Except there was a fourth mortal who was given the same choice. Also an Argonaut. He chose immortality as well, but after learning his soul mate was dying, he escaped from the Underworld and rushed back to find a way to save her. According to my father, their reunion did just that. It restored the life energy and soul mate balance between them."

That word…reunion…floated in Nick's head, but his mind was spinning with questions. He'd never heard of anyone escaping the Underworld and living to tell about it, except for Orpheus and Gryphon. "You're saying this Argonaut bested the gods."

"No," Natasa answered. "Ultimately he didn't. Zeus found him, and, as punishment for abandoning his immortal duties, he turned him into a daemon. But his soul mate lived on."

Nick's brow lowered. "Who was the Argonaut?"

Across the room, Demetrius slowed his frantic pacing.

"Meleager," Titus said behind Natasa. "The Argonaut was Meleager."

The name bounced around Nick's brain, pinging like tiny pinballs smacking into each other in a vast empty space. Meleager. *Meleager...*

And then the name finally registered, and his wide-eyed gaze shot to his brother. "Atalanta's lover. You're telling me she—our mother—was this Argonaut's soul mate?"

Natasa nodded, drawing his attention. "She didn't know Zeus had turned Meleager into a daemon. She thought he'd gone back to the Argonauts, and when he disappeared and no one could find him, she blamed the order for not searching harder for him. Years went by with no word from him, and, eventually, she accepted his death and gave in to her grief. But she never stopped blaming the Argonauts. And eventually, that grief pushed her to make her pact with Hades for immortality and revenge."

Perspiration formed on Nick's forehead. He wasn't sure what to say. What to think for that matter. This was all way more than he'd expected when Theron had dragged him back here. His mother's vendetta against the Argonauts hadn't just been because they'd passed her over for induction into the order based on her gender as everyone thought, but because she'd blamed the Argonauts for her mate's death.

Reunion.

The word trickled back into his jumbled thoughts like a cog stuck in a wheel, trying to break free.

Reunion...

Re—

Vibrations rippled all along his spine as his gaze shifted to Callia. "What do Atalanta and Meleager have to do with Isadora?"

Callia shot a worried look toward Zander. Her mate nodded, then she turned her violet eyes on Nick once more. "It proves that what nearly killed Atalanta is the same as what's happening to Isadora. It's all about life-force energy and the soul mate balance. Whether you or Isadora want to accept it, she is your soul mate, and as any of the Argonauts will attest, the soul mate bond is the strongest bond there is."

Nick looked toward his brother, but Demetrius was no longer watching him. He was pacing again, this time raking his hand through his hair as if just the thought of standing still might kill him.

"We've tried everything else," Callia went on, drawing Nick's attention back to her. "We've had Isadora hold the Orb of Krónos, hoping the powers contained in the disk would help, but they haven't. We've confirmed that she gets an increase in energy when you're in the same room. Touching you amplifies that increase. We've even tried infusing your blood into hers, which worked for an hour or so to bring her vitals back to normal, but the effects slowly wore off. We know that you're the key to her being healthy again, but nothing we've done so far has worked. This, though…" She glanced toward Natasa, then looked back at Nick. "This proves there's really only one way to solve this problem."

Nick waited for the healer to tell him what that one way was, but Callia didn't go on. She just stared at him with a sorrowful expression. Everyone did, actually. Everyone but Isadora, who sat still behind her desk, as silent as she'd been through the whole conversation, glancing repeatedly toward her mate across the room, and Demetrius, who, Nick was pretty sure, was going to wear a path in the marble floor if he didn't slow his steps soon.

Nick's brow dropped. "I don't think I'm follow—"

Reunion…

The word. The meaning. This intense powwow. Everything suddenly clicked.

Nick's gaze shot to Isadora, then to Demetrius again—neither of whom were looking at him—then finally back to Callia. "Someone tell me this is a practical joke."

An eerie silence settled over the room.

"Seriously," Nick said, looking from face to face. "This isn't funny."

"Do you see Orpheus in the room anywhere?" Zander muttered. "If this were a joke, that lunatic would be here dragging it out, loving every minute of it. This is no joke, man."

No way. Nick's chest stretched tight as a drum. No way they were implying that the only way to save Isadora's life was for him to…

He took a big step back and rested his suddenly sweaty hands on his hips, unable to even think the words. Yeah, there might have been a time when he'd considered it, even fantasized about it because the soul mate curse had been tormenting him and seeing Isadora so happy with his brother had been like a knife to the chest, but no way in hell would he ever have acted on it.

His attention shot toward Demetrius. "You, of all people, can't be listening to this insanity. Please, Demetrius, for the love of all that's holy, tell me this is a fucking joke."

Demetrius's feet stilled. His back was to Nick, and he didn't turn to face him. But every muscle in his body was clenched and rigid, and the way he reached up, the way he grabbed a fistful of his dark hair and pulled hard, as if he were trying to will away reality with pain, reignited those vibrations all along Nick's scars.

"It's not a joke," Theron said in a hard voice to Nick's left. "Every Argonaut knows the power of sex."

Nick cringed. Holy fuck, someone had actually said it. Just the use of the word made his stomach roll and all of this seem that much more real. And fucking deranged.

"Sex solidifies the soul mate bond," Theron went on. "It's how we each knew who our soul mate was, without doubt. Callia's right. The soul mate bond is the strongest force out there. And your newfound god powers are fucking with that bond in a negative way. No one's saying this has to be a repeat event. Once was all it took to save Atalanta's life, and since she was your mother, once should be all that's needed here."

The leader of the Argonauts made it sound like they were talking about swapping recipes, not Nick *fucking his brother's wife*.

That dark energy inside rumbled to life with a burst of excitement, but Nick fought it back. Raking a hand through his hair, he grabbed his own damn locks, wanting a little pain to dull the throbbing in his skull.

"If this is a"—gods almighty, he couldn't believe he was saying this—"a sperm issue—"

"It's not a sperm issue," Callia said. "It has nothing to do with fertility or even biology. That's why the blood transfusion didn't work. It's about solidifying a bond. A connection. One that balances energy."

Holy shit. They really did expect him to have sex with Isadora. Everyone in the room was waiting for him to say yes as if it were no big deal. He glanced toward Isadora. She still hadn't met his eyes, just kept flicking worried glances toward Demetrius. But just the fact she wasn't freaking out told him she'd either already accepted this insanity or wasn't about to make a scene in front of her family and friends.

Disbelief rushed through him. How the hell could she accept it? He shot a look at Demetrius, who was still fucking pacing. How the hell could he? They were in love. Madly in love. He'd seen it up close and personal. This wasn't something two people in love would ever agree to.

He wasn't doing it. He couldn't. Now that he knew what love felt like, he couldn't—wouldn't—do anything to jeopardize theirs.

Nick's gaze shifted to the windows in search of Cynna. Only she wasn't there. He looked around the room but couldn't find her. She'd left. At some point when he'd been wrapped up in all this nonsense, she'd slipped out, and he hadn't even noticed.

Panic pushed at his chest. Had she left before or after they'd decided he needed to sleep with Isadora, the one person Cynna hated more than anyone else in the world?

"I...I'm not doing this." Nick turned for the door. "This is nuts. You are all fucking nuts."

Footsteps shuffled behind him. Theron called, "Wait." But Nick ignored him. He needed to get out of this crazy house before he went completely insane himself.

Zander lurched forward and put his big body between Nick and the door, blocking Nick's exit.

"Move," Nick said, ready to be done with this.

"No, you *are* doing this." Zander's eyes shifted to a dark, stormy gray, one that indicated his legendary rage was just waiting to be set free.

As if Nick freakin' cared. He had his own darkness to deal with. "No, I'm not. And none of you can make me."

He moved to step around Zander, but the guardian slapped a hand on Nick's chest and pushed him back. "This isn't just about you. People are going to die if you don't do the right thing."

"Zander," Callia said softly from the opposite side of the room.

"No, *thea*. He needs to know the fucking truth."

"And what truth is that?" Nick tossed back, that shadow energy now a roaring thunder in his veins. "That you're all fucked in the head because you want me to screw my brother's wife? I'm sorry, but I'm not into your sick and twisted games."

"No." Zander blocked Nick's path, still not letting him by. "This is the truth. If Isadora dies, so do Callia and Casey, because they're linked through the Horae. And I'll be gone too, since my mate is my weakness. But forget about me. Forget about what this will do to my children or Isadora's child, or even Casey's baby, if it survives. Have you ever seen what happens to an Argonaut when he loses his mate?"

Ari's insanity flashed in Nick's mind. The crazed look in his eyes. His thirst for vengeance. His unpredictability and irrational recklessness.

"Theron and Demetrius won't be of any use anymore if they lose Casey and Isadora. That leaves, what? Orpheus, Gryphon, and a handful of other guys to protect the human realm? Orpheus is unpredictable at best. Gryphon's still pretty well fucked in the head from being your parents' plaything in Tartarus. And the other guys are tough as shit, but how effective can they be without the rest of us to back them up? And what happens if Argolea loses its queen? Did you stop for one minute to think about that? The Council will rush in and abolish the monarchy. Isadora's daughter will never be allowed to rule. And your people... Just what the hell do you think the Council is going to do to the Misos when Isadora isn't here to protect them? When we're not around to help her?"

A cold chill settled hard in the center of Nick's chest. He knew exactly what the Council would do. The same damn thing they'd tried to do to him. Only his people weren't half as strong as he'd been, even as a child. They'd never survive.

A buzzing sounded all through his ears. One that sent his stomach swirling.

"This isn't just about you." Zander dropped his hand from Nick's chest. "This isn't even about sex. This is bigger than all of us. If you were half the leader your people think you are, you'd man up and do the right thing this time and save them like you should have done before."

Nick's gaze shot up, and all that rolling darkness surged forward. "Why, you son of a—"

"All right, enough," Isadora pushing to her feet. "Zander, you've said your piece, now back off. This isn't Nick's problem, it's ours. And this isn't his fault, so stop heaping blame where it doesn't belong. If you want to blame someone, blame the gods. Nick." Her voice gentled, just a touch. But it was still strained, telling him she was just as anxious about this whole nightmare as he was. "No one's telling you what you need to do, least of all me. As far as I'm concerned, this is one gigantic mess with no right or wrong solution."

She stepped back from the table, looking even thinner than she'd appeared yesterday when Nick had arrived in Argolea. "I'm going upstairs to check on my daughter." She glanced toward Demetrius, and Nick couldn't help but see the hurt and lingering fear in her eyes. "If anyone needs me, you know where to find me."

She stalked past Nick, then disappeared into the hall. As silence settled over the room, Zander moved back, but he didn't cut his glare from Nick. And Nick knew everyone was staring at him, waiting for him to say something, to do something, to make it all right. But he didn't know what the fuck to do. And all he could think about was getting to Cynna, where things made sense.

He moved out into the hall, and headed for the stairs. This time, thankfully, no one tried to stop him.

"Niko, wait."

Fuck.

Nick stilled at the sound of Demetrius's voice. With one hand on the banister, he slowly turned to face his brother.

Shadows covered Demetrius's face, but as he drew closer, Nick saw what he'd missed in Isadora's office because the guardian had been looking away the whole time. Agony. Pure, unrestrained agony. The kind that could rip a person apart. The kind Nick had seen on so many prisoners' faces in Zagreus's lair.

"You have to do this."

Nick let go of the banister. "No. Just…no."

"She's going to die. I can't save her. Only you can. You have to."

Nick pinched his forehead with his thumb and forefinger. "Holy shit. Do you realize what you're asking me to do?"

"I know exactly what I'm asking," Demetrius said in a low voice. "Do I hate it? You fucking bet I do. But she's running out of time, and I can't stop it. We've tried everything. I need her to live, Niko. Elysia needs her to live. This country needs her to live. And if that means I have to share her with you"—he swallowed hard as

if just the thought sickened him, which Nick knew it had to—
"then I'll do it. I'll do anything to save her."

Nick dropped his hand, still unable to believe—unwilling to
accept—that Demetrius was asking him...no begging him...to...

Shit.

He leveled a look on his brother. "No one in that damn office
mentioned the elephant in the room. If the soul mate bond is
affecting her in the opposite way, you know what could happen.
You know what might result."

Demetrius's dark gaze never wavered from Nick's. "The soul
mate bond amplifies emotional entanglements. Yeah. I know."

"Which means she could fall in love with me."

Demetrius's jaw ticked.

"And you're okay with that?" Nick asked, wide-eyed.

"No, I'm not fucking okay with it," Demetrius snapped. "But I
don't have a damn choice here. It's either this or death. And I
can't—I won't—lose her. You have to do this. She'll be in the red
suite, on the fifth floor at nine o'clock. I'll make sure she's there."

"Tonight?" Nick stepped back. "Holy fuck. Isn't that like
rushing things just a little?"

"You want her to suffer? Because that's all you're doing by
making her wait."

"What if everyone in that room is wrong?"

"They're not. You and I both know deep inside this is about
the soul mate curse. I can feel it. I know you can too. She grows
weaker every hour. There's no telling how long she has left. If the
stress on her body gets to be too great, it could push her into
cardiac arrest. Callia's given me every gruesome detail, and I
can't... I don't..." He drew in a shaky breath. "Meet her tonight
and finish this, Niko."

There was a time, not all that long ago, when Nick would have
relished those words from his estranged brother, but not now. This
wasn't any kind of victory. And he knew if he agreed to this, none
of them were going to walk away unscathed.

Nick closed his eyes. He'd gladly trade time in Zagreus's
torture chambers for this fucked-up mess. "I don't want this. I
don't...want to hurt you."

"Then don't let her die. Do the right thing."

Holy hell. Nick didn't know what the right thing was anymore.
He didn't want anyone to die, not his people, not Casey and Callia,

and especially not Isadora. But this… What they were all asking him to do…

Pressure built in his chest, made him feel like he was being sucked under a rolling, brutal wave. He needed Cynna. Needed to see her and touch her. Needed her to center him, like she'd always been able to do. Needed her to tell him what the hell he was supposed to do next.

"I'll…" *Fuck.* He couldn't believe he was actually about to say it. "I'll think about it."

"Don't think too long," Demetrius said as Nick turned for the stairs. "Our soul mate doesn't have much time."

Cynna stared out at the darkening view from the window seat in the room she'd shared with Nick last night. A wide beach stretched beyond the castle walls and disappeared in rolling waves that lapped at the shore. But her gaze was fixed on the horizon, where the clouds had parted just enough to let a few shrinking rays of sunlight pass through as the sun set low in the distance, drawing everything into darkness.

She closed her eyes and breathed deep. She'd been silly to think she could have any of that sunshine in her life. The dark was all she knew. Since her parents had died, it was the only thing that was consistent.

The door behind her opened and closed, but she didn't turn to look. Couldn't. Not with the tumultuous way she was feeling at the moment.

"I thought maybe you'd left," Nick said in a quiet voice.

Cynna blinked back the useless sting of tears and told herself all wasn't lost…yet. He could very well be here to announce that he'd told the queen and everyone else in that room to fuck off. "The last time I did that, I didn't make it very far."

The sound of his footsteps drifted across the carpeted floor, then he sank next to her on the window seat, where she sat with her back to the wall and her knees pulled up to her chest. But he didn't touch her. And a little voice in the back of her head whispered that was not exactly a good sign.

He leaned forward and rested his forearms against his thighs. "How much of that craziness did you hear?"

Skata. He hadn't told them to fuck off. If he had, his shoulders wouldn't be bunched and that guilty look wouldn't be pulling at the corners of his eyes.

What little hope she'd been clinging too dropped like a stone into the pit of her stomach, and that voice mocked, *What the hell did you expect? She's his soul mate.* "Enough."

He looked down at the floor and clasped his hands together. "It's nuts, right? I mean…really…outrageous."

No, it wasn't just outrageous. It was completely sick and twisted, but it wasn't Cynna's place to say so. She had no hold on him. She wasn't his soul mate. And she'd known that from the moment she'd gotten emotionally involved with him. She'd just stupidly let herself fantasize that it didn't matter.

"So I take it she really is going to die."

He still didn't lift his head. Just continued to stare down at the floor with that blank, unreadable expression. "It looks that way."

Steeling herself against a conversation she didn't want to have, she dropped her feet to the floor, careful not to touch him, then pushed to standing. "Well, it looks like you're getting everything you ever wanted then. Even with your brother's blessing."

"I don't want this," Nick said as she crossed to the bed. "I never really did."

She looked down at the lightweight jacket Skyla had given her that first day, laid out on the mattress. She'd already thrown the denim jacket she'd been wearing earlier away. It was ripped at the shoulder from the scene in the alley, and she couldn't stand to look at it anymore. Couldn't handle remembering the way Nick had finally kissed her after she'd dragged him back from the edge, the tenderness in his voice, the sweet way he'd touched her, and his urgent need to be close to her. Not his soul mate, but her. "I guess it doesn't really matter what any of us want, now does it?"

He pushed to his feet. "Cynna—"

"No, you know, it's…fine." She closed her eyes and pressed her fingers against her pulsing temple. She was lying. It wasn't fine. It would *never* be fine, but what the hell could she do about it? "She's your soul mate, and though I might not get the whole soul mate draw…thing, I've definitely noticed how you can't say no to her. So fine. Do what you have to do." She dropped her hand and reached for the jacket. "You don't owe me any explanation."

"It's not what you think." He stepped toward her.

She tried not to look but couldn't keep from glancing up. His eyes were shadowed, his brow furrowed. He was probably the strongest man she'd ever met, even stronger than Zagreus because of everything he'd lived through, but at the moment, he didn't look strong. He looked wrecked. And her foolish heart went out to him.

"It's not just about her," he went on. "It's about what happens to her sisters if she dies, and the people of Argolea if there's no ruling monarchy, and what the Council will do to my people in the settlement if the queen isn't around to stop them."

He was justifying his decision. A decision he'd clearly already made. Her eyes slid closed, and her heart—or what was left of it—felt like it burst into flames in the center of her chest.

Drawing a deep breath, she pulled herself together as best she could, opened her eyes, and tugged on her jacket. "Then I guess that's all there is to say."

She turned for the door, but he moved quickly, stepping in her way. "Wait."

Angry now—that this was happening, that she couldn't change it, that she wasn't enough for *him* to want to find a way to change it—she glared at him. "For what?"

"Just… I still need you."

Frustration and hurt and betrayal all swirled inside her. "You never needed me. Not really. I was just a distraction from reality. In Zagreus's lair, when we got to the colony…here. I've never had any magical power over you, Nick, not like your soul mate, and you know it. So I'm sure if a nobody like me can distract you for whatever it is that you *need*, then your soul mate will do an even better job."

She stepped around him, but he grasped her upper arm, the heat of his fingertips burning into her skin beneath her jacket as he turned her to face him.

Godsdammit… She was past the point of understanding. She wanted to lash out, to tell him to leave her the hell alone, to run. But when she glared up at him, the anguish she saw on his scarred face nearly did her in.

"I don't…want you to leave," he said in a pained voice.

Oh gods. Everything hurt—her stomach, her chest, her limbs, her head. And she found herself wanting to sink in and comfort him the way she needed to be comforted right this very second. But she couldn't. Because something told her when he eventually left her to be with Isadora, that willpower that she'd held on to so tightly all those months with Zagreus would finally break. And she'd spiral even deeper into the depths of a despair that had pushed her toward revenge in the first place. To a place she'd never break free from.

"Neither do I," she managed. "But I've never gotten what I want out of life. And this time, I'm not willing to compromise."

Gently, she pulled her arm from his and straightened her spine. "It's selfish of me. I know it is. But I won't share you with someone else, especially her. I just...can't. If you do this, then you have to do it without me."

CHAPTER TWENTY-TWO

Zagreus stalked out of the cavern where Lykos was tormenting a particularly naughty nymph chained to the wall. Nothing pleased him lately. Not the sounds of agony in his lair, not watching Lykos—now that he was healed from his wounds—work his special talents on a nymph who'd tried to run away. Not even toying with the trio of Maenad nymphs he'd taken to his bedchamber last night.

He headed for his office, pushed the door open, and dropped into the chair behind his massive desk. The underwater window cast shades of blue and green over the dark room, and he stared at the fish swimming by, wondering if ripping a few to shreds would do anything to bolster his mood.

Probably not. The only person who could lift his spirits was an entire world away, probably fucking his uncle right this very minute.

His mood slid deeper into darkness. He clenched his jaw and drummed his fingers along the stone surface of his desk. The tracking device in Cynna's arm had been a diversion, so that she and Nick would think that was how he was monitoring their escape. But he didn't need it to know where she was or what she was feeling. Thanks to his blood, which now circulated in her veins, he was privy to her emotions. And those emotions—those disgusting, abhorrent emotions—were currently fucking with his plans.

His sweet Cynna felt strongly for Nick. Yet instead of being overjoyed by that feeling, she was currently brimming with anger, something that infuriated Zagreus beyond reason. Until he felt the burst of joy and excitement he knew came only from that useless emotion Argoleans and humans called love, he couldn't tell if his uncle had truly fallen for her yet.

He loathed the fact that he needed that to happen, but breaking the son of a bitch emotionally was the only way he was going to harness Nick's powers once and for all. Still…the thought of Cynna fucking the bastard, of her enjoying it, of knowing that she was falling in love with the asshole made Zagreus see nothing but blinding red.

"Did you think you could double-cross me and I would not find out?"

Startled out of his rage by the sound of the menacing voice, Zagreus jolted and glanced to his left, where Hades sat in a chair in the dark corner of the room, his black-as-sin eyes like daggers boring into his son.

Fuuuuck. Play it cool.

Zagreus glared right back at dear old Dad. "You've got nothing better to do than bother me? Things must be slow in the Underworld."

"Don't play coy with me, son. Where is your female? The one you so like to fuck in this deplorable lair you call home?"

Zagreus's blood heated, but he forced himself not to react. "Around."

Hades pushed out of his chair, his gaze never once wavering from Zagreus's face. "Your female is in Argolea with my prize."

A bead of apprehension slid down Zagreus's spine. "Why would you ever think that?"

"Because I have spies within the Argolean Council who keep me abreast of what's happening in their realm, and the two were recently spotted there together." He slammed his hands on Zagreus's desk, making Zagreus inch back from his father's rolling, heated fury. "There's no way they could have escaped from your control unless you let them go. The demigod's powers may continue to grow, but he's not as strong as you. Not yet. Not unless he breaks. And something tells me if you released your bitch with him, it means you're about to claim something that does not belong to you."

Zagreus's pulse pounded hard as he stared up into Hades's enraged face. As a god, Zagreus was immortal. His father couldn't kill him even if he wanted to. He couldn't even strip him of his powers. But he could destroy everything Zagreus had built, and he knew where Cynna was located. In retaliation for what he considered betrayal, Hades wouldn't hesitate to take the only thing Zagreus really cared about.

"I'm not waiting to claim anything," Zagreus lied. "This is all part of my plan. He cares for the female. Physical pain didn't break him. Sexual pain didn't seem to faze him. Emotional pain is the only thing that will work. The female is on our side. In fact," he went on, extending the lie, "this was all her idea. As soon as the demigod falls in love with her, she'll alert me. My presence will signal the ultimate betrayal. And that will be enough to finally break him the way we want."

Hades eased back, his eyes full of distrust. But Zagreus knew the god wanted Nick more than he wanted anything else. And this explanation—even if not completely true—made perfect sense. He breathed a little easier. Yeah, he might just have lost Nick's powers for himself, but if he played his cards right, he could keep his lair and Cynna too.

Rage covered Hades's features, and he slammed his foot into the floor. A massive earthquake shook the tunnels, knocking over the stone desk, dropping pictures from the walls, making rocks crumble from the ceiling and crash against the ground.

Zagreus lurched back from being pummeled by falling stones. When the shaking finally subsided, Hades's booming voice roared through the cavern.

"I will not be fucked with. I warned you what would happen if you double-crossed me."

"I'm not double-crossing you," Zagreus lied, pushing to his feet. "He's going to break."

Hades stalked forward, forcing Zagreus to scramble back until his spine hit the wall. The god-king of the Underworld glared into his son's eyes.

"You're right, he will. But you, my lecherous son, will never claim him. And when he finally breaks, Krónos's powers will transfer to me. I want him back. Now. If you ever want to see your precious bitch again, you'll do exactly as I say. Gather your satyr army and be ready to march at midnight."

* * *

Nick's hands were sweating.

Standing outside the bedroom door in the empty hall on the fifth floor of the castle, he swiped his damp palms against the thighs of his jeans, lifted his hand to knock, then lowered it quickly and stepped back.

Holy fuck. What the hell was he doing? His chest grew so tight he couldn't breathe. Bracing his hands on his hips, he paced away, focusing on the push and pull of air in his lungs until he could think again.

He'd been putting this off for fifteen minutes, pacing back and forth in this corridor, trying to convince himself to just go in there and get it over with. But every time he tried, he pictured Cynna as she'd looked just before she walked away from him, her eyes no longer dead and flat as they'd been in Zagreus's lair, but filled with so much pain and heartbreak, he hadn't known what to say or do to make this better for her.

He stopped. Raked a hand through his short hair. Fisted the locks and pulled so hard, pain spiraled all through his skull. He loved her. *Loved* her. Not with candy and flowers, but with his whole heart and mind. And he was about to step into this room and screw another woman, all because the gods enjoyed fucking with his life.

He couldn't do it. He didn't want to do it. He didn't care if his soul was linked to someone else. It wasn't right. It wasn't fair. It wasn't—

"Come into the room, Nick." Surprised, Nick looked up to see Isadora, dressed in loose jeans and a thick cream-colored sweater, standing in the open doorway to the suite. "I can't stand listening to you pace out here anymore."

The soul mate draw he'd always felt with her tugged at something deep inside him, and before he even realized it, his feet were moving, carrying him from the hall into the entry of the suite, then into a living room with walls steeped all in red.

His pulse raced. He glanced around the room, expecting to see nothing but a bed, but to his relief, he discovered he was standing in a living area. White plush furnishings were set out in front of a whitewashed fireplace, flames already flickering in the hearth, and black-and-white framed photographs of flowers and hillsides decorated the walls.

Wrong. So fucking wrong. This whole thing is just—

Isadora sat on the couch and tucked one bare foot up under her, looking petite against the enormous piece of furniture, and swiped her blonde hair away from her face. "Why don't we just…sit for a little bit."

Before the fucking began? Nick's legs felt suddenly wobbly. He rubbed his damp hands on his thighs once more and sat in a side chair across from her. "Okay."

Silence settled over the room. Somewhere close, a clock ticked, but Nick's mind was drifting. To his brother, wondering where Demetrius was right this moment and what the hell he was thinking. To Cynna, and whether or not she'd ever talk to him again after this night.

"I heard you went out to the settlement," Isadora said softly.

Small talk. Shit. Part of him was thankful for it. Part of him just wanted to get this damn thing over with so he could get the hell out of here.

He cleared his throat, shifted in his chair. "Yeah. I did."

"I bet that was difficult."

A lump formed in his throat. Seeing his people, what had happened to them, learning about his friends who had died… It was more difficult than anything he'd ever done. His memory slid to the alley and the moment he'd nearly lost it for good. And the way Cynna had pulled him back, comforted him, cared nothing about what might happen to her, and given everything to him.

He closed his eyes. And a warm wetness burned the backs of his eyelids. One he'd never felt before.

"You don't want to do this, do you?" Isadora asked in a quiet voice.

Nick didn't answer. Didn't know what to say. He felt torn between his heart and his soul. Two things he'd always thought were connected.

He opened his eyes and looked over at his soul mate. At the female he would always be drawn to. And though that pull to her was still there, pushing him toward her, to help her, to save her, what he felt in his heart was stronger. "If you'd asked me six months ago if I wanted this, I would have said yes. Absolutely. But now… Everything's different now. I'm different. And I don't…"

Shit. How did he say this?

"I don't want it either," Isadora blurted.

"You don't?"

She shook her head and blinked back the sheen of tears in her eyes. "Demetrius and I argued about it. I know it's the right thing to do, but I just…"

"You can't do it," he finished for her.

"No," she whispered. "I don't want anyone to die because of me. Casey, Callia, Zander…" She closed her eyes tight, opened them again. "I don't want them to get hurt. And I don't want anything bad to happen to the people of this realm or to the Misos, but I'm tired of doing the right thing for everyone else. I know it's selfish, but all I can think about is what this will do to my family. To Elysia. To Demetrius. If we go through with this, Nick, it will kill Demetrius. Maybe not at first, but it will eat away at him until the man I fell in love with is gone. He already hates that he couldn't save me from Hades's contract on my life. He'll blame himself that he couldn't fix this too."

"None of this is Demetrius's fault."

"It's not yours either."

No, it wasn't. It was the gods'. And they were all nothing more than pawns in their fucking game.

He pushed from the chair, crossed to the couch, and sat next to her. Leaning forward, he reached for her hand, feeling how cold her skin was and the way her pulse jumped against his fingers.

Yes, she was growing weaker because of him. He knew that in his soul. And yes, he could tell that his touch had a positive effect on her. But he wasn't convinced sex was the solution. There had to be another way. Something they'd all missed.

He cradled her palm against his and smoothed his fingers over the back of her hand, feeling her skin warm the longer he held her. And when he looked up into her chocolate eyes to ask if she felt it too, a jolt of familiarity shot through him. The same familiarity he'd felt when he'd been in Zagreus's tunnels looking…into Cynna's eyes.

"What is it?" Isadora's brow dropped low. "Are you okay?"

He gave his head a swift shake, but the scars on his back were tingling again, and puzzle pieces were shifting around in his mind, trying to find a fit. "Yeah. I'm…I'm fine."

She shot him a look that said she wasn't quite sure she believed him, then sighed and looked down at their joined hands. "So what are we going to do?"

He really had no idea what they should do, but he knew exactly what he couldn't do. "You know, something no one's thought of is the fact those four Argonauts everyone's basing this theory on were given their immortality. I was born with it, even if it's taken this long to come out. That might not seem like a big difference, but in the eyes of the gods, it might be enough. No one truly knows if the same thing that happened to those Argonauts' soul mates will happen to you."

"I know. Theron, Zander, Demetrius... They're all desperate, grasping for a solution."

He knew that. Understood it. But he didn't want to accidentally make things worse basing all this on a guess. He nodded toward their joined hands. "This helps, doesn't it? My touch?"

"Yes."

"Then we'll continue to do this."

She eyed him warily. "You're going to sit here and hold my hand all day?"

"For several hours a day, if that's what it takes. Whatever we can do to slow this thing down until we can come up with a different solution. Because there has to be one. I can't come between you and Demetrius, Isadora. I might have tried once, but it was wrong of me. I know that now."

Isadora stared at him for several long seconds, then quietly said, "You're in love with her, aren't you? The female you escaped with. Cynna."

Nick's heart picked up speed. And memories of Cynna bombarded him from every side. The way she'd tended his wound in Zagreus's lair, the moment she'd freed him from his cell, the strength it had taken for her to put herself between him and his darkness at the colony, and, ultimately, the hurt in her eyes when she'd left him tonight.

He drew in a deep breath that did nothing to ease the growing ache in his chest. "Yeah, I am. Which is pretty freakin' strange, because I've never been in love before."

"It changes the way you see the world, doesn't it?"

He looked into her eyes, for the first time understanding her. "It changes everything."

"Then go to her."

His brow dropped. "What?"

Gently, she pulled her hand from his. "I won't come between you and her either. I might have been willing to consider it when I thought your heart wasn't on the line, but now that I know the truth…" She shook her head. "I won't destroy both of the men I care most for in this life all because the gods will it to be done."

Something in his soul relaxed. All the pent-up frustration he'd felt through the years because he couldn't have her leaked away. He reached for her without thinking, wrapped his arms around her and drew her against his chest. Her arms wound around his back, her cheek pressed against his shoulder. And as his body heat seeped into her, easing the chill of her skin, he realized this was the first time he'd ever held her. The only other time he'd been this close to her was when he'd foolishly kissed her, thinking he could force her to care for him.

What an idiot he'd been. She already had cared for him. He'd just been too stupid to realize her heart would always belong to his brother. Which was exactly where it was meant to be.

"We'll find a way to fix this," he said over her head.

"Maybe." She eased out of his arms and rose. "Maybe not. But it's not your responsibility. And I don't want you to worry about me anymore tonight." Her expression softened. "Go to her, Nick. And tell her… Tell her I'm sorry. For all of this."

He pushed to his feet. "What about you?"

She smiled, but the expression didn't reach her eyes. "I'll be fine. Like you said, we've still got time. Go. Before Cynna leaves and you can't find her."

Warmth and need and hope pulsed through Nick's chest. His hands grew sweaty all over again, but this time not with apprehension. With anticipation. And at the first thought of Cynna, he knew exactly where she'd gone. Knew he'd always be able to find her because she held *his* heart.

"I'll come back," he said. "We'll figure this out."

"Yes," Isadora said softly as he flashed from the room. "Someday maybe we will. But not tonight."

Cynna knelt in front of the remembrance stones in the field behind what was left of her parents' home on the outskirts of Kyrenia and brushed the dirt and leaves from her parents' names.

Moonlight shone down, enough light to illuminate the pale pink, gray, and white flowers that bloomed around the stones year round.

Asphodel. The ghostly wildflower grew around all the remembrance stones of the dead in Argolea. Food for the souls of the deceased, her mother had once told her. She'd always found it morbid that life should spring from death. But tonight that thought eased the pain she was feeling. If only a touch.

Shuffling sounded behind her, and without looking, she knew Nick had found her. Knew because no one else would even think to come out here for her. Not even Delia.

She swiped at her eyes and slowly pushed to her feet. She'd carefully kept the truth from Nick as soon as she'd realized his connection to the Argonauts, but tonight that secret no longer mattered. And maybe if he knew who she really was, he'd stop following her. Because, gods knew, she couldn't handle being near him after what he'd just done.

"My mother's name was Andromeda," she said without turning. "She lived in Argolea most of her life. She knew my father there when he served with the Council of Elders. She was bound to a very powerful *ándras* at the time who clearly didn't love her back. She told me once she tried to make him happy, tried to give him sons, but the Fates were never on her side, and he blamed her for that. For what he called her liability. She stayed with him for hundreds of years, even though she was miserable. Divorce, from someone as powerful as him, wasn't only frowned upon, it wasn't allowed."

Nick didn't say anything, but Cynna told herself that was for the best. The sooner she got through this, the sooner they could be done. In the silence, she stared down at the remembrance stone and her mother's name, the engraving worn from the weather of the years. Her mother had been gone so long, it was hard for Cynna to call up her image, something that made her heart ache even more.

She swallowed back the pain and forced herself to go on. "He had many affairs, but when she realized he'd been sleeping with her closest confidante, and that the female was pregnant, she couldn't take it anymore. She left him. My father was her friend, and he helped her escape. But when her husband learned of what had happened, he wasn't happy. He sent his soldiers to bring her back, only they couldn't find her. To save face, he publicly announced that she'd crossed into the human realm on a shopping spree and was killed by a pack of daemons."

"Cynna," Nick finally said after several seconds, "are you saying—"

"Yes." She turned to face him. He was wearing a thick gray Henley, jeans, boots, and a dark jacket. And standing before her in the moonlight with his blond hair mussed and that sexy scruff on his jaw, her heart did a little flip. Then dropped into the pit of her stomach all over again because, as much as she wanted him, she couldn't have him. Never again.

She pushed aside the hurt. His confused expression said he'd obviously heard the stories. But knowing Demetrius was his brother, of course he'd have heard them all.

"My mother was Andromeda, the queen of Argolea. She left the king, came here, and started over. With my father's help. They were never bound, not legally at least, but the witches didn't care. They took them in as their own, gave them a place to live, and in return, my parents helped hundreds of other refugees who were persecuted or banished by the monarchy and the Council for different reasons."

She crossed her arms over her chest, rubbed the chill at her arms, and looked down at the asphodel all around her feet. Life from death. She hoped that was true, because her life seemed to be filled with nothing but misery.

"I was born a few years later. I grew up with two parents who loved each other more than life itself. They didn't have much, but they had each other. And that was all that mattered. Until the Council's spies discovered the queen was living in Kyrenia and who she was with. They claimed it was the witches they were trying to eradicate, but it wasn't. It was her and the former Council member she'd left with. The one who'd defied them. And the king knew. He gave his permission. He sat back and did nothing as his wife was murdered."

"Gods." Nick rubbed a hand over his face. "Isadora is your sister. I knew your eyes were familiar. I even noticed it tonight."

A wave of betrayal and hurt rushed through Cynna. She didn't want to think of him with Isadora tonight. Didn't want the image of what they'd done together anywhere in her mind. She turned away and stalked across the field, back toward the ruins of her parents' house. "Half sister. And now you know why I hate her so much."

"Because her father took everything from you."

Her feet stilled. He was behind her. Close, but not too close. And her heart pounded hard with the desire to touch him and the need to push him away. "Yes," she whispered. "And like father, like daughter, she's doing it again. Which is why I need you to go and never follow me again." Her throat grew thick. "I know revenge isn't the answer anymore, but I can't...be around you. Not after all this. It's too much."

She stepped forward, desperate to get away from him.

"I didn't sleep with her."

She stopped, sure she had to have imagined those words.

"I couldn't," he said softly. "Because my heart belongs to you."

Cynna's pulse sped up until it was a whir in her ears, and wide-eyed, she turned to face him.

"I love you, Cynna." He moved toward her. "Not because the gods say I should. Not because some curse tells me to. I love you because I choose to."

He stopped inches away, and her stomach tightened, her head felt light. She was too afraid to speak, too afraid any kind of sound would wake her and prove this was a dream and not reality.

His fingers brushed the hair away from her temple. "And because you're the only person in my life who's never wanted anything from me except me."

"I..." She swallowed hard. This wasn't a dream. He was standing here. Looking down at her in the moonlight like she was...everything. Her skin grew hot. "What about Isadora?"

Sadness crept into his amber eyes, and he trailed his finger down her cheek until she trembled. "I don't know. I can't change the soul mate pull. I'll always feel the need to help her if I can. But being with her like that is not the answer."

He lifted his other hand to her face, cradling her jaw in his big palms. And his eyes grew so soft and dreamy as he gazed down at her, her heart burst to life in her chest. "You're my answer, though. To every struggle, every heartache, every question I was too afraid to ask. You've drawn me back from the edge so many times, not because you have some magical quality but because you understand me. No one, not in two hundred years, has ever cared for me the way you do. Because of you, I know I can fight the darkness inside and win. All I have to do is think of you, and I'm free."

He shifted closer until his body brushed hers, and his heat seeped into her skin, making her ache, not with loss this time, but with…hope. "I want to be that same answer for you. I know your life has been filled with pain and darkness, but I can be your balance the way you've been mine. If it takes my whole life, Cynna, through all of eternity, I promise to be that and more for you."

Tears burned. Tears she couldn't hold back. She closed her eyes as the first droplet slid down her cheek. "You big jerk. You already are."

He lowered his mouth to hers, and she held her breath. Then sighed as his lips brushed hers and she drew him into her mouth.

She didn't deserve this. She didn't deserve him after all the bad shit she'd done in her life, but she wanted him. He might have thought she'd saved him from a bitter darkness, but the truth was, he'd saved her. Because without him, she'd have become a hard, empty shell of a person. She'd have become someone just like Zagreus.

"Nick…"

He tipped his head, kissed her deeper, wrapped his arms around her and pulled her into the warmth and protection of his body. And as she returned his kiss with every ounce of passion inside her, she opened the last bit of her heart to him.

Her head grew light. Her skin tingled. She felt as if his kisses were shaking the ground. And then her knees wobbled, and she drew back from his mouth and realized they weren't standing in the field behind the ruins of her parents' old house. They were in a bedroom. One with pale blue walls, a queen-size bed covered with a gray-and-white-checked quilt, and a small window that looked out over a dark street.

"Where…?" She glanced around and recognized the symbol hanging over the bed. The crescent moon tipped on its side with three droplets falling beneath it. The witch's symbol for blessing. Her gaze shot back to his face. "We're in Delia's house. You flashed me through walls."

A sexy, powerful grin curled his lips, pulling on the scar across his cheek. "I'm telling you, these gifts are coming in mighty handy."

He leaned close, brushed his tempting mouth over hers again, and pushed the lightweight jacket from her shoulders, then dropped it on the floor. "But right now I don't want to use them. I want to unwrap you like the gift that you are."

She sucked in a breath as he drew back, as his fingers found the hem of her T-shirt and lifted it above her head. His eyes raked over the swell of her breasts, and her nipples tightened when she saw the desire in his features. He licked his lips and leaned down to kiss her again.

She pushed the jacket from his shoulder as he walked her backward toward the bed, every part of her aching for his touch. He laved his tongue over hers and flipped the clasp on her bra free, then tugged it from her arm and tossed it behind him.

The backs of her legs hit the mattress, but he caught her around the waist before she fell, then lowered her to the bed, never once breaking their kiss, never once letting her go.

She'd never wanted anyone to protect her. Never thought she'd needed it. But with Nick, she felt safe. Cherished. And even in his darkest hour, she knew in the depths of her heart that he'd never hurt her.

She reached for his shirt as he climbed over her. He eased back long enough for her to pull the soft cotton free of his body. Then his mouth was on hers once more, the muscles in his back rippling beneath her fingers as he kissed her again and again, as she opened her legs and he pressed her into the mattress.

"Mm, Cynna." His hand slid up her side to cup her breast and brush his thumb over her nipple. "I'm lost without you."

Her fingers found his waistband, and she reached between them, unbuttoning his jeans. "Then don't ever be without me."

He groaned into her mouth as she slipped her hand into his pants and closed her fingers around his length. He was hard, hot, already pulsing in her grip. And as he licked into her mouth and pressed into her hand, she stroked him, loving the way he trembled against her, loving that she did this to him, that she was the one who could make him weak.

He drew back from her before she was ready to let him go, crawled back off the bed, and stripped her of her own pants. Heart pounding, she pressed up on her elbows and watched as his gaze skipped across her naked flesh, as his features darkened, as he licked his lips again, then lowered to his knees and tugged her hips to the edge of the bed.

"This is what I want," he whispered.

Anticipation and heat swirled inside her as he pushed her legs apart, as he leaned close. And then he licked the swollen flesh between her legs, and she was gone.

Pleasure rushed down her spine. She dropped her head back as that pleasure trickled through her body, groaned when he did it again and again, sending her spinning toward a release only he could make her reach. He knew exactly where to touch her with his tongue, with his fingers, knew just when to suckle to make her cry out and when to back off to heighten her arousal. Sweat slicked her skin. She fisted the quilt at her sides. Lifted to meet his wicked tongue as he pushed her closer toward oblivion. And when he finally let her go, the ecstasy was like nothing she'd ever known, so completely soul shattering, she knew nothing else but him.

He kissed his way up her body and captured her mouth before she had a chance to catch her breath. But she didn't care, because his frantic tongue dancing across hers reignited her need, her lust, her desire. Groaning, she scrambled to free him from his jeans. He kicked them off and climbed between her legs.

"I'm not going to make love to you," he whispered. "I'm not going to fuck you." The head of his cock slid into her slick heat, sending pleasure arcing down her spine. "I'm going to own you, Cynna. Mind, body, soul. The way you own me."

Her body trembled. Zagreus had wanted that—to own her. But it was nothing like this. That had been dark and controlling and one-sided. This was light and love and a mutual need to belong. To each other.

Every inch of her skin tingled. Desire roared in her veins at the sound of his husky words, from the heated, intense expression on his focused, handsome face. It was all she could do to hold still. "Nick—"

He lowered his mouth to hers and pushed forward until the tip of his cock pressed a fraction of an inch inside her. "You're mine," he whispered against her lips. "The only one I want. The only female I've ever loved."

He drove deep, drew back then shoved in again, moving faster with every thrust. She groaned at the delicious friction, hooked one leg around his hip, and lifted to meet every plunge, every thrust, every press and glide and retreat. Gods, she needed him. Needed this. Was desperate for more. Desperate for him. Desperate to be his everything.

He was right. Her life had been nothing but darkness and despair up until this point, but no more.

"I am yours," she whispered.

His thrusts grew harder. Faster. Longer. As if her words excited him even more. And his arousal ignited her own, pushing her right back to the peak. She held on tighter. Clenched all around him, lifted her mouth to his, and whispered, "Only yours."

He groaned, his whole body contracted with his release, and the second his orgasm slammed into him, so did hers, twisting them down together until he was all that mattered. Until she knew he was the lone bright light dragging her back to the person she was meant to be.

He fell against her, and she wrapped her arms around him, kissed his cheek, his temple, sifted her fingers into his hair and held him close for as long as she could. Her heart pounded hard as the bliss settled, and a warm happiness encircled her heart in the silence. One that brought a smile to her lips. One she'd never experienced before. Because this—he—was everything she'd never been strong enough to hope for.

But even as that happiness spread through her veins, a tiny voice whispered this was too good to be true. That love, for someone like her, would never last. And though she fought it, something in the center of her chest grew deathly afraid the voice might be right.

He pushed up on his elbow and looked down at her, his brows drawing together in concern. "What's wrong?"

"Nothing." Thankful that he couldn't read her mind, she swallowed back the fear and told herself that tonight she wouldn't worry about the future. Tonight all that mattered was this. Him. Them. This moment. Everything else could wait.

She lifted her lips back to his. "Just kiss me again."

A slow, sexy smile curled his mouth as he rolled to his back, pulling her on top of all his muscular heat. "Mm, baby." He tangled his hand in her hair and tugged her down toward his tantalizing mouth. "That is never something you have to ask for twice."

She held her breath and kissed him. And for the first time in she couldn't remember how long, she prayed.

She prayed that he was right.

CHAPTER TWENTY-THREE

Isadora stood in the dark closet in the run-down apartment on the outskirts of Tiyrns and lowered the hood of her cloak. Looking up the long metal rungs of the ladder toward the trapdoor above, she drew a steadying breath. She wasn't sure she had the strength to climb, but she wasn't going back to the castle. Not yet, at least.

She'd known exactly where Demetrius would go. Knew his thoughts and what he was feeling better than he did. As she pulled herself up the ladder, she wondered how he was able to get his big body through this small space. How he'd done it for so many years when he'd chosen to live in this tiny place instead of in the luxury each Argonaut deserved.

She wasn't letting him revert back to this. Not to thinking he didn't matter. Because he did. More than anyone else in this world or the next.

Breathless, she reached the top and pressed her hand against the door. Metal hinges creaked. The muscles in her arms burned. But before she even pushed the door up two inches, it swung back, and strong male hands gripped her, pulling her up to the wood decking of the octagonal room, then tugged her into a sea of strength and heat.

"*Kardia*." Demetrius dragged her so close, he was all she felt. "What the hell are you doing here? Are you crazy?"

"Yes," she said against him, holding on and not letting go. "Crazy for you."

He released a long breath above her head, but didn't seem to want to let go of her either, and for that she was glad. So very glad.

"How in the name of the gods did you get out of the castle unnoticed?"

"Orpheus's invisibility cloak."

"Damn daemon," he muttered. "I'm gonna burn that thing."

"No, you won't. I won't let you." She hugged him tighter, digging her fingertips into the muscles of his back. "I looked everywhere for you."

He swallowed hard. "I couldn't stay. I would have come back. I just—"

"I didn't do it."

He stilled against her. "You didn't?"

She shook her head and beat back the tears that wanted to fall. "I couldn't. I don't want anyone but you."

His arms tightened around her with the strength of a vise, and he lifted her feet from the floor, turning his face into her neck as he held her to him. "Stupid female," he whispered against her. "So, so stupid…"

Those tears spilled over. She couldn't stop them. She sifted her fingers into his hair. "We'll have to find another way, because I can't be with anyone else. I would rather die than do that to us. I love you. Just you. Always."

His mouth found hers. And she clung to him as he kissed her, knowing that this, their love, was stronger than any soul mate bond. His strength would keep her alive. It had to.

"Love me, Demetrius," she said against his mouth. "Love me right now."

He pulled her toward a pile of blankets on the far side of the small room and lowered them to the floor, tugging her on top of all his strong, delicious heat. After swiping the cloak from her shoulders, he slid his fingers up under her sweater, lifted his mouth back to hers, and whispered, "Ah, *kardia*. I already do. I'll love you forever. No matter what."

Cynna lay in bed, staring up at the dark ceiling, unable to sleep. Again.

She glanced down at Nick softly dozing against her, his head pillowed on her chest, his legs intertwined with hers in the sheets, his arms wrapped around her, holding her close. Love blossomed all through her heart as she ran her fingers through his silky hair, but it didn't ease her worry or stop that niggling voice in the back of her head.

Sighing, she looked back up at the ceiling. The voice was right. Even if Nick didn't wise up to reality and leave her on his own, there were still a hundred reasons why they just wouldn't work in the long run. The biggest of which, that voice whispered, was Zagreus.

A shudder ran through her as her mind drifted to the Prince of Darkness. He was still out there. Probably pissed that she'd left. And though she wanted to believe they'd escaped from his prison on their own, she knew if he hadn't wanted them to go, they'd still be locked in that hellhole. Which meant he was biding his time, waiting for…something.

Disjointed memories swam through her head. She tried to pull them into view. Couldn't quite make them connect. She remembered being in her room in the caves. Remembered someone holding her down. Remembered Zagreus's menacing voice echoing in her ears.

"You're going to make him fall for you. And when he finally turns his back on that useless hero honor and chooses you, then we'll have what we want. Then I'll come and reclaim you both."

That shudder turned to icy fingers rushing down her spine. She'd been so focused on Isadora and what was happening with Nick and his soul mate these last few days, she'd ignored the biggest threat of all.

She glanced down at Nick again, her heart racing. And remembered Zander's words earlier in the queen's office.

"Have you ever seen what happens to an Argonaut when his soul mate dies?"

Yes, she had seen it. She'd seen Ari. The former Argonaut was completely broken. Nick was strong enough to fight the darkness but not a shattered soul. What would happen to him if Isadora died? What would he do?

In a firestorm of understanding, Zagreus's plan made sense. The reason he'd let them go. The reason he hadn't come after them yet. The reason he'd made her drink his blood that night in her room.

A new, more crucial urgency pushed at her from every direction. Slowly, so she didn't wake Nick, she climbed out from under him, dropped to the floor, and found her clothes. Tiptoeing out into the hall, she pulled them on while her fingers shook with both fear and dread.

She didn't bother with her jacket, just rushed downstairs and out onto Delia's porch before it was too late. Picturing the castle, she closed her eyes and flashed to the front gates.

The guards let her pass with hardly a look, something she was grateful for now. She raced into the castle, then stopped in the massive foyer. It was past midnight. Everyone was likely asleep. But this couldn't wait until morning. Gripping the banister, she skipped stairs and raced for the upper floors.

She sprinted down the long corridor toward the queen's suite, then slammed on her brakes and jerked back when she heard voices in the same sitting area where she'd encountered Isadora and her daughter.

Her chest rose and fell as she stepped under the archway and peered inside. Demetrius sat back in the corner of a plush couch with one leg on each side of Isadora. She lay back against his chest cradling Elysia and feeding her a bottle. The baby cooed and tried to grab the bottle. Isadora laughed. Demetrius closed his eyes and pressed his lips against the queen's temple, holding her close and breathing deep.

Happy. They were happy. A family unit. The way Cynna's parents had once been with her. And she was about to destroy them for all eternity.

"Cynna?" Isadora looked up. "Is everything okay?"

Cynna swallowed the lump in her throat. Guilt washed through her. For a sister she'd always hated. And for a moment, she considered turning around, going back to Nick. But she couldn't. Because this was too important.

She stepped into the room. "You have to do it. You can't let Nick talk you out of it."

Demetrius stiffened, but Isadora only frowned. "Nick and I both decided that is not something either of us is willing to do. That solution is off the table, permanently."

Panic pushed Cynna forward. "You don't understand what's happening here. Zagreus couldn't break Nick physically or sexually to gain his god powers, so he let us go. He knew Nick was already interested in me. He's been waiting for Nick to fall in love with me so he can swoop in and tell Nick how I betrayed him, thinking that will be enough to break him emotionally. But he's wrong. Nick's too strong to break from that. But if you die, it'll push him over the edge. The soul mate bond is stronger than anything. You've all said it. I've seen what a broken Argonaut looks like. If Nick loses you, it'll be too much. It'll—"

"Cynna, stop."

She jerked around at the sound of Nick's voice. He stood in the archway to the hall, wearing jeans and the same long-sleeved shirt she'd pulled off his chiseled chest only hours ago, staring at her with intense amber eyes that seemed to see right through her.

That panic swelled, making her throat tight and her fingers tingle.

"I didn't know what he had planned." Perspiration dotted her forehead with every step he took toward her. "I only just figured it out when I remembered what he said to me in my room before I blacked out. I wasn't in on this stupid plan with him, I swear it. I—"

Nick stopped in front of her and lifted his hand to her face. "I already know that."

Her gaze searched his face. His very calm, not the least bit angry face. "You do?"

"I figured out his plan a long time ago. I know you weren't part of it."

Relief and pain and heartache swirled inside her, and her eyelids fell closed. Gods, she loved this man. Loved him so damn much she was willing to sacrifice everything she wanted to keep him safe.

Forcing herself to turn away, she looked toward Isadora, who'd pushed to her feet and was watching their conversation with interest. Demetrius stood behind her, holding the baby.

"You have to do whatever you need to do so you don't die and he doesn't break," Cynna said to the queen. "I don't care about the consequences. None of you should."

"Cynna." Pity filled Isadora's chocolate eyes. "I know you're upset, but Nick and I being together is not the answer. We've already discussed it. Maybe if we weren't already a family. Maybe if this wasn't all so intertwined things would be different, but—"

"Oh, fuck family." Cynna threw her arm out to the side. "What does family have to do with anything? This is about Krónos and what he'll do with Nick once he breaks him and—"

"She didn't tell you, did she?" Nick said at Cynna's back.

Isadora's gaze darted past Cynna, focusing on Nick. "Tell me what?"

"About your mother."

A buzzing erupted in Cynna's ears. She whipped around, but Nick barely spared her a glance.

"My mother?" Isadora's voice lifted at Cynna's back. "What about my mother?"

Cynna's eyes widened as she stared up at Nick. "What the hell are you doing?"

"Looking out for your best interests." His gaze shifted to focus on her. "She would never choose me because of Demetrius. But even if he were gone, she still wouldn't agree to something that would ultimately hurt her sister."

"My...sister?" Isadora asked in a dazed voice.

Holy shit, he'd said it. Cynna's eyes slammed shut.

"Your mother wasn't killed by daemons," Nick said. "She escaped. She started a new life, fell in love, had another child. A girl. A girl who she ultimately had to leave when the king approved the Council's war on the witches and destroyed Kyrenia."

Cynna's eyes open, and she glared up at Nick while a hundred different emotions prickled her skin. "You son of a bitch."

He grinned. The bastard *grinned*. Then he leaned down and kissed her. "That's love-of-your-life son of a bitch. And get this through your stubborn head, female. I love you. That wasn't just a declaration, it was truth. And that means I'll do what's best for you even when you can't. Isadora and me... It's not happening. Ever. But this—you and me—this *is* happening. And as long as I have you by my side, I know we can find the answer to this mess."

Tears burned behind Cynna's eyelids. She was trying to do the right thing. Trying to save him the way he'd saved her, and he was making it so damn difficult.

Before she could move into the strength of his arms and tell him what an idiot he was, Isadora grasped her arm and turned her around. "I have another sister?"

The queen's eyes grew damp, and she threw her arms around Cynna, hugging her so tight, Cynna gasped. "I didn't know. If I had known..."

She pushed back and stared at Cynna, her face brimming with a mixture of happiness and sorrow that tugged on Cynna's heart in a way she wasn't ready for. "She was happy? Our mother was actually happy?" One tear spilled over her lower lashes and slid down her cheek. "I never saw her happy. Not once. My father made her so miserable. He made both of us miserable. He never even looked for her after she disappeared. He wouldn't let me look for her. I used to daydream that she left me to start over, but I never imagined she actually had. I so desperately wanted her to find love, to be free of his prison, to—"

Horror flashed across her face. "She was in Kyrenia? Oh my gods. *You* were in Kyrenia?"

She hugged Cynna again. "I'm sorry. Oh gods. I'm so sorry."

All that resentment rushed out of Cynna on a wave. Because, in that moment, she realized that her jealousy and anger had been misplaced. Isadora's life hadn't been perfect. She'd suffered and hurt just as much as Cynna. Maybe more, because she'd never known the love of a real family. Not until she'd created her own with Demetrius.

Isadora drew back and pressed her hands to Cynna's cheeks, swiping away tears Cynna hadn't even realized were sliding down her own cheeks. "Nick's right. This changes everything. And I'm so very glad he told me. I have another sister." A warm smile brightened her damp eyes. Eyes that were the same color and shape as Cynna's. "We'll figure this out. Together we'll all figure this out."

The queen finally let go of her, and when she did, Cynna's legs felt like gelatin from the rush of emotions. But Nick was right there to catch her before they went out from under her. Just as she needed.

He wrapped one thick arm around her, pulled her against him, and tipped her chin up with his finger. "Stop running from me, okay? I'm getting tired of chasing you. I almost flashed butt-ass naked because I didn't know what you had planned. Trust me, I'm pretty sure that's not something the castle guards want to see."

"No." She leaned into him, fighting back the smile on her lips. "I'm sure they don't." Her heart felt light. As if a giant weight had been lifted. Which was just ludicrous, because there were still so many things left unresolved. "But I definitely wouldn't mind seeing that naked ass again. Soon."

His amber eyes darkened, and desire slid across his features. A desire she knew was meant only for her. He leaned down toward her mouth. "There are plenty of rooms in this castle where I can give you a private showing."

She pushed to her toes and kissed him, desperate to get him alone again. To show him how much she loved him. But footsteps pounded across the floor, growing louder by the second. She drew back from his mouth.

Nick turned. Cynna peered past him toward a tall, dark, and handsome Argonaut she didn't remember meeting.

The male skidded to a stop in the doorway, gulped in a breath of air, and said, "I'm glad I found you. All of you."

"Phin?" Demetrius stepped forward, still cradling Elysia in his arms. "What's wrong?"

The Argonaut's face was flushed, his chest rising and falling as if he'd been sprinting. He sucked in one breath, then said, "Daemons. And satyrs. In Tiyrns. Hades's and Zagreus's armies are attacking."

Nick gripped Cynna's hand tightly in his as they hurried down the stairs toward the lowest level of the castle, afraid to let go of her for even a second. Pandemonium had already broken out. People ran right and left. They zigzagged between bodies and drew to a stop at the end of the balcony.

Gripping the banister, Nick peered over to the grand foyer below. Weaponry had been hauled into the foyer. A castle guard was organizing soldiers and volunteers and handing out swords. Nick scanned the faces, searching for Theron, but the only Argonaut he could see was Gryphon, already armed and ready for battle, standing in the middle of the great Alpha seal, embracing Maelea, his mate.

The Argonaut drew back, his light blue eyes hard, his face taut and rigid, and his voice drifted up to Nick's sensitive ears when he said, "Stay with Natasa."

The crowd parted, and Nick watched as Gryphon nodded to a redhead at Maelea's side. One who was whispering something to her own mate, Titus.

"Hades will be looking for you," Gryphon added.

"I can stay and fight," Maelea protested.

"No." Gryphon's eyes flew wide with a panic Nick understood and was fighting back himself, but the Argonaut pulled it together, cupped her face, and said softer, "No, *sotiria*. I'll be useless if you're here. Please. Do this for me. Get to Prometheus. He'll know how to keep you hidden. I need to know you're safe."

Tears filled Maelea's dark eyes, and the pair embraced. Beside them, Titus held Natasa just as tightly, whispering words so softly in her ear, Nick couldn't make them out.

Cynna stiffened at Nick's side. "There are more, right? More who can fight?"

"I don't know." But worry gnawed at his gut. One army, maybe they could handle, but not two. Hades and Zagreus joining forces in this land clearly wasn't a contingency any of them had ever planned for.

To the right, Orpheus stalked into the foyer with Skyla at his side, both dressed in fighting gear, Orpheus with a blade strapped to his back and Skyla with a bow slung over her shoulder. He sidestepped a boy who looked no more than fifteen lining up to be armed, shook his head, then continued moving toward the Argonauts.

Nick tugged on Cynna's hand. "Come on."

By the time they reached the center of the room, Gryphon, Titus, and their mates were gone. The females, hopefully, to safety; the Argonauts already out into the battle. He and Cynna met up with Orpheus and Skyla.

"Where's Theron?" Nick asked.

"Threatening Phineus within an inch of his life," Orpheus muttered, looking around the foyer. "Do you see these volunteers? Too fucking young."

"Theron's entrusting the queen, her sisters, and the kids into Phineus's care," Skyla clarified. "He's taking them to Delia, who's going to hide them all in the mountains until this is over."

A good plan. One Nick suddenly wanted in on. "Where?"

"In the tunnels below the castle," Orpheus answered. "They lead out into the mountains."

Nick looked down at Cynna. "You should go with them."

"What?" Cynna's eyes widened. "No. I'm staying right here."

"Cynna, be smart. She's your sis—"

"And I can fight, she can't. Look around you, Nick. You're arming babies. You need all the hands you can get." She turned to the Siren. "I need a blade."

"Dagger or sword?" Skyla asked.

"Both."

Skyla stepped back and motioned Cynna to follow. "Come on. We don't have much time."

As the two headed over to gather weaponry, Nick raked a hand through his hair. She was right, but dammit, he didn't want her anywhere near this battle. "Son of a bitch."

Orpheus whistled toward a guard rushing by and told him which weapons he wanted the *ándras* to bring for Nick. As the frightened guard scurried off, Orpheus's expression hardened. "They came in through the west. The city gates are holding, but they won't last long. Zander and Cerek are already at the wall."

"What about Kyrenia?"

"Delia's evacuating the Misos to the Temerus Caves. They run for miles in the Aegis Mountains. That's where Isa, Casey, Callia, and the kids are all heading. The witches have been hiding there for eons. They'll all be safe."

Nick hoped like hell Orpheus was right. Pressure built in his chest. Duty pulled at his soul. And that dark energy popped and sizzled, just waiting to be unleashed.

He needed to be with his people, helping them get to safety, but he knew Zagreus and Hades were here for him. If he went to the settlement, their armies would likely follow.

He could leave, get the hell out of Argolea, try to draw the gods away from this realm, but he didn't even know if Hades and Zagreus were close or if that was what the gods were waiting for him to do. And even if he left, there was no telling when, or if, the gods would pull their armies. He could run and hope for the best, but his honor wouldn't—couldn't—let him leave his friends to die alone. Not this time.

Cynna and Skyla returned. Cynna had pulled her dark hair back into a tight tail and tugged on a lightweight jacket. A blade was strapped to her back and two daggers were sheathed at her hips, reminding him of the deadly warrior she'd been in those tunnels when they'd escaped from Zagreus's lair.

Orpheus looked down at the Siren. "Ready?"

Skyla's green eyes sparked. "You bet your ass I'm ready."

She stepped past her mate toward the front door. And moving into step beside her, Orpheus smacked his hand against the Siren's backside, then whispered, "Keep this ass in one piece, Siren. I'm more than a little attached to it. And to you."

"Don't worry, Daemon." She leaned into him. "I'm not planning on going anywhere without you."

The two disappeared out the door, and Cynna took a step to follow, but Nick pulled her back. "Wait."

Irritation flashed in her dark eyes. "Don't tell me to hide again."

"I won't. I just… Dammit." He closed his arms around her in a fierce hug, drawing her against his chest, wishing he could pull her inside him where he knew she'd always be safe. But he couldn't. All he could do was hope and pray and trust.

"Stay close to me," he said into her hair. "If Zagreus is here, he'll be looking for you."

Her arms wound around his back, her fingertips digging into his muscles to hold him just as tightly as he was holding her. "I will."

"I'm not kidding, Cynna." Tears burned his eyes as he tightened his grip. "This won't be the same as when he let us go."

"I know. And I'm not ready to die today, trust me. Not when I finally have something to live for. But I can't sit back and do nothing. We brought them to this world, Nick. We have to do something to stop them."

He closed his eyes and clung to her, needing every bit of her strength, her courage, and her love to get him through this. Because she was wrong. He alone had brought this hell to her people and to his. And something in his gut told him he was the only one who was going to be able to end it.

He just didn't know how yet.

CHAPTER TWENTY-FOUR

Nick pulled his blade from the chest of the daemon he'd just taken down, whipped around, and decapitated the beast, then turned to look for Cynna as the body fell to the hard ground.

Dammit, he'd told her to stay close. He swiped the sweat out of his eyes and scanned the battlefield, searching for her. Panic reformed beneath his ribs when he couldn't find her. Argonauts, soldiers, and any able-bodied volunteers the castle had been able to round up clashed with satyrs and daemons in the moonlight outside the city walls, but they were losing the battle. It was only a matter of time before the monsters broke through the gates. And this was only the first wave. Hades and Zagreus—wherever the fuckers might be—hadn't even unleashed the brunt of their armies yet.

His gaze found Zander, sinking his blade deep into a satyr's belly; Demetrius battling two daemons, both as big as him; Theron rolling across the ground, then lurching to his feet behind a satyr, grabbing him by the throat, and using his blade to slice the beast's throat open wide. But he still couldn't find Cynna. She'd been beside him only minutes ago. When that satyr had charged him from the back and knocked him to the ground.

Something whirred through the air near his head. His instincts kicked in. He ducked, missing being decapitated himself, then swiveled and sank his sword into the back of another daemon. The daemon went down on all fours. Nick jerked his blade back and was just about to chop the fucker's head off when his sensitive hearing picked up a high-pitched yelp, followed by a growl somewhere off to his right.

"Cynna…"

He sprinted over the small rise and spotted her, forty yards away, swinging her blade with both hands while a satyr ducked and rolled, then kicked her leg out from under her.

She hit the ground with a grunt.

The satyr circled around her and growled. "Now who knows more about the people of this world, *Mistress*?" He nodded down at her, his lips turning in a nasty sneer. "Look at you. You're nothing but Zagreus's hired slut."

Fury erupted across Cynna's face. She grasped her blade and scrambled to her feet. Tendrils of hair fell over her eyes. Her forehead was covered by a sheen of sweat. Her pants and boots caked with mud. But she didn't seem to notice or care. Holding the blade in front of her, she stepped to the side, moving with the satyr. "Better to be a hired slut than a bitch who can't follow a simple order. Tell me, Lykos. How's that wound in your belly? Did it heal yet? I bet Zagreus was thrilled when you showed up looking like a stuck pig thanks to the female you were clearly told to let go."

"Why, you little cunt." The satyr's eyes blazed, and he lifted his weapon. "It's way past time someone taught you a lesson."

The satyr charged, and Nick's heart lurched into his throat as Cynna stepped back and her blade clanged against the satyr's.

He'd never reach her in time. Not unless he flashed.

He didn't think; he reacted. Power surged through his limbs. He felt his body flying. When his feet hit solid ground behind the satyr, he opened his eyes to find the beast on his knees, and Cynna standing over him, her blade sunk deep into his chest.

Blood splattered across her cheek. She shoved the blade deeper, making the monster howl. "I've already learned my lesson. And I'm not your mistress. Not anymore."

The satyr fell back onto the ground and coughed up blood. Nick kicked the weapon away from the beast and stalked toward Cynna. Grasping her around the waist while the battle raged on the other side of the small hill, he pulled her close and kissed her hard. "I couldn't see you. Don't scare me like that again."

She sagged when he released her. "I didn't exactly have a choice. This fucker was about to gut a kid who has no business being out here."

Nick knew exactly who she was talking about. A youngling, no more than twelve, who'd been thrown into the battle by some asshole Nick wished he could find and throttle.

"You won't win this," the satyr rasped from the ground.

Nick glanced down. Blood seeped from the satyr's wounds, pooled at the corners of his mouth, and stained his grotesque body.

"They haven't even started yet." The beast coughed, and even more blood sputtered from his mouth. Then the motherfucker looked at Nick and grinned. "You'll never be as strong as Zagreus. He'll break you yet. And every single soul in this realm. He and Hades won't be happy with just you. They'll win. Wait and see."

The dark energy surged to the surface, coloring Nick's vision red, and he lurched toward the satyr, but Cynna grasped his arm and pulled him back.

"Don't. He's not worth it. Look." She nodded toward the satyr, who sputtered one more time, then went still, his lifeless eyes staring up at the stars.

But Nick didn't care that the beast was dead. All he could focus on was the fact that the satyr was right. They were outnumbered, outmaneuvered, and as soon as those city gates gave, they wouldn't be able to stop Hades's and Zagreus's armies from sweeping over the land.

Cynna grasped Nick's arms and turned him to face her. "He's wrong. Do you hear me? You're stronger than Zagreus; you always were. I know it. Hades knows it. Even Zagreus knows it. That's why he hates you so much. Because you conquered the darkness, which is something he could never do." Her hands tightened around his arms. "This isn't over. We won't let it be."

The clouds parted above, spilling moonlight over her face. And as Nick stared down at her, awe and love swept through him. She always knew exactly what he needed, sometimes even before he did, and he would forever draw courage from that. But she was wrong this time. This battle would be over in a matter of minutes the way it was heading.

She picked up her blade and motioned him to follow her up the hill. Reluctantly, he did, but as they climbed to the top of the small ridge, part of him wished he could just give in to all the darkness so his people could use it to their advantage.

They stopped at the crest, and his gaze swept over the battlefield. Bodies littered the ground. Blood and dirt stained hands and arms and legs and clothing. The clash of weapon against weapon echoed through the darkness. As did grunts, growls, and cries of agony. Of pain. Of death.

"Look." Cynna pointed toward Orpheus, swinging out with his blade, taking down a daemon, then a satyr, and finally another daemon as if they were nothing but paper dolls. "See? This isn't finished."

No, but as Nick took it all in, he suddenly knew how it could be.

A surge of energy, of hope rushed through him. "I can stop this."

Cynna looked over. "How?"

"I need to find Skyla." He scanned the battle once more, his feet already dragging him down the hill.

"Nick. Wait."

He spotted the Siren, fifteen yards from Orpheus, lifting her bow and releasing an arrow dead center into a satyr's chest. A daemon bared its fangs and lunged for her. Skyla lowered the bow with her left hand, reached for the dagger from her hip, and whirled, her blonde hair flying as she sliced the monster across the jugular.

"Skyla!" Nick shoved a satyr to the ground, stabbed him through the heart with his sword, stepped over him and sliced out again, taking down another charging from his right. It was like swimming through a sea of bodies. Every time he'd get by one, another would appear. When he finally reached her, Skyla was as breathless as him. She kicked a dead satyr to the ground and swiped her bloody forearm across her brow.

"I need you to get me to Olympus," Nick told her.

"Why?"

"Because Zeus will know how to unleash my powers. I can't do it on my own."

"*What?*" Cynna's voice lifted at Nick's back. Nick turned to her. Damp hair stuck to her temples, droplets of sweat slid down her neck, and her jacket was ripped at the shoulder and shredded along one side. But her eyes were wide and frightened. More scared than he'd ever seen them. "No."

"I have to go, Cynna. It's the only way we stand a chance. We don't have enough manpower. You said so yourself."

"What about Krónos?" Skyla asked. "If you release your powers, won't that free him?"

In theory, yeah. But Nick knew deep inside that wasn't going to happen. Not this time. Because this was his choice. It wasn't being forced upon him. He wasn't breaking, he was accepting. "I can control it."

Skyla stared at him several seconds, her green eyes searching his features as if looking for truth. Abruptly, she swiveled away. "Orpheus!"

Orpheus kicked the last of a group of daemons he'd been fighting. The beast growled and lunged forward. Ducking under the monster's arm, Orpheus whirled around and stabbed the daemon through the back. The beast dropped to the ground. Orpheus glared down at the limp body. "I told you to stay down, motherfucker."

"Orpheus!" Skyla fought her way to her mate. Nick and Cynna followed. Orpheus looked up at the sound of Skyla's voice, his expression instantly morphing to concern.

He met her halfway, in a section of ground littered with bodies. The battle raged behind them, but they'd beaten back most of the monsters in this small area, and for the moment they could breathe.

Orpheus grabbed Skyla by the forearm as soon as he reached her. "What's wrong? What happened? Are you okay?"

"I'm fine." Her fingers slid along his arm. "I'm taking Nick to Olympus."

"*What?*" Orpheus's eyes widened, mimicking Cynna's reaction. "No."

"He's right," Skyla told her mate. "It's the only way. Nick has the power to stop this. He just has to be able to release it."

Orpheus's gaze shot past Skyla and locked on Nick. "I'll take him."

"No," Skyla said.

"I know the way as well as you, Siren. Zeus and Athena are still pissed you left the Siren order. You're not safe on Olympus."

"Fuck Zeus," Skyla snapped. "There's no guarantee he'll even help Nick, and if he doesn't, we still need more fighters. Athena hates Zagreus more than she hates me right now. His satyrs have been screwing with the Sirens for years. I can rally my sisters, you can't. Athena will agree to it. She won't be able to pass up the opportunity to destroy Zagreus's army, but only if *I* convince her."

Indecision crossed Orpheus's face. Seconds ticked by in agonizing silence. Then his eyes darkened, and he grasped Skyla hard, pulling her against his chest. "You better fucking come back. Do you hear me? I'm not losing you to the gods again."

"I'll be back." She wrapped her arms around his shoulders. "I promise. I promise," she said stronger.

"This is a stupid plan," Cynna said at Nick's side. "Zeus will try to take your powers for himself."

"Well, he can't have them." He turned to her. "You were right. I can control it. I can control it, because you showed me how."

Her eyes softened. "I won't let him break you."

"No, you won't." He sheathed his sword at his back. "Because you're not going."

"What? Why not? You'll need me there more than ev—"

"You were right about something else, Cynna." Nick reached for her arms. "I am a leader, whether I want to be one or not. It's who I am. I should have been with my people tonight instead of here, but I couldn't go because I brought this nightmare to them. And because of that, I have to be the one to stop it. But I can't be in two places at once. They still need someone strong to lead them. Someone who understands strategy and how the gods think. And I need it to be someone who's not going to quit on them. No matter what. I need it to be you."

"I…" Her gaze darted around, then shot back to his face. "I'm not a half-breed."

"Race doesn't matter. You know that. The measure of a person's strength isn't what they were born into but what they become. And you, Cynna. You're the strongest person I know. You understand what it means to be a refugee. To be alone. That's the definition of my people. That's us."

She stared up at him in the moonlight. And slowly, tears filled her eyes. Tears he felt in his own eyes. "You're not coming back, are you?"

"I don't know." His heart squeezed so hard, pain echoed everywhere. "I don't know what Zeus will do. But I have to try. I can't stand back and watch everyone die because of me."

She rose to her toes and wrapped her arms around his shoulders, burying her face in his neck. And as he held her close, he knew in the pit of his soul that no matter how horrendous his time in Zagreus's prison had been, he was thankful for all those months. Because if he hadn't been there, if he hadn't suffered, he wouldn't have realized what he could become. And he never would have found her.

"I love you," she whispered against him. "I'll love you across the ages. No matter where you go or what you do, I'll love you always."

His heart swelled. He tipped her chin up, captured her lips, and kissed her with everything he had in him. "Only you, Cynna. I have only ever loved you. I *will* only love you."

"Nick," Skyla said at his back. "We need to go."

Slowly, Cynna let go of him. But her eyes were red-rimmed and filled with tears when she lowered to her feet. And as Nick stepped back, he took a snapshot of her face and stored it in his mind. Because he knew no matter what happened, if he ever felt out of control or on the edge of insanity, all he had to do was focus on all the love swirling in her eyes at this moment, and he'd be saved.

The way she'd always been able to save him.

Cynna swiped the tears from her cheeks after Nick and Skyla flashed to Olympus. She had just enough time to pull in one shuddering breath before Orpheus screamed her name.

She grasped her sword and looked up to see three daemons charging right for them, their horns glinting in the moonlight, their fangs dripping something vile.

Orpheus stepped to the side, his weapon in his hand, urgency across his face. "Get the hell out of here. Get to the settlement like Nick wanted."

Cynna's mind was a sea of confusing thoughts as Orpheus hollered at the monsters and took off at a run, drawing them away from her. Yes, she needed to save Nick's people. Needed to do for him what he'd done for her. But as her gaze swept out over the battle, over satyr after satyr and daemon after daemon swinging weapons and clashing with Argonauts, Argoleans, and anyone who was willing to stand up and fight, defeat washed through her.

She was one person. What could one person do in the middle of so much evil?

And then, in a rush, she knew.

Her gaze shot up to the hillsides, searching. He had to be close. He always liked to watch. And this—all this misery and death—this was everything he craved.

She spotted Hades on a hilltop high above the city, watching the battle from a cluster of trees, his dark eyes fixated on the bloodletting below, his massive arms crossed over his chest. Her heart rate spiked, and she searched all around him for any sign of Zagreus, but she couldn't find him.

Panic gnawed at her spine as her gaze shot to the left of the battlefield, to the hills and trees on the opposite side of the small valley. He wasn't there either. But she knew he had to be close. He had to be—

Her eyes locked on him. Standing behind a tree, half his face shadowed in darkness. Staring directly at her.

"What the hell are you looking for?" Orpheus yelled, slicing his blade through a satyr's throat. "Get the fuck out of here!"

Cynna swallowed hard. Didn't move. Terror swept through her, but she beat it back. Because Nick was worth the sacrifice.

Orpheus swiveled around to see what she was staring at, then muttered, "Fuck me." He whirled back to face her. "Don't even think about it, Cy—"

Cynna closed her eyes and flashed to the hillside.

Zagreus didn't move a single muscle when she appeared. But he didn't have to. She felt his fury raging across the distance between them.

"So the coward flees, and you finally decide to come back to me," he sneered.

"Pull your army from this land."

The muscles around his dead eyes contracted. "And why would I do that? We're about to win."

She took a step toward him, her heart pounding, her stomach swirling. "Because if you do, I'll go back with you. Willingly."

Interest and desire flared in his eyes, telling her exactly what she'd hoped. He still wanted her. More than he wanted to win this war.

"I won't run," she added. "I won't run ever again."

He was on her so fast, she didn't even see him move. His hands closed around her arms, like metal cuffs snapping shut. "You won't run again, because I *own* you."

Pain spiraled down her spine, but she drew on every ounce of courage she had left. "You don't own me. You never did. I was with you because I chose to be. And if you pull your armies from this land and agree not to return, I'll choose to be with you again. But you'll never break me. And you'll never ever own me. Because my will is stronger than yours."

He stared hard into her eyes. And she knew he was searching for a way to prove to her she was wrong. But she wasn't. And she wasn't backing down.

He released her and stepped back, a careless expression crossing his chiseled features. "I can't stop what's already begun."

"Yes, you can." Cynna stumbled but righted herself before she went down. Lifting her chin, she glared at him. "But know this. If those city walls are breached, this offer is rescinded. I'll fight to the death and take as many satyrs as I can with me along the way. And you'll never have me again. You'll never have what I'm willingly giving you here and now."

Fury filled his dead eyes, and he advanced on her once more. But she didn't turn and run. She stood her ground. And hoped like hell this worked.

Skyla grasped Nick's arm, stopping him in the massive hallway of Zeus's temple on Olympus. "Wait. What about Isadora?"

Nick's mind skipped back to his soul mate in Argolea being ushered into the caves with his people. That pull to her he always felt tugged on something in his chest, but he knew in the center of his soul that Isadora would tell him to do this if she were here. She loved her family, but she was a leader, like him. And though she might not have been able to sleep with him to save herself, she'd be the first to put her life on the line for her country.

"I don't know. I have to hope that Callia and everyone else were wrong and that she won't die when this happens. But I do know if I don't try, everyone dies."

Skyla's gaze held his, then she nodded and released his arm. "Good luck."

"Good luck to you."

They parted ways. She heading to plead with Athena for the Sirens' help in the battle, he to find Zeus and demand he become a god.

Holy...*fuck*. There was something he never thought he'd want. Ever.

He stopped in front of a set of massive gold double doors with Zeus's legendary lightning bolt carved into the sleek surface. Drawing one deep breath, he braced his hands against the cool metal, pushed both doors open, and stepped inside a circular room with a marble dome, columns that rose to an elaborately painted ceiling, and gold-plated everything.

A god he instantly recognized as Poseidon lounged on a plush purple sofa with gold trim in the middle of the room, his surfer-blond hair falling in his eyes, his massive body stretched out across the piece of furniture, making it look tiny. Across the room, where he stood with his hands clasped behind his back as he stared out at the view far below, Zeus turned his head.

"Nikomedes," Zeus said in a low, commanding voice. But then, being the King of the Gods, of course he was commanding. He was the big shit here and everywhere. "I see you brought the traitor with you."

Nick's spine stiffened at the use of his full given name. "Skyla's no traitor. She just didn't want to be part of all this anymore. Free will. Isn't that why you're so fascinated with humanity?"

Zeus turned to fully face him. "She left the Sirens and betrayed me."

"She left for love. You, of all people, should be able to understand that choice. You fall in love every other damn day."

"Ah, he's got you there," Poseidon quipped from the couch.

Zeus didn't respond. Just clenched his jaw, moved to a desk across the room, and leaned back against the white marble surface. "So you want me to unleash your god powers so you can save your people."

Of course he already knew. He was Zeus, the king of fucking everything.

"Yes," Nick said.

"Pretty ballsy," Poseidon muttered. "What's stopping us from smiting you and just taking those pretty powers?"

Nick glanced to his right toward the god—his brother.

And wow, wasn't that just totally fucking wicked?

"Because you can't." Strength and understanding surged in Nick's veins. Of course they couldn't take them. If they could, they'd have tried long ago. Hades and his son had just been too stupid and greedy to accept reality. "I'm as strong as both of you. Maybe more, because what I have came directly from our father. And because I've already learned how to control it."

Poseidon glanced toward Zeus. The two exchanged silent words, then Zeus focused on Nick once more. "It wasn't the act of becoming a god that killed the soul mates of the three Argonauts I offered immortality. It was their selfish choice for power. That desire tipped the scales away from the balance between the heart and the soul. Everything in our world is about balance, but something tells me you already know that. Your coming here to Olympus for selfless reasons proves your worthiness. We'll help you unleash your immortality to defeat Hades and Zagreus, but if we do so, you owe us a favor."

Relief pulsed through Nick, followed by a whisper of apprehension. Any kind of obligation to the King of the Gods couldn't be good, and his mind instantly shot to Cynna. Mortals weren't allowed to live on Olympus unless they served in one of Zeus's armies, like the Sirens. If they forced him to stay here, to somehow join forces with them where he couldn't be with her…

"What kind of favor?" he asked warily.

Zeus glanced toward Poseidon once more. The God of the Sea waggled his brows, then grinned with a sinister turn of his lips.

Zeus looked back at Nick. "There's someone we're looking for. A female. One of great interest. You're going to find her for us."

CHAPTER TWENTY-FIVE

Nick flashed to the middle of the battlefield in Argolea. Strength and power surged in his veins thanks to the little Kumbaya handholding ritual Zeus and Poseidon had made him do on Olympus. There was great power in three, and somehow, forming a trifecta—three sons of Krónos—had been enough to unleash what was hidden inside him. That and, as Zeus explained, the fact he was choosing to unleash it, rather than it being taken.

For as much as everything in this world seemed to be governed by destiny and prophesies and fate, when it came down to it, free will was the force that kept the world moving. And it, above all else, had the power to defeat the darkness.

His gaze swept over the battlefield. Theron and Zander and Demetrius fought a pack of daemons to his left. Orpheus and Cerek did the same to his right. At his back, he spotted Gryphon and Titus swinging out with their swords, taking down one monster after the next, and ahead, Sirens—Zeus's elite kickass female army—unleashed arrow after arrow into the daemons rushing the gates to the city of Tiyrns. But there were no satyrs.

Confusion dragged at his brow. He turned a slow circle, looking closer.

"Nick!"

He whipped around and found Skyla near the gates, her bow at her side, her eyes wide with *a what the hell are you waiting for?* expression. Then his gaze shot toward the wall, where daemons had launched ropes and were climbing steadily to the top, about to infiltrate the city.

They were out of time.

He centered himself, just as he always had when Cynna had pulled him back from the edge, then held his hands out in front of him and focused on all that fucking darkness.

Power surged in his hands, and an arc of light erupted from his fingertips, rippling outward, targeting anything holding on to that darkness.

A shock wave blasted the daemons backward. They went down like dominos, starting in the center of the battlefield and spreading outward. Screams of agony rose up in the dark as they crumpled to the ground. Once they hit the surface, their bodies went up in flames then finally smoked out until all that was left behind was ash.

Gasps of surprise rose up from the bloody battlefield. Followed by an eerie silence. And finally, an eruption of cheers, and one menacing growl.

Nick peered up to the dark hillside where Hades stood staring down at him, absolutely fuming.

Take that, fucker. Nick pointed his index and middle fingers toward his own eyes, then toward Hades. *You're next, asshole. Better get the hell out of here.*

Fury erupted over the god's face. Dark smoke swirled all around him. And when it cleared, the god was gone.

"Holy shit!" Skyla was the first one to reach Nick. She launched herself into his arms, then dropped to her feet, her green eyes alight with excitement and victory. "You did it. I didn't think you could actually do it."

Nick let go of her and nodded toward the Sirens, several of whom turned to look their way. "You did it too."

"Yeah, well." She grinned. "Athena was more than willing to fuck with a few satyrs, but they were all gone by the time we got here."

That didn't make sense. "All of them?"

A rolling, bellowing laugh rumbled behind Nick before she could answer.

Nick turned just as Orpheus swept Skyla up into his arms and spun her around. "Hell, yeah. Did you see the way those fuckers went up in flames? Thank the Fates I got rid of my damn daemon. I'd be toast right now."

Skyla laughed as he lowered her to her feet. "Not toast. Definitely not toast. Just mine. Mine, all mine."

Footsteps echoed as the two kissed. Theron, Zander, and the rest of the Argonauts moved up to join them, breathless, bloody, scraped, and sweaty. But thankfully, none were seriously injured.

"Where's D?" Cerek asked.

"He already flashed to the settlement to check on the queen." Titus swiped the damp hair out of his eyes. "He was out of here as soon as the daemons went down. Said something felt different."

"Different isn't always good," Gryphon muttered.

"No, good different," Titus answered. "D was excited. Said it felt like she was better."

Nick was relieved to hear that. Because he could no longer feel anything from Isadora. It was as if the soul mate bond that had connected him to her for so long had completely vanished the moment he'd gained the full use of his powers. Which, actually, made sense, since gods didn't have soul mates.

And holy fucking A. He was a god.

He looked around, frantic now to find Cynna, to share it with her, only he still couldn't see her.

"Nick. Dude." Orpheus said at his side. "She's gone."

Nick turned to face him. "What do you mean gone?"

With one arm slung over Skyla's shoulders, Orpheus frowned. "I was wrong about her. Somehow she convinced Zagreus to pull his army. He and his satyrs left just after you and Skyla did, which gave us the upper hand once Skyla returned with the Sirens. Man, Hades was pissed."

Nick didn't give a flying fuck about Hades. Panic clawed at his chest. "What about Cynna?"

"She left with Zagreus too."

Everything inside Nick stilled as he searched for her. Not with his head but with his heart. The heart that belonged to her. And when he found her, when he realized where she'd gone, he knew exactly what she'd sacrificed. And why.

* * *

Zagreus couldn't shake the doldrums.

His gaze followed Cynna as she rose from the seat beside him where they'd been watching Altair, his newest second in command now that Lykos was dead, torment a nymph chained to the wall in the main chamber of his lair. His *agapi* was as slutty and hot as she'd ever been, her trim waist and plump breasts encased in the tight leather corset, her long stems stretching beneath the skimpy miniskirt and ending in the knee-high black stiletto boots that always made him hard.

Except...he wasn't hard right now. He watched her disappear out the door where he'd sent her to fetch his wine. In fact, since they'd been back in his lair the last few hours, he couldn't seem to muster up enough enjoyment to get it up for her at all. Which was fucking wrong, because he was totally hot for her in every way. In all the ways he used to be.

"She seems unhappy, my prince." Altair settled onto the seat to Zagreus's right, giving the nymph a break from his flogger.

Not that Zagreus cared what the satyr was doing with the nymph. Even that didn't bring him pleasure anymore.

He shifted in his seat and gripped the armrest of his throne chair. "She's just tired, that's all. By tomorrow, she'll be back to her old self."

"Right," Altair muttered. "Tired. That's it."

Cynna walked back into the room, her head held high, her breasts pushed out, and her spine straight, but there was something missing from her eyes. Stopping in front of his chair, she handed the goblet to Zagreus and said, "Your wine, my prince."

"Thank you, *agapi*."

His fingertips brushed hers as he accepted the wine, but there was no reaction from her. Not even disgust. She didn't answer. Didn't even look at him. Just sat in the seat next to him and stared off into space, as if she were seeing something or some*one* else.

Zagreus's mood slid darker. His enjoyment of her had always come from her defiance, her headstrong attitude, her strength. But this female was only a shadow of the one he'd known before. It was as if she no longer cared.

"Nick," she whispered.

Zagreus's head came up, and his eyes grew wide at the sight of his former prisoner standing in the middle of his chamber. He shoved his goblet at Altair, gripped the armrests of his chair, and lunged to his feet. "You."

"Me," Nick said.

From the corner of his vision, Zagreus watched excitement and joy burst across Cynna's face. She pushed to her feet.

Zagreus threw his arm out to the side, sending a burst of energy all around her, forcing her to stand still. "She's not yours anymore."

"That's where you're wrong, *nephew*," Nick said in a calm voice. "I'm hers."

Zagreus felt his hold on Cynna slipping. As if prying one finger back at a time, the energy around her slowly crumbled. When it shattered at her feet, she lurched forward, right into Nick's arms.

The two whispered disgusting things that turned Zagreus's stomach. He scowled as he watched them embracing, seeing Cynna in a whole new light. The female had never hugged him like that. She'd never lovingly run her fingertips over his jaw as she was now doing to Nick. And that light hadn't once shone in her eyes when she'd looked up at him.

The dark knot of vileness tightened inside him. Love was the disgusting emotion he felt emanating from both of them, pushing him even deeper into despondence, because it was something he was never going to experience for himself.

Nick fixed his amber eyes on Zagreus. His amber *god* eyes. Oh yeah, Zagreus could feel the power pumping off the god now. There was no more weak mortal left anywhere inside him.

"Your lair is surrounded. The Argonauts and the Sirens are outside. Either free every last prisoner in this hellhole, or we'll do it for you."

Rage rushed through Zagreus. He lurched down the three stone steps to tell Nick just what he and his posse could do, then drew to a stop when a rolling dark energy swept through the tunnels and raced over his skin. "Hades."

"Hades is here?" Cynna turned to face him.

"It's okay," Nick said beside her.

"But it's Hades. He's a god. A powerful one."

"So am I."

Cynna looked up at Nick. And Zagreus focused on her face. On the awe and compassion reflected in her eyes. He didn't doubt that Nick was as strong as his fucking father, and he wasn't opposed to letting the two duke it out, even if it meant losing his lair. But as he stared at the female he'd coveted longer than any other, he realized if he tried to hold on to her, she'd get caught in the middle of an immortal battle, and, ultimately, she'd die. As much as he wanted to keep her as his own special pet, her death was not something he was willing to gamble with. Not when he knew Hades would likely kill her just to punish his son for pulling his satyrs from that battle.

"Go," Zagreus growled.

Surprise rushed over Cynna's smooth face as she looked at him. "What did you say?"

Zagreus stalked back up the steps and dropped into his chair, slumping against the arm. "Go now. Before I change my mind."

"The prisoners," Nick said.

"You don't have time for any damn prisoners." Zagreus waved his arm. "Get the hell out before my father arrives."

Nick grasped Cynna's hand. "We'll be back for them."

Zagreus scowled, propped his elbow on the armrest, and glared toward the far rock wall. "Pretty sure there won't be anything left to come back to."

Soft fingers brushing his hand drew his head around. Surprise spread through his chest as he looked up at Cynna, standing a foot away, touching him.

"Thank you," she whispered.

The ground shook. Rocks broke free from the ceiling and shattered to the ground. Screams rose up in the cavern, and Altair scrambled to free the nymph from her chains, then rushed out of the room with the female in his arms.

"Cynna," Nick called.

Cynna's eyes softened with gratitude and an emotion Zagreus couldn't name. And in that second, as she stared at him, as his chest grew tight, he knew what it felt like to do the right thing.

She rushed toward Nick before Zagreus could stop her. Nick grasped her hand. The two turned to look at him once more, and then they were gone in a pop and sizzle of energy.

"You fucked with me," Hades growled from the doorway.

Slowly, Zagreus swiveled to look toward his father. But he no longer cared what the hell Hades wanted. All he could focus on was the pulsing warmth in the center of his chest, growing larger by the second.

"I told you what would happen if you betrayed me," Hades roared.

A sound like rolling thunder boomed through the cavern. Zagreus looked up toward the ceiling. Before he could push out of his chair, the ground opened up, dragging him and everything down into darkness.

Cynna stumbled the second her feet hit solid ground. Dust filled her lungs, and she coughed, trying to clear it away. Blinking several times in the early morning sunlight, she realized she stood on the edge of a giant sinkhole. Water rushed in over the rocks, submerging Zagreus's lair, sweeping over everything until there was nothing left.

"Holy *skata*," she whispered. "If you'd been a few minutes later…"

Nick drew her back from the edge. "I needed everyone in position before we came to get you."

On the other side of the giant sinkhole, voices drifted to her ears. She glanced across the distance toward several Argonauts and a few Sirens staring at the destruction.

"I wasn't worried about taking down Zagreus," Nick said. "But I couldn't get to you and everyone else at the same time."

"Oh my gods," Cynna whispered, looking back at the water. "All those prisoners."

"Don't look." He pulled her into his arms. "We tried. I didn't know Hades was going to show."

She closed her eyes and sank into him, relieved and thankful and—

She jerked back and looked up. "Isadora?"

"Fine. Better than fine. Cured."

"Cured?"

He held out his forearm and showed her his unmarked skin. "I'm not an Argonaut anymore. Which means there's no more soul mate pull between us."

"No more soul mate pull. That means—"

"That means I am yours, female. Every part of me. If you still want me."

"If I still want you?" She grasped his neck and pulled him down to her. "Are you kidding?"

He chuckled, but that laugh turned to a groan when she closed her mouth over his and kissed him.

His hands framed her face, and he tipped her head and kissed her deeper, making every doubt and fear and worry she'd had since the moment he'd left her for Olympus disappear into the ether.

When she was breathless, he drew back and rested his forehead against hers. "Did you really think I wouldn't come for you?"

Her heart rolled. "I didn't know if Zeus was going to let you go. Convincing Zagreus to take his army and leave was the only thing I knew to do to help."

"It was a smart move. Smart and stupid all at the same time. I freaked when I came back and found you gone."

"I'm sorry for that. But it was no stupider than you challenging Zeus."

A half smile curled his lips. "Agreed. But it worked. Right now, though, I'm ready for a whole lot less excitement. At least of the cataclysmic variety."

Cynna brushed her fingers over his sexy jaw. "How does it feel? Being immortal?"

"Pretty much the same." He fingered a lock of hair near her cheek and smoothed it back near her ear. "Though I've heard sex is pretty fucking awesome for a god. And I'm itching to try that out."

She laughed and lifted her mouth to his once more, but a soft cough drew her back.

She glanced to the right toward the elderly woman wearing diaphanous white, sitting on a rock beside them. Cynna startled, but Nick smoothed his hand down her arm and said, "Relax. It's just Lachesis."

Cynna nearly choked. "The Fate?"

"One and the same," the Fate answered. "Well done, Niko." A victorious grin curled her lips. "Very well done."

Nick smirked. "You could have…oh, I don't know…hinted that all I had to do was go see Zeus to finish this."

"Fates can't give answers. Only lead you to the choice. But you didn't even need me for that. You had her." She nodded toward Cynna.

Cynna swallowed hard. She'd never met a Fate before. Was this normal for a god?

"Take care of him, child." Lachesis's blue eyes grew serious. "He may be immortal now, but he will still be challenged. By his brothers. By his father. By his duty. Krónos will become even more determined now to break free from Tartarus. The search for the last element needed to complete the Orb will intensify, and darkness will try to win out. He will need you more than you think. Especially as he works to protect his people. The Council of Elders in Argolea is corrupt, as you know. But do not run from the fight. Embrace it. Together. And make a difference in your world."

"I will," Cynna managed.

To Nick, she said, "And take care of her, warrior. She is a special one."

Nick smiled down at Cynna, a warm, loving, for-her-only smile that heated every inch of Cynna's skin. "I already know that."

Lachesis floated to her feet. "When she passes from this world into the next, the choice to stay or pass with her rests in you."

Nick looked back at Lachesis. "It does? I thought immortality meant…immortality."

"Choice is always with you, Niko. No one controls you. No one ever did. Every god has the same choice. Most are simply too caught up in the trappings of power to be anything but selfish. If love is your guide, however, I know you'll make the right choice when the time comes. Live and be happy. Use your gifts for good. But be wary of Zeus and Poseidon."

She disappeared as abruptly as she'd arrived, and as soon as she was gone, Cynna looked up at Nick. "Zeus and Poseidon?"

"I'll explain later." When she lifted her brows, a wary expression crept over his face, and he added, "In exchange for their help, I agreed to do them a favor."

Being indebted to the gods could not be good. "That sounds ominous."

He glanced toward the sinkhole filled with water and frowned. "It might be. Now."

Before she could ask more, he wrapped his arms around her and whispered, "Enough about them."

She lifted to his kiss. Reveled in his strength, his warmth. His love. And as she slid her arms around his neck and stroked her tongue along his, she felt herself flying and knew he was flashing them away from Zagreus's lair forever.

She opened her eyes and discovered he'd brought her back to the same bedroom where they'd stayed together last night. The one at Delia's house in the settlement. "Don't you have work to do? Helping move your people back from the mountains?"

"Someone else can deal with that. For the next few hours I plan to work only on you."

She smiled, loving that answer. But before she could ease up and show him just how much she loved that with her mouth, a shiver rippled across her spine. One look told her he'd obliterated her clothing again.

Her brow lifted. "Not interested in unwrapping?"

"Not right now." He lowered her to the bed, and warmth bloomed all through her belly when she realized he was already naked too. "Right now I just need you."

Love and happiness filled her soul. "You have me, Nick." She stroked her fingertips over the scar on his cheek. "You always will."

He rolled to his back and pulled her on top of him so she was straddling his legs, then slid his hands to her bare hips. "Prove it to me, my strong, sexy, sinful Cynna. Show me that I am yours and you are mine. I'm completely at your mercy, exactly as I was before."

A wicked, erotic smile pulled at her mouth. He was remembering the tunnels, when she'd pleasured him with her hand. Her whole body tingled with a surge of white-hot lust as she thought back to that moment too. Only this time, she planned to use way more than her fingers to bring him to a soul-shattering release.

She grasped his wrists and pinned them to the mattress above his head, then leaned down and gently brushed her lips across his. "Brace yourself, handsome. I can't promise this won't hurt."

His lust-filled grin consumed his entire face. And as she pressed her lips to his neck, his collarbone, his chest, and worked her way south, he groaned. "Mm... That's it, baby. That's exactly how I like it. Don't you dare stop."

She wouldn't. If it took the rest of her life, she'd show him just how much his love meant to her. Because, thanks to him, she was finally home.

ETERNAL GAURDIANS LEXICON

adelfos. Brother

agapi. Term of endearment; my love.

ándras; pl. *ándres.* Male Argolean

archdaemon. Head of the daemon order; has enhanced powers from Atalanta

Argolea. Realm established by Zeus for the blessed heroes and their descendants

Argonauts. Eternal guardian warriors who protect Argolea. In every generation, one from the original seven bloodlines (Heracles, Achilles, Jason, Odysseus, Perseus, Theseus, and Bellerophon) is chosen to continue the guardian tradition.

Chosen. One Argolean, one human; two individuals who, when united, completed the Argolean Prophecy and broke Atalanta's contract with Hades, thereby ejecting her from the Underworld and ending her immortality.

Council of Elders. Twelve lords of Argolea who advise the king

daemons. Beasts who were once human, recruited from the Fields of Asphodel (purgatory) by Atalanta to join her army.

*Dimiourgo*s. Creator

doulas. Slave

élencho. Mind-control technique Argonauts use on humans

Fates. Three goddesses who control the thread of life for all mortals from birth until death

Fields of Asphodel. Purgatory

fotia. Term of endearment. My fire.

gigia. Grandmother

gynaíka; pl. *gynaíkes.* Female Argolean

Horae. Three goddesses of balance controlling life and order

Isles of the Blessed. Heaven

ilithios. Idiot

kardia. Term of endearment; my heart

Kore. Another name for the goddess Persephone. "The maiden"

ligos-Vesuvius. Term of endearment; little volcano

matéras. Mother

meli. Term of endearment; beloved

Misos. Half-human/half-Argolean race that lives hidden among humans

Olympians. Current ruling gods of the Greek pantheon, led by Zeus; meddle in human life

oraios. Beautiful

Orb of Krónos. Four-chambered disk that, when filled with the four classic elements—earth, wind, fire, and water—has the power to release the Titans from Tartarus

patéras. Father

sotiria. Term of endearment; my salvation

Siren Order. Zeus's elite band of personal warriors. Commanded by Athena

skata. Swearword

syzygos. Wife

Tartarus. Realm of the Underworld similar to hell

therillium. Invisibility ore, sought after by all the gods

Titans. The ruling gods before the Olympians

Titanomachy. The war between the Olympians and the Titans, which resulted in Krónos being cast into Tartarus and the Olympians becoming the ruling gods.

thea. Term of endearment; goddess

yios. Son

**Read on for a sneak peek at
EXTREME MEASURES
The first book in Elisabeth Naughton's
steamy new Aegis Series**

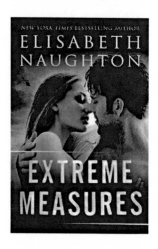

Being prepared for any scenario is the trademark of any good CIA operative, and Eve Wolfe is one of the best. But when her latest mission literally explodes in her face, she wakes up labeled a traitor and—even more surprising—in the custody of elite Aegis Security operative and ex-lover Zane Archer. Although she still secretly has feelings for Zane, he's now demanding the one thing that she can't give him: the truth.

When he caught her breaking the rules years ago, Zane let Eve walk away without an explanation. Now someone has not only sabotaged Aegis but also turned an American city into a war zone, and all signs point to Eve. Zane needs answers that can come only from Eve's still-tempting lips, and he finally has the elusive operative right where he wants her—at his mercy.

The first full-length book in bestselling author Elisabeth Naughton's new steamy romantic suspense series brings a spy in from the cold…and sets her heart ablaze.

EXTREME MEASURES

CHAPTER ONE

Guatemala
ETA to extraction: Twelve minutes and counting.

Zane Archer scanned the darkened compound from the trees just beyond the perimeter wall and tried to ignore the sweltering jungle heat.

Too bad it didn't work.

Sweat gathered under his fatigues and beneath his helmet, but he knew soon the temperature would be the least of his worries. Wiping a hand over the moisture dripping into his eyes, he looked through the scope. At this hour—nearly three A.M.—the only lights flickering were in two windows on the second floor of the Mediterranean-style mansion. A guard roamed the portico outside the first floor, and other than a few howler monkeys chirping in the jungle canopy nearby, no other sound besides leaves and palm fronds rustling met his ears.

He glanced at his watch again. *ETA to extraction: Eleven minutes, Twenty-five seconds.*

Nerves fluttered in his belly, but he ignored those too. Keeping the M4 carbine rifle trained on the guard, he tipped his head toward the com unit near his shoulder. "Look alive, boys. We're coming up on go time."

In his earpiece, the radio squawked. "You're sure he's in there?"

Jake Ryder's skepticism was nothing new. But on this, Zane was confident. "Carter's intel is sound."

"It'd better be," Jake muttered. "Our balls are dangling out here in the breeze, Archer."

Zane bit back the smartass comment because Jake had let him take the lead on this one and looked through his scope again, scanning the perimeter once more.

His heart picked up speed and adrenaline flooded his system. Ryder and Hedley should have their men in position on the far side of the compound by now. Though Zane was confident this extraction was going to go down without a hitch, he knew Jake Ryder—CEO of Aegis Security, the private company comprised of Zane and a handful of elite specialists from around the globe—wasn't so sure. Jake didn't know "Carter" from a fart in the wind. And though he was aware Zane and Carter had teamed together during Zane's five years with the CIA, he still questioned the fact this whole op hinged on the intel Carter had passed along to Zane. Intel that said one Adam Humbolt, Ph.D. and specialist in chemical weaponry, was being held in this Guatemalan compound by a gang of thugs who worked for Central American drug lord Roberto Contosa.

"Humbolt's in there," he said into his com unit. "Trust me, Carter and the Company want this guy free as much as we do."

Not as much. *More.* Humbolt "officially" didn't work for the U.S. government, but word on the street was the scientist knew some super top secret shit the U.S. didn't want shared with anyone, Central American drug lords included. And though logic said this extraction probably should have fallen to a SEAL or DELTA team, because the State Department didn't want this op on record, the job had been handed off to Aegis with its superior track record. Their orders were simple: get the job done quietly and quickly and with no link back to the U.S. government whatsoever.

Ryder didn't respond, and Zane knew his boss was thinking, *we'll see*, but facts were facts. Sure, there were a whole lot of people who wanted the science percolating in Humbolt's genius mind, another bunch who'd like to see him dead, but the ones who mattered just wanted him back in the States alive and in one piece.

Time ticked by slowly in the oppressive early morning heat. Zane could all but feel the adrenaline from his teammates stationed around the compound. And though he tried to stay focused as he waited, he couldn't stop his mind from drifting back to the last time he'd worked with Carter. To being stuck in that run-down apartment in Beirut he'd shared with Carter and Juliet. To the months of running surveillance, blending in, fighting back the boredom. To the nights he'd been alone with Juliet when Carter had been out. To the laughs, the looks, the heated moments that never should have happened.

"Jesus," he whispered. "You are such a fucking moron."

"You say something?" Hedley piped in his ear.

Shit, he was talking to himself. He cleared his throat, peered through the scope again, and put all thoughts of Juliet out of his mind for good. "Remember, boys," he said, drawing on his military training. "Slow is smooth. Smooth is fast."

"Ooh-rah," Landon Miller murmured, the only communication the former Marine had uttered since they'd set up the perimeter.

As the team went black, Zane said a quick prayer they'd be in and out in seconds rather than minutes or hours. Said another that no one got dead.

He shifted his finger from guard to trigger. Lined up the compound sentry in his crosshairs. And just as the last second passed on his watch, he fired once, killing the south end sentry with a barely audible pop. On the north end, he was confident Ryder had just accomplished the same.

He was out of the tree and across the wall before the sentry's body hit the ground, rappelling the cement structure as quickly as possible and bracing his rifle against his shoulder as he crossed the dew-covered grass. At the southwest corner of the compound, he caught up with Hedley's group coming in from the side and pointed up, signaling the hostage room they'd identified earlier on the second floor.

Miller and Stone tossed ropes up and over the second story balcony, the grappling hooks catching the balustrade and securing tight. Zane followed Hedley to the second floor, waited in silence as the other two men climbed up and over the railing. As a silent unit, they made their way across the balcony and lined up outside the hostage room.

Hedley signaled with his finger, counted to three, then pulled an M84 flash grenade from his pack. When he got the nod from Hedley, Zane used his rifle to blow open the door of the compound. Hedley jerked the pin from his grenade and tossed it into the room.

EXTREME MEASURES

A roar shook the building and echoed through the darkness, followed by a blinding flash of light, intended to disorient those inside.

Zane was the first through the door, sweeping the right side of the room with his gun. Hedley came in on his tail, scanning the left while Miller and Stone followed through the middle zone. Shouts echoed around them. Zane caught sight of two hostages, tied in chairs in the center of the room, then the tangos, two on the right, one on the left, all three scrambling for weapons in their confusion.

He fired two double-taps, shifted his weapon to the second target, and fired again. The shots hit dead center in the chest, dropping the captors with quick pops. "Clear right," he said into his shoulder.

To his left, he heard two more pops and saw the last captor go down. "Clear left," Hedley echoed in his earpiece.

"All clear," Miller followed from the middle of the room.

"Who's there?" The man in the chair turned his head from side to side, his vision obstructed by a black bandana tied at the back of his head

"The cavalry." Zane yanked the blindfold from Humbolt's head. The man blinked several times. He was thin from weeks in captivity, and he looked like he'd taken a major beating. Bruises and dried blood covered one whole side of his face.

In the chair beside him, the brunette vibrated with fear. Zane shot her a look and then refocused on the job at hand. "Mr. Humbolt, we're here to get you out."

"Thank God," Humbolt breathed.

Hedley cut the hostages' ties while Zane and the other two got them to their feet.

"How did you find us?" the woman asked in a shaky voice as Zane ushered her toward the door. She didn't look much steadier on her feet than Humbolt, but at least she wasn't black and blue.

Zane didn't know who she was, but there'd be plenty of time for intros later. "We'll fill you in once we're secure. Right now just focus on keeping up."

The woman nodded, and Zane glanced at his watch. Time from start of op to apprehension of hostages: Three minutes, thirty-seven seconds.

They were ahead of schedule.

"We're on our way out," he said into his com unit. "Plus two."

"Roger that," Ryder echoed back.

Slow is smooth, smooth is fast, Zane repeated the phrase in his head as he lifted the rifle to his shoulder again and turned back for the door. Miller and Stone took up position on either side of the hostages. Hedley brought up the rear.

They moved with stealth back to the balcony where Zane and Hedley provided cover and Miller and Stone took the hostages over the railing and down to the ground. In the jungle around them, nothing moved, just like they'd planned. The lack of noise from the front of the compound confirmed Ryder's team had taken out their targets and that everything was downhill from here.

When they were safely on the ground, they resumed position and headed for the southwest corner of the compound again, where Ryder's team of four waited.

Just as they rounded the corner, an explosion rocked the compound. The force of the blast shot Zane's body backward. He landed on his back with a crunch, his ears ringing. Coughing through the smoke pouring out of a giant hole in the first floor, he rolled to his stomach. Gunfire lit up the night sky. Something sharp ripped through his left quad.

He struggled to his feet. Swayed but found his balance. Disbelief rushed through him as he held up a hand to block the smoke and dust from getting in his eyes while he scanned the blown out building. When his gaze caught sight of Humbolt, five feet away on the ground, blood oozing from multiple cuts and scrapes over his arms and face and seeping like a river from his ears, his entire body went still.

The man's eyes were wide and lifeless, his body, limp. Draped over his torso, the woman also lay dead, her eyes staring out into space, a hole the size of a melon in her abdomen.

No. Disbelief churned to panic, then boiling rage. *No!*

"Goddammit, Archer! Get back!"

A hand grasped his fatigues, dragging him tight to the side of the blown-open building. He stumbled then fell to his ass. His back hit the crumbling stucco. A burn like dynamite lit up his left leg, and his vision swam. Struggling to see, he found Miller through the smoke, covered in soot, pulled Stone back in the same manner.

The ringing in his ears prevented Zane from hearing shit going on around him, but he recognized the ricochet of bullets hitting dirt, thought maybe he'd been hit—somewhere—but still couldn't focus on anything except Humbolt lying dead against the earth.

His principal. Four minutes, twenty-three seconds after the start of the op.

"…Humbolt's fucking dead!" Hedley hollered into his com unit. "No. One man down. Leg. I don't know. It's gushing. We need to get the bloody fuck out of here!"

In Zane's earpiece, Ryder's muffled voice rattled off commands, but the words were too dim to make out. They always had a backup plan ready to go in case things went wrong. Their backup in this case was to haul ass out before anyone else got dead, then reconnoiter two klicks south of the compound and rendezvous with the chopper.

How had it gone so wrong? Zane had led the planning phase of the mission himself. They'd known exactly how many guards would be on site, what kind of weapons they'd be up against. The firepower raining down around, them and the carefully timed explosion, signaled they'd been compromised.

Hedley dragged him to his feet, braced an arm under Zane's to hold him up. Through the smoky haze, Zane saw Hedley's mouth moving as the Aussie screamed directions, but that fucking ringing was growing louder, drowning out most sound. In the distance, two bodies rushed toward them through the smoke. Zane lifted a hand that held no gun. Shit, where was his rifle? He pointed, had no idea if he screamed or not. Hedley whipped around with his weapon just as Jake Ryder and Pierce Bentley appeared through the debris.

Zane nearly went down as soon as Hedley let go, but somehow managed to prop himself against what was left of the wall. Dirt and sweat slid into his eyes and messed with his vision. His lungs burned. The scent of searing flesh and rubber was all he could focus on. Ryder signaled the roundup as the rest of his team fired back at the tangos spraying bullets from the second floor and the outer wall where Zane and his team had just been. Hedley wrapped an arm around Zane's waist, pulled Zane's wrist over his shoulder and forced him low as they moved under the balcony and stayed out of the line of fire. Behind him, Stone hauled Humbolt's body through the debris and followed.

Zane lost track of time, wasn't sure how the hell they made it through the jungle and to the chopper alive. All he knew when he got there was that he was sweating like a motherfucker, he couldn't feel his leg anymore and his principal was dead.

Dead.

Hedley threw him in the Huey, turned and yelled at the others behind them. The chopper's blades whipped everything around them—trees, grass, palms. Seconds later, they were loaded, and the chopper lifted off, banking to the left into the inky darkness. Zane shifted where he was lying on the chopper's floor and glanced out the open door down to the compound below, alive with flames and billowing smoke.

It looked like the world was on fire. One simple extraction had gone violently wrong. His gaze strayed to Humbolt's lifeless body.

Nausea rolled through his stomach. He dropped onto his back again, stared up at the Huey's ceiling, and worked not to lose his dinner. Somehow, he clawed himself free of his helmet, dropped it on the floor, and focused simply on sucking air into his suddenly-too-small lungs. It took several seconds before he realized someone was screaming his name over the whir of the blades. His gaze shifted to the side where Ryder was holding a sat phone out to him. "Says they want to talk to you!"

Zane took the phone, pressed it to his ear while Stone cut through his fatigues and started work on his leg.

"I need a tourniquet!" Stone yelled.

Hands moved in unison. Blood spurted. Someone tied a strip of cloth or rubber—or, holy *fuck*, that felt like metal—across his thigh. Pain returned with the force of a Mac truck moving at a hundred and twenty miles per hour. Zane gritted his teeth to keep from screaming just as the familiar voice said, "Sawyer? You survived?"

He knew that voice. He recognized the breathy cadence and the use of his CIA alias. But more than anything he understood the sound of victory.

Juliet.

In that second, he knew. He knew just who'd fucked their mission and why.

"How—?"

"How is not important." Her voice hardened. "It's the why you should really be concerned with. But then you know the why, don't you?"

He pushed up to sitting even though Stone pressed against his shoulder with one bloody hand and hollered at him to lie down. The pain in his leg morphed to a blinding red, which erupted behind his eyes. "When I find you—"

"You won't. I trained with the best, and I never lose." He could almost see those amber eyes of hers when she was in black ops mode, hard and cold and as soulless as any terrorist. No wonder she'd made such a good operative. She was just like them. A venomous black widow, waiting to strike.

The phone went dead in his ear before he could respond. As dead as Humbolt on the floor beside him. Zane dropped back to the ground with a groan. The cell fell from his fingers to roll across the floor. And as they flew over the jungle and Stone packed his leg wound, Zane vaguely heard their medic tell the pilot to haul ass or they were gonna run out of time.

But Zane didn't care. As his vision blurred and darkness threatened, only one thing revolved in his mind. Only one goal remained.

No matter what it took, no matter how long, he'd find her. He'd find her, and he'd make her pay.

Learn more about
EXTREME MEASURES
at ElisabethNaughton.com

ABOUT THE AUTHOR

Photo by Almquist Studios

Before topping multiple bestseller lists—including those of the New York Times, USA Today, and the Wall Street Journal—Elisabeth Naughton taught middle school science. A rabid reader, she soon discovered she had a knack for creating stories with a chemistry of their own. The spark turned to a flame, and Naughton now writes full-time. Besides topping bestseller lists, her books have been nominated for some of the industry's most prestigious awards, such as the RITA® and Golden Heart Awards from Romance Writers of America, the Australian Romance Reader Awards, and the Golden Leaf Award. When not dreaming up new stories, Naughton can be found spending time with her husband and three children in their western Oregon home.

Visit her at www.ElisabethNaughton.com to learn more about her books.

CPSIA information can be obtained at www.ICGtesting.com
Printed in the USA
LVOW11s0235080816

499397LV00013B/612/P